A cold wind suddenly ⸻ ⸻ ⸻n ordered to by Andrew's outburst. It cut through the trees and chilled Andrew's flesh. Everything was now strangely still, since the new wind did not even seem to stir the leaves. Then he heard a noise like a wild boar crashing through the undergrowth.

'What is it?' he cried, alarmed. 'Is anyone there?'

In that moment he observed two forms moving determinedly through the moonshadows. He recognised them straight away. One was a hanged murderer and the other was his victim. He wanted to run but his legs froze solid and his breath quickened as the two figures stepped into the glade.

'What do you want with me?' asked Andrew. To his chagrin he was still shaking violently. The smell of decay was appalling and made him feel unwell. 'Are you here to take me away?'

'Know this,' said the murderer, turning his darkly-ravaged features to look down upon Andrew's own, 'that one day you will become a famous knight, a Templar, who will distinguish himself on the battlefields of the Holy Land.'

RICHARD ARGENT

WINTER'S KNIGHT

www.atombooks.co.uk

ATOM

First published in Great Britain in 2010 by Atom

Copyright © 2010 Richard Argent

The moral right of the author has been asserted.

A CIP catalogue record for this book
is available from the British Library.

ISBN 978-1-905654-54-3

Typeset in Melior by Palimpsest Book Production Ltd, Grangemouth, Stirlingshire

Printed and bound in Great Britain by CPI Mackays, Chatham, ME5 8TD

Papers used by Atom are natural, renewable and recyclable
products sourced from well-managed forests and certified
in accordance with the rules of the Forest Stewardship Council.

Mixed Sources
Product group from well-managed
forests and other controlled sources
www.fsc.org Cert no. SGS-COC-004081
© 1996 Forest Stewardship Council

Atom
An imprint of
Little, Brown Book Group
100 Victoria Embankment
London EC4Y 0DY

An Hachette UK Company
www.hachette.co.uk
www.atombooks.co.uk

For Anna and Emily Monk.
May good fortune go with you both.

PART ONE

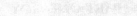

1. THE HORKEY BOY

It all began when he met the two dead men in the forest. His life changed with just a few hollow words from the mouths of a hanged murderer and his unfortunate victim. But that's how these things happen. One day you're a simple lad, the son of a lowly farrier, disliked and bullied by the other youths of the village. The next your world has become this shining, golden place. And you? You've become golden, too, with promises heaped on your shoulders, and great things on the road ahead. That's how the Horkey Boy felt, though later, much later, long after he'd passed the hour on the day his fortunes changed.

There were two great barns, both as big as four large houses stacked together. The crowd was moving from one barn to the other. In the middle of the mass of villagers, knights, monks and men-at-arms was Andrew, the Horkey Boy chosen by lot.

Some of the knights and monks ruffled his hair and were saying, 'Well done, lad, that's the Barley Barn. Now for the Wheat Barn.'

However, the youths of the village gave him black looks. Several were digging at his back and ribs surreptitiously, with sharp flints. These boys were jealous, envious of the attention Andrew was getting from the knights and monks. His peers did not like him. They had never liked him. One boy in particular kept treading on his heels and trying to step on the backs of his sandals to trip him up.

These youths were hissing in his ears when no one was looking, keeping their threats under the noise of the crowd.

'We'll get you, witchboy. You're in for a beating tonight,' snarled one big lout.

'Yeah,' said another, breathing in his ear with hot, stinking breath, 'I'm going to enjoy making you squeal like a stuck pig.'

Andrew paid no heed to these remarks, which were common enough, coming from his hated foes. He shrugged them off as he marched to the second great barn. One day he would show them. One day he would leave Cressing village, make his fortune, become rich and famous and return to destroy them all. One day . . .

'Up you go then, boy,' whispered a monk in his ear.

He immediately came out of his reverie. They were now within the second enormous barn with its vertical supporting beams soaring to the ceiling above, where many other massive beams and rafters criss-crossed each other, holding up the high roof.

'Oh – yes.'

He shinned up a ladder into the rafters. In his right hand he held the Horkey Branch which was to go at the apex of the inner roof.

Andrew glanced down from the dizzying heights. Below him, monks, common people and the Templar knights in their white robes with red crosses were now craning their necks, staring back up at him. He could see eager white faces, wide eyes, expectant, open mouths. They were gathered in the middle of this huge construction of massive oak timbers. Andrew had a small green oak branch in his right hand. He now concentrated on tying this symbol, known as the Horkey Bough, to one of the roof timbers. Andrew had already performed this harvest ritual in the great Barley Barn. Now, as the Horkey Boy, he was doing the same in the second of the famous Cressing barns.

A loud cheer went up from below.

'Well done, boy,' called a warrior-monk.

Andrew looked down and smiled, enjoying his moment of glory. He was at the very top of the barn, which was the height of six tall men. A dizzying height, that seemed to be almost in the clouds. Fear suddenly gripped his heart. His hold on the beam tightened, forcing a splinter to pierce his palm, making him wince. In that second he almost slipped, just managing to clutch a beam in time to stop himself falling. A sallow-faced boy in the crowd pointed and laughed.

'Look at 'im. Agile as a donkey.'

A knight struck the speaker behind the ear with his open hand.

'Quiet, idiot!' snarled the knight. 'This is a religious ceremony, not a game.'

The Norman knight was right, of course. It was a religious rite. But not, as he mistakenly believed, a Christian one. It was one of those Anglo-Saxon pagan rituals that had survived the onslaught of Christianity and had now embedded itself into the new calendar.

The boy rubbed his head and glared up at Andrew, blaming him for the blow. His companions narrowed their eyes and muttered in support of the boy who had been struck. Andrew knew he was going to get beaten later. He was not popular with the youths of Cressing village. They called him 'witchboy' and other similar names. There was a story that he had been delivered at birth by a witch in the forest, during the winter snows. There were the dark marks of the witch's hands on his ankles where the old hag had gripped him when she pulled him out the wrong way round from his mother's womb. Worse, some of his toes were webbed and this marked him out as something of a demon's offspring. Ever since he could remember Andrew had been bullied and abused by the other village children.

Now that he had been chosen as the Horkey Boy he was hated by their parents as well. They all wanted their sons to be given the privilege of tying the Horkey Boughs to the rafters of the two great barns. No one except his own parents, and perhaps Friar Nottidge, whom he often helped in the walled garden, would be concerned if Andrew was beaten senseless by the other youths. The Templar knights themselves expected a boy to stand up for himself. If he could not, they believed he deserved to be beaten. The girls of the village would just watch and taunt him when he fell to the ground. This was the year of Our Lord 1175 and brutality was a part of life. Cruel men became powerful men. Kindness was seen as a weakness.

'Come on down now, son,' called Andrew's father, gesturing. 'Friar Nottidge wants your assistance.'

He moved towards a side door at the back.

Andrew's father was a farrier for the Templar knights, with the rank of sergeant-at-arms. He shoed their chargers, their cart ponies and the heavy horses used in the fields. Cressing was a good village to be born in. The Templars as an Order were extremely rich. Though they had personally taken vows of poverty, the Templar barns were always full of grain. They owned much land. They had castles and great houses. As individuals they were poor, but as a group they were immensely wealthy. They were rich enough to loan money to princes and kings.

'Don't be long now! Work awaits.'

Down below the other adults were beginning to drift out through the huge barn doorways. One knight was saying, 'Let's pray the harvest next year is as good as this one.' That's what the Horkey Branch was for, to ensure a good following harvest. Men and women were supposed to be Christians now, but the former gods and superstitions had not been cast aside. Frigg and Thunor, Tiw and Woden, the old Anglo-Saxon gods, they were still part of village life. People were careful to keep some of the rituals associated with these deities, just in case. If the milk went sour Andrew's mother blamed Robin Good-fellow, sometimes called Puck, rather than fallen angels. If father slipped on a frozen puddle in the winter, he cursed Jack Frost, not Satan and his hordes. Blaming the Devil was reserved for much larger calamities, like serious illness.

A band of older boys remained in the barn, waiting for Andrew to come down from the rafters.

'Come on, cloth-ears,' snarled Harold, the boy who had been struck by the knight, 'come and get your reward.'

Harold the butcher's son was one of the most popular lads in the village despite the fact he was a bit of a bully. He was tall, good-looking and strong. His smile was broad and infectious, and his cheery greeting uplifting. The girls were fond of him. The other youths looked up to him. Adults liked him because he was helpful and would lend a shoulder to any task if requested by a neighbour. They forgave him his nasty jealous streak because it was usually only directed at one or two boys of no consequence. He didn't like Andrew because Andrew could outrun him and he could swim, too. Over the years he had made Andrew's life a misery, with his bullying ways.

'What, so you can throw me in the pond again?' replied Andrew.

'Nah, not since you learned the Devil's trick of walking on water,' replied Harold. 'We'll just throw you in a hawthorn hedge. See if you can walk on spikes.'

Thanks to repeated duckings in the village pond and the local river, Andrew had been forced to learn to swim. None of the other village boys were able to do this and they regarded the skill as another dubious gift from the warlock's wife who had assisted at Andrew's birth. Remaining on the surface of water, without the help of a boat, was highly suspicious to ignorant, simple villagers who had no need of such a talent. Even the adults regarded Andrew's ability to swim with great mistrust.

'I think I'll stay here,' Andrew called down, 'if it's all the same to you.'

'I'll come up there and get you.'

'I wish you would. I'll kick you down again. You think you can fight me without the others helping you?'

Harold considered this challenge with a frown and finally decided that his valour deserted him.

'Well, then, I think I'll just wait.' He folded his arms and set himself in a determined pose.

With that, Andrew took a crust of bread from his pocket, settled himself astride a rafter and began chewing.

'Please yourself.'

Fairly soon, as Andrew knew would happen, the other boys began to get bored. At first they started larking around in the barn itself, but after a while they left. Harold stayed for a short time, still smouldering with annoyance at being struck by the knight. Then he, too, became restless and went to leave, but instructed a young girl of about six years old to 'scream out when he comes down'.

The youngster was an urchin in a filthy smock, her arms and legs covered in grime and her hair matted with cooking grease. Once Harold had gone the girl, whose name was Imogen, scuffed about on the dirt floor below. She had just recovered from elf-water disease and still had the spots all over her dirty face. She looked up at Andrew and said, 'If you give me a farthin', I won't do nothin'.'

'I haven't got a farthing.'

'That bit of bread then?'

Andrew stopped chewing the crust and looked at it. What was left was about the size of his hand. He held his arm out and dropped the crust down on to the dirt floor. Imogen reached down and snatched up the heel of loaf, sucking on it almost immediately.

Andrew descended warily, not at all sure that the girl wouldn't yell for the youths now that she had the crust.

'I won't scream,' she said. 'I said I wouldn't.'

'Thank you.'

Andrew dropped to the floor, ran through the small doorway at the back and round the barn, heading for the walled garden tended by the monks. Once inside he would be safe from attack. Unfortunately for Andrew, however, the other boys had foreseen his plan and were waiting at the entrance to the garden. Harold saw him, too, and grinned.

A stone struck Andrew on the back as he tried to get away, then another. Two boys were waiting behind trees as he ran between them. They came out with cudgels and laughed as they swung at his legs, catching him painfully on the shins. He knew he had to stay on his feet, though, or they would be on him like a pack of dogs.

'How's that?' cried a thick-set youth called Carter, as he struck Andrew on the knee with his stick. 'Want more of *this* Horkey Branch, witchboy?'

Andrew flung out an arm and caught the youth on the mouth, causing it to gush with blood. His assailant yelled in pain and humiliation. But then the other boy struck Andrew hard across the shoulders with his cudgel and Andrew stumbled, almost going down. He regained his feet and ran away from the two, while those following behind pelted him with stones. Fortunately he was not hit again.

He raced for a part of the high wall overhung by the branches of a medlar tree. Leaping from the ground at a run, he caught hold of a bough and gripped it firmly. For a moment he thought his fingers were going to slip, but he managed to hold on. Quickly he hauled himself up until he was astride the top of the wall. Harold arrived, panting and almost foaming at the mouth with frustration. Andrew stared down at his enemy, who now looked like the thwarted cur that he was.

'Not today, coward,' Andrew said to Harold. 'Try your luck tomorrow, you thick-headed oaf.' Then he dropped down into the garden, where he rubbed his painful bruises and cursed those who made his life a misery.

Finally, he looked around him.

Friar Nottidge was there, as always.

The thin, eternally distracted friar was in charge of the gardens, with their herb beds, an orchard of fruit trees and several vegetable patches. There was a fish pool there, and an ornamental knot garden where the Templar knights would go and sit and meditate by its central fount, the only one in all England which had a puff-cheeked image of a Green Woman in bronze on one of its four sides, the other three featuring the usual Green Men. The children of the village believed the Green Woman's head came to life at night. They said she went out in search of sleepers' limbs hanging outside the bedclothes. When she found one she would sink her teeth into the white flesh, biting deep and hard.

As soon as Andrew was within the walls of the garden, the scent of herbs and flowers enveloped him in an invisible blanket of richness. He let out a sigh. He found a sense of peace in the walled garden that was not to be had anywhere else, even in the church. He breathed in the smells deeply, filling his body with them. They seemed to cleanse him, to purify his blood. The autumn colours washed over him, too, for the earth was getting ready to sleep.

The good friar was standing among the quinces when Andrew approached him.

'Hello, friar.'

Friar Nottidge paled and visibly jumped, putting a rough hand over his fast-beating heart.

'Oh my goodness, where did you come from, Andrew?'

'I climbed over the wall by the medlar tree.'

'Oh? I didn't see you. You were quiet in doing so, then.' In truth, the good friar was almost deaf and he glanced towards the spot where the medlar and quince trees grew, as if mildly suspicious of the story, then he turned back to the figure before him. 'Oh well, here you are and all's right, I suppose. So, let's forget your sudden entrance into the world. Will you help me gather some household herbs?'

Andrew ignored the implication that he had appeared suddenly, as if by magic. He knew that even the monks believed he had been corrupted by a witch. If the friar wanted to think Andrew had the power of making himself invisible, so be it. After all this time, to protest and deny would only make matters worse. It was best simply to take no notice and to act as if there had been no unspoken accusation.

'Yes, friar, that's what I came to you for. What do you want me to fetch?'

'Hmmm. Fly repellent, for a start – you know that one?'

'Yellow loosestrife, friar.'

'Good, good. And some mugwort, to flavour the ale. Woodruff, mullein for candlewicks, pennyroyal to strew on the prior's bed – he does love the scent of it – oh, and some orris to repair the chairs . . .'

The list was quite long and included gillyflowers, old red clove, Caesar's mantle, chard, heartsease, vervain and Good King Henry. Andrew enjoyed working and gathering in the walled garden. He liked the names of the herbs, he liked the scents they gave off and he thought it was wonderful that they had so many uses. Most important of all were the Nine Sacred Herbs:

Wergula
Mugwort
Waybread
Maythen
Fennel
Stime
Crab
Chervil
Atterlothe.

It was quite different from helping his pa at the forge, which was heavy, solid work, hammering white-hot metal and showering the dark corners of the room with sparks. The smell of burning was always in the air at the forge. It was not a thoroughly unpleasant odour, but neither was it a smell that left one feeling good. It was Andrew's job to operate the cowhorn handle of the bellows to send a blast of air down a pipe into the heart of the fire and make it blaze. Occasionally he would be allowed to punch the holes in the horseshoes, but was never permitted to shape them to the hooves, that being a farrier's art. Andrew had always lived with the ringing of hammer on anvil, an alarm that raised him from his bed in the morning, an accompaniment that sent him to sleep at night, as his father reworked old iron horseshoes into shepherds' crooks, or wheel-hub collars, or axe heads – anything to make an extra penny.

Andrew worked the rest of the day in the walled garden with Friar Nottidge, but there came a time when he knew he would have to leave for the hovel in which his parents lived. His mother would be wondering where he was and Andrew started feeling guilty. It was his job to bring in water from the well and fetch wood for the fire. He bade good evening to the friar and then climbed over the back wall, fearful that his earlier tormentors would be waiting for him by the gardens' entrance. Then he slipped past stables and priory, where the knights and their retainers were milling around, some busy, others idle. The village itself was a fair distance from the Templar enclave, but he reached his home without incident.

'Water,' said his mother when he appeared in the doorway, 'then the wood, if you please, Mister Horkey!'

There was pride in her voice, however. It had been a great honour, being the Horkey Boy. And knights would often slip the chosen one a coin or two for luck when they recognised him around the place. Andrew would have to make himself visible in the village tomorrow morning to take advantage of his good fortune. It would mean braving the bullies but it would probably be worth it.

'Yes, Ma.'

He took the wooden pail and ran to the well, filling it in a few minutes and returning with it. Then, grabbing another crust from the table where his mother stood preparing the evening meal, he set out for the woodland. Overhead, gloomy looking clouds were scudding across the darkening sky. It was said that Frigg used a beech broom to sweep them over the heavens. Andrew did not stare upwards too long, in case he should catch sight of the goddess. That would be bad luck indeed, and sure to bring catastrophe on the household. For the same reason he tried to banish thoughts of ditch fairies out of his head, for one certain way of getting them to appear was to allow your thoughts to dwell on their presence. If you became too concerned about them, they would pour out of ratholes and rabbit warrens and carry you off to their lands. If you protested they bit you with their tiny poisonous teeth.

There was plenty of dead wood on the edge of the forest and Andrew soon had an armful. However, when he turned back towards the village he saw his way was blocked. A gang of boys headed by Harold were coming up the dirty track. Several held cudgels in their hands, and some carried stones. Andrew could see there was violence in the hearts of these bullies: they were intent on beating him senseless. It had happened before and Andrew had been ill for a long time afterwards. Some had hoped he would not recover. They wished him dead. The monks might say something afterwards, especially Friar Nottidge, but most of the peasants in the village were as suspicious of Andrew as their children, and in the end nothing would be done about the crime.

'What do you want?' he called to the boys. 'I'm meeting someone here – one of the knights . . .'

'Liar,' called Harold, his simpleton's face twisted into a visage of hate. 'A lot of lies from a witch's spawn. It's time we sent you back to the Devil where you belong, you festering boil. No one's goin' to help you this time. I'll see you . . .'

Harold's sentence was cut short as his legs buckled and he dropped to the ground, his forehead spurting blood. Andrew had let go of the sticks and in a moment had picked up a stone and flung it as hard as he could. The flint had struck his enemy square above the eyes. The youth's burly frame had folded like an empty sack to the ground. Harold's friends were at first stunned by the swiftness of the attack, but they soon rallied and charged, yelling and waving their clubs.

15

Indeed, they would have been on Andrew and beaten him senseless, probably to death, if something untoward had not then occurred. A strange shape suddenly launched itself from the edge of the woodland and swept between Andrew and his attackers. It had a white, hideous face and it screeched loudly. The village boys ran back in terror and Andrew jumped away in fright himself. Then they all saw what it was – nothing more than a barn owl, which swept away over the meadow.

'Witchboy,' cried the village youths.

For once Andrew did not blame them. It had indeed seemed like dark magic, conjuring a bird of prey to defend himself. This was not the first time a raptor had appeared to come to his aid. One or two incidents in the past had seen a kestrel and a goshawk come to his rescue, as if called by someone, or sent by someone.

Missiles were again launched at Andrew and he turned and ran into the darkness of the great forest, stones striking the trees around him.

The boys followed him only a short way in, then they turned back and ran out again as he knew they would. Beyond the woods were fens and marshes where grotesque and blood-thirsty monsters lived, creatures that fed on children and tore adults from limb to limb. These fearsome beings sometimes wandered out of the bogs and into the woodland. This was 'Hunter's-moon' month in the old Saxon calendar, when hungry spirits roamed abroad. Ghosts could smell fresh blood and Harold would certainly not dare enter the wood with his wound running red.

Andrew kept walking, though, in case there were braver souls among those cowards on the edge of the forest. The trees seemed deeply black and hostile as darkness fell. They had not yet lost their leaves so the canopy blocked out any light from the sky. Nettles and brambles brushed his legs, stinging and pricking them. He was, like all the boys of that age, wearing a simple smock and his legs were bare. But his physical discomfort did not concern him as much as his mind and spirit. Andrew was afraid, he admitted it to himself. No one with any good sense wandered in a woodland after dark.

A little while later the moon rose and light came through the forest's branches. There was enough to follow a path to a log in a small glade, where he sat down and miserably contemplated his problems. The boys – and some of the girls – would never leave him alone. He was destined to be bullied while he stayed in Cressing village. Yet what else could he do? He had nowhere else to go. The world outside Cressing was a mystery to him. He had heard of the great city of London, and the nearer town of Chelmsford, but which way did they lie? And what would he do once he got to either of them? He had no real skills apart from a little gardening knowledge and something of his father's trade. Farriers were in demand, of course, but it took years to gather the expertise to fashion things from heated iron. Perhaps he could offer himself as an assistant to some farrier, but often men of trade took their own sons into the business and had no need of strangers.

'I'm not staying here in this dull village,' he cried out, loudly, his voice ringing sharp and clear even in the tree-clustered wood. 'I need to leave, to get out into the wide world, where I can make my fortune.'

A cold wind suddenly sprang up, almost as if it had been summoned by Andrew's outburst. It cut through the trees and chilled Andrew's flesh. He hugged himself with his arms, wondering where it had come from just like that, and why it penetrated so deeply into his bones. The moon above edged behind a cloud, not disappearing altogether, but its light was now considerably paler than before. He became aware that the sounds of the forest had ceased. A tawny owl's hooting in the distance had stopped. The cold coughing bark of a fox had fallen silent. Everything was now strangely still, the new wind not even seeming to stir the leaves. Then he heard a noise like a wild boar crashing through the undergrowth.

'What is it?' he cried, alarmed. 'Is anyone there?'

In that moment he observed two forms moving determinedly through the moonshadows. He wanted to run but his legs froze solid and his breath quickened as the two figures stepped into the glade. He recognised them straight away. One was a hanged murderer and the other was his victim. They were talking to each other in low voices, arguing, gesturing as they paced along, heading towards the same log which Andrew had chosen as his seat.

'I tell you,' muttered the hunched murderer in an angry tone, 'I cannot forgive you. I was wronged by you in life and you deserved what you got.'

The victim, a tall, gaunt fellow, pointed to the ugly cleft in his skull which had been left by the axe wielded by the other.

'No man deserves this. I may have cheated you, yes, I *did* cheat you, but then it was the same for everyone. You were not especially chosen. I cheated everyone, equally.'

The murderer was heavy-set, burly, with a hump upon his shoulders and a head that lolled forward with its own weight. His torso had been opened from neck to belly and loose flaps of skin curtained an empty hole which his soft organs had once occupied. There were no eyes in his head and his lips were in tatters, revealing long pegs of yellow teeth, jutting from gums that shone with slime.

Andrew recalled that this man was a tenant farmer and had employed the victim, a casual labourer, to help him with harvesting his grain. He paid the labourer by the weight of the gathered grain, only later to find rocks in the bottom of the sacks when he came to empty them. Incensed, the farmer had set out to retrieve his money, only to find the labourer had spent it all on drink for himself and others at an inn. The farmer then took an axe and clove the man's head, felling him like an animal bred for slaughter. The labourer's drinking companions bayed for his blood and the local baron, who was fond of hangings, obliged them by sending the murderer to the gallows, and thence to a gibbet.

The murderer argued, 'Then you deserved to have a dozen axes buried in your head. How can I show remorse for an act which I believe to have been justified?'

'Because, you oaf, you was found guilty of murder by the baron himself, and was dangled for it. Murder is a monstrous crime, unchristian and against the law of the land. How can that be justified . . .?'

Andrew watched this exchange in terror. He was so frightened he was almost choking on his own breath, but to his credit he did not leap up and run away. There was a curiosity in him which sometimes got him into trouble, but at other times provided him with valuable experiences.

Andrew knew that dead men walked. It was common knowledge, but he had never before witnessed such a ghastly sight. These two decaying beings were between worlds. One, or both, deserved to be in Hell. In the moonlight he could see the rotting flesh was liquefying and beginning to slip in gobbets from their bones to the ground beneath. Andrew kept quite still, hoping he would not be noticed, but eventually both dead men turned his way and the murderer addressed him in a mournful voice.

'Ah, but we should not argue in front of the living – here's the shaveling. Let's sit and talk.'

And they sat, one either side of him, stiffly upright.

'What do you want with me?' asked Andrew. To his chagrin he was still shaking violently. The smell of decay was appalling and made him feel unwell. 'Are you here to take me away?'

'Not that, lad,' said the victim, in hollow tones, as if he were speaking from somewhere deep down in a well. 'Someone who has your interest at heart sent us with a message. We've come to tell you something you might want to know. We have knowledge of your future, boy, being as we are not of your world, but looking in on it, so to speak, from another. When you entered the wood, we felt your sorrow which entered our damned souls and courses hot and deep through our empty veins. We feel your pain and have some-thing of a remedy.'

'Know this,' said the murderer, turning his darkly ravaged features to look down upon Andrew's own, 'that one day you will become a famous knight, a Templar, who will distinguish himself on the battlefields of the Holy Land. So cease this self-pity, for it sears through what's left of our poor mortal remains. It burns, boy, it burns. Now, we'll leave you to the owls and foxes, and be on our way . . . Josiah Buncart, you poor excuse for a cadaver' – the murderer had now risen from the log along with his victim and they moved off together again, into the tangle of shadows on the edge of the glade – 'let me say once more, clear and precise, I cannot, I will not, rescind. Guilty by the baron, or no, I feel in my heart, or rather in the place where that organ once dwelt before the crows ate it, that I am right in this matter.'

'Wait,' cried the murdered man from the edge of the glade. He stopped suddenly, turned to the murderer, then pointed back at Andrew. 'We have to tell the boy a *secret*.'

'No, no. We was particularly asked *not* to tell the boy the secret. If you remember, Josiah, we was told to keep mum on that account.'

'Was we?'

'Indeed we was. You will remember the words, "Seal your dead lips on the matter of the secret." I'm surprised you don't remember that, Josiah, I really am. Your memory seems to have got much worse since you died. It never was very good when you was alive, but now it's all shot to pieces.'

'I didn't just die, I was horribly murdered. Suffering such a deed is bound to affect a man's memory . . .'

'What secret?' cried Andrew, interrupting them. 'Is it something I need to know?'

'As to that,' said the murderer, 'you might *need* to know, but are we the ones to tell you? The answer to that question is *no*. It's not in our writ. Goodbye.'

The two men faded into the darkness.

Once the glade was quiet again Andrew's heart began to slow to its normal pace. How horrible to witness the dead walking! Yet, they had given him a message. He would be a knight! Was that possible? Andrew was a lowly farrier's son. To be a knight of the realm one needed to be of noble birth, surely? Yet he had it from the mouths of the dead, that this was his destiny. Had they said he would be a prince, he would be loath to believe it. What a wondrous prophecy, if it were to come true. In an instant his life had changed. There was a great light at the end of the road, instead of just bleakness, darkness. Once he was a famous knight, of course, he would return and wreak vengeance on those who had tortured him in his youth. They would suffer as he had suffered – worse, they would wish they had never been born.

But then again, what was this secret they had spoken of? Was it the key to riches? Or to immortality? Something good and valuable? Or was it a bad thing, a thing to watch out for and avoid if possible? Andrew would never know now that the dead men had gone. And who had sent this gruesome pair? Had they come at the bidding of the warlock's wife? Or some angel or demon? Perhaps he would never know that either. A secret, a secret. What could it be? Yet why worry? How silly to concentrate on just those words! His whole future life was a secret, wasn't it? Death was a secret. There were thousands of secrets around, some of which never would be revealed.

The main thing was the prophecy.

He was to be a knight one day.

Andrew stayed in the forest until the early hours of the morning and then slipped out, down the dew-sprinkled meadows to the village. He went straight to Friar Nottidge's cell and woke him with a gentle hand. The good friar was still in his filthy habit, which he wore day and night, and woke with a startled shout, 'What? Who? Why?'

'It's me, friar,' whispered Andrew. 'I've come to say goodbye.'

Friar Nottidge sat up and rubbed his bristly face.

'You're leaving? That's wise, boy.'

'How so, friar?'

'They're after your hide. They say you struck a youth with a stone. His head is broken and he's at present a simpleton who talks in riddles.'

Andrew sighed. 'Will he recover, friar?'

'Oh, I expect so.'

'I did strike him, friar, but he deserved it. They were going to kill me, I'm sure they were. There must have been twenty of them. They had rocks and cudgels. I was simply defending myself.'

'That's not the story I heard. The boy was walking by himself, on his way to fish in the pond, when you attacked him.'

'They're lying,' said Andrew, fiercely. 'They've always lied.'

'Well now, you say you're leaving. What will you do, Andrew?'

'I am to become a knight,' replied Andrew, proudly. 'It was told to me by two dead men.'

The friar stiffened. 'Careful boy – no sacrilege.'

''Tis true, friar. I spoke with a murderer and his victim. They walk the forest, arguing about who was right and who was wrong.'

'And the names of these ghouls?'

Andrew gave them.

The friar nodded, scratching at the flea bites which covered his abdomen and bottom. 'Ahhh,' he murmured, 'their bodies will need to be exhumed from the earth. There is only one cure for walking dead who can't resolve their differences. We must cut the heads off their corpses and rebury them with their skulls between their legs. That's a sure cure for such evil practices. Only one corpse will be in the churchyard, of course. The other won't be buried in consecrated ground, being a murderer. I must ask the baron where his mortal remains have been placed. But you, young Andrew, a knight? I think not. You have not the right colour blood for such an elevation in the world.'

'But they said . . .'

'Forget what you've been told by the Devil's spawn, boy. How can you trust a murderer and a cheat? Don't fool yourself with such inflated ideas. You'll only be disappointed. You're not worth a pig's bladder, unfortunately, being of such lowly birth.'

'Yes, friar,' replied Andrew, thinking the fool was the priest, for he was now certain he was destined for fame. 'Now I have to go. Please speak with my ma and pa. Tell them not to worry, for I will find work and one day return. I don't know where I shall go now, but the Lord will look after me, provide for me, won't he, friar?'

'Oh,' replied the friar, laying back down and closing his eyes again, 'I wouldn't bank on that, boy. He's not that reliable, whatever monks like me tell you. I've seen beggars die of starvation while they've been praying at the altars of great churches and women die of thirst with their arms around a holy cross bearing the image of Christ Jesus himself.'

'Thank you, friar, you're a great comfort,' said Andrew, not without a note of sarcasm in his tone.

'You're welcome, my boy. No point in going out into the world with false hopes. Look to your good sense, your able hands – and try not to thieve, even when you're hungry.'

'Yes, friar, goodbye friar.'

But Friar Nottidge was already asleep.

2. THE PLAYERS

Andrew set out on the road, leaving his parents and two sisters behind him with a heavy heart. He had no idea where he was going or what he was going to do once he had decided. It seemed natural just to follow the dirt track wherever it went, hoping his luck would lead him to fortune. On the road that day he was passed by several knights and their retainers, some on foot, some on horseback. They took absolutely no notice of him. He might have been invisible for all they cared. He passed through one or two villages, but those occupants who saw him stared at him with distrust, since they knew by his smock that he was a peasant, and peasants did not normally travel on the open lanes. If they were serfs, they were bound to their masters, and, if free men, locked to their workplace.

Five miles from home he came across a shack which was not much more than a lean-to. Outside, with a log for a stool, sat a woman who had once lived in the village of Cressing. She had been turned out by her husband and driven from the village with sticks and stones. Andrew felt they had a little in common, since he had to all intents and purposes been banished, too. Her name was Ruth, the baker's wife, and her crime had been to give birth to twins.

Ruth was old and lined of face before her time. She appeared thin and wasted, clad only in a dress made out of old flour sacks and a threadbare shawl. She was stirring a pot over a fire. The pot appeared to contain nothing but potato water.

'Hello, mistress,' said Andrew.

She looked up, her eyes empty of all expression.

'What? Andrew, the farrier's son? Have they sent you to torment me further?'

'No, mistress, no. I'm running away.'

'Well, run as far away as you can, boy, for you'll get no mercy from that lot.' She nodded in the direction of the village.

'I – I'm sorry for your misfortune,' said Andrew.

There did not seem anything more to say, so he walked on. He was upset, now that he had seen the woman's plight, though he had not thought of her at all while he had been in Cressing. It was only a year since Ruth the baker's wife had produced her twins. They were both killed instantly, of course, because everyone knew that one of any pair of twins must have been conceived by the Devil. Since no one knew which of the two was the evil one, it was safest to kill both. And the woman who bore them had obviously consorted with Satan, or she would not have brought such creatures into the world. So her husband and neighbours felt quite justified in banishing her from her own home.

By midday Andrew found he was hungry and crawled through a hedge and stole a turnip from a field. If he had been caught, he would have been hanged there and then from the nearest tree or signpost. However, he managed to gnaw his way through the vegetable and fill his stomach without being caught. Towards evening, however, he found himself joined by a middle-aged man called Jake, a fellow in tattered clothing which had once been good material. Jake was lean with crafty eyes that never looked into your face. He was always looking sideways, as if he had caught sight of something in that direction, on the ground.

'You an' me, we could do well together,' sniffed Jake, as they found a ditch to sleep in. 'We could watch each other's backs.' Jake filled a dirty green hat with sods of earth and grass torn from the banks of the ditch and pummelled the result with his fist into a makeshift pillow.

'Why would we do that?' asked Andrew.

'So's no one takes us for fools. Protection, see, from them as would harm us.'

'Who would that be? Who would harm us?'

'Anyone what didn't like us,' replied Jake in an exasperated tone of voice. 'Look,' he explained, 'perhaps someone would want to rob you, but I'd be there to stop 'im, wouldn't I?'

'I've got nothing to steal.'

Jake, who had rested his head back on his turf-filled hat, sat up quickly and seemed upset by this news.

He frowned. 'What, nothin' at all?'

'Not a penny. Not a crust of bread. Nothing.'

'Oh?' This caused his new companion brief consternation, but Jake rallied quickly. 'Well, that makes us close, so to speak, for I also have nought in my purse. We are bosom companions, you an' me. We must seek our fortunes together.'

'Have you anything to eat?' asked Andrew. 'If we're bosom friends, we ought to share our food.'

'What have you got then?' asked Jake.

'Nothing.'

28

'What, nothin' at all?'

'Nothing at all.'

'Then neither 'ave I.'

But later, after dark, Andrew heard munching and could smell the juice of an apple.

'Can I have some?' he asked.

'Wot?' Jake snapped.

'Apple.'

'Oh, that,' came the casual reply out of the dark, 'that's a rat what's found a crab, you know. Nothin' to do with me.'

Andrew knew the man was lying but, wisely, did not argue. During the night he felt the rank breath of someone leaning over him and unfriendly hands exploring the pocket on the front of his smock. Opening one eye he caught the glint of moonlight on a small knife that was poised over his face. He closed the eye again, quickly, and pretended he was still asleep, worried that if he showed any signs of being awake he would get his throat cut. After a while there were grunts from the would-be thief, when nothing was discovered on his person, and then he was left alone. Andrew did not go to sleep again. When at last he heard snoring he rose softly and began walking along the lane, putting distance between himself and his erstwhile travelling companion.

Jake caught up with him around mid-morning.

'That weren't very friendly, boy,' growled Jake. 'Goin' off like that without a by-your-leave.'

Andrew knew he would have to assert himself or he would never rid himself of this foul pest. He stepped aside and picked up a heavy stone from the edge of the track.

'Get away from me,' he said, firmly, 'or I'll cave your head.'

29

Jake's head jerked backwards. 'Hey, no need for such – I'm just a lonely man who wants company.'

'Find it elsewhere.' Andrew knew he was bigger and stronger than this sly, skinny creature, even though he was a mere boy. 'Be very sure I will use this rock on your head, you maggot. The reason I'm on this road is because I broke another boy's skull. I'm happy to do the same for you, if you don't leave me alone. No more talk now. Just walk on.'

'But . . .' Jake started to argue, but on looking into Andrew's eyes saw danger and wisely skittered away, along the lane. 'I'll see you get yours,' Jake cried, when he was at a safe distance. 'You just wait, boy. You're not finished with me yet.'

Andrew threw the stone which missed Jake's head by a whisker. Jake's legs suddenly became animated and he skipped away and was soon out of sight. Andrew followed at a measured pace, hoping that Jake would run all the way to the next town. Andrew made a mental note to bypass the next place he came to, in case Jake decided he would camp there to make trouble. Though why the man should bother with a penniless youth was beyond him. There was nothing to gain from it except malicious pleasure.

'If he wants to make an enemy of me,' muttered Andrew, 'he'll surely regret it.'

By noon the next day, Andrew was once again ravenously hungry. There were no crops in the fields he passed by; rather, they were pastures for cattle and sheep. He tried knocking on the door of a hovel, but was chased away by a woman clutching a fire poker who narrowly missed striking his head. He began to eye the birds in the hedgerows, thinking he might eat them raw if he could just manage to catch one. He did see a fox with a pigeon in its jaws but did not have a hope of catching the beast and wrenching its prey from its mouth. A few blackthorn sloes only made him feel worse, his mouth becoming dry and puckered after he'd bitten into them. He drank from a pond a while later and was immediately sick.

One day he came across the body of a man lying in a rocky gully. He had been dead for some time, for the flesh was rotten on the bones. The corpse had been eaten by crows and other wildlife. No one had even cared enough to bury the remains. This was the world outside the village. If you were in a community, there was always someone who would show concern for your welfare. If you were out in the wide world, you were on your own. No one was responsible for your well being, no one cared whether you lived or died. You were a stranger, and strangers were suspicious people who were harried or hustled out of the district, before they did something unspeakable. No one was aware that Andrew was a good, honest lad. Not out here. All they saw was a lone young rascal in a dirty smock who was probably going to steal from them, or worse. Someone who was not where he should be.

On the fourth night he lay once again in a ditch, wondering whether he would rather not wake the next morning, for he had found nothing but misery on the open road. Knighthood was the last thing on his mind now. Survival was paramount, if that indeed was what he desired. Wretched and desperately unhappy, the loneliness was the thing that raked his soul and left it bleeding. He had not even been out of his own village less than a week, yet he missed it desperately. All his life he had been surrounded by people he knew. Some he had loved, some he had not. But he had known them all.

31

Out here every man, woman and child was unfamiliar to him. They stared at him with hard eyes. They curled their lips as they watched him pass. He yearned for a kind word but got nothing but snarls. He felt like a leper, shunned by all, despised by all. This was his land, ruled over by one king, and these were his countrymen, his fellow Englishmen. Yet they treated him like a rabid dog which had wandered into their domain.

In the early dawn he woke feeling woozy and strange. A figure came walking out of a field towards him. He thought at first it was Jake come back. He was just about to yell at him, to tell him to go away, when he saw he was mistaken. It was a scarecrow. The scarecrow, a man composed of crossed sticks, a tattered cape and a turnip head, stood before him.

'What do you want?' asked Andrew, less concerned by this weird happening than perhaps he ought to be. 'You want to persecute me, too?'

The scarecrow's smock waved in the wind as the creature answered him: 'You look hungry.'

'Of course I'm hungry. I could eat your head.'

'You could, but it's been out in the wind and the rain too long – it's as hard as brick.'

'Just now I could eat a brick.'

At that moment a gust of wind caught the scarecrow, filling his cape like a sail. The creature was lifted off its feet and carried away like a rag on the back of a gale. Andrew watched it go, wondering if its head had indeed been too hard to eat.

Falling asleep again, he dreamed of bread and chicken, only to wake with his stomach feeling as if it were full of flints.

'Oh God, please help me,' he said, as he fell into an illness-drugged sleep. 'Who else is there?'

Andrew was now at his lowest ebb. He was weak through starvation, his head was full of thoughts akin to wild birds, and he saw things. Everyone knew that there existed a race of spirit beings which lived invisibly in the same world as men. He began to catch passing glimpses of these creatures out of the corners of his eyes, wispy wraiths which appeared to be mocking him. These he knew were *scuccas*, demons from the Under World which often appeared on Earth in the form of dogs or rooks. Then there were shining misty beings that flitted before him and chased the demons away. These he knew to be angels. Sometimes the demons and angels fought a fierce but silent battle around him. The angels always won these encounters. Andrew knew if they ever lost his soul would be carried off by the loathsome, fiery-eyed *scuccas* and taken somewhere dreadful.

The next dawn came, as dawns always do. Andrew crawled out of the ditch and walked a short way to a market town. There he washed under the cold water of the pump and drank to fill his empty stomach. When he had finished he went and sat on the steps of the wooden hall where the heads of the guilds met to discuss trade, nursing his misery. Shortly afterwards three youths came sauntering down the street. They were chattering to one another in animated voices, obviously good friends. Unlike Andrew, in his country-boy smock, they were dressed in woollen leggings and overtunics, though clearly the clothes were not new, for they were ragged at the edges. One of the boys, the one who was doing the most talking, wore a jaunty green hat with a long, pointed cloth peak. The boys went first to a horse trough in the middle of the square, then caught sight of the pump and drank from that instead.

Andrew noticed that the shortest of them had a lute slung over his right shoulder, while the largest youth carried a bundle which no doubt contained the worldly belongings of all three boys.

Like Andrew, they were obviously passing through.

Gathering his courage, Andrew smoothed down his smock and then stumbled across the square to confront the new arrivals.

'Hello, what have we here?' said the boy with the hat. 'Mr Turnip-Shoes seems to want a word with us.'

Andrew stood and swayed, clearing his throat.

'You – you drank from the town pump without permission. My master is the . . . the person responsible for the pump. I'm afraid it will cost you a penny each.'

Two of the boys laughed and the one with the hat grinned, saying, 'Oh, it will, will it, Sir Cabbage-Drawers?'

'Why are you making fun of me?' asked Andrew, incensed by their mirth at his expense. 'I have explained this troubled situation to you. If you prefer jail or the stocks, by all means keep up your jibes and taunts. But you would be well advised to heed my friendly warning. Pay now, or face a good deal of regret.' He drew himself up to his full height. 'I'm a patient man, sir, but my patience has its limits.'

'Oh, you are, are you? Well, sir, I'm all atremble.' He opened the worn leather purse at his belt. 'It seems I must give you your due, or I will be thrown in the dungeon and tortured for my penny.' He fumbled for a minute then withdrew a ball of fluff. 'Here, sir. I pay my fine with interest. Keep the change.'

'Patrick,' said the largest of the three youths, his pleasant features sporting a wide grin, 'leave the lad alone. Can't you see he's hungry?'

'Yes, Patrick,' said the other youth, a small, wiry-looking boy with a frizzy little beard projecting from his chin, 'let's be on our way.'

Patrick, who was of medium height and well proportioned, looked Andrew up and down with pity in his eyes, then nodded. As all three turned and began to walk away, Andrew panicked and called out, 'I shall have to inform the authorities of your reluctance to follow the law. You shall have future cause to regret your impulsiveness, sirs, believe me.'

Patrick now turned again. He looked angry now. He seemed about to give Andrew a mouthful of abuse, when his expression suddenly changed.

'Now where,' he said, 'does a country bumpkin like you learn such full-blown speech? Long words, well-formed, delivered with aplomb? Look, boy, we know you're not in charge of the pump. Town pumps are for the use of all men, whether citizen or stranger. So you can let go of your false indignation. Is it food you want? Are you indeed hungry? Here,' he reached into his purse and drew out a small, bright coin that flashed in the weak autumn sunshine, 'go and buy yourself a pie, for goodness' sakes. There's a baker just along the street. Just follow the smell of newly baked bread and you'll find him eager to sell you his goods. We know. We've just paid him a visit ourselves.'

Andrew looked at the shiny coin. 'I – I'm no beggar, sir.'

'Oh for the Lord's sake,' cried Patrick, 'now he doesn't want it! Take the silver farthin', lad. I've no use for it. Fill your belly with pastry and meat and then go home, wherever that is.'

With tears of humiliation in his eyes, Andrew snatched the coin from the youth's hand.

'I learned my speech,' he said, in a gravelly voice, 'from my friend Friar Nottidge. He taught me the meanings of many fine words, and he gave me lessons in figures and geometry.'

'Good for Friar Nottidge. Now, boy, go and get that pie.'

Andrew did as he was bidden, running along the streets until he came to a pie shop. The baker sold Andrew a day-old pie and watched with round eyes as the boy wolfed it, hardly pausing for breath. There was enough for a second stale pastry which went the way of the first. Now that his belly was full, Andrew went looking for the three youths again. They were sitting outside an inn drinking weak ale, arguing among themselves over some trivial subject. They looked up at him as he approached.

'I've come to say thank you,' said Andrew. 'You were right, I was starving.'

'Tell us your story, lad, for Arthur and Toby here are eager to hear it,' said Patrick, sipping his jug.

'I have run away from Cressing village to seek my fortune.'

'Cressing? Isn't that the Templars' manor?'

'It is.'

'And where have you been looking for this fortune you hope to find? In ditch-row rabbit holes?'

'Now you're making fun of me again,' said Andrew, stiffly, 'and I won't stand for that. You'll oblige me by meeting me at single-sticks on the town green, if you please.'

The three youths roared with laughter. 'He's a one, an't he?' cried Toby, the giant among the trio. 'We should have him with us.'

Patrick raised his eyebrows below the fancy hat, then nodded in approval. 'So we should. We need a smooth-chinned boy, do we not, since Arthur has grown that foul fuzz on his face? This youth is slim and would be more beguiling with a bit of rouge. How about it, runaway, would you like to join us?'

Andrew was puzzled, looking from one to another.

'Join you at what?'

'Why, at play-acting, you simple fellow. We're players. Do you not recognise our craft by our noble looks?'

All three instantly turned their heads sideways and froze, so that Andrew could admire their profiles. Then they turned back again, laughing and slapping their knees. Indeed, they seemed a merry crew and suddenly Andrew's heart lifted from the darkness, where it had lain for many days, into the light again.

'I had thought of becoming a knight,' Andrew confessed, 'but it would do no harm to earn a little money on the way.'

'Only a knight?' cried Patrick. 'Well, why aim so low? Why not a prince or a king, boy? Show a little ambition, if you please.'

'Do you always turn things into jokes?'

'Why certainly, lad, it's my profession to entertain, after all. If I'm not making people laugh, I'm making them cry. Shall I do my impression of Dido being spurned by Aeneas? Or Troilus after Cressida has run away to the Greeks? No, no, I cannot. It would tear your heart in two. Better to make you smile than make you weep, eh?'

Andrew found himself smiling now.

'Can I really join you?'

'Of course. Show him his costume, Toby, while Arthur orders the poor thirsty boy a drink.'

Toby undid the bundle he was carrying and took out an item of clothing. He let it unfurl in front of Andrew, while Patrick strummed a chord on the lute and sang, 'Tra-la-la!'

Andrew grimaced. It was a woman's dress. Quite an attractive blue frock with a lace collar, full length to the ground, though with a dirty hem that no doubt often trailed in the dirt.

'But why . . .?'

'We need a young female player,' said Patrick, sipping his ale. 'Arthur looks like a goat these days and fails to convince our audiences even of his inner beauty. You, my boy, have the looks of a strumpet – or will have, once we've powdered and rouged you, put a wig on you and Arthur's shown you his favourite mincing walk. Rough men will fall in love with you and women will envy you your deportment. You will be famous throughout the length and breadth of the land. Knights will soon be asking, "Who is she, this divine creature? I must make her my lady." While princes and kings will curse the fact that you are not of royal blood and are therefore unmarryable.'

'I – I don't know.'

Arthur placed a jug of ale in Andrew's fist.

'Would you rather starve?'

'No, of course not – but to impersonate a woman . . .'

'What do you think it's about, this acting?'

'I thought I might make a good villain – I can be quite savage in my demeanour, you know.'

Toby said, 'We already have villains and savages aplenty

38

– there are three of them here in front of you, for a start. Fine ladies with squeaky voices, however, are in short supply. Take it or leave it, lad. If you join us, it will be in silks and jewels, with ochre eyelids and bright red lips. No one will recognise you, now will they? Your own mother would pass you by on the street. Your father might give you a second glance, but it would be a lecherous stare, not one of "what's my boy all done up like a dog's dinner for?". Sit down, sup your ale, and thank God you met three generous players who took pity on you.'

So Andrew did just that, telling them his name and saying he was indebted to them forever.

'Of course you are,' Patrick agreed. 'When you become a knight, you'll remember your player friends and reward them with great riches and power, won't you? Until then, my friend, let's be thankful for an audience with a few coins in their pockets. We'll play this town tonight, then leave for the next. We never stay long in one place. A day or two at the most. If anything goes amiss in a neighbourhood – a murder or a robbery – the first people they look to blame are travelling players and gypsies. So it's best always to be on the move. Such evil crimes are usually committed by brothers or fathers of the victims, but players are vulnerable people, easily singled out by mobs. Remember that, young Andrew. If we wake you in the middle of the night and say 'Run', be sure you leap to your feet and follow us on our way.'

'I will indeed remember.'

The performance the troupe gave that evening was not an inspired one. Andrew's embarrassment at having to put on a female voice ruined the opening scene. He kept slipping back into a mumbled, apologetic male tone which had the audience shrieking and jeering. The piece was a serious Greek tragedy, but as always Patrick was quick to gauge the mood of the audience. Not long after they had begun he encouraged the others to overact and play the evening for laughs, which they received in plenty. Whenever the audience looked like it was turning away from them, Patrick would come to the rescue with the lute, singing a ludicrous love song to Andrew, who would cringe and look for an escape from the stage which was not to be had. The 'stage' was in fact simply the yard in front of the local alehouse. Once the audience had surrounded this area there was no retreat for the actors. When Andrew looked for an avenue to dive down, the audience would close it with a great guffaw, and push him back into the limelight.

'Well,' said Patrick afterwards, as they counted the coins, 'we got away with that one, but Andrew,' he wagged a finger in his new companion's face, 'this must not happen again or we'll have to part company.'

'I need some practice,' Andrew said, plaintively. 'You must teach me how to detach myself from myself. I watched you all, when I had no part to play, and saw that you became different people. How is that done? Will one of you please show me how to lie to myself? How to make Andrew believe he is Rosamund?'

The other three were impressed by Andrew's grasp of his problem and Toby said he would 'take him in hand'.

That night they slept in a barn on the edge of town, but were up just before dawn and on the road. They were headed for the great Essex town of Chelmsford, where Patrick felt they could attract a large audience. Using the open road as his stage Toby went through various changes of character, right in front of the fascinated Andrew, and gave Andrew some advice on how to get out of himself and into character.

'Say to yourself,' he told Andrew, 'that the sheriff is looking for Andrew of Cressing, believing him to have committed a serious crime. Say to yourself, "I must pretend I am not this person they seek, but another man, or woman, and I must convince them of that lie or I will be hanged, drawn and quartered before the sun goes down." Never look into the faces of your audience. Let them become a sea of pale, unrecognisable blobs. You are not playing the part for them, you are playing it for *yourself*. When the performance is over you must be in the frame of mind in which you have great difficulty in believing you are not Captain Black, the notorious pirate, but indeed simple Andrew.'

'I am not simple,' muttered Andrew.

Toby's face clouded over and became dark. 'And I say you are.'

Andrew stared at the giant youth before him.

'Why do you insult me, Toby?'

'Because you are a grub, a maggot, a slimy worm,' snarled Toby, viciously.

'I – I thought you liked me, Toby.'

'You?' growled Toby. 'I loathe you, you toad. In just a moment I might stamp on you, like the slug you are. What? You stare at me with starting eyes like a lunatic? How dare you put your gaze on me, the great Caesar? Is a mighty warrior to be ogled by a peasant, a goatboy from nowhere? I have commanded armies of thousands. You, you have ministered to stinking nannies and their offspring. Away with you.'

41

Andrew suddenly grasped what was happening.

'Maggot, you call me?' he leapt up and roared in Toby's face, a centimetre from his nose. 'Slug? Have you fought with lions with only a staff? Have you chased wolves from the flock with mere stones? Have you wrestled with bears to save a lost kid? Oh, you with your fine suit of armour, your mighty sword, your bodyguard of hundreds. If I, a simple goatboy, had your weapons, your army at my back, I too would be a great warrior. Think on this, when you have stood alone, in sandals and shift, with nought but stick and stone to protect you, *then* you can call yourself a man!'

Toby grinned and shouted, 'Bravo!'

The other two clapped their appreciation.

'Was that good?' said Andrew. 'Was that good acting?'

'Terrible,' cried Patrick, 'but it was the best you've managed so far – we'll make a player of you yet – in a thousand years.'

They howled with laughter at a crestfallen Andrew.

Angelique de Sonnac was a lonely young woman. Her mother had died in giving birth to her and her father had never remarried. She had no brothers or sisters and all her female companions were elderly. Her father, Sir Robert, kept promising to bring some young people to the mansion, but the knight was quite wrapped up in affairs of state. He was adviser to King Henry and that great soldier and statesman kept Sir Robert busy enough to cause him to neglect his daughter. Consequently, Angelique was always hatching plots, trying to find ways of visiting her cousins on the far side of London. They lived in one of the many timber-and-thatch houses which lined the road north, out of the city.

'It's not so far away,' she told her pet spaniel, Minstrel. 'We could easily get there and back in a day.'

Matthew and Andrea were younger than her, and really she wished for someone of her own age to talk to, but there was no one else. Once or twice, noblemen had visited her father, bringing with them their families, but their visits were always short and no one had been for a long time now.

Her father was not a cruel man. On the contrary, Robert de Sonnac was a kind, gentle man who loved his daughter to distraction. Probably too much, for he was afraid to let her leave the house without him in case something awful happened to her. But he was so entangled with the king's business that he hardly had time to sleep, let alone take his daughter on visits to cousins. And, of course, his work took him away from home a great deal, which left Angelique feeling somewhat abandoned.

'We're quite grown up now, Minstrel,' Angelique said to the spaniel, who turned his urgent liquid-brown eyes to her face on hearing his name, 'and don't need to bother father with our problems. I shall visit our cousins on my own when father is doing his rounds of the estate. Ah, you wonder how I can do that, when the servants will not allow it? Well, there is quill and ink on the dresser. I shall write to my cousins and tell them to expect my visit. And there is one other document I shall write . . . but perhaps you'd better not know the contents of that particular missive.'

Minstrel, having his ear scratched and being spoken to in such a low conspiratorial voice, decided an energetic response was required. He barked his approval of whatever it was that his mistress found so interesting to talk about.

Angelique went first to her father's library, with Minstrel padding behind her. There she found one or two letters which her father had written to her mother while she was still alive. Angelique had read them many times before and had shed tears over the sentiments expressed by her father to the mother she had never known. Robert de Sonnac was one of those knights who were more comfortable writing poetry than stabbing Saracens through the heart. His words were quite beautiful and his expressions of the love he bore for his wife again brought tears to his young daughter's eyes. But Angelique had not collected these letters to feed her emotions. She had a practical use for them.

She took the letters back to her writing desk and there began to compose a letter from Sir Robert to his steward. In the letter 'Sir Robert' ordered that during his absence his steward should arrange a carriage to take Angelique on a visit to her cousins. Angelique was also an expert with the quill, but her true skill lay in forgery. She copied her father's hand perfectly, knowing her talent was good enough to fool a half-blind elderly man like the household steward.

'There,' she said, shaking sand over the ink to help it dry, 'that looks much like father's writing, doesn't it?'

Minstrel, wondering what it was he was supposed to be looking at, nevertheless barked his approval once again.

3. LONDON

'Now, Andrew,' said Patrick, as they approached Chelmsford, 'we are still in the county of Essex and there may be men out looking for you. We must be wary and ready to run.'

Andrew was puzzled. 'Out looking for me? Why?'

'Because,' answered Arthur, 'you're a runaway.'

Andrew shook his head. 'No one will miss me, except my parents. Why, the baron doesn't even know I exist, I'm sure. It's true the lord of our village, who is a mere knight, will hear of my running away, but he will not care. Besides, my father is a freeman.'

'Be sure of this: the lord of your region knows the name of every man on his estates. Barons are grasping creatures who keep account of every penny, every piglet, every man, woman and child who they believe belongs to them. That's how they become barons in the first place. They are thick-headed, strong-limbed creatures and the code they live by is greed. Your father may be a freeman, but until you take over his business you are probably listed as a potential serf. You know what your rights are as a serf, I suppose?'

'None?'

'Very few, anyway. You are nought but a baron's slave, unable to leave his employ or village without his permission. You have broken the law and, if you're caught, you'll suffer for it. One of the ways in which you will suffer will be to

45

lose your freedom altogether. They will drag you back and put you to work in the fields, my friend, and I doubt you'll ever reach the status of your father, who you say is a freeman.'

'What am I to do?' asked Andrew, dismayed. 'There will surely be men from Cressing here, in the county town. There will be traders and merchants, if not others.'

Toby smiled. 'We must make sure they do not recognise you, Mistress Quickly.'

'Oh,' said Andrew, realising what was in store for him. 'Am I to spend the whole time in a dress?'

Patrick laughed. 'Don't worry, our next stop is in London – there are so many people there, it's unlikely you'll meet anyone from your small village.'

'How many people?'

'They say there are over fifty thousand who live in the city, not counting visitors to the capital.'

Andrew whistled. 'So many? I had not thought there would be that number in the whole country.'

So, before entering Chelmsford, they dressed Andrew in woman's clothing and plastered his face with powder, rouge and ochre, until not even his own mother would have recognised him. It rather had the opposite effect to what was desired, for passers-by stopped to stare at this bizarre female in the street, taking him for a madwoman. Andrew played up to this by singing ballads in a high voice, talking to the trees and birds and trying to kiss the cheeks of respectable elderly gentlemen without their leave. Soon the players had a crowd around them and they began to perform one of their set pieces. Indeed, it was lucky that Patrick had warned Andrew of the danger he was in, for one of the first to stop and watch the show was a Templar from Cressing. Andrew knew him by sight and it was likely that the knight would have recognised Andrew, but for his comely disguise.

The knight, however, seemed to disapprove of the play for he pursed his lips and moved on, heading towards the market square.

Andrew remained in costume the whole day and part of that night. It was most uncomfortable for him and he began to hate his role. However, he was aware that it was necessary. Late in the evening a drunkard picked a fight with Patrick and tried to strike the youth with his metal tankard. Patrick skipped out of range and picked up a bottle, throwing it at the drunkard. The bottle missed its target and hit another gentleman, a butcher by his garb. The butcher drew a large knife from his waistband and threatened to slice some bacon from Patrick's body. Toby hit the butcher on the head with his fist, flattening the man, and Arthur kicked the drunkard's legs from under him, sending him tumbling to the ground. All four players then ran from the scene, Andrew having to lift his skirts way above his ankles, all the while pursued by a mob.

The boys ran out into the countryside and found a place to sleep in a hay loft. In the morning they called in at a farm and bought breakfast with their earnings. The farmer's wife was amazed to see how much 'the young lass' ate, as Andrew – still recovering from a week's fasting – shovelled his eggs down his throat.

'I apologise for my sister,' said Patrick, with a wave of his hand; 'she has the manners of a sow. I blame my mother and father, God bless their memory, for not instilling any decorum in this unruly wench. Hoyden she was born and hoyden she remains to this day. We are sorely oppressed by her behaviour, madam, and are most sorry to subject you to her unruly eating habits.'

'Oh, never mind that,' said the farmer's wife, understanding only a small part of Patrick's high-falutin' speech, 'she's enjoying her food.'

And enjoying it Andrew certainly was. Though knighthood still seemed as far off as it ever had, the three boys he had met had changed his whole outlook on life. Why, if he had known that being on the road could be such fun, Andrew would have run away years ago. Of course, he had not known that he was breaking the law by leaving the village. Would it have made any difference if he had? He thought not. Harold and his parents were probably raising such a stink that Andrew would without doubt have been put in the stocks anyway. And that would have been the end of him, for the village bully boys would have thrown heavy flints at him (later protesting that they had only thrown vegetables) and would have stoned the life out of him.

Now he was far away from all the petty politics of village life. He was on his way to the great city of London, where King Henry and his sons and daughters could sometimes be seen. Andrew was excited to think he might actually set eyes on some of these royal persons. There were the younger Henry, Richard, Geoffrey and John, princes all. Then there were the princesses, Matilda, Eleanor and Joan, but Andrew did not know if royal ladies travelled or were kept in one place. However, King Henry was often in France, where he was also duke or count of a number of provinces. Or Ireland, of which

he was lord. The Plantagenet king ruled over many lands
outside the British Isles. Patrick explained that Henry, who
was often called 'Curtmantle', was of Norman stock, married
to a French queen, Eleanor of Aquitaine. All quite dizzying
for a country boy whose father made horseshoes.

Once Andrew reached London he could think about
pursuing his dream of knighthood, for in the capital city
anything could happen. Why, that was where fortunes were
made. One day a man could be penniless, the next wealthy.
He had heard such stories of youths who had risen to power
on the whim of a nobleman. Perhaps some great man might
take a shine to Andrew and put him on the road to his goal?

It was on a Wednesday that Andrew entered London.

The sights and sounds were amazing. And the denseness
of the crowds. The *noise* of the mob. The rumble of wheels,
the clatter of hooves. Pans clanking. Shutters rattling.
Tradesmen yelling. Fishwives shrieking. The narrow streets
were thronged with people, animals, carts, waggons, men on
horseback. They wore clothes of brilliant colours. Such clothes
as he had never seen before, on the backs of strangers from
unknown lands. Black-skinned people, people with ever-
smiling eyes, people with hair like passing clouds, olive-
skinned people. There was colour on the rooftops, on the
towers. Fluttering flags, waving banners. There was colour on
the river in the many-shaped sails.

'A Saracen!' cried Andrew, reaching for the dagger in
Patrick's belt as a man in a white smock and turban
approached.

Patrick gripped the hilt of his knife.

'Just another visitor, Andrew. Calm yourself. Not all men

of the East are Saracens. He is but an Arab sailor or merchant.'

It was a dizzying experience. The place stank of animal dung and human excrement. Men were openly urinating in the narrow alleys. Dogs were defecating on doorsteps. Vegetables rotted at the roadside. Rats ran hither and thither, chased by scrawny mogs. Donkey breath and horse sweat clogged the air. Drunkards sprawled on the walkways and corners of roads. Thin, hawk-eyed urchins prowled as silently as cats looking for opportunities to steal. Rouged women plucked at tunics and whispered in men's ears. Here and there stood a dignified person in expensive clothes, surveying the scene with a haughty, disdainful look on his face, as if he were not part of this unholy congregation.

Every so often there was an open square, surrounded by brick or wooden houses, the upper storeys of which jutted out over the street. It was also a town of many steeples, with scores of churches only paces away from one another. And convents. And monasteries. So many people, so many buildings, yet crammed so tightly together. Andrew could not understand why, when there was so much space out in the country. Surely they could have put the houses further apart? Instead they locked into one another, leaned over towards one another, pushed against one another. Almost all of London was on the north bank of a bend in the great River Thames, but there was one wooden bridge which crossed the water to a place called Southwark on the far side.

'They say they are building a stone bridge, next year,' Toby announced, 'to replace that old wooden one.'

'I'm not surprised,' cried Andrew. 'Fifty thousand people!

Why, if they all decided to cross the river at once, the wooden bridge would collapse under their weight.'

The others laughed. 'Why would everyone want to cross the river at once?' asked Arthur. 'Why, I'll wager half of the population has never crossed it at all.'

They weaved around a pavement scribe, who asked Patrick if he wished to write a letter to his mother.

Patrick declined, saying that unless the scribe could write in the language of the dead the letter would never be read.

'What, not ever?' said Andrew, replying to Arthur.

'Most have no need, unless they're travelling down to some-where like Southampton, or one of the other southern ports.'

'I suppose so, but you'd think they'd do it just once in their lives, just to be able to say they had been across.'

Patrick said, 'Not everyone is as curious as you, Andrew. Most of them wake up thinking about money and go to bed with the same thought in their head. Money is their god and rules their lives. Once they have a house to live in, they want a better house to live in. Once they have food in their larders, they want another larder, and another. Men will die rich without parting with a penny, even though their money is worthless to them once they're in the grave. If they won't be at least a farthing richer by crossing the Thames, they won't bother to do it.'

There were many dangerous characters in the streets of London, but the four youths watched each other's backs. If Andrew had wandered into this wicked city as gullible as the day he'd left home, he might have been murdered within a day simply for the sandals on his feet. All the boys sported daggers on their belts, which they openly displayed as a warning to footpads and thieves. Evil lurked on every corner, within the shadows of the churches, under the eves of overhanging buildings, certainly in every alehouse. Andrew was twice shouldered into a street dangerous with traffic by some careless ruffian, before learning to sidestep or give as good as he got.

People here in the city often appeared surly and bad-tempered, unwilling to give passage. On one corner Andrew almost ran into a man whose shiny skin was entirely black. Andrew stood amazed, staring rudely at the fellow, only to receive his first London smile. He grinned back at the man, who might have been a savage if he had not worn a tunic and hose, and looked for all the world like an ordinary citizen.

'Did you see that?' he asked Toby. 'Where did that man come from, do you think?'

'There are many such foreigners in London,' Toby replied. 'I think that one was from Afrik, which is a land that neighbours Jerusalem. You will see dark men here, though, with lighter skins than him. Not all from the Holy Land either. The world is a big place, Andrew, and there are many countries with many tribes. See, there is a man with a sallow look and narrow eyes, from some place even further off than Afrik – and over there one with a milky appearance, probably from a cold region. This world has far more wonders than you can learn from me, Andrew. You should best talk to sailors and wandering merchants. They go everywhere. And the beasts they've seen are so frightening you would not even like to see a picture – the nightmares I have had, of dragons and sea monsters, and creatures called tigers that eat you!'

Andrew's mind began to open like a flower in spring, while walking through London, and it filled his heart with wonder.

That night they played to a full audience until a watchman chased them from the square. Not all the people who saw the play paid their penny, but still the four made enough for beds and a meal in the house of a Jewish family, who treated them with great courtesy. The boys all slept on the stone floor of the parlour, but they had beds of sacking to cushion them from the hard ground and it was warm and dry. In the morning they breakfasted on hot milk and bread fresh from the oven.

Their host told them they were good lads, not given to drunkenness like some he had given shelter to, and they were welcome any time. It was true that Patrick and Toby, especially, liked to imbibe ale when it suited them, but they were usually jolly rather than argumentative after doing so. Arthur was religious, so did not 'swill the Devil's brew', and Andrew found he did not like the taste.

'I must walk on the bridge,' Andrew announced to his friends. 'I have to cross from here to there.'

'What in Heaven's name for?' asked Arthur. 'The dirt on that side of the bridge is the same colour, the same texture, and has the same foul odour as the dirt on this side.'

'It is a wonder of Nature,' Andrew argued.

'Not of Nature, but of Man,' Patrick corrected him. 'Man made that bridge.'

'And is not Man a natural beast?' replied Andrew, learning to counter-argue.

'Certainly, but one usually refers to natural things as those that are made by Nature and God, such as seashells and trees.'

'Is not the bridge made of wood?'

'Certainly, but . . .'

'And does not wood come from trees?'

'Yes, of course . . .'

'I rest my argument,' Andrew said, quickly, before Patrick, who was intricately clever with words, could offer a riposte.

The four boys then made their way to the bridge which spanned the Thames. When they approached it they saw that it was crammed with people on foot and traffic. Men and women squeezed by each other irritably, the bigger, stronger ones pushing the smaller ones out of the way. Waggons, carriages, carts and horses took up the left side, while the flow of raw humanity took up the right.

'You want to join in that stinking parade?' said Arthur, shaking his head. 'Well, I'll wait for you here.'

'Me too,' Patrick said, firmly.

Toby sighed. 'I'll come with you, Andrew – you need someone to cleave a path.'

So just two of the four stepped on to the bridge and began to join the flow from north to south. When they were just a third of the way across there came a shout of alarm. Suddenly, out of the weak sun came a kestrel which flew right in front of a carriage horse. The horse shied, whinnying, and kicked back with its hind legs which caught the nearside wheel. The wheel splintered, shattered, and the carriage lurched violently towards the bridge rail. A figure was thrown from the carriage over the rail and seemed to float down to the racing waters below on a cloud of lace. It was a young woman and her frightened expression turned to terrified shock as she hit the cold water. She was carried immediately under the bridge by the current, to the side where Toby and Andrew were forcing their way through the mass.

Andrew threw off his sandals and leapt up on to the rail.

'Stop!' cried a horrified Toby. 'You'll drown.'

Without any thought for Toby's warning, or his own good sense, Andrew jumped. He hit the water and gasped at the extreme cold which squeezed his chest with pain. His arms and legs felt like frozen logs of wood. He floundered a little but then came up and trod water while he looked around him. Where was the girl? He stared about him wildly as the current swept him along. As fortune would have it, he caught a brief glimpse of white cloth on the surface near to him. The girl was only just under the water, the hem of her skirt floating above her. Andrew struck out with sure, even strokes towards this item of clothing, gripped it and held on. The girl surfaced, spluttering and coughing.

She clung to him tightly, almost dragging him under, but Andrew was much stronger than this lass and he pinioned her arms with one of his own. She went limp almost immediately. He then grabbed her long hair, using it to hold her head above the surface and to keep her at a distance. Then he began kicking out towards the south bank. The river took a bend at that point and carried them towards a moored rowing boat. As they passed this craft Andrew clutched the mooring line and held on for dear life. The girl was now stretched out on the current as if on the end of a rope. Her face kept bobbing down below the surface of the water every few seconds. Her very life depended on the thick, long coils of her hair, the ends of which were in Andrew's firm grip.

Andrew held on, and held on, and held on, thinking that at any moment he would have to let go of the girl or release his grip on the line. One or the other, or both. He was utterly exhausted and he could not feel any of his limbs. There was no way he could heave himself and his charge out of the water into the boat. That was an impossibility. All he could do was remain where he was, hoping for a miracle.

The miracle duly came. A fisherman ran down to the river's edge, gripped the mooring line and began pulling it in. Others came to help. Soon Andrew felt himself being dragged up the bank. He still had hold of the girl's hair and someone had to prise his frozen fingers apart to release her. Then he passed out. When he came to and sat up, shivering violently, he saw that the girl was motionless on the ground. Someone had covered her with coats. Andrew noticed he had a coat draped around his own shoulders, too. He stared at her lifeless form and choked out some words.

'Is she dead? Was she drowned?'

It was Patrick who answered him.

'No, Andrew – she still breathes. You saved her life.'

'Thank the Lord.'

'Yes, I suppose so,' murmured Patrick, 'assuming it *is* the Lord who is to be thanked.'

This enigmatic statement went over Andrew's head, as he was led away by his friends. When they were not more than fifty metres from the scene several horsemen arrived at the gallop. There followed a shout and one rider, an older man in full livery, rode towards the four youths.

'Who was the saviour?' asked the man from high in the saddle.

'Andrew. Andrew of Cressing,' blurted Toby, pointing at his friend.

The rider nodded, grimly. 'And where will I find this Andrew of Cressing if I have need of him later?'

'A-a-at the i-inn of the Cr-cr-crossed Keys,' stammered Andrew, through chattering teeth, 'if he l-lives that long to reach its fire.'

Once the rider had returned to the girl, who was now being lifted and carried off on a litter, Patrick remonstrated with Andrew and Toby.

'Better not to have given your name, or the place where you might be reached. If the girl dies they may look for a scapegoat.'

'But he saved her life,' protested Toby.

'Do not underestimate the insanity brought on by grief,' replied Patrick, wisely. 'At this moment Andrew is a hero, but if she dies of the cold they will start to say, "If he had done this, or done that, she would still be alive." They will begin to question Andrew's method, his speed of action, his choices. "Why did he not lift her into the boat?" they will ask. "A few minutes might have made all the difference." Before you know it Andrew will be to blame by his negligence.'

'B-b-but it was impossible to l-lift her,' stammered Andrew, his teeth chattering. 'I couldn't l-lift a babe I was so weak.'

'And,' Patrick seemed to hesitate as they came to the doors of the inn in question, 'and also they might question why this yokel from an inland country village can walk on the river where others would sink and drown to death. Is it God who gave him this power, or the Devil? Toby, can you stay afloat on water? Or you, Arthur?'

The two boys solemnly shook their heads.

'Neither can I,' Patrick continued. 'Nor do I know anyone who can.'

'You know me,' protested Andrew, heading towards the fire as they entered the inn. 'It's called *swimming*. You have surely heard of that art, Patrick. There are sailors who can swim. Not many, I'm told, but they do exist. I learned the trick when the village bullies threw me into the pond. If I had not done so, I would have drowned. There's nothing magical about the act of swimming. You simply move your arms and legs in the right way. Tell me, Patrick, can you walk?'

'Of course I can walk.'

'Why "of course"? You couldn't walk at birth. You learned the art because you needed to, or you would not have been able to move through the world. You didn't need to learn to swim, because you don't live in the water. I did, often, being thrown there by rough youths.'

'But are these things you tell us right?' said Patrick. 'I only met you a short while ago. In fact, the only things I know about you are what you've told me. You could be the biggest liar in the kingdom. How would I know? Everything about you must be treated as a mystery, for we only have your word that you are a farrier's boy, the son of a sergeant-at-arms in a Templar village in Essex, who ran away from bullies. I would like to know where that kestrel came from, the one that flew in the horse's face and made it shy. I would like to know where you get those dark marks, like shadow-fingers on your ankles. I would like to know why your toes are webbed like those of a duck. Where I come from you would have been burned as a witchboy at birth.'

Toby went red and said furiously, 'You leave him be, Patrick. Why would the Devil wish to save the life of an innocent girl? It was no doubt the Devil who spooked the horse, but

Andrew went to her rescue and saved her life, and perhaps even her soul. Andrew is our friend. You should be ashamed of yourself, Patrick.'

Andrew, beginning to warm through now that he was sitting in front of burning logs, shook his head.

'No, Toby, Patrick has a right to ask these questions. And I fear you will not like all the answers. The truth is I am Andrew of Cressing, my father is indeed a farrier for the Templars, but my mother was out collecting wood in the winter the moment I was born. Someone helped her with the birth, a woman they call "the warlock's wife" and it is said her hands burned these marks into my feet when she pulled me out the wrong way round, feet first. They also say that my webbed toes are a consequence of having a witch for a midwife.'

Andrew did not tell his friends about the two dead men, who had said they had a message from the warlock's wife. That would indeed have turned the most ardent friend into a doubter. He felt he had said enough already.

Toby said, extremely seriously, 'These are strange things you tell us, Andrew, but they don't make you a witchboy. You were born of ordinary parents, just as I was. It wasn't your fault, or the fault of your mother, that she was caught out in the winter snows. Nor was it the fault of either of you that the nearest person to hand was a warlock's wife. You've suffered for it, in the hands of your village. If you had magic at your disposal, you would surely have destroyed your enemies with it. That makes sense, doesn't it, Patrick? Why would he suffer all the ills he has put up with, if he has dark magic to protect him?'

Patrick shrugged. 'There's logic in that, Toby boy, but I'm

not sure logic helps when others are out for blood. We must hope that girl lives. If she doesn't, we shall have to skip this inn in good time to thwart the mob, for I'm certain they'll come after Andrew if she dies.'

The grapevine in King Henry's London was a swift form of communication. Very soon the young players learned that the girl was alive and well. The boys based their play that evening on the tragic Greek myth of Leander swimming the Hellespont every night to meet his love, Hero, on the far side. He was guided across by the lamp Hero always lit upon her tower. But one night a storm blew out the flame and Leander lost his way in the darkness and drowned. It had been Patrick's idea to do this tragedy and it worked like a dream. They had their largest ever audience and the pot was overflowing with coins at the end.

They went back to the inn in riotous mood, forsaking the good Jew's accommodation for a parlour where ale was to be had. That evening Andrew tried to explain to his companions that any good fortune which had come to him via the midwife who had assisted at his birth was thanks neither to God nor to Satan, but another deity who was around before Christianity came to the shores of England.

'We call him *Woodwose*, but some know him as the Green Man. Lord of the forest and vale, he is a natural being of this world, so none need fear him, for there is no evil in his bones. Indeed, we have also an image of the Green Woman in our walled garden at Cressing, which the monks acknowledge, as well as the villagers. These are creatures of Nature and well thought of, the dark green spirits of mossy hollows and turf dikes. They bring the sunlight to tangled undergrowth and the night's moonshadows to the dank woodlands.'

'Superstition,' muttered Patrick.

'No, no,' affirmed Toby. 'My uncle once saw a Green Man. He had wide-spread antlers on his head . . .'

'What, your uncle?' said Arthur, first looking to Patrick for approval of this jest, but Toby frowned so hard that Arthur quickly turned his stare to the wall.

'. . . wide-spread antlers on his head,' continued Toby, doggedly, 'and the hooves of a deer for feet. He had breath that frosted the morning grasses. He moved like the shadow of a flying crow on the ground or the gliding of a russet fox through dead bracken.'

Patrick sighed. 'You're bumpkins, both of you, but I'll never change your minds. Now get some sleep. It would be better to be up early and out of the city, before someone robs us of the money we earned tonight. You can't gather coin in the city without a hundred eyes noting the fact and marking it down as tempting. I made sure we weren't followed here from the square, but tomorrow the footpads will be on the lookout for us and will try to catch us in some alley.'

The boys had been given the kitchen to sleep in, the warmest place in the inn, and they bedded down under benches and pan racks, spreading the thin blankets given them by the landlord.

Two hours before cockcrow the door to the kitchen was noisily flung open and several men-at-arms came tramping in, their metal-clad feet harsh on the stone floor.

'Andrew of Cressing?'

All had woken with the sharp entrance. Arthur pointed. Andrew rolled out from under the meat-cutting bench.

'I am Andrew of Cressing.'

'You must come with us, now,' ordered one of the men-at-arms. 'Sir Robert de Sonnac wishes to speak with you.'

'At four o'clock in the morning?' said Patrick.

'The master does not sleep well,' replied the man with a wry grimace, 'and bends the world to his own hours.' To Andrew, then, 'Come, boy. Gather your wits quickly. The master does not like to be kept waiting, even if none of us has yet broken our fast.'

4. SIR ROBERT DE SONNAC

Andrew went through the doorway with the men, leaving the rest of the players wondering if they would ever see him again.

'Get up behind me, boy,' said the man-at-arms, as he mounted his horse in the street.

Andrew did as he was told. The other men, none of whom had said a word, climbed into their own saddles. They set off towards the bridge across the Thames. Indeed, they crossed it when they reached it and rode a short way out into the countryside, beyond the village of Southwark. Finally, they reached a large estate deep in a woodland. It had a magnificent dwelling and took Andrew's breath away. Andrew was led inside and on into a great hall. At the end of a long table sat a lean, fair-bearded man with shoulder-length hair. This man's eyes studied Andrew as the youth walked towards him. The men-at-arms did not linger. They left the two together. Andrew stopped in front of the gentleman and allowed himself to be appraised. He wondered if he was meeting the steward or the head servant. Surely the owner of this mansion would not be interested in a youth of his stamp?

'Well, then,' said the elder in a quiet voice, 'don't be alarmed, boy, you're here to be rewarded not chastised.'

'Thank you, sire, but I was not afraid.'

This brought a slight smile to the man's lips.

'Why not?'

'Because you have a kind face, sire.'

This raised a laconic laugh. 'Have I? Well, it may interest you to know I've killed a good few men in my time, many of 'em without sorrow or regret.'

There was a fire blazing in the great hearth. The fuel shifted and a burning log fell from the top of it and rolled out on to the hall floor. Andrew went and picked it up by the unburned end and tossed it back into the flames. This interruption gave him time to think and he replied, 'They must surely have deserved it, sire?'

A slow nod from the older man, shadows travelling over his face in the candlelight. 'A lot of them did, to be sure. You know who I am?'

'No, sire, but I would suppose the master's steward?'

'Humph! My steward Ruben is an ancient retainer, but I keep him on because I have a kind heart as well as a kind face. I am Robert de Sonnac, the knight who owns this little country box and the father of the young woman you saved from drowning. I was on the king's business when this affair happened, but thankfully my steward saw fit to recall me instantly, which is why you find my hose still spattered with mud.'

'Oh.' Andrew had not noticed the dirt the knight spoke of. He was still in a state of bewilderment. He did not know what to think. Though there were several at Cressing, he was unused to having intimate conversation with knights of the realm. They normally gave him a curt answer, if he dared to speak in the first place.

'Because you are her saviour, I shall tell you her name,

boy, and then you shall tell me yours. She is called Angelique and she is the apple of my eye. What you did for me today means more to me than all my wealth, which is considerable. Her mother died of a fever some five years ago. Angelique has been my comfort. One day soon some knight with fire in his eyes is going to ask for her hand, and I shall lose her to him, as I must. These days with her are precious to me and I shudder to think what would have happened to me if she had died yesterday.'

'Sire, your love for your daughter is to be commended,' said Andrew, not knowing what else to say.

This brought a frown to Sir Robert's face and Andrew realised he had overstepped the boundaries of intimacy. Hastily, he tried to make amends. 'I meant, sire, that many knights do not have any great regard for the females of their household, only for their sons.'

Another slow nod. 'Sadly, this is true.'

Andrew kept talking, hoping to race away from his error of judgement. 'Though most of the knights I have seen are not married men, for they are Templars who have taken a vow of – of cel . . .' Andrew struggled for the word.

'Celibacy?' finished the knight. 'You are familiar with the Templars?'

'I am from the village of Cressing, where Templars have their great grain stores. My name is Andrew, sire, and my father is a farrier for the Knights Templar, being a respectable sergeant-at-arms.'

'Well, I am just an ordinary knight, Andrew. I am not entitled to wear the white robe with its red cross, not being one of that fierce sect of warrior-monks with whom you seem so familiar. Their vows of chastity, poverty and obedience would be beyond my capabilities. I enjoyed my marriage to my beloved wife, I like being rich and my obedience is to King Henry alone, and not to some Grand Master. It's true the Templars, like the Hospitallers, fight like lunatics and do not seem afraid of death in any way, but a good healthy love of life never did a man harm in the long run. I'm not sure we couldn't do without fanatics like the Templars, leaving a trail of blood across distant lands.'

Andrew felt a hot indignation rise in him.

'The Templars are protectors of helpless pilgrims, sire, on their way to the Holy Land. They save many men from attack by wild animals, bandits and heathens.'

'They began as protectors of the weak, but they seem to have extended their original brief to include killing all Seljuk Turks and Saracens they come across. I take it you approve of the Knights Templar, or you would not be annoyed with me for criticising them.'

Andrew realised he was again overstepping the mark.

'Sire, I would not dare to do such a thing. It's just that – well, I have grown up in my village respecting the Order of the Knights Templar. My own father is their devoted servant . . .'

At this moment there was a sound from the doorway. Robert de Sonnac looked up. Andrew turned to see a figure standing there holding a candle, the light of which fell on charming features. Even with her hair in disarray and a thick, ugly woollen robe covering her form, she was pretty enough to make Andrew stare. He had seen her once before, but her skin had then been puckered by the cold, her face pallid and shrunken, her lips drooling river water. Now she looked young and lovely, her tangled golden hair falling around her shoulders and down her breast.

Her feet were bare and drew the attention of her father, who frowned.

'Go back to bed, Angelique. You have not yet fully recovered and here you are wandering abroad in the foul humours of the night. No coverings on your feet? Fie, child.'

'I wish to see the gentleman who saved my life,' said the girl, stepping forward, 'and to thank him from the bottom of my heart.'

Robert de Sonnac raised his eyebrows, but said, 'See him then, daughter, but he's no gentleman. He's a rough-cast peasant from a small village in Essex.'

'At the moment he pulled me from the cold, wet claws of that river I would not have cared if he had been a slave, Father. What is his name?'

'He's called Andrew, apparently.'

'Andrew,' she said, staring straight into Andrew's eyes and turning his heart to melting butter, 'I thank you for my life. If you are indeed a peasant, you have fine looks. . .'

'Daughter!' came a warning father's voice.

'. . . and a noble bearing.'

'Thank you, mistress,' murmured Andrew, entirely overwhelmed by all this attention. 'I am glad to be of service.'

He wanted to tell her how pretty she was, and how astonishing were her eyes, and how well her small nose went with her perfect complexion, and what lovely, dove-like hands she owned, tipped with such clean nails, and how her feet were so small and neat they did not deserve to be clad in boots, and how her voice was to him like the chimes of a song-thrush. He wanted to tell her all these things, but, of course, could not, for her father would have swatted him like a fly for his insolence and audacity, and would have been right to do so.

'Tell me, Andrew. How is that you can swim as you do? None of my father's men can swim. Nor can my father, who is able to do almost anything that I can think of.'

'I learned as a child, when I was thrown into the village pond by older boys.'

Her eyes widened. 'And why would they do such a thing?'

'Because they say I was delivered at birth by a warlock's wife – they call her a witch, though she is not.'

'Well, if she delivered such a handsome child, she must have been a very nice witch,' replied Angelique.

'Daughter!' came the stern warning voice again. 'This talk is unseemly in a young woman. In *any* female, if it comes to that. I have not raised you to be a hoyden. Now, go to bed. You've rendered your thanks to the youth, now do as you're bidden.'

'Yes, Father,' she said, dipping her head, but before leaving the room she called quietly to Andrew, 'Ask for anything. My father is rich and he loves me a great deal.'

Robert grunted and Andrew smiled.

'I'm aware he's a wealthy knight, mistress, for I noticed the candles were of beeswax and not of cheap tallow.'

She smiled back at him. A wonderful sun-lit, moon-lit smile that further melted Andrew's heart.

'Ah,' she said, 'you are making fun of me – that's all right, isn't it, Father? – for I have a cheerful disposition.'

'Go to bed, child,' growled the father. 'Bed, bed, bed.'

She left them, taking with her more than the light of a candle.

'Now then, boy,' said Robert de Sonnac, 'what is it that you want in the way of reward?'

The prophecy of his becoming a knight immediately came to mind.

'Sire, this may seem bold to you – believe me, indeed it does to me also – but I have been told it is my destiny to be a knight. I want this with all my heart and soul. I wish to join the Templars in their duty of guarding the pilgrims and fighting the heathen in the Holy Land.'

'A knight? No small matter, then?'

'It has been said to me, sire, that my ambitions are so lofty as to be impossible.'

'I would say so.'

'Yet I could not settle for less, sire,' continued Andrew, fervently. 'I have been told this is my destiny and will strive for that end for as long as I hold breath.'

'Andrew,' said Sir Robert de Sonnac, 'I cannot give you what you ask and I think you know that. However, what I can do is give you the trappings of a knight, and an introduction to a friend of mine, a good friend, who is a Templar knight at Cressing. His name is Gondemar de Blois. Have you heard of him?'

Andrew's heart was racing. 'Sire, he is one of the most respected of knights at Cressing.'

'Indeed, I have known him since he was a snot-nosed squire and I always felt him to be a little above himself, but that's neither here nor there. He regards me as a friend and that's what's important here. Andrew, I'm going to supply you with a suit of armour, a good horse and a letter to de Blois asking him to take you on as a squire. Even if he does so I doubt you'll advance any further in rank, not being of noble blood, but at least you'll be among those you seem to admire so much. You'll probably get to the Holy Land and will fight with Saracens, God help you, for already over three hundred thousand knights have been killed crossing the plains of Turkomania alone – Frenchmen, Germans, English, Italians – prey to Seljuk Turks, beasts and bandits. Think of that number, Andrew. By the by, what are you? Of Norman or Saxon descent?'

'Both, sire. My father is a Norman and my mother from a Saxon family.'

'Good combination for a new Englishman. My own wife was of Saxon stock. Well, what do you say to my offer?'

'I – I'm overwhelmed with happiness, sire, but I feel unworthy. It was but chance that led me to save your daughter. I don't feel I really deserve such great fortune. I gave no deep thought to my action. I simply did it without thinking. I heard a shout for help, and jumped over the rail. My feelings are all mixed up at this moment, sire, so you must forgive me for my weak words.'

'Yet you did not leap instantly for you had time to remove your sandals. Andrew, it pleases me that you have truth and modesty in you as well as courage. Bravery is often a spurred rather than a considered action. Now, you'll need to go back to your companions and tell them I'm not going to hang you, then return here. Over the next two or three weeks we'll equip you. My sergeant-at-arms will give you some basic instruction on weaponry, but you'll not learn much within that period of time. If de Blois accepts you, as I think he will, then he'll see to it that you continue your training. Can you ride?'

'A little, sire. I have fetched horses for my father to shoe, from farmers and the like.'

'Shire horses?' snorted Robert, contemptuously. 'No thoroughbreds, I suppose?'

'Who would let a village boy ride a stallion or good mare, sire?'

'Point taken. But you have at least been on a mount, which is something. I hope you're a quick learner, for I must leave with my daughter for France in less than a month. Andrew, you did me a great service and I'm deeply thankful. Learn well, stripling, and we'll make something of you, eh, if not a fully-fledged knight.'

'Thank you, sire.'

Andrew's head was swimming with thoughts and his spirit was soaring when he went to say goodbye to his friends. By the time he reached the inn, morning had arrived and people were up and about. His friends were lounging around the parlour eating pottage and drinking weak ale when he walked through the door. They looked up and stared at him. He strode towards them, eager to tell them his news.

Patrick, lying across a bench seat by the fire, said to his companions, 'Would you say that's more of a strut, or a swagger?'

'A strut, definitely,' said Arthur. 'He hasn't the broad shoulders worthy of a swagger.'

'Guess what?' cried Andrew, hardly able to contain himself.

Toby said, 'They let you off with a warning?'

'I'm to be a squire,' cried Andrew. 'Sir Robert de Sonnac has given me a horse, a suit of armour and a letter to Sir Gondemar de Blois, recommending me as his squire.'

The three other boys looked at him in astonishment.

Patrick said, 'You're serious?'

'Of course – would I joke about something so wonderful.'

'Wonderful,' repeated Arthur, knocking Toby's feet off his lap, when the big fellow tried to rest them there. 'Is that meant in the sense that your fate is full of wonder?'

Andrew was suddenly bashful.

'I must sound like a braggart. Forgive me, lads. I don't mean to make you envious,' Andrew said, 'and I'm sorry it can't be all of us, but of course that's impossible.'

Patrick said indolently, 'We are so envious we're as green as my hat.'

'Absolutely,' agreed Arthur with a forced yawn. 'Green as the vales of Cheshire.'

Andrew frowned. He had the distinct feeling that the other players were neither joyful at his news, nor even upset because his good fortune had eclipsed theirs. They did not seem impressed in the least.

Toby now gave him the reasons why.

'Andrew,' said the big, amiable youth, 'you mean to say you prefer the rigours of squirehood to being a player, free and wild with no responsibilities and with wonderful companions? They will put you through hell, my dear friend, and if you fail they'll cast you aside and think no more about you. If indeed you pass their insane tests, they'll stuff you in the hold of some stinking ship and carry you to a foreign land where they speak a vile tongue and where everything is different. Once there you might stay alive long enough to regret your fate, but sooner rather than later you will succumb to some awful disease, or be eaten by a lion, or have some Saracen slice off your head.'

'You're not jealous?' Andrew asked, in a flat tone.

'Not in the least, my poor Andrew,' Patrick said, smiling. 'In fact we would regard your future as being the one path to avoid if at all possible. We would hate to be squires. Andrew, I am from a good family – my father is a respected hatmaker in Stratford-upon-Avon – with his influence he could have acquired a squireship for me at the drop of – of one of his hats.' Arthur laughed and Patrick continued: 'I would have hated it. Hell's kitchen, my friend. What? Lumbering around in an iron suit, with swords and maces crashing on my helmet trying to beat the sense out of me? Then to be shipped off to some hellhole east of the sun with an arrogant knight who would think nothing of throwing me to the wolves if it suited his purpose? Fie!'

'But,' blurted Andrew, 'what about duty? What about fighting for the Holy Land? What about bravery and *honour*? What about the fact that one day you could be a *knight*?'

'Keep it,' said Arthur. 'In just one week I can be king, prince or the most villainous knight who ever trod the soil of England. Tonight I am playing a ruler in the Mystery Play *Herod the Great*, tomorrow Patrick says we shall be doing *Noah's Flood*, and mine will be the voice of God. Thus today I rule the world, and tomorrow all of Heaven and Earth – and – and Andrew, *at no danger to my life or limb.*'

'But it's all make-believe. I wish for reality.'

Patrick said, 'Then you must embrace it, Andrew, but do

73

not feel pity or sorrow for those you leave behind. We are happy doing what we love best. Good luck, young friend. We shall miss our mistress with her rouged cheeks and fluttering lashes. I have to say, Andrew, you made a better girl than you'll ever make a rough squire. Will you say the line once more for us all, *"Kiss me, my sweet, for my lips are honey-coated and will send you soaring with the birds."*'

'I will not,' replied Andrew hotly, 'it took all my courage to say it the once in front of a crowd of hairy drunkards.'

The boys laughed at this. They clustered around Andrew then and wished him all that he desired himself. They slapped him on the back and congratulated him, said they would miss him sorely, and sent him on his way with all the good feelings necessary for someone parting from friends of whom he had grown fond.

He left them and made his way back to the house of his benefactor. There he was introduced by the master to Old Foggarty, who was to accompany him to Cressing. Old Foggarty had only one arm, was as skinny as a peddler's dog but as strong as an ancient oak. With his one good arm he could wield a sword along with the best soldier and regaled Andrew with an exhibition of his thrusting and cutting strokes. Old Foggarty had a white beard as long as a lance, and rheumy eyes, but his brain was sharp and keen, and there was no loss of muscle.

'One day I shall be as weak as a kitten,' he told Andrew, 'and on that day I'll thank you to put me to my rest.'

'I can't do that. I've only just met you.'

'Better a stranger than a friend.'

'Why?'

Old Foggarty had no answer for this. It seemed he made sayings up as he went along, to suit his needs.

'Now, the master has said you'll need a palfrey,' Old Foggarty told Andrew, as he led him to the stables. 'I know which one he has in mind.'

'A palfrey is a woman's mount,' Andrew complained. 'I'm not riding a woman's horse. I was promised a steed. I'll have to fight dragons where I'm going.'

'Dragons, is it?'

Andrew had been told there were dragons out there in the world, somewhere, which killed for the sake of hearing men scream.

'There are dragons in foreign lands, aren't there?'

'Yes, yes,' Old Foggarty muttered, waving his hand, 'so I've been told, though I've never seen a scale or tooth of one. It's said we used to have them in Cymru.'

'So you see, I can't go against dragons on a pony.'

But when he showed Andrew the mount Robert de Sonnac had chosen for him, Andrew was delighted. It was a sleek gelding, chestnut brown, with a high, noble head and a silken mane. It was a beast any knight would have been proud to own. Andrew stroked the animal's nose. The beast scraped the earth with its right forefoot, as if responding to Andrew's touch. Andrew was filled with joy at being given such a wonderful gift. A live blood horse. A mount that was so beautiful a sultan would have given jewels to own it. It was the most stunning steed Andrew had ever set eyes on.

'You're mine,' he whispered in the gelding's twitching ear. 'You're mine and mine alone.'

'His name . . .' began Old Foggarty, but Andrew stopped him.

'I don't want to hear the name he used to be called by.'

'Used to be?'

'Yes, I have a name for him myself. He's mine so I have a right to call him what I wish. His name – his name – is – is Warlock.'

Old Foggarty sucked in his cheeks. 'That's an unlucky name for a horse, that is.'

'Nevertheless . . .'

Old Foggarty shrugged. 'Warlock it is, then. I'll leave you two to become acquainted. Don't try to ride him just yet. Visit him for a few days in the stables, lead him out into the morning air, make a little fuss of him first. When he gets used to you, when he likes your smell, then we'll think of getting you in the saddle. He'll make a fine charger. You'll need to become his master, of course, but I'll show you how to do that. Now, tomorrow at ten of the clock, you will need to be in the great hall. The armourer is coming and he doesn't like to be kept waiting.'

'Bit uppity for an armourer, isn't he?' said Andrew.

Old Foggarty sucked in his cheeks again.

'Uppity? He just happens to be Helmschmid of Austria, one of the finest armourers there is. Helmschmid has been armourer to kings and satraps, to emperors and oligarchs. The master heard that he was in London and has asked for this great craftsman to make you a suit of armour that would make a prince proud. There: what do you think of that? A snot-nosed boy with a shining suit of Helmschmid armour on his back. You'll make the king's knights, jealous, you will. The master loves his daughter with all his heart. You saved her life and he wishes to repay that deed with anything you desire.

I heard him say he wished you'd just asked for a bag of gold and left it at that, but you didn't, eh? You had to go and make a lot of fuss about wanting to be a knight.'

'It *is* what I desire.'

Old Foggarty walked off, muttering, 'Uppity, is it? Seems to me the peasants are getting way above themselves, never mind the armourers.'

The next day Andrew was indeed awestruck by the Austrian armourer, who spoke no English and was dressed in the finest of clothes and had a fierce manner. Helmschmid received nothing but open-mouthed looks as answers to his questions. He tutted, sighed deeply, and then spoke through an interpreter. The famous armourer used only short, sharp sentences. He did not look Andrew in the face again while he made his measurements for the suit of armour. He simply held his conversation, such as it was, with his interpreter. The interpreter then shouted the translation up at the vaulted ceiling of the great hall. It was as if Andrew were not present in the room and they were communicating with some invisible being in the rafters.

Helmschmid was clearly not one to waste his valuable time on ignorant English boys who could not be bothered to learn the fine language of his home country. On top of this, Angelique poked her head in to see how he was getting on, which unsettled Andrew somewhat. Happily, everyone else stayed away.

'*Achselhohle bequem?*' snapped Helmschmid.

'Armpit good?' yelled the interpreter.

'Sorry?' said Andrew.

'Is the underarm feeling loose and comfortable?'

'I think so.'

'Think so is not *yes*. Our armourer is an artist. We are carrying his art on our body, young man. If some great warrior were to ask us, "Is that armour from Helmschmid?" and we say, "Yes, but it feels a little tight under here, whenever I raise my battleaxe to lop off an enemy's head", my master would be shamed, would he not? We must be exact, young man. Remember, too, that we are still a boy. We still have some growth in our body. We will need more room in the armour than if we were a man full grown. We do not want "think so's" – please answer the questions exactly. Now, is the feeling good under the arms?'

'Just a little too tight.'

'Ah – now we know what to say to our master.'

And so it went on, all morning and into the afternoon, until Andrew was exhausted and felt he had been through a battle rather than a fitting for a suit of armour. In the evening he was glad to get away to walk Warlock around the paddock. He told his horse everything that had occurred that day and the creature's eyes showed that he understood the agonies Andrew had gone through. The youth could have sworn that once or twice Warlock even nodded in sympathy.

'You too will have to go through this, old fellow,' said Andrew, stroking his mount's neck. 'Chargers wear armour, too.'

A look of alarm appeared in the gelding's eyes.

5. RETURN TO CRESSING

Over the next few weeks Andrew was tutored by Old Foggarty in the exact science of killing the enemies of God, Henry and England. Despite the absence of an arm, Old Foggarty was an expert with the sword, the dagger, and – his own particular favourite – the mace and chain. The latter was a spiked iron ball the size of a man's fist, connected to a short rod by a long chain. The user held the rod and whirled the iron ball around his head. He either throttled his opponent by winding the chain around his neck, or battered his head in with the spiked ball.

'No frenzy, nothin' wild and whiskery, shaveling. Just swing her smoothly, nice an' easy, nice long, looping swirls, and let the ball take the chain round his throat and choke the life out of him. Man whose coughing for air, his face goin' black and his hands scrabbling at the chain's not able to fight anyhows, so if you think he's not goin' to expire through lack of God's air, you just stab him somewhere vital.'

Andrew could not get the hang of this unwieldy weapon and, though Old Foggarty kept trying to make him an expert with it, secretly he decided he would never use one in battle. Andrew much preferred the noble sword and the furtive dagger as his weapons of choice. He did not like crashing iron balls on to helmets or shields. There was no finesse in such an action. And as for throttling a man: why, even in his imagination he was appalled by the image of someone trying to tear the chain from his throat while his eyes popped out of his head. Strangulation was a repugnant thing to watch and a horrible way to die.

'What about the lance?' asked Andrew of his tutor, during lessons in the courtyard. 'Are you going to teach me the lance?'

'The lance is for jousting at tourneys. You want to carry around a piece of timber the length of a barn rafter? No, of course you don't. Forget the lance. Leave the lance for the showgrounds of England's princes. As for the rest of a warrior's tools, battleaxes are for brutes with inflated muscles and pottage for brains. Pikestaffs and clubs are for cack-handed peasants. The bow might be a noble weapon, but knights do find it a bit tricky pulling on bits of string while galloping around in a suit of iron on the back of a charger. No, my little shaveling, you become expert with the sword and mace and chain and you won't go far wrong . . .'

The sword it had to be, then, thought Andrew, with the dagger as a standby if the longer blade ever failed him.

On many of the days while he was practising in the court-yard he was aware of being watched from one of the windows of the mansion. He soon came to learn this was the day room of Angelique, the beautiful daughter of his benefactor. Andrew was excited by the fact that he was the object of her atten-tion. He devised ways of passing Angelique 'by accident' in passages and other unfrequented places. He discovered she gathered flowers from the garden most mornings and 'happened' to bump into her on his way to the pump. The meetings were quite innocent and only allowed the two to exchange meaningful looks and the odd 'Your servant, mistress', answered by 'Good morrow, sir'.

Even just these words made his heart race and the blood pound in his temples. It allowed him, too, to whip off his hat and sweep down in a low, courtly bow, hose-covered right leg thrust forward, which he felt showed him at great advantage. He had the sort of figure which could carry off such an action with grace and elegance, tinged with rakishness. Maidens' hearts were often conquered by displays of fine manners and Angelique's was no exception to this general rule.

Could he ever dream of capturing such a heart?

One day Robert de Sonnac's steward called him to the knight's library. Andrew had never been in this room and he was amazed by the number of illuminated books and charts. The monks had a library at Cressing, but that contained only a fraction of the volumes Andrew could see here. The shelves and tabletops were covered with them. Andrew opened a huge tome with a gold-embossed leather cover and peered at the neat black script within. He could not read, of course, never having been to school, but Friar Nottidge had taught him to recognise some of the letters. There was an 'M', the sound you made when you pressed your lips together. And there an 'L', which was a clucking motion with the tongue. And the 'S' shape that made you hiss like a serpent. Oh yes, and that wonderful character the 'X', which looked quite dark and dramatic. Peasants often used that one to sign their names.

'You find that passage interesting?'

Andrew jumped on hearing the voice behind him and, turning, found himself facing his patron.

'I – I'm sorry, sir. I have not damaged the paper.'

Robert laughed. 'I'm pleased to hear it. You looked fascinated by the content. Can you read?'

'No, my lord, I cannot,' confessed Andrew. 'I was studying some of the letters, which my friend the friar taught me.'

'Ah, yes.' Robert opened the volume himself and stared at the writing on the page. 'Bizarre and magical, aren't they, those cryptic squiggles? Those marks, so strange to illiterate eyes, are little black keys to doors which lead to a wonderful world, Andrew. But I doubt we have time to teach you how to open the locks. It took me several years to learn to read. I'm trying to teach my daughter now and she's much faster than I was at grasping the skill. One really needs to be a member of the clergy – learning to read and write seems to go with being a churchman – or a king with time on his hands. Knights have their heads full of other things, like the practical management of estates, while leaving the writing and number work to learned stewards and clerks.'

'Yes, my lord.'

Sir Robert now put his hands behind his back and his face became serious.

'Now, Andrew, I am here to talk to you of my daughter.'

Andrew felt himself going hot and knew his face was on fire.

'Oh, sir . . .'

'Yes, indeed, "Oh, sir". One or two meetings might have been passed off as coincidence – but *every* day, Andrew?'

Andrew hung his head. 'I'm – I'm very sorry, Sir Robert. It – it won't happen again.'

'You find her beautiful?'

The 'yes' came out as a croak.

Robert nodded as he paced the floor, speaking in a quiet, controlled voice. 'Indeed she is, which is both a delight and a worry to me. You know, of course, that she has to marry the man I wish her to marry? Yes, of course. So does she. Maids of her age, from noble families, accept it. They sometimes fall in love, of course. One hopes with the chosen husband, but not always. Love is no great follower of rules and regulations. I believe Angelique has formed an attachment to her saviour, you, Andrew, which is natural. A youth performs a great act of self-sacrifice – you could easily have drowned yourself – and becomes a hero to the person who was saved. I believe she is infatuated with her saviour, rather than with the stripling I have before me, and her eyes are clouded by her admiration of the act you performed for her.

'Andrew, you must put all thought out of your head of ever winning my daughter as your bride.'

'My lord, I am too young . . .' Andrew blurted.

'Well, you may say so, but others have fallen in love at your age and have remained in love until death. I myself – well, let's not have a history lesson. The fact is, Andrew, much as I am grateful to you for your great service to me and my daughter, I cannot allow this infatuation to continue. I thought you were set on becoming a Templar?'

'I am, sir, I am.'

'Templars are chaste. They are warrior-priests. I'm sure you know the code of the Templars? *Chastity, poverty and obedience.* Chastity, Andrew. You cannot fall in love and woo a maiden if you wish to be one of the Knights Templar. You must put aside worldly things.'

'I know I must.'

'Then these meetings with my daughter will cease. I don't want to be angry with you, Andrew. I don't want to send you to Sir Gondemar before you are ready. But I can't have my daughter's head full of romantic notions either. I hope we understand one another?'

'We have done nothing wrong.'

'Of that I am sure, Andrew, for though I know very little about the youth who stands before me, I know and trust my daughter.'

'Of course, my lord. I'm sorry.'

Robert sighed. 'Well, youth is youth. But you must learn to control passion and longing, and become a staunch man of iron. Even as a Templar's squire you will need to save all the power of your mind and body to protect the pilgrims on the way to the Holy Land. They're being slaughtered in their hundreds on their way from the port of Jaffa to Jerusalem, by bandits and savage tribes. It will be your duty to save as many souls as possible and for that you need to be single-minded.'

'I will not – not look on Angelique again,' said Andrew, fired by this image of himself as a protector of the pilgrims. 'I will devote myself to my studies of warfare.'

'Good, good.' Robert laid a hand on the youth's shoulder. 'Old Foggarty tells me you are an excellent pupil.'

'He does?' replied a surprised Andrew. 'He tells me all the time I am a clumsy oaf with horse meal for brains.'

The knight laughed. 'That's to stop you becoming too confident. Just listen to Old Foggarty. He has all the skills necessary for you to keep yourself alive, once you leave for Outremer.'

'What is Outremer?'

'It's the name the Knights Templar give to the foreign lands where they use their talent as warriors, first to stay alive themselves, and next to keep others from being massacred. Now, despite our talk this morning I have a gift for you. A sword.' Sir Robert paused for a while, as he studied Andrew closely. Andrew felt he was being judged, but he knew not what for. Then Sir Robert continued: 'A knight's sword defines him as a man of honour. It is his badge. Yes, he may carry a pennant and, yes, he might have his coat of arms on his shield. But it is his sword which is the symbol of his knighthood. There-fore it needs to be a good sword, one which is both strong and durable. A shining example of workmanship at its highest and best.'

He turned and reached for something behind him.

'This blade,' he said, turning back, 'is such a weapon. It was mine, but I am giving it to you.'

Andrew was a little disappointed. A second-hand sword, then? No doubt Sir Robert was going to get himself a new one to replace this old sword. He took the sword, still in its scabbard, and with a belt attached.

'Thank you,' he replied, simply.

Sir Robert had not noticed Andrew's lack of enthusiasm on receiving the gift, for he was still talking.

'You see the name embossed on the hilt?'

Andrew looked and saw a word. It meant nothing to him. This time Sir Robert did take notice of his expression.

'You don't know an Ulfberht sword? No? Well, I suppose there's no reason why you should, given that you come from a small village. Yet I should have thought one of the Templars would have told you . . . no, well, never mind. I shall educate you in the way of such things.

'Ulfberht swords have been the best of weapons since the

Vikings and Franks discovered them. They are fashioned from pattern-welded steel in the Rhineland. The crucible steel itself comes from Persia or the land of the Afghans and it can be honed to a sharpness not possible in other swords. It has a reputation for strength and invincibility. There are fakes out there, copies, but a genuine Ulfberht is worth its weight in gold. In fact, if I remember rightly, I paid as much for this one.'

Andrew tried to look impressed but he still felt he was being fobbed off with an old blade no longer wanted.

'Thank you, sire. I shall treasure this weapon. I am mindful of the great service you do me.'

The words came out with some feeling, but deep down there was doubt about the quality of the blade.

Andrew went away from the meeting feeling uncomfortable. He did not like having angered his benefactor. But also he did not like the fact that he could not look at or speak to Angelique again. Of course he had not even considered her as a potential bride – the thought had not entered his head. But he had thought they might become friends. However, he could see now that he was not going to be allowed to become friends with a lady, the daughter of a knight. God forbid, certainly not secret lovers, who exchanged notes and poetry, and yearned for the impossible. No, no. That thought had *never* been there. Perhaps, if he could ever learn to write notes and poetry he might send *someone* such things one day. But he saw how ungrateful he looked in the eyes of his patron and now resolved to become 'a man of iron'.

Back in the hands of Old Foggarty, Andrew threw himself into his studies of war with such a passion that he chopped the head clean off a painted wooden Saracen. Old Foggarty looked at the damaged effigy and clucked like a hen. 'Took me three weeks to make that stat-too,' he grumbled, 'and you go an' knock off his noddle in half a minute.'

'Sorry.'

'Sorry it is, eh? You got to learn to control that there temper, boy, 'cause it'll be the death of you. Cool and calm is what a warrior needs to be. No hot-headed slashing and hacking. Clean, skilful strokes.'

'I cut off his head, didn't I?'

'You did that, but there won't be just one standin' afront of you. There'll be ten. You go hackin' and bashin' like you did, full of fury and wasting your strength, chopping away ten to the dozen, and you'll have killed only one when you needed to kill ten. Single thrust, to the heart, was all as what was needed. Not a storm of chops and hacks, like some mad beast with a thorn up his bum.' He picked up the severed head and stared at its face, shaking his own grey skull. 'Poor old Ashface. Took me a week to paint that lovely turban on him. Can't stick it back on again now, can I? You've done for him, good and proper.'

Andrew apologised once again, but Old Foggarty was not to be appeased. He grumbled the rest of the day.

Finally the day came when Andrew had to leave the mansion and with Old Foggarty set forth towards Cressing. The silver-hued suit of armour crafted by Helmschmid of Austria was breathtaking. It shone with a blinding light, was perfect in its proportions, and was inlaid with exquisite gilt centripetal designs. The shoulder epaulieres were fashioned like an eagle's wings, the visor on the helmet was a lion's mouth, and the breastplate bore the picture of a dragon. Every piece of it – the cuissards, gauntlets, palletes, gorget, brassards, cuirass, tasses – all, all were magnificent in their design. Never had Andrew seen such a beautiful suit, not even on the knights of Cressing.

'I shall look like a prince, riding into my village wearing this,' cried Andrew in delight.

'You're not wearing that to Cressing,' said Old Foggarty, firmly. 'You'll go in these.' He showed Andrew an old rusting hauberk, a pair of soiled gauntlets and some dented elbow and knee protectors.

'What?' shouted the dismayed youth. 'Why?'

'Have some sense, shaveling. Do you want them to hate you as soon as they see you again? You go in all pricked out with pomp and pomegranates, eh? *Braggart,* they'll think. *Too uppish, by half.* You'll make knights jealous and contemptuous monks will think you vain, which you damn well are, of course. The villagers will all but choke on their indignation, offence and loathing. They'll find an excuse to burn you at the stake within a week and throw dice to see who gets to keep the Helmschmid armour. With your witchboy birth, they won't have far to look for an excuse, neither. No, boy, you go in with humility and grace, and leave this for me to carry in a sack. Lord a-mighty, I'm dealin' with an infant. Give me strength or give me leave to go.'

Andrew immediately saw the sense in all this, but he was nonetheless distraught. He had seen himself entering the village like some war god, high and glitteringly magnificent in the saddle of his dazzling charger, Warlock. He *wanted* them to choke on their envy. He wanted them to look on him and feel he was better than them. He *was* better. He had saved the life of a knight's daughter and his reward was to rise above his roots and look down on the unfortunate masses. He, Andrew of Cressing, was now one of the privileged few.

But he knew Old Foggarty was right. The duck pond was still there, ready and willing to welcome its victims. They might put him in his envied suit of armour, chuck him in the water and say, 'Let's see if you can swim with *that* lot on.'

'Oh, all right. I'll wear the rotten chain-mail vest. Haven't you got one a little less rusty?'

'It was good enough for me, back in '53, so it's good enough for a bloody blacksmith's son. See those bent links? A Frenchman tried to stick me with his dagger there, but I strangled him with my bare hands before he could pierce the vest.'

'That was when you had two hands to strangle with.'

Old Foggarty nodded. 'Two hands, two arms.'

Andrew was suddenly curious. 'How did you lose the one?'

'Got mangled under the wheel of a siege engine.'

'And you cut it off?'

'Palestine healer did it, with a little saw. Said the wound would turn rotten if not. Told me green slime would get took by my blood to this heart,' he thumped his chest, 'and rot that too, and I'd die else. They're better at that kind of healering, them Arab-land folk. They've studied medicines for longer than us. They know what they're talking of in that way.'

'Is that what happens, with a crushed hand?'

'Crushed anything. Goes black and green, and stinks like a putrid cabbage. Poison gets in your veins, turns the blood foul. Goes into your chest and your heart melts away to nothing. Ugly death. You got to cut off the offence and stick the bloody end of your limb into a fire, to seal it off. That's what this Arab physician did for me.'

'You rewarded him, of course?'

'Gave him my best drinking horn. He didn't drink ale or wine with it, o'course, 'cause with their religion they're not allowed. But he sold it for a good few coins, bein' as it had precious decorations – gold leaf around the lip and a nice silver tip to the point of the horn.'

During his training Andrew had noticed another figure had suddenly appeared around the estate, a young man who seemed interested in Andrew's progress. The youth, a slim, lithe young fellow, seemed well dressed and was therefore no mere stable boy or gardener's son. Andrew also noticed that the boy took good care not to let Old Foggarty see him. Perhaps he had wandered in from some neighbouring estate, hoping to get a glimpse of Angelique. Thinking on this, Andrew felt a hot stream of jealousy sear through him, which surprised him. Why should he worry if another young man was interested in Angelique?

But he did.

The intruder, Andrew noticed, was always accompanied by a dog. It was not the sort of beast a real man would be proud of owning. Not a large hunting hound. Not a deer chaser, or a killer of foxes. It was one of those silly lapdogs that young French princes were probably given as companions. A horrible thought then struck him. Perhaps this boy *was* a prince? A foreign prince visiting England? Indeed, he looked pale and red-lipped enough to be a soppy French prince. What chance, then, did he, Andrew, stand against royalty? None. None at all.

'Who cares,' he lied to himself, crossly, 'I'm not interested in her anyway. I'm to be a Templar.'

The next time he saw the figure, dangling from the limb of an apple tree which, being winter, was bare of leaves, he shook his fist at him.

The visiting prince returned the gesture and laughed.

Andrew was infuriated and for two farthings would have dragged the boy out of the tree and pummelled him until he wept.

Finally the moment came when Andrew and Old Foggarty were to set out for Cressing in Essex. Andrew, on one knee, took his leave of Sir Robert and thanked him profusely for his many favours. Sir Robert in turn thanked Andrew for the hundredth time for saving the life of his daughter. He then gave Andrew some advice.

'Do not allow arrogance to rule your soul, Andrew. Always remember who you are and where you came from. Always remember your parents and take every opportunity to remain humble in the eyes of men and God. Only a fool lets himself believe he is special and is entitled to look down on his fellows. Arrogance is the curse of the knight. Some like to call it pride. Pride in their country, pride in their race, pride in their worth. Do not be fooled. It remains arrogance.'

'I will try, my lord.'

Robert placed his right hand on Andrew's left shoulder.

'I hope you will, my boy, because I like you. You have good looks, a good mind, and I think you'll do well. Just don't get above yourself. If you do, it will eventually destroy your soul.'

Shortly afterwards Andrew and Old Foggarty rode away

from the mansion. Andrew looked back, hoping to see a beautiful face at one of the windows. But there was no figure at the window. He felt a bitter streak run through him, a streak that widened when he saw that damned, handsome youth again, the one who had been watching his training. The boy was standing in the shadows of the treeline as Andrew and Old Foggarty rode out of Sir Robert's estate. Old Foggarty had his eyes on the track ahead, but Andrew noticed the boy all right. The youth waved.

Andrew frowned. What did that mean? *Goodbye, the way is now open for me?*

He shrugged. All right, he would play a casual 'who cares' game with this pasty-faced fellow. Why give the youth the satisfaction of knowing he was concerned about his presence? Andrew threw the boy a wan smile and waved back, whereupon the youth ran off into the trees, the small, useless dog close on his heels.

'Good riddance,' muttered Andrew. 'I hope you both get eaten by woodland orcs.'

'What's that?' said Old Foggarty.

'Nothing.'

'Nothing, eh? I never knew a youth who spoke more about nothing. Well now, talker-of-nothing, we're on the road. I have to tell you something. In my pack are two important items. One is a long tube, the other is a small bell. If I should die, or be killed in your company, let them bury me where I fall.'

'You won't die,' Andrew said, shocked. 'Why should you die?'

'I'm an old man, and the thieves of sleep have been robbing me for years. I have to die one day and it might be today.

Listen, boy, this is important. When they bury me I want you to make sure they put my breathing tube from the coffin to the surface of the earth. Then, if I should wake unexpected, I'll be able to breathe.'

'If you're dead, why would you wake?'

'Some do, once they're in their graves. They've dug up coffins and found scratches inside the lids where the dead have tried to claw their way out.'

'They have?'

'Oh yes, indeed they have. And you'll oblige me by putting a string through the tube and to hang my bell at the other end of it, so that if I *do* awake, I can ring the bell and you can dig me up.'

Andrew tried to imagine standing by Old Foggarty's grave and then hearing the tinkling of his bell. Would he have enough courage to dig? He doubted it. Perhaps those with scratches on their coffin lids had not woken up, but were actually still dead? He had already met two dead men and the meeting had not been pleasant. He still had nightmares about it. Those trapped between life and death were not nice to look at. They had horrible, haunted eyes in which you could see Hell staring out at you. Their faces were hollow, drawn and a sickly grey colour, and their mouths seemed like wet pits that led nowhere. Would he be able to resist the bell? Probably not. How ghastly!

'Promise me, boy.'

'I'll – I'll try . . .'

'Try?' Old Foggarty turned round to look him in the eye. 'You'll do more than *try*. Promise me you'll take me up again. How'd you think I will feel, buried alive? Full of dread, that's what. And what's to be scared of? It'll only be me, down in the grave earth, not some monster from Ifurin.'

Andrew knew that Ifurin was an older Hell, the one the Celts once believed in. A place of freezing winds, snow and ice, and horrible monsters roaming, looking for dead men to eat. If Old Foggarty was destined to go there, then Andrew had no choice but to dig him up as fast as he could, before the old man was dragged down into an otherworld of winter and savage scavengers, eaters of souls and flesh.

'Are you a Welshman, Old Foggarty?'

'I should say so, boy.'

That night they stayed at an inn in Chelmsford. Andrew had been hoping to see his friends the players again – Patrick, Toby and Arthur – but did not come across them. He and Old Foggarty had a lean, narrow room where they slept topped and tailed in a long bed. Andrew hated the feel of Old Foggarty's callused feet, so curled himself up in a tight S shape. Later in the night he was woken by the sound of Old Foggarty grumbling.

'There's one of 'em here, I know it.'

'One what?' asked Andrew, sleepily.

'A thief of sleep.'

Andrew recalled Old Foggarty saying those words earlier in the day, but he had not taken a great deal of notice. Old Foggarty was always saying strange things.

'What's a sleep thief?'

'There are those who can't sleep themselves, so they steal the sleep of others,' growled Old Foggarty. 'There's one here in this inn.'

Andrew opened his eyes. It was pitch-black in the room.

94

Not a glimmer or glow of light anywhere. He stared into the darkness.

'How do you know?'

''Cause I can't sleep. Damn his eyes and liver,' snarled the old man. 'I should go and seek him out and put an end to his thieving.'

Andrew had visions of Old Foggarty sneaking around the inn, entering bedrooms until he found a likely victim, then starting a fight or even murdering someone. It was not a pleasant thought. The pair of them might end up as guests of the Sheriff of Chelmsford in his jail. They might even find themselves on the gibbet.

'Look, take some of my sleep,' said Andrew, sitting up. 'I've had enough. I don't need any more tonight.'

'How do I do that, boy?'

'Just close your eyes, relax and let it come to you. I've done this for my own father, when he hasn't been able to drop off.'

'All right, but if this doesn't work I'm going to find that thief and get my own sleep back.'

Andrew stayed bolt upright in the darkness, looking down towards his elderly companion. A little later he was relieved to hear snores coming from the far end of the long, narrow bed. His trick had worked. In allowing Old Foggarty to think he could borrow rest from another person, he had enabled the elderly man to relax and fall away into the nether world he desired. It was a good thing they would reach Cressing tomorrow, using the good road which led to Silver End. Andrew didn't think he could spend another night wondering whether Old Foggarty was going to rise up and plunge his dagger into someone. What if he imagined

Andrew himself was stealing his sleep? He shuddered at the thought.

Dawn came and they set off from the inn after a good breakfast. On this day they passed a ditch where Andrew had slept on his way down to London. In that ditch he had been the most miserable person on Earth, chock full of woes and troubles. He had been ill-clothed, cold, wet and starving, with legs like sodden logs. Now here he was, on a beautiful charger, well fed, free of cares. How quickly things changed in the world! Of course, he might also be dead, drowned in the River Thames, or hunted by an enraged, grief-stricken Robert de Sonnac if he had failed to hold on to his daughter's hair that day and *she* had drowned.

The pair approached the village of Cressing in the mid-afternoon. The tops of the great barns came into view above the stark trees, towering above the houses. Snow had settled on the ground in light patches and a chill wind had sprung up, so both men were wrapped in woollen blankets. Breath was steaming out of horsy nostrils like winter blossom. Andrew's face was pinched with the cold, but he was both excited and afraid. How would he be greeted? The villagers had chased him out of Cressing because he had wounded one of its most popular boys. Would that charge still stand against him? Would Robert de Sonnac's 'good word' be enough to keep the wolves at bay?

Then there were his parents. He had missed his mother and father a good deal lately. And also his sisters. Without question he loved all of his small family. When he had left the village he believed he would never see them again. His parents had been good to him and he had let them down by retaliating against Harold. No matter that Harold was to blame: Andrew's parents would have suffered snubs and insults because their son had attacked one of the village favourites. No doubt Harold had grown even more into the stalwart figure his youth had promised. People liked strong, handsome young men who treated their elders with respect. They did not like lean, intense youths who bragged that they were better than any of the other boys and would one day become famous.

'Is this it?' murmured Old Foggarty.

'This is it,' replied Andrew, his breath coming out quickly. 'Cressing.'

Old Foggarty pointed with a bony finger.

'I like the barns. I seen them from a long way off. I ain't never beheld such big barns, young 'un. They could be castles from their size. Two of 'em, eh? Some building they must have took. Beams the size of full oaks, by the look. Walls as thick as those of Troy. These Templars are surely as rich as a Turk to construct barns that size.'

'The Templars are poor, Old Foggarty, as well you know.'

'Individually, yes – but as a group – rich as sultans.'

So, here Andrew was, going back to a place which had cast him out. There was the home of the shoemaker, Joshua. And there the hovels of the field workers. Further on was the priory, smoke climbing in a spiral from its chimney. And there the walled garden which had been his sanctuary as a small boy, in the company of Friar Nottidge. Yet – yet the whole village looked smaller now that he had seen other towns. So much smaller. And the people seemed smaller, too, not at all worldly. They looked drab and downtrodden. A people to be pitied for their narrow lives. They had not seen what he had seen. London.

And yet again, this was his home, where he had been raised, and he still had that spark of fondness for it. He rode into the main thoroughfare, a muddy track that ran between the houses, and tried not to peer into the glassless windows. There were villagers in the street he recognised, who studied his horse curiously, not yet looking right up into his face and seeing him as one of their rejected sons.

Then one of them did look up and let out a startled shout. That was the only sound Andrew heard, as his heart began thumping in his chest, for once he had been recognised the villagers dropped their loads and gawped openly at him. One of them was Harold. Harold's mouth hung open. Andrew glared down at his old enemy with what he hoped were baleful eyes. Harold blinked in disbelief. One of the other youths dropped his bundle of wood, collected from the forest for the fire, and ran off, probably to tell others that the witchboy was back.

Angelique de Sonnac's life suddenly felt empty again. Her intriguing visitor, the youth who had saved her life, had now gone. There was no need for her to dress in boy's clothes any more. She had enjoyed disguising herself in order to watch Andrew crashing around in his armour and hacking at wooden enemies with his sword. A deep sadness descended on her. Then she rallied. Well, there was plenty of time now to plan her next escapade. It was true she caused her dear father a great deal of anxiety with such pranks but life would have been very very dull indeed if it had nothing in it but embroidery and weaving.

6. SQUIRE

As befitting a Knight Templar, Sir Gondemar de Blois lived in a simple dwelling. It was not a hovel, of course, but it was nowhere like as grand as Robert de Sonnac's mansion. Andrew knew which was de Blois' house and he led Old Foggarty there. Then Andrew was left outside, holding the horses. Old Foggarty was gone quite a long time, then a servant came out of the house and told Andrew he was wanted inside. A groom also appeared and led the steeds away to stables behind the house. Andrew entered a hall to find his companion sitting with a middle-aged knight at a table set in front of a roaring log fire. They had obviously just eaten a fine meal, for bones were scattered on the floor among the hounds, which were crunching away on them.

Obviously, thought Andrew, I get fed after the dogs.

'You, boy, come here!' ordered Sir Gondemar. 'Let's have a look at you.'

Andrew stepped forward and stood in front of the knight.

Gondemar was a tall, swarthy man with dark, glittering eyes. His face bore the marks of smallpox on cheeks and nose. His hair was bushy and black as charcoal, as was his beard. There was a stern expression on his face as he studied the parchment in his hand, then looked up again to run his eyes over the figure of the youth before him.

'You know me, sire. I used to live in the village.'

This was greeted with derision and scorn.

'Know *you*? Why should I know a peasant not even of my household?'

Andrew's heart sank. 'No reason, my lord.'

'No reason indeed. Am I expected to recognise the woman who does my laundry, or the oaf who delivers oats for my steed?'

Old Foggarty cleared his throat and interrupted him. 'It's what they call a phenomenon, sire.'

'What is?'

'The fact that the boy believes you should recognise him. You see, *he* knows you very well, having seen you riding through the village many times. Since you are a familiar figure to him, his brain tells him you are known to each other, which of course is not the case. Famous men suffer greatly from this delusion among the masses.'

This appealed to Sir Gondemar, since it inferred that he was a famous man.

'Oh, quite. I see the connection.' He turned back to Andrew. 'So you wish to be my squire?'

'If it please you, sire.'

'Well, it doesn't please me and it doesn't displease me. It's really of no consequence. I already have two squires, so another one is neither here nor there. Have you any training?'

'Yes sir,' Andrew glanced towards Old Foggarty, but the elderly man shook his head slightly, so Andrew said without naming his tutor, 'Sir Robert de Sonnac has given me some training. I know the duties of a squire, my lord.'

'Which are?'

Andrew recited. 'To carry the knight's armour, shield and

weapons. To carry the knight's banner. To dress the knight in his armour. To rescue the knight should he be taken prisoner. To protect the knight if he is in danger of losing his life. To guard any prisoners the knight might take. To take the knight to safety and tend the knight if he is wounded or loses his horse.' Andrew paused, then added, 'Oh, and to ensure an honourable burial if the knight falls in battle.'

'Very important duty, that last one,' said Gondemar, waving a chicken bone in Andrew's face. 'Not that I plan to get killed in the near future, you understand. But one never knows God's plan for one. Right, you'll do. Quarter yourself with the other two squires at the back of the house. One is called Gareth, the other . . . I don't recall the name of the other one, but you'll find out for yourself. Here, you look hungry,' he tossed Andrew a half-loaf and a drumstick, 'gnaw on those. And', he was thrown a flaccid wine skin, empty but for the dregs.

Then, just before he was dismissed, Sir Gondemar called Andrew forward again and stared at the sword by his side.

'Let me see that!'

Andrew drew the blade and placed it hilt first in the knight's waiting hand.

Sir Gondemar's expression changed to one of astonishment as he felt along the raised letters on the hilt. He then touched the blade lightly with a finger. A fine line of blood appeared on that finger, as thin as a seamster's thread. Indeed, Andrew knew the sword was as sharp as the edge of a shadow. And strong. A heavy rock had bounced from it as if shot from a catapult.

It was now being turned over in the knight's hands. 'Is this one of those cheap iron copies?' Sir Gondemar asked.

'I don't know,' replied Andrew, staring at the sword himself. 'It was given to me by Sir Robert. It's second-hand.'

'By God,' breathed Sir Gondemar, swishing the air with it, 'it is *his* Ulfberht. He *gave* it to you? A genuine Ulfberht?'

He looked down at Andrew with something akin to dislike.

'You're a lucky fellow, boy. Any time you wish to sell this blade, come to me first. You hear?'

'I don't think I could sell it, sire. It was a gift.'

'Well, when we get to Outremer you might be glad of some gold – I will give you gold for it. Once abroad you may find Sir Robert's influence waning a little and feel more free to do as you wish with your weapons, eh? I should think so. With what I will pay you, you'll be able to purchase a good sword in its stead and have plenty left over for carousing and fine clothes. To be frank with you, boy, this one is out of your class. Wasted on a squire, certainly.' The envy in his voice was thick enough to slice into rashers. 'But remember, to me first, none other, or you'll be looking for another squireship, understand?'

'I understand, sire.'

'Good.'

The sword was handed back, reluctantly.

With that he found himself dismissed. It seemed everyone was impressed with this sword but him. Perhaps he had better start admiring his own weapon? It seemed so. He went and found the steward who showed him to a stone room behind the kitchen. Being situated thus it was at least a warm place, behind the cook's large oven. There he found two boys around fourteen years old. One was a huge lad with a lopsided jaw. The other was built more like Andrew himself.

'Who're you?' asked lopsided jaw, when Andrew walked through the doorway. 'Don't you knock?'

'I'm to join you,' Andrew said. 'You must be the Other One.'

Both boys stared at him and Andrew explained, 'The knight said I'm to bunk with Gareth and the Other One.'

Gareth grinned and said to his companion in a Welsh accent, 'He never remembers your name.'

'Why?' cried lopsided jaw, continuing to polish the breast-plate armour he had on his lap. 'My name is Gondemar, same as his!'

'There you have it,' replied Andrew, taking off his riding blanket and scattering the drops from melted snow on a cot next to the wall. 'He won't like someone having the same name as his, which he regards as special. Why don't you change yours to John?'

'I was named for a rich uncle,' grumbled the boy, 'who never gave us a penny in his will at the end. You're right, I should change my name. Henceforth I shall be John.'

'So Gareth, so John, my name is Andrew. I'm squire number three. Where do I sleep?'

'Where you wish, you scruffy fellow,' replied Gareth, pleas-antly. 'Look, you take the corner over there. You'll need a cot and some straw for a mattress.'

'One of the servants is bringing that. I'm tired. I've been riding all day on my horse, Warlock.'

They stared at him enviously. 'We have to ride Sir Gondemar's nags. You have your own horse?' said Gareth. 'Are you a rich man's son?'

'No,' he decided to keep to the truth, 'I'm the local farrier's boy. No great pretensions. But I saved a knight's maid from

103

drowning and so earned my right to be a squire. The maid's father gave me a horse, armour and the chance to make something of myself.'

'Oh, not from nobility then? My father's a knight.'

'A very poor one,' added Gareth, 'whereas my father is a baron and owns a great deal of land.'

'All Welsh rocks and hillsides, though, no decent pastures,' said the newly named John.

'Still and all, *noble*.'

They both gave Andrew knowing looks and he realised that his background definitely made him the lesser squire of the three. It was something he already knew. You could not simply *earn* the right to knighthood. You had to come from a good family. He bit his tongue. There was no use arguing with these youths. He was what he was and nothing could change that, especially in Cressing, where he had been born and raised. Reminders of who he had once been were all around him. There was the hovel. There his mother and father. He would give himself away every time he acknowledged his parents. No doubt the village ruffians would sneer at him, until he taught them otherwise. His troubles were not over, he realised; they were just beginning.

'Right,' he said, 'two knaves and a peasant, but I'm sure we'll all get along extremely well, won't we?'

John said, 'So long as you can stand it.'

'What do you mean?'

'Well, we can't all three hold Sir Gondemar's shield for him.'

Competition. They were talking about competition. Of course. The best jobs would go to the favourite squire. Shield-bearer was the top job. Andrew suddenly realised he coveted the chance to bear the shield for his lord as much as the other two. He could remain on cordial terms with his fellow squires, but when it came to Sir Gondemar they were serious rivals. No doubt they all wanted to be knights, all three of them, and that meant getting sponsorship from their lord and master. Certainly he could not sponsor them all.

'We can still be friends, can't we?'

When the other two paid his words no heed, but returned to their former tasks, Andrew realised the answer was 'no'.

Later that evening Andrew was summoned by Sir Gondemar and Old Foggarty. His duties were outlined to him. He wanted to ask if he would ever be allowed to bear the knight's shield, but instinct warned him not to be so forward. Patience and time were of greatest importance here. Not so long ago he had been a nobody. Now at least he was squire to one of the most respected knights on the Templar estates of Cressing. He should be thankful for that and keep his peace for a while.

'May I visit my parents, sire?' he asked the knight, who raised an eyebrow at this question.

'If you must, but they know you are here.'

'I simply wish to ask their forgiveness for running away and leaving no message.'

Sir Gondemar gave an amused grunt. 'I suspect they knew why you absconded, squire – you broke a youth's head with a flint.'

'Ah, you have heard of that?'

'Tattle travels just as fast in the upward direction,' said Gondemar, more for the benefit of Old Foggarty than Andrew, 'as it does down or sideways. The boy's misdemeanours were known to me before you arrived with the letter.'

'I am not to be punished?' said Andrew, wonderingly.

'You might have been, had you returned as yourself,' replied Gondemar, 'but since you came back in the guise of a hero, all has been forgiven.'

Andrew was happy. He left the hall and, taking a firebrand for light, made his way to the house of his father and mother. When he entered they were sitting at the battered old table eating bread and cheese by candlelight. The first to greet him was the family hound, Beowulf, whose ears came up and whose tail wagged in joy. Here was his favourite human returned! The golden-haired Beowulf leapt from the floor and rushed at Andrew, almost knocking him off his feet. Andrew laughed, rubbing the dog's ears with affection. The rest of the family watched this display without pausing in their meal.

Once he was able to, Andrew turned to his parents. His father was drinking ale. His two younger sisters, Rachel and Marion, were now both squealing and pointing at him. Andrew's mother had half risen from her seat, but was waved down by father. Father turned a face scarred by sparks and red-hot flecks of metal towards his son.

'Well, Andrew?'

'I'm sorry, Pa. I left a message with the friar, so that you'd know why I had gone.'

'You tried to murder that Harold. That's why you went.'

'That's not true, Pa. I – I was simply defending myself. The others would have beaten me had I not done so.'

Father turned the bulk of his body – a massive body it was, too, with its huge barrel chest and muscular arms – towards his son.

'Your crime,' said his father, 'was not to succeed.'

Then he roared with laughter and slapped the table with the palm of one hand, making the plates and mugs jump and rattle.

'You can't mean that, Father,' said Andrew. 'I'm sorry to have worried you, Mother. And you two,' he wagged a finger at his two young sisters, 'don't let them bully you at the pump either.' He puffed out his chest. 'I am squire now, to Sir Gondemar de Blois. One day I shall be a famous knight and we shall all eat grapes off silver platters.'

'That'll be nice,' murmured his mother, 'but in the meantime sit down and have some of the monks' goat's cheese. It's strong and will help you grow taller and even more handsome.' She smiled shyly. 'Are you really a squire, then, Andrew? My goodness, that's going up in the world, isn't it? We're all very proud of you, very proud, even though the other villagers . . . well, they don't understand, do they? They have silly notions about . . . sit down, son, sit down. Next to your father. That's it, see how he beams at you. And Rachel, stop sniggering, it's unbecoming in a maid. And Marion, take your thumb out of your mouth. That's it.' Her voice took on a note of satisfaction. 'The whole family together, round the meal table . . .' She smiled broadly, blinked, then burst into a flood of tears, her face buried in her apron. Everyone rushed to comfort her, knowing that she was crying because her lost son, believed gone forever, had returned home and was alive and well. Not only well, but had risen vastly in status to become a lord's squire. It was all too much for her in one evening, she said through her sobs; she would be better able to cope with such wonderful news in the morning.

'But,' she added, 'you must visit your godmother and tell her the good tidings, too.'

'My –?' Andrew paled. 'Oh, you mean *her*. But – but she's – she's a warlock's wife. All she did was help to deliver me. That doesn't make her my godmother, does it?'

'She was present at your baptism, which was given you by Friar Nottidge, deep in the forest, using the water from a woodland pool. Godmother she is, most definite, son. You must visit her and the warlock and tell them of your good fortune.'

'If he's any kind of a warlock,' Father interrupted, 'he'll know already, won't he?'

'I'm talking about manners,' replied Mother. 'Politeness and manners.'

'Oh, them,' muttered Father.

'I'll do it tomorrow, Mother,' promised Andrew, unhappy about carrying out this duty in the dark hours. 'When it's light. Did Friar Nottidge tell you I met two dead men in the woods? Well, I did and I don't want to meet them again, for they were horrible to look at. So, I'll go in the morning, if that will suit, and tonight I'll entertain my sisters with gruesome tales of flesh hanging from yellowed bones and grinning skulls with empty sockets.'

The two girls were staring at him round-eyed.

'Or perhaps not,' he murmured. 'Let's eat the cheese.'

While the farrier's family were tucking into a good meal of cheese and bread, a young man of Andrew's age had just met Patrick and his fellow players. He was just what they had been looking for. His long silken hair was ash-blond, his eyes were a startling blue colour and his skin was as pale as sea-washed, sun-bleached wood. His figure was lean and somehow delicate. Patrick, Arthur and Toby had come across the youth walking down a dirt road in the direction of Cambridge. They had asked him if he would join them as they still needed a female for the troupe.

'Yes, I can be a girl for you, if you wish.'

He was perfect for the female parts, being so fresh-skinned and azure-eyed, but they found he was just a little mad.

'Where are you from?' asked Patrick.

'Heaven,' came the reply.

Patrick glanced at his two friends who just widened their eyes and shrugged.

'So, Heaven, eh? What were you doing there?'

'My name is Tomas. I am an angel.'

'Oh, an angel. Not an archangel, then?'

'No, sir, just an ordinary angel, but I can bless this troupe if you wish? I have a little divine power.'

Patrick said, 'If it please you.'

The blessing was duly administered.

Toby asked, as they walked along together, 'How did you get down here – from Heaven?'

'I fell.'

'So,' said Arthur, 'you're a *fallen* angel.'

The full force of those blue eyes were turned on him and Arthur almost stumbled in his walk. Tomas was no fool. In fact, he was highly intelligent.

'Not in that sense. I simply lost my hold on the clouds.'

'What's it like up there?' asked Toby. 'Is there music?'

'Such music you have never heard. It charms nightingales into silence, knowing they can never match it. Such sweet singing. Such melodies from heavenly harp string and lute.'

'What about dancing?'

'Dancing isn't allowed,' explained Tomas.

Arthur said, 'Pity, that – I like a good hop and a skip.'

'And where's your wings?' Patrick said. 'Aren't you supposed to have wings?'

'Some do, some don't. If I had wings I wouldn't have fallen, would I?'

Patrick agreed with him. 'That's logical,' he said, adding, 'not much else is, but who am I to question an angel's logic?'

Toby hesitantly asked the inevitable question.

'Have you seen – you know?'

'Him? No, of course not. I have no wish to be blinded by the radiance of His being.'

Thereafter the three youths stopped questioning Tomas. Toby was inclined to believe that the young man was indeed an angel. Arthur remained sceptical. Patrick thought he was a mild lunatic touched by too many nights sleeping under a full moon. It mattered not. The boy was a willing player and still perfect for the parts they wanted him to play. He proved to be a much more accomplished actor than the one they had lost, Andrew of Cressing, whose fortunes had changed for the better. Andrew, bless his soul, had not been the best female impersonator to trip and simper around the stage. His acting had barely reached adequate on the best of nights. Tomas, however, proved to be in a class of his own, even when playing a ruffian and a villain. He was a born player, better even (it has to be said) than the leader, Patrick, himself.

7.   GRINDEL AND BLODWYN

Andrew set off the next morning, sword at his left side, across a landscape covered in hoar frost. Beowulf trotted happily at his side, pausing only to investigate rabbit holes and mole hills as the fancy took him. Halfway across a field a hare sprang up out of nowhere and zigzagged for the far ditch. Beowulf was after it like a bolt from a crossbow, both creatures kicking up clouds of frost that sparkled in the sunlight. That was the last Andrew saw of his hound that morning. The dog was happy to see his young master, but there were other important issues which could not be ignored. One was a running hare.

The world glittered in the dawn light with a million tiny crystals. Andrew's feet crunched on frozen grass. White dust turned to droplets of water, then to mist. Andrew was cold. The old chain-mail vest he wore had lain gathering coldness to its metal links all night long. Under it was only a leather jerkin. Only his head was warm where he had thought to wear a woollen cap rather than his helmet. His eyes were watering badly and his breath was billowing before his face.

'I should have ridden out,' he told himself, 'and made it quicker.'

But he knew he would have had to tether Warlock on the edge of the woodland, for the trees grew too thickly within. The brambles would have scratched the charger's legs and

111

flanks. A horse left on the edge of a wood was vulnerable to accident or theft.

There was one thing he was glad of. It was at least daylight.

This was 'Blood-month', the eleventh in the old thirteen-month calendar, when the slaughter of surplus livestock took place before winter arrived. Bullocks, goats, pigs and sheep fell under the knife. The old lunar calendar had not been abandoned by farmers, for wrapped up in that calendar were many festivals and rituals. The new Christian calendar was regarded seriously by monks, gentry, craftsmen and merchants – but farming folk overlaid it with the old one. Without the ancient rituals, the crops would undoubtedly fail. Without the festivals there would be no fertility and so no good harvest. The farmers were convinced that following purely Christian ways would bring famine to the land.

So, this was *Blót-mónath*, when fresh blood was on the wind and thirsty ghosts would smell it and come forth looking to drink. To go out during the dark hours before 'Yule-month' arrived was suicide. Even Norman lords and their house-swains would not venture out of the village on such nights as these. Why tempt fate?

Nearing the dark wood, Andrew hesitated, but then he knew he had a task to perform and forced his feet forward. He entered the wood by a narrow, winding path which had been overlaid with birch twigs to cover the mud. Around him stood oak trees and hornbeams: mighty trees with big souls. Elves and dwarves would be watching. It was best not to look for them, best to ignore them. Men had been blinded by the silvery dazzle of elves who stood as tall as Andrew himself.

A hart suddenly flew out of the undergrowth, panicked by

Andrew's approach. Andrew jumped with fright and his pulse raced at the sudden flight of the stag.

'Don't *do* that,' he said, fighting for breath.

Thankfully he came at last to the A-frame hut covered in damp thatch and moss. There was a fire going outside the rough dwelling. A pot was hanging from a tripod of sticks. Steam rose from the pot, which carried the scent of cooking pottage.

'Hello?' called Andrew. 'Anyone there?'

A rat emerged from the near end of the thatch, ran along the ridge of the roof, and then disappeared at the far end.

'All right, I'm leaving,' Andrew said, relieved. 'No one here.'

Just then a tall, dark man appeared in the doorway of the hut. He was dressed in a thick robe. Just behind him a woman half his size poked her head round the man's buttocks to stare at Andrew. She was dressed in a ragged dress and had a shawl around her head. They were elderly people, with at least fifty winters behind them, but their faces were not as lined as those of the farmers and field workers.

'It's a shaveling,' said the warlock, 'carrying a man's sword.'

'It's *my* sword,' retorted Andrew, hotly, stung by the word that Old Foggarty always used to describe him.

The woman's eyes brightened. 'It's young Andrew,' she said. 'Don't you recognise your own godson, Grindel?'

She came out from behind the magician's robe as he was remarking that he didn't even recognise gods, let alone their sons.

'Greetings, Blodwyn,' said Andrew, in faltering tones. 'I – I came to thank you for the good fortune.'

To his consternation she sidled forward and gripped him by the head and planted a kiss on his temples, one on either side. He wondered if she would leave burn marks there, as she had done on his ankles. When she released him, Andrew squirmed away.

'Ah, an old lady's kisses are not as welcome as those of a comely lass, eh?' she cackled.

Andrew blushed. 'What do you know about Angelique de Sonnac?' he cried.

Blodwyn laughed again. 'Only what you've just told me. Angelique de Sonnac? That sounds like a genteel name. The daughter of a nobleman, no doubt. Our shaveling is reaching high, is he not, Grindel? And what is this good fortune you speak of? Let me guess. You've managed to murder young Harold at last. Pity about the last time. Your failure to do so then was a matter of great regret to those like myself and Grindel. Harold is growing into a rather troublesome youth, who would like to see me and my husband burned at the stake for witchcraft.'

'No, it's not about Harold, Blodwyn. It's about me.' He puffed out his chest. 'I am a squire, perhaps to be a knight one day.'

Grindel's face took on the ghost of a smile.

'You received a message, eh?'

'From two dead men?'

There was no sign from Grindel's expression that he already knew this fact.

'Anyway, I thank you both. As for witchcraft, well you are practising the black arts, aren't you, Blodwyn?'

'Hmm, a little of this and a little of that. But we also do a lot of good with herbs and healing balms, which is why the Templars have protected us for so long. We cure their wounds and headaches. One day, though, someone is going to say our gifts *all* come from the Devil. On that day they'll march up here with pitchforks and firebrands, and take us away to be burned on a fire. Harold will see to that. Now, have some breakfast with us, boy, for we have plenty of pottage.'

Andrew looked at the pot and frowned. 'Is – is it *regular* pottage?' He knew that Blodwyn sometimes slipped hazel-wort into the pottage she gave to her guests. Andrew knew from working in Friar Nottidge's garden that hazelwort was a purgative that loosened the bowels.

Grindel said, 'No magic potions in this pot. Just ordinary food, halfling. It'll build your strength. Blodwyn's pottage is almost as solid as clay. You have to carve it with a knife and eat it like hot cake. There's honey to spread on it – and a little butter. Sit, boy, on that log over there. A squire, eh? Well, a small way to becoming a knight. One day you'll ride into Cressing with a crest and coat of arms. Shall you come inside the hut to eat your breakfast?'

Andrew recalled the last and only time he had been inside their dwelling. He remembered fetid air which stank of name-less concoctions and things half rotten. There had been fear-some objects hanging in the sooty roof timbers of the inner thatch which had made him blanch. He could not tell you *what* exactly, but thereafter they had fed his nightmares. On that occasion he had disgraced himself by vomiting over their dirt floor and running with a giddy head through the doorway to the fresh air beyond. Andrew had no desire to repeat that day's performance.

'I – I'd rather stay out here, if you please.'

Andrew found a seat on the frost-covered log and was soon given a trencher with a slice of Blodwyn's pottage. It looked a little pink and he immediately thought of blood. He looked at Blodwyn, who read his mind.

'Wild berries,' she said, 'not blood.'

'Oh – yes, I thought so.'

'Did you now.'

When he had eaten his pottage, which tasted much like any other pottage, he asked a question.

'Those two dead men, they said there was a secret – to do with me.'

Blodwyn looked up quickly.

'A secret?'

'Yes, I got the feeling that they meant it was about me, personally, but they wouldn't tell me what it was.'

Grindel and Blodwyn exchanged looks.

'As to that,' replied Blodwyn at last, 'I don't know of any secret to do with you alone.'

Andrew had the uncomfortable feeling that she was lying, but he did not dare accuse her of such. Blodwyn was a formidable woman when roused to anger. Even indignation. And magic was not something to be trifled with. There were toads in the ditches that had once been respectable citizens of town and country. There were rats which hunted forest fairies for food because, being cursed, they could eat nothing else. You did not rouse the indignation of a warlock's wife, even if she was your godmother.

When Andrew left, Grindel called after him, 'Don't forget your prayers to the old gods, in Up World.'

Andrew turned and said, 'We're not supposed to pray to them any more – you know that.'

'Bah. What makes you think this new god is the right one? How can he handle a whole world on his own, eh? Doesn't make sense, does it? Be a bit lonely on his own in Up World.'

'He doesn't live there – he's – he's everywhere.'

'Big fellah, eh? Or pretty nippy?'

Andrew knew it was useless to argue with Grindel and said no more.

After his visit, Andrew left the strange pair, walked quickly through the woodland and then descended the slope to the village. On the way down he passed the graveyard. There were two new tombstones, one inside, one outside the low, dry wall. That would be the murderer and his victim, disinterred and reburied with their heads cut off and placed between their legs, to stop them walking abroad again. The murderer would be the one outside the wall, since he could not be buried in consecrated ground.

As he approached the two great barns he saw Harold waiting for him, along with his cronies. Harold had always been brawnier than Andrew and the squire could see his old adversary flexing his muscles. Harold's father was a butcher and therefore he had *some* importance in the village. Not that Andrew could have killed a serf just like that, without a great deal of fuss ensuing. The mob were picking up large flints now, but to show fear would have been the worst thing to do. Andrew strode towards them in a determined fashion, hand on sword hilt, causing several of the youths to look at each other with doubt in their eyes.

'That weapon doesn't scare us,' cried Harold. 'You don't know how to use it properly.'

Andrew confounded this statement by immediately unsheathing his sword with a metallic ring, then making several swift flourishes which Old Foggarty had taught him. Clearly he *did* know how to use the blade, and with some skill. Harold was taken aback for a moment. Andrew sheathed the weapon without even taking his eyes off the youth.

Andrew cleverly directed his remarks at Harold alone, ignoring the rest of the mob completely.

'Out of my path, churl. I am Sir Gondemar's squire and have been about his business. If you block me, I shall cut you down.'

'Better do as he says,' whispered a peasant's son in Harold's ear. 'I did hear of his becoming a squire.'

Harold ignored this. 'I am entitled to my revenge. You struck me with a stone before you ran away. It's my right.'

'So, throw your flint,' replied Andrew.

Harold raised his right arm and, after taking aim, hurled the knobbled flint at Andrew's head. Andrew blocked the stone with his mailed arm. The missile struck him on the elbow and was deflected away over his right shoulder.

'Now you've had your chance, step aside,' the squire ordered, 'or I will surely cut off that arm.'

Harold said in a frustrated voice, 'But the stone didn't strike your head.'

Andrew smiled. 'Is it my fault you're such a rotten shot?'

The other boys laughed at this, infuriating Harold even more. He turned a deep red.

'One day, Andrew Farrier, I'll knock you down to size.'

'One day, Harold Butcher, pigs will fly.'

With that, Andrew strode through the youths, shouldering Harold aside as he did so. Coming towards the group were the other two squires of Sir Gondemar, Gareth and John. They stepped purposefully across Andrew's path of retreat. Gareth said in a bored tone, 'Is there trouble here, Squire Andrew? Do you need assistance?'

At this the other village youths began to drift away, unwilling to become involved in Harold's war any more. Clearly, Andrew Farrier was now untouchable. He was a knight's squire, a member of the Templar fraternity, and they were simple country folk. It was certain that Harold now had to give up his feud with Andrew or walk on dangerous ground. They themselves remembered the times they had personally bullied Andrew and hoped he had forgotten or at least forgiven their cruelty towards him. Those who had laid hands on him to toss him into pond or river, or who had pelted him with pebbles, now regretted their actions and were busy thinking up ways of laying the blame on others.

Andrew replied, 'No, I thank you, Squire Gareth – I believe these churls have to be about their own business now.'

Andrew himself wanted to get back to his parents, to do something about his elbow. It was extremely painful. He could feel the bruise forming where the flint had struck. Yes, the chain mail had saved him from a broken bone, but it had still hurt like mad. Harold was no weakling and when he threw something it went with force. Andrew had not wanted to reveal his pain to his enemy, so had kept a straight face when he had wanted to yell and dance about with agony. He quickly left the scene and went to find his mother, who knew how to cure bruised bones and cuts and all those minor injuries of childhood.

When he finally went back to his quarters, he was sent for by Sir Gondemar. The knight did not seem in a good mood. He glowered when Andrew entered the hall.

'You missed the departure of your tutor,' said Sir Gondemar. 'Is it not polite to say farewell to one who has taught you?'

Andrew's heart sank. 'Old Foggarty has gone?'

'He left early this morning. You were sent for but you were not in your quarters with the other squires.'

Andrew hung his head. 'Forgive me, sire, I was at the house of my parents. I have not seen them for a long time.'

Sir Gondemar looked extremely severe. 'You were not there either, boy – where were you?'

Andrew's head came up with a jerk. 'Oh, yes. Early morning. Well, the weather seemed . . . there was a good frost. I – I went for a walk – in the forest, above the village with my old hound.'

Sir Gondemar's face lost its severity for a moment when he heard the word 'hound'.

'For what purpose?'

Instinct warned him not to mention the warlock and his wife.

'Sire, I – I was exercising Beowulf – that's the dog's name.'

Sir Gondemar stared hard at him. Then, to Andrew's relief, the knight nodded slowly. 'A good reason for an early morning stroll. My own hounds,' he gestured at the dogs lying by the great fire behind him, 'often need a walk. You will walk them twice a day from now on.'

'Of course, sire. I will do your bidding.'

'You will also confine your activities to this household.'

'My lord?'

'I do not want you visiting your parents again. You are my squire now. I have a reputation to consider. Do you think I want my squires hobnobbing with a sergeant-at-arms farrier and his family, visiting hovels in the village during the dark hours? These things do not go unnoticed. I will not be the object of jibes from my peers.'

Andrew's crestfallen look must have touched the knight somewhere in his deeply buried heart.

'Oh, come, boy, you'll soon have to leave for Outremer. We shall be going to the Holy Land in the near future. Your family cannot come with us there, now can they? You may take the horses to be shoed when it is necessary. That will be one of your duties. You may see your father in the course of his business, but then only. If you are out and about, you will ignore any attempt at recognition. Am I understood?'

'Yes, sire,' said Andrew, almost in a whisper.

To forsake his parents and his sisters! To have to walk past them without passing the time of day, or even waving! That was going to be difficult. They would understand, of course. His father and mother were not stupid. Indeed, they would probably not acknowledge him unless he turned aside to speak to them. They knew their place, which was now far below his. A farrier was a craftsman, well respected in any village. His father was a sergeant-at-arms, an honorary title given him by the Templars who gave him most of his work. But a farrier was not of a knight's household, was still a yokel, far, far beneath a knight, and a good way below a knight's retainers. Andrew would have to learn to ignore the fact that his parents lived just a stone's throw away.

'Now, there is something more serious, boy.'

Andrew's attention was once again sharply on his lord and master.

'Sire?' he said, his voice cracking.

'This name they call you – "witchboy" – how has that come about?'

'It's – it's nothing, sire.'

'It's something. Witches are evil creatures, the spawn of the Devil.' Sir Gondemar visibly shuddered. 'Is your mother thought to be a witch?'

Andrew replied quickly, 'My mother? No, sire. Not her. It was said Ma gave birth to me while on her way to the village church across the fields. It was a winter's day, sire. My father called for help and the warlock's wife came – she who lives in the,' Andrew suddenly realised it would not be politic to use the word 'forest', where he had already admitted to walking that morning, 'the, er, holt at the top of Aethelred's meadow – she came and helped my ma. That's all. There are youths in the village who hate me because – because I was chosen for the Horkey Boy. They make up these tales to fuel their jealousy, sire.'

'The warlock's woman. She was your mother's midwife?'

'Only by accident, sire. She helped deliver me and then was gone. It was nothing, my lord.'

'A birth is not *nothing*. I have seen women give birth out in the fields and they suffer great pain in the delivery. I cannot say I like this connection, youngling. I don't like it at all. But my friend has asked me to take you on as my squire and that I will do, for the sake our bond. You saved his daughter's life. No mean achievement in a river which flows swiftly at the change of tide. So, we must stamp on this name-calling. Which of the youths jeer at you in this way?'

Andrew mentioned the names of the worst of his tormentors, including that of Harold.

'I shall send some men-at-arms to their homes. They will not use the insult again. Now, you – if I am bothered by anything concerning you again, be it small or large, you are dismissed. You hear me? No more of your parents. No more witchery, or anything like. Already you have been more troublesome than the other two squires put together. You will behave – exemplary behaviour – or you will go. Understood?'

'Yes, sire. Forgive me, my lord.'

'Now, you shall exercise the hounds.'

Yuletide came and went.

Andrew had to bear the pain of having to ignore his parents and sisters. He had been right about them, however. It was clear from their faces that they both understood and sympathised. They knew why he was ignoring them and they in turn neither spoke to nor acknowledged him in passing. Andrew was able to speak to Friar Nottidge, though, and sent messages to his mother and father through this good man. Friar Nottidge also kept Andrew informed of other matters.

'Your master, Sir Gondemar, is threatening to bring the warlock and his wife to trial,' said the friar to Andrew, as they sat on the camomile seat looking across at the knot garden and fountain. 'He says he wants them burned at the stake.'

'What?' cried Andrew, leaping up. 'But they're harmless.'

'They consort with the Devil, Andrew.'

The squire could not argue with this.

'But – but they never really hurt anyone.'

'I believe this is true. Oh, don't worry, Sir Gondemar will probably never carry out his threat. He's terrified of witch-craft. He's too afraid they'll curse him as they die.'

'Then why is he threatening them?'

'He's hoping they'll pack up and leave for some other part of the country and so be out of his hair.'

'They won't, you know.'

Friar Nottidge nodded. 'Andrew, you must distance your-self from those people. The taunts you received as a young boy will return otherwise and now that you're an adult they'll be all the more dangerous to you.'

'I know that.'

'Good.'

Spring arrived and the youths of the village were all out in the fields, or working at the mill, or butchering, or doing other jobs. Gareth, John and Andrew had spent the winter months in idleness. Winter was no time for a knight to be out and about. He huddled down in front of his fire and waited for warmth to come back to the earth. His servants, his swains, did likewise. Only when the first wild flowers began to show did Sir Gondemar send two of his squires northwards to York as armed escorts for waggons of grain. Gareth and Andrew were selected for the mission.

The boys were excited. This was Andrew's first expedition and he felt like a man as he rode beside the waggons he was guarding. *Just let them try to rob our caravan*, he said to himself. *They'll have Andrew of Cressing to answer to.* His pride in his own prowess, as yet untested, was considerable. It was a thing of youth, especially of untried youth, to feel it necessary to ride puffed up and vain. Gareth was much the same. They were like two cockerels in a yard of old roosters. They thought they knew everything; they certainly felt they were the best fighters the world had ever had the pleasure of knowing. They believed they would die for each other, for their lord, for their kingdom.

The caravan had to pass through Sherwood Forest, in Nottingham county. Sherwood was notorious for sheltering outlaws and the soldiers and horsemen of the caravan kept a sharp eye on the riffling leaves of the trees, which danced with sunlight and shadows. At first the two youths jumped at every gust of wind that shook a bough, but after a while they relaxed and actually became better guardians for it. With their minds more settled, they were keener of observation and more ready to deal with any ambush from the notorious ruffians of this forest.

At noon they were attacked, outlaws dropping from the overhead branches of trees, and rushing out from the shadows of thorn bushes. Their yells were bloodcurdling and chilling, but the two boys did not hesitate to meet the onslaught.

'To your right Andrew – beware the cudgel!'

'And you, Gareth, mind your back!'

In the dim light of the forest no one quite knew what was going on, especially those who were being attacked. Soldiers flayed about themselves wildly with their swords, in danger of striking each other rather than the enemy. Arrows and bolts were fired in panic, hit trees, ricocheted everywhere. Outlaws rushed out of the shadows, shrieking and yelling, causing one or two startled men-at-arms to run away in fright. Waggon bullocks bolted with the grain and overturned their loads. Horses danced in fear, screaming like men when they were wounded. One man-at-arms was convinced they were being attacked by witches and kept calling for a friar to bring down the wrath of God on his long-haired, wild-eyed opponents. Men were stabbed in the buttocks; had their feet trodden on and crushed by skittish steeds; were bowled over by stampeding bullocks; ran full pelt in panic straight into tree trunks and were knocked cold. It was not at all the glorious action that Andrew had thought a battle should be.

One lithe outlaw leapt from the ground and locked his thick, hairy arms around Andrew's neck. Choking, Andrew struck back with the pommel of his sword, catching the man in the gut. Still the stinking figure hung on, tightening his grip. Andrew sheathed his sword, drew his dagger and struck again. The wounded outlaw slid from the back of the horse and fell to the ground, where he was trampled by Gareth's steed. Andrew fought for breath, feeling his bruised throat, but knew that he could not retire from the fight. Drawing his sword again, he rejoined the fray, sweeping this way and that. The fierce outlaws had them outnumbered, but their weapons were not as good.

Gareth was then struck by a club and fell from his mount.

'Hold on, Gareth,' cried Andrew.

He swiftly dismounted and stood over his comrade, fighting off any villain that came close. Eventually Gareth was up on his feet and the two fought together, back-to-back, until finally the outlaws gave up and ran off into the forest again, having captured only one waggon out of the twenty that made up the caravan.

Three men-at-arms with the waggons had been killed and seven outlaws lost their lives. Sherwood was a dense, tangled forest, the paths through it narrow and overhung with huge oaks. The way was still dark and dangerous, despite their victory. Both squires were glad when they finally emerged on the far side, without any further loss of their cargo.

It was the first time Andrew had drawn his sword with actual intent to cause harm. The experience had been exciting but not at all as he had imagined it would be. He had not foreseen the bungled blundering of such an action. In his mind he had visions of everything being clear and clean-cut, but it had been far from that. It had been chaos.

Still, he had acquitted himself well. He was congratulated by the leading sergeant-at-arms of the waggon caravan. After a while he began to see more clearly how valiantly he had fought and was quite proud of himself. The two soldiers who had deserted were caught, tried and summarily hanged from an oak. This affected Andrew more than the fight itself. How quickly life was taken from a man. There were always these two instinctive reactions when a man was surprised by danger. One was to freeze, the other was to run. Andrew knew it could have gone either way with him. The fact that he froze was not due to courage. After the initial shock, of course, one unfroze and joined the melee. Had he run away, though, he might have joined those now swinging from trees. How easily it could have tipped either way.

'They say,' said Gareth, as they rode side by side, 'that there is a knight controlling these grubby gangs of outlaws.'

'A knight?'

'One Sir Robin of Loxley, though it's unproven.'

127

'Why would a knight want to rob people?'

'Not all knights are honourable, Andrew. Loxley is of old Anglo-Saxon stock and, as you know, most knights are from Norman families. His father was an earl but lost most of his lands and the son is seething with rage, wanting revenge as well as a return to wealth.'

Andrew was stunned by this. 'But we're all Englishmen, aren't we?'

'Some are more English than others and you've obviously forgotten, old sausage, I'm Welsh.'

With this cryptic remark, Gareth rode on, leaving Andrew to ponder on the vagaries of national identity. The outlaws who had been killed had been scrawny, filthy peasants, closer in their appearance to animals rather than men. But they must have had the hearts of men, to attack a well-armed waggon caravan. Surely it was out of hunger and want, rather than desire for riches? Who would bother with a grain waggon when there were merchants with gold in their purses?

Andrew thought Gareth was wrong about the outlaws having a noble leader. He himself was convinced they were a disorganised rabble. If they had a leader at all he was like themselves, an uneducated lout. Surely, surely not a nobleman? That would be like throwing away your entire heritage, your entire family pride, your bloodline. Some of the Anglo-Saxon royal families traced their bloodline back to ancient gods. Woden, Tiw or Ing. To throw all that away? Unthinkable.

The grain was eventually delivered and Andrew had received a lesson in the reality of fighting. The two squires returned to Cressing. There Andrew received an astonishing piece of news. He was to leave Cressing, to go ahead of Sir Gondemar and make his way to Jerusalem, to prepare for things before the arrival of his lord and master.

'I will follow in three months,' said Sir Gondemar. 'You must arrange accommodations for me and one other squire.'

'Just one?'

'Gareth will be with me. I am dismissing the other.'

Andrew was not impertinent. He did not ask why John, or, rather, Gondemar-the-squire, was being sent away. There were a number of reasons, but mostly it was because Sir Gondemar did not like him. You could not argue with that. John would probably be glad to go, if it were not that his livelihood was being wrenched from him. Better a master who loathed you than no master at all.

'I shall do my best to please you, sire.'

A hand went on his shoulder. 'Good, good. I trust you, Andrew, despite your low birth.'

At this moment Sir Gondemar de Blois looked magnificent. He was wearing his best armour, which shone in the sunlight. But most of all Andrew envied the knight his Templar robe. It was pure white, the white of Heaven, with a blood-red cross on the front. The warrior-monk looked like one of the Host, come down to avenge the Lord. Andrew desired the right to wear that robe above all things. To be a Templar! The Knights Hospitallers wore black robes with white crosses of eight points above their hearts, but their order was nowhere near as splendid as the Order of the Templars. Hospitallers had been formed to care for sick and injured pilgrims on their way to the Holy Land. The Templars were the protectors, guardians of the pilgrims.

Andrew knew which he would rather be.

It was surely the most worthy ambition a youth could have, to be a Templar Knight. Oh yes, he wanted it so badly he shivered at the thought of it. One day. *One day*. He had been promised, had he not, by those who could see into the future. His godparents? His devilparents? What did it matter? The prophecy of the two dead men would come to pass. He would wear the white robe with the red cross over his heart and ordinary men would admire and envy him.

Before he left the village, he was accosted by Harold.

'I hear you're going away,' said Harold, with a sneer. 'Don't bother to come back again. If you do, I shall kill you, squire or not. I'll cut your throat while you sleep and take what comes.'

'*When* I come back, I shall seek you out, Harold, and cut you down where you stand, in front of witnesses.'

The pair stood there, breathing hate at each other, until finally Harold was called to his father's workplace.

'You won't come back,' called the bully, over his shoulder. 'You'll die in some fly-infested land and your corpse will rot under a foreign sun. But remember what I said. If you do manage to live, and come back, you'll wish you had died over there.'

Andrew set out seven days later, heading for the port of Dunwich on the east coast. There he would take a ship to a place called Venice, which he had been told was an island city in the Mediterranean Sea. Old Foggarty had given him some lessons in geography, but not much of it had sunk in. It was difficult to picture other lands and cities when you had only been as far as London. Even London had been an extraordinary experience for a country yokel, with its bustling streets, its many odd characters and its big wooden buildings and churches.

Trying to picture places like Venice and Jerusalem in his mind was almost impossible. They sounded like fairylands. It seemed Venice floated on the sea like a water lily made of coloured bricks and tiles. Its buildings were all palaces, towers and cathedrals made of gold, silver and precious stones. Jerusalem had strange animals called camels with humps on their backs wandering the streets. In Jerusalem there were buildings with domes, called mosques, which had open spaces inside them as big as a village square. There the towers were tall and thin, with globes on top of them. The markets were full of fabrics of brilliant colours and there were gems clustered on dirty plates for sale.

'You should look at a chart, a map,' Old Foggarty had told him. 'I don't have any in my possession, but they are like pictures of the world spread flat. You can see how each country fits on to the Earth. Ask the master if he's got one.'

But Andrew had never dared to request a look at a 'map' and so was still ignorant of the jigsaw patterns of the world.

Andrew's excitement, as he made his way across country on his charger, could hardly be contained. He was but a yokel and here he was on his way to exotic lands! He wore a sword, rode a fine horse, led a donkey behind on which he carried his magnificent armour, and ordinary peasants stepped obligingly out of his path. Even being a squire was something undreamed of by a boy of his birth. However, as he came along a narrow dirt lane near a small river port called Woodbridge, four youths blocked the way, sauntering along without a thought for other users of the highway. Andrew's indignation rose.

'Hi there,' he called, as he rode up behind, 'clear the way.'

They took no notice of him and he stared at their backs with annoyance.

'Did you hear me, churls? Clear the way, or I will ride through you, by Heaven.'

One of the youths flung an arm above his shoulder as if to say, 'Go to hell!'

'In that case, I shall ride through.'

Now one of the youths turned around and cried, 'Oh, you will, will you, sir – in which case we shall be obliged to drag you from that nag and pummel you . . .' Then the youth's face changed from annoyance into a smile and he cried, 'Andrew!'

The speaker was none other than Patrick. And there was Arthur. And his good friend Toby. The other boy, a strange looking creature of pale appearance, was not known to Andrew.

'Lads!' he cried. 'Where are you bound?'

'Why, we've been summoned to a castle in a remote place called Orford, to give them a performance. And you?'

'To the port of Dunwich. I'm bound for the Holy Land.'

'Ah,' said big Toby, 'you are a knight already?'

Andrew smiled wryly. 'No, things do not move that fast, Toby. I'm still a squire. I go to prepare the way for my master, who joins the other Templars in Jerusalem in three months. But who is this new player? Did he take my place as the leading female?'

Patrick laughed. 'He did indeed. Andrew, come down off that old hack and meet Tomas.'

Andrew leapt from Warlock and shook hands with the new

youth, whose palm and fingers were as slim as a girl's. In fact, he looked a delicate creature, with his whitish hair and brilliant blue eyes. The boy was looking at Andrew with wonder in those eyes.

'Oh Andrew,' he said with great reverence and awe in his voice, 'you are going to Jerusalem?'

'That I am, by way of a city called Venice.'

'Andrew, I would give the Earth to go with you.'

Arthur said, winking secretly to Andrew, 'Tomas is an angel – Jerusalem is his dream.'

They all began walking down the lane together, with Toby leading Andrew's horse and donkey.

'So,' said Andrew, cheerily, 'give me the Earth then and I'll take you with pleasure.'

Tomas looked upset and lost, and Andrew immediately regretted his joke.

'Ah, I see the problem. You don't *have* the Earth, do you?'

Tomas said, 'I – I could come with you as your squire.'

Andrew laughed. 'But I *am* a squire. I never heard of a squire's squire.'

'Your servant then, and your squire when you become a knight.'

'You don't know me, Tomas. I could prove to be a highly demanding master.'

Tomas smiled and shook his head. 'No, I can see by your face that you are a kind person, Andrew. And Patrick, Arthur and Toby have spoken of you. Toby's account of you is best, while Patrick thinks you would have made a good player. Arthur speaks of you the least and when he does there's a dismissive tone to his voice.'

Arthur blushed at this and said, 'Oh, not so, Tomas.'

But Andrew knew all this. Tomas had put it into words, but he knew the feelings of each of his erstwhile comrades. It was true that Arthur liked him the least and Toby liked him the best. And it was also true that Patrick thought of nothing but the troupe and measured all things by the success it might give to the players. Tomas had merely put into words what everyone present knew to be the case.

The friends walked along, chattering to one another, without Andrew having to give Tomas a straight yes or no answer. That night they stayed in the river port of Ipswich. In the morning they would all be ready to travel to their individual destinations.

In Jerusalem a young man by the name of Walter Pughson was buying fruit in the market. Walter had been sold four times so far during his short life, the last time when he was seven years old. The man who purchased him that time was a swordsmith by the name of Pugh. Now he was almost fifteen and had been the swordsmith's apprentice for five years. Pugh treated him with kindness and indeed called him his own son. The swordsmith was unmarried and had taken himself and Walter to the Holy Land to further his trade, there being too many swordmakers in England at the time.

Now Walter was haggling with the stallholder over the price of a basket of dates.

'You will cause my children to starve,' grumbled the man, as a price was settled on. 'I make no profit on such a bargain.'

'Let them eat fruit,' replied Walter. 'It will serve them better than flatbread.'

The stall owner rolled his eyes. He was, of course, not actually interested in feeding children, he just wanted to moan about his loss of profit.

Walter enjoyed his life in Jerusalem. The sun shone most days. With continual strife against the enemies of King Baldwin IV of Jerusalem there was plenty of work for his master. Walter had many friends among the Islamic peoples of the city and liked their way of life. He found people of this region light of foot and touched with fire. In England the weather had been dreary much of the time. The people there seemed heavy and overburdened with troubles. Keeping warm was one problem. Keeping a roof over one's head was another. And the food! What was better, a plate of succulent dates or a bowl of turnip stew? Why, a life in Jerusalem was much the better one. In most weathers you could sleep on a rooftop with just a blanket.

Humming to himself Walter turned into a side street, intent on carrying the basket of dates back to his master's forge. Turning a corner, he almost collided with a large man. Then out of the shadows came four others. He was about to protest when one of them smiled then hit him on the head with some sort of soft club. The blow was heavy enough to knock him cold. When he came to he found himself tied by the legs to the back of a mule in a place where there was nothing but rocks and sand. The men who had captured him were riding camels. They were heavily bearded, turbaned fellows from some other region. All five were dressed in black. They had cruel faces and humourless eyes. One of them, on seeing Walter was awake, tossed him a goatskin of water.

Walter gulped down the cool liquid, then addressed his captors.

'What am I doing here?' asked the distressed youth. 'I have no money. Is it to ransom me? I am worthless.'

The men said nothing. They simply stared straight ahead.

'Please, sirs, tell me where we are going.'

One of the men, a tall creature with a large, hawk-beak nose, turned his head and muttered a word. Walter sighed and began to weep. The men took no notice of his distress. They were a hard people, raised to suppress any feelings of compassion. Had he been the son of any one of them he could not have expected to be treated any less harshly.

The word the man had spoken was 'Masyaf'.

Masyaf was the fortress of a bloody and fanatical sect of warriors famous for their fearless murders.

It was located in a place known as the Valley of the Assassins.

These rough-hewn men were Assassins.

8. BOUND FOR JERUSALEM

When morning came Tomas once again pleaded with Andrew.

'Please take me with you to Outremer, sir. I shall make an excellent servant. You won't ever need to lift a hand again. I believe you will make a wonderful master. And when you become a knight, as I know you will, I shall be your most proper, obedient squire.'

This constant feeding of his ego eventually wore down Andrew's resistance. He was flattered by the attentions of this strange youth. When he thought about it, he decided it would be good to have a companion to share his highs and lows. An angel was better than a demon. Problems always seemed less worrying when there were two heads. And Sir Gondemar had given him plenty of money for travelling. Of course, he would have to account for that money when he next saw his lord, but a servant would cost little for passage and food.

Finally he said to Tomas, 'Yes, you may join me as my servant.'

Tomas was ecstatic. 'Of all things wonderful – I am going to Venice and Jerusalem! Thank you, sire.'

'Well, as to that, I'd rather you called me "Andrew", for I am not yet a knight. Yes, I think "Andrew" will be fine until I am elevated to knighthood.'

Andrew felt quite uplifted by his own decision. Tomas seemed an undemanding youth. It would be pleasant to share new experiences with someone as excited as he was. And, unlike Gareth, Tomas was in no way a rival. They could enjoy a companionship that had no edge to it. And, of course, Andrew would have assistance in looking after his horse and carrying out his duties as charged by Sir Gondemar.

Patrick was not so happy about the whole affair.

'Two leading ladies lost within the year,' he groaned. 'How can you do this to me, Andrew? First you take yourself off on a hare-brained scheme and now your replacement joins you. Good female players are hard to find – there are so many ugly, rough churls around.'

'Oh, someone will come along,' cried Andrew, airily. 'You'll see.'

But before he left Andrew gave each of the players two gold coins: enough to keep them in food and drink for months to come.

'Is this your money, Andrew?' asked Patrick. 'Won't you get into trouble, just giving it away?'

'Oh, I'll think of something. I'll say I've been robbed.'

'Not by us,' cried Toby. 'We'll be hanged.'

'No, no, by some bandit in a foreign land. It'll be fine, don't you worry. I want you to be happy.'

'You shouldn't lie to your master, Andrew,' suggested Tomas. 'What about your honour.'

Stung by this remark, Andrew snapped, 'Oh, well, I'll tell him the truth, then. Sir Gondemar can take it out of my wages, or something.'

He and Tomas parted from the players at around nine of the clock on a cold and wintery morning. Since the donkey was so heavily laden with Andrew's armour, Tomas climbed up behind Andrew on Warlock. Only Andrew was aware of the fact that they were imitating the emblem of the Knights Templar: two men sharing one horse symbolised the Templar dedication to frugality and emphasised their vow of poverty. The youths then made their way east, to Dunwich. On the way they stopped to buy bread and it was then that Tomas 'blessed' Andrew's armour.

'Nor sword, nor spear, nor arrow shall attempt to pierce this breastplate,' intoned Tomas, 'or the wrath of God will come down upon the attacker as holy fire. This armour will have the protection of the Lord and will be girded about by an invisible force, which will turn away points of weapons and will blind enemies with its brilliance. With this armour the wearer will be safe from harm.'

'Well,' said Andrew, remaining inwardly sceptical, 'it seems I need never fear for my life again.'

'Oh yes,' said the prayerful Tomas, seriously, 'you can of course drown, for such heavy armour will drag you down to the depths of the ocean, where monsters and horrible fiends lurk.'

Dunwich was a thriving port gradually being eaten away by the sea. However, building was still going on, for this was the tenth largest town in England, its deep river delta making a perfect harbour for ships of all shapes and sizes. There was a label of treason attached to its history. Two years earlier, Robert, Earl of Leicester, had landed at Dunwich with three thousand Flemish mercenaries in an attempt to overthrow King Henry II. Poor Robert had failed miserably.

The town itself boasted a monastery, more than a handful of churches and a leper colony. Tomas wanted to go into the colony and bless the lepers there. Andrew, however, said that the horrors of their sickness had been sent down as punishment from Heaven, and forbade Tomas to bless them, saying the creatures must suffer for their sins. Tomas spoke surprisingly sternly to Andrew, saying he knew some fine people who had been visited by leprosy and he knew them to be men of God. In the end the length of their quarrel made it impossible for Tomas to visit the colony, for they ran out of time.

The two boys found a boat bound for Venice. It was called the *Willow*. Andrew was to sleep down in the hold where Warlock was tethered, while Tomas had to make do with a space on the open deck with slaves and servants. They set sail on the turn of the tide. After some hours they were being tossed like a cork in a great storm in the Bay of Biscay.

Andrew, thrown about violently from stem to stern, was a very sick young man for hours. Warlock, too, suffered terribly and thrashed and kicked below decks, seriously damaging some of the soggy timbers. These two were not alone. Other men, other horses, were in a similar plight. Water gushed in through the hatches, swirling about the hold. It was freezing cold, wet and dark down there. Andrew thought he was going to die. Warlock thought he was already dead.

'Surely,' said the naïve, unaffected Tomas, who visited his master on occasion to care for him, 'you must have sinned badly to be so afflicted?'

Andrew could not answer his servant since his head was permanently in a bucket.

Tomas spent most of his hours on deck, which was his

home while on board. It was true the tempest frightened him, with its jagged lightning and loud thunder, but he did not feel ill. He clung to the rigging and swallowed down salt spray with fresh air. Both seemed to do him a power of good. It was cold, to be sure, but there was no horrible smell of vomit and faeces; no struggling, moaning men; no darkness deeper than a bottomless pit. Out in the open the winds might cut through a man, but they were clean and wholesome. Tomas suggested to his master that he, too, might feel better on deck.

Andrew, however, remembered Tomas's words, after he had blessed his armour. It would be easy to be thrown overboard in such furious waves. Andrew, despite his swimming ability, knew he would drown in such conditions. He cursed his servant for the vivid picture left in his mind, of a man plunging to his death in a green hell of giant sea serpents and name-less demons. He stayed where he was, in that dank hole below decks, shivering madly and heaving up nothing but pain once his stomach had emptied itself.

After a few days of blundering about the big ocean, they found themselves passing through the Pillars of Hercules and into a calmer Mediterranean Sea. There was a warmer, sweeter air above decks. Andrew dragged himself up there and hung over the rail, marvelling at the blueness of the waters. He was still weak but less miserable. Able to think now, he looked across at the coast of Africa and shivered for a very different reason. That was a dark land, full of unknown horrors. He had heard of men there without heads, their noses, eyes and mouths being in their chests. This was a strange human race, but there were also bizarre beasts of every form. Dragons, naturally, and unicorns, basilisks, gryphons and chimeras. But other creatures, indescribable creatures, also lurked in and roamed the landscape. It was best not to dwell too much on such things in case the ship foundered.

'Can you smell the spices, Andrew?' sighed Tomas, coming up alongside his master. 'Can you smell the red earth of yonder?'

'My nose has given up smelling after what happened down below.'

'Well, that's no more. Now you are in the light.'

This was true and Andrew took heart from it. On the other side he could see the coast of Andalucía. Despite the fact that this land was ruled by the Moors, it looked more inviting. At least one could make a landfall there without immediately being eaten by men or monsters.

'Why, this is better than a winter at Cressing,' agreed Andrew. 'Here at least it's not bitter cold. A chill wind, yes, but bearable. And look at all those boats, with their three-cornered sails!'

'Like wounded butterflies on the water,' said Tomas. 'What are they doing, Andrew?'

'Fishing the waters! Hundreds of them. Dark men pulling on their nets. Heathens, no doubt. How lean and supple they look. It must be the sun that darkens their skins. Tomas, do you think we will have skin like that when we return home?'

Tomas, his skin as pale as flour, shook his head, not knowing the answer to this question.

While their ship was in motion smaller boats began to cluster around it. The masters of these vessels called up to those on board the *Willow*, asking if they wanted fish, cloth, whips, curved Arabian daggers and a thousand other goods. Certainly fish was purchased by the ship's cook and passengers bought a number of other items. The sale was effected by the buyer putting his money in a leather bucket which was see-sawed to and from the ship's deck by means of ropes tied to the handles either side of the bucket. The money went down in the bucket, was taken out, and the purchased goods put in its place to be hauled back up to the deck. A certain amount of trust was needed to make this commerce possible, but those in the boats below knew that if they cheated they would lose all future sales, not only for themselves but for their fellow traders. Thus bargains were struck and executed without so much as the smallest hitch.

Now that Andrew was back on his feet and convinced he was actually going to live, he appreciated what his servant Tomas had done for him while he had been sick.

'I thank you, Tomas. Do you know, I think you must be the secret the dead men spoke of!'

When asked to explain, he told Tomas about the words of the murderer and his victim. 'One said to the other, "Shall we tell him the secret?" and his fellow said, "No, we haven't been charged with that task." So they wouldn't tell me what it was. I think, Tomas, you must be the secret of which they spoke, since I had no thought I would find someone as useful and as energetic as you.'

'Andrew, I don't think I can be your "secret" – I'm not that important. If the dead men spoke about it in such hushed tones, it must have been something of real import.'

'But you say you're an angel, Tomas. That's quite important in the grand scheme of things.'

'Well, an angel *is* important, that's true, but this secret of yours sounds like something momentous in your life. I feel I was *meant* to be your servant. It was all planned in Heaven and was certain to happen, so there would be no need for it to be a secret. A secret is something that has to be uncovered by accident or will. We must keep attentive for signs of this secret and be ready to discover it when it lurks nearby, Andrew.'

Andrew thought about this and decided his companion-servant was probably right. The dead men had spoken of the secret in tremulous tones and it had sounded an earth-shattering thing. Tomas was also right about keeping a keen eye open for this secret. It could perhaps pass one by without one knowing it was even there ready to be unveiled.

The ship sailed on, down through the Mediterranean, pausing to take on board two Knights Hospitaller at Malta, then round the boot of Italy and up the Adriatic to Venice.

At the first sight of the fabulous city of Venice Tomas could hardly contain himself.

'Oh, Andrew, we are surely in Heaven,' he cried. 'Look, look at all the marvellous buildings! How they flash like fire in the sun. Look at the brave lions on the fluttering banners. See the basilicas, the cupolas, the towers! White and shining. The red bricks. The dazzling tiles. Gold everywhere. Silver over all. Glass, brilliant glass. The glint of old bronze. I think I could find rest here in this wonderful city. This is God's sculpture; his hands have worked this art, I am sure.'

Andrew was just as excited as Tomas, but did not have the same skill with words, so contained his joy.

Later, when they were walking through the streets, the

squares, alongside canals teeming with craft, he said, 'What a wonder, Tomas – when I think of my village of Cressing, how dull it seems beside this island city which seems to have sprung from the very waves of the ocean. Even London can't match it, you know. There are more marble statues here than there are people in Cressing.'

'Oh, yes, Andrew. Look at that bridge, it crosses the Grand Canal with such sweeping grace.'

'Well, as to that,' replied Andrew, huffily, outdone once again by the eloquence of his servant, 'I couldn't say. But when you look around you, you can see more wealth on the outside of these buildings than in all the coffers of all the rich earls of England. These stones, the way the citizens of this city dress, no wonder they're so . . . so . . .'

'Arrogant? I agree, Andrew. They look down their long noses at us and you can see them wrinkle the ends as they pass. One would think we smelled of dung the way they turn their haughty heads aside. It is a great city, to be sure, but the people are no more special than we are, despite their fine clothes and silver shoes. Andrew, you are as good as they – and I – I am one of the High Host, so I have it over them, you see.'

'Yes, they are glum looking. They have all this and still they look as if they're in the pit of despair.'

'Money does not bring happiness, Andrew.'

'No, indeed, for I have none and yet I am happy.'

Andrew, a little piqued by Tomas's displays of philosophy and learning, asked him how he knew so much.

'I learned it in Heaven,' Tomas told his master.

'Were you then born in that place?'

145

'Oh no,' confessed Tomas. 'My parents abandoned me as a young child and I had to fend for myself. I was forever hungry and could only eat what I could find in the forest. Sometimes that was acorns and strange-looking mushrooms. One time, after I had not eaten for a long while, I went to sleep in a cave and there I saw some golden steps leading up through a hole in the roof of the cave to the sky above. I climbed the steps one by one, for it was quite difficult with the rise in each step being half my own height. Once I was in the clouds, though, my form became lighter and easier to manage, so that sometimes I was almost able to float from one step of gold up to the next.

'Eventually I came to a great arch, also of gold, which I knew to be the gateway to Heaven. Beyond Heaven's gate was a world of blinding light, so bright I could not see into it. Ghostly forms moved in this brilliance, but it shone with such fierceness it was impossible to hold my gaze. I made as if to enter beneath the arch, but there were angels guarding the gate who tried to tell me to turn back, since I was still mortal and not really permitted to cross into God's kingdom.

'However, an old man – his beard fell hundreds of feet down through the clouds, but being white seemed part of them – ordered the angels to let me pass.

'"I am Adam," said the ancient man, "your ancestor of many grandfathers ago."

'Then he touched my head, like a bishop blessing a sinner, and I became an angel such as those guarding the gate, though unlike them I was not yet fully grown. Great knowledge flowed as liquid instantly into my form: wonderful words, wise sayings, magical numbers, the power of blessing. Once I had become one of the Heavenly Host, I was able to look around me and saw other angels, archangels, cherubim and seraphim and also saints. These were all gilded, some with silver, some with gold. There were dead souls there, too, those who had passed through the fine-meshed golden sieve – more closely woven than muslin – which separates good from evil. Their forms were also luminous but not with precious materials. They were more like moonbeams alongside the rays of the sun.

'There were paths covered in crushed diamonds and the dust of powdered rubies drifted around our feet. Someone had taken pure sunbeams and bent them into balustrades which hemmed the walkways. Towers of glistening crystal soared above our heads and portals of amber led us into rooms open to the soft air of Heaven. In these rooms sat alchemists and wizards, poring over books and parchments, finding there the answers to those secrets they had so desperately desired while on Earth – of how to turn base metals to gold and how to make life everlasting – but which secrets had come too late. They struck their temples with their fists in frustration. They stamped their feet in agony. Why? Because they could now see how close they had come to those priceless secrets when they were in the world of mortals.

'I would have stayed in Heaven, Andrew, if I had not slipped while trying to find my footing on the clouds. It is like trying to walk on shifting sand up there and I was new and quite young. I fell to Earth as a wounded bird or a leaf falls, not with any great speed but with a kind of side-to-side drifting movement. This allowed me to land with a lightness which prevented any hurt to my recently changed form. That,

Andrew, was how I became what I am today, an angel and a child of wisdom.'

Andrew accepted this description of heaven without comment, having heard one or two others like it before in his life.

Before the two set sail from Venice they learned why the Venetians looked so dejected. It seemed that Turkish enemies were not enough for the Emperor Manuel of Byzantium. Jealous of the great trading nation of Venice, he had recently ordered the arrest of all Venetian merchants in his domains and had confiscated their wares. The sum of this 'theft' was enormous and set back the island city considerably. Venetians were quite rightly furious and upset by this un-Christian act and swore to get revenge on Manuel's rival city of Constantinople. However, for the present that was impossible, and Venetians had been left to fume helplessly while their best merchants languished in a foreign jail and their goods were sold to profit the sly and crafty Manuel.

Andrew and Tomas left the city of Venice to its grief, sailing on the tide for the port of Jaffa in the Kingdom of Jerusalem. Andrew learned that the realm was ruled by King Baldwin, a young man the same age as himself, just fifteen years old. He was also told that the king was known as 'Baldwin the Leper' because of the disease he had been born with. Andrew recalled his words about lepers at Dunwich and was worried that Tomas would throw them in his face. However, Tomas did no such thing, even when they also learned that, despite his illness and lack of years, King Baldwin was known to be a very able general. Knights flocked to his banner, from all over Europe, and beyond.

*   *   *

While Andrew and Tomas were enjoying the sea breezes riffling through the rigging, one Walter Pughson was going through hell. After his capture by the tribesmen he had indeed been taken to the fortress of Masyaf in the Valley of the Assassins.

Who were these people? Walter knew of them from talk in the marketplace. They were men of deadly intent. The sole purpose of all Assassins was dedicated to murder. They were sent out alone, a single individual, to slay this great leader or that high ruler. No one was safe from their long reach: not king, not emperor, not despot, though all of these high-born rulers might have thousands of warriors nearby. If the first Assassin failed, another would be sent, and another, and another, until finally a knife was plunged into the victim's breast, or poison laced his wine, or a garrotte strangled him in his bed.

The Assassins murdered by stealth. They were faceless. They were anonymous. No one knew them until the blade flashed and a monarch lay bleeding on the floor of his throne room, surrounded by bewildered guards. A victim could lock himself away with strong, utterly loyal protectors, and still he would eventually fall to the ground with sightless eyes. Very, very few escaped the final touch of the Assassins, if their name was marked.

Walter Pughson had been thrown in an oubliette, a dungeon below the floor of the room where gathered Assassins ate their food. Scraps fell through a grille in the floor and this was all Walter got to eat. The word 'oubliette' comes from the French *oublier*, 'to forget' which was exactly what his captors did with Walter. They forgot him. He licked the dirty water that ran down the walls of his dungeon, and ate the filthy bits of meat and bread which fell from above. No one answered his cries for pity. No one even looked down through the bars. He could not even touch the soles of the sandals over his head. The foulness of hunting dogs dropped through the grille, but no kind words.

One thought kept Walter alive.

Why had the tribesmen risked their lives to enter Jerusalem simply to take him captive? They surely had a use for him or they would have simply cut his throat long ago. He resolved to promise to do whatever they had in mind for him – if indeed it was a task and he was going to be more than just a sacrifice – then go back on that promise once he was free. He would feel no dishonour in lying to thieves and murderers. After all, what could they do to him then that they could not do now? In his misery there was hope and he prayed he would see Jerusalem again.

9. CITY OF GOD

What a harum-scarum port was Jaffa!

Ships and boats of all description on the water. On the dockside, people of all shades and nations. Traders, craftsmen, merchants, knights, monks, pilgrims, rich men, poor men, beggars and (no doubt) thieves thronged the wharves. A score of modes of dress were evident, from brilliant-hued robes to grey habits. Camels crooned, asses bayed, curs howled. They and their masters and mistresses churned the dust into clouds which mingled with perfumed smoke from hookahs. Here and there were men whose cheeks bulged as they chewed a weed which Andrew was told was called qat, which turned common occurrences into fantastic dreams. Water sellers were every-where, their cries ringing through the streets which led into the town. Lean cats slinked hither and thither, seeking scraps of food. Musicians played on corners, poets read their works aloud to passers-by, scribes scribbled letters for illiterate customers, fruit sellers sold golden pears and silver nuts.

What a cacophony! What sights! What *smells*!

And it was surprisingly cold, with a sharp wind that cut through a man like a blade of ice.

Andrew was once more thoroughly overwhelmed. First there had been London, then Venice, now Jaffa. Jerusalem was yet to come. His senses were on fire as he smelled the musky scents of the East, saw the ochre colours of the East, heard the strange music of the East. An English village boy exposed to these exotic assailants of his senses, he was in a whirl of excitement, trepidation and amazement. It was as if his body had been thrown into a land where everything had changed, all his familiar and known senses had been shaken free and others had taken their places.

'What a land!' he exclaimed to Tomas, as they stepped ashore, leading Warlock and the donkey by their bridles. 'It seems like madness.'

'Indeed it does, Andrew. Look there. I do not know even one-tenth of the names of those fruits. That one is what I'm sure is called a *date*. But they are so many and various. And the fabrics on that stall! So brilliant in colour. This is almost like Heaven, except it is full of people, not angels and saints.

'And strange beasts – that must be a camel. How it glares at me! See, there is its water sack on its back. It chews like my uncle, who had no teeth, the jaws going from side to side. Indeed, it looks like, and *is*, my uncle Joshua, reborn. Hello, Uncle Joshua!' Tomas shouted. 'How long have you been in Jaffa? My, your hair has grown back on your head quite profusely since last I saw you. But your eyes are just as rheumy.'

'What a fool you are, Tomas,' laughed Andrew. 'See how the beast stares at you.'

An elderly Arab in a red turban sidled up to them.

'*Salaam ali kum.* Can I help you, masters? I am Yusuf. I can find you good lodgings for a pittance, sirs.'

The boys accepted the offer, but Andrew kept a close watch on his purse. After all, he told himself, this was the country of Infidels. These people were not his people. He did not know whether they had a sense of honour, or if stealing was an accepted sport among them. In fact, in his eagerness to be careful, as happens so often he was quite careless. He hid his purse all right, but failed to check his clothing before sleeping. In the morning he found his tunic had been washed and hung over a fire to dry. Two silver coins which had been in his tunic pocket had been carefully placed on the small stool by his bed.

'You didn't steal my money,' he said to Yusuf, when the elderly man brought the youths tea. 'You could have.'

Yusuf looked at him with contempt.

'I do not take that which does not belong to me by right.'

Andrew said he was sorry for his thoughts, but that he was not familiar with the peoples of lands other than his own.

'I have found,' came the reply, 'that most people in most lands are much the same, for in my lifetime I have been to Egypt, Al Yemen, Rum, Persia, Cyprus, Venice, England . . .'

Andrew interrupted him: 'Wait – you have been to England?'

'I have been many more places, if you will let me finish the list, for I was a sailor on a trading dhow when I was a younger man. What you see here is an old man, but you only see the wrapping. You must never think you know what is inside from the wrapping, sir, for it tells you nothing but the age of the package. I have done many things, fought many battles, sailed many seas, and therefore am able better to judge men than you, a green boy who has not yet tasted of life.

'I know, for instance, that in your country there are a great many honest men, but you also have one or two robbers and thieves there, as we do here. You must judge a man by what he does and trust that man until he does something wrong. Always begin by favouring the stranger with your trust, young master, and you will enrich your soul thereby.'

'But what if he *is* a bad man?'

'Then you will have lost something of worldly value, but your immortal soul will still be pure. Which is more important to you? Your goods or your true self?'

'The answer to that is obvious.'

'*Aiwa*. And here, let me tell you, thieves are punished by the loss of their right hand. Even if I had a dark way within me, which I do not, I like my right hand too much to risk losing it for two silver coins.'

'That sounds barbaric to me,' said Andrew.

'And how is it with thieves in your country?'

'We hang them.'

'Ah,' said the sage old man, smiling and pouring more tea for Andrew, 'and, of course, that is not barbaric.'

That morning they took their leave of Yusuf.

'You are a good man for an Infidel,' said Andrew.

Yusuf replied, 'And so are you.'

'I am not the unbeliever, you are,' exclaimed the squire.

'We are both Infidels to each other,' said Yusuf, 'which is why there is bloodshed over this ancient land.'

'Ah, I understand your meaning.'

'Never fear, young master, there will always be men like us who can see over the tops of such barriers.'

'I hope so, Yusuf. I think you would like my godfather, who is a warlock and lives in a wood. You are both – what is the word I want, Tomas? – someone who speaks wisely . . . ?'

'Philosophers.'

'Yes, that's what you are, Yusuf, a philosopher, like my godfather, the warlock. Farewell, old man.'

'Goodbye, boys – stay alive.'

The pair set out for the city of Jerusalem, both astride Warlock.

For his part the horse, in his horse-like way, was pleased to be on dry land. He had hated the journey in the hollowed oak, tossed upon violent waves, trapped in a dark, stinking stable, saltwater swilling around his hooves. He stepped out, lively as a colt, along the road to the Holy City, sucking the strange smelling air down into his lungs through his cavernous, silken nostrils. His mane flowed softer than a maiden's hair in the wind. His high tail flicked at the insistent flies. The two young human animals were light upon his back, the armour being borne along behind by the ever-suffering donkey. It was, once again, a good life.

After two days' journey, one night spent out in the open in cold weather, they at last saw the walls of Jerusalem. Tomas became emotional, sobbing with joy at the sight. Andrew was simply overawed. They entered the city gate which was guarded by several bored looking soldiers, and found themselves immediately in narrow streets crowded with people, both Muslims and Christians, stone arches over their heads every few metres. Andrew asked the way to the Temple of Solomon, the headquarters of the Knights Templar. When they reached it his heart was pounding in his chest. Here it was, the great temple, and he was about to enter it. He knew the stables were underground and told Tomas to lead his horse to them and give the beast a rub-down and something to eat.

He was walking along a passage, the walls of which were covered in tapestries, when he was accosted by a coarse-skinned knight.

'Hello, boy – what are you doing here? Do you not know this is the Temple of Solomon? Be off with you.'

'Sire, I am the squire of Sir Gondemar de Blois, who has sent me ahead of him to ease his arrival.'

'Ah, you're that stripling, are you? Well, in that case I have a message for you,' said the big, dark-haired man. 'Your master is yet on his way overland, doing his duty of protecting pilgrims on the route to this holy city. You are to ride out and meet him at Antioch. Good luck, boy, and watch your back. There are Saracens who would have your head out there, and bandits, and wild beasts which would tear out your innards.'

Andrew's jaw dropped. 'How far is Antioch?' he asked.

'Some four hundred miles.'

'Why, that is as long as England!' Or so the friar had told him.

The black-bearded knight laughed.

'Wait a minute,' said Andrew, suspiciously, 'how did such a message reach here before I did?'

'By a faster boat?' suggested the knight. 'I hope you're not calling me a liar, shaveling?'

Andrew realised his misjudgement.

'No, sire. Forgive me. I have only just this hour come to Jerusalem and now I find I have to leave. It is hard.'

'You're a squire, boy. You do as you're bidden, though I do pity you. Gondemar must think little of your life to make you go on such a dangerous journey alone. And only just arrived? How green you must be, boy. You will surely win your spurs if you get to Antioch alive. Look,' the knight had compassion in his eyes, 'I know of a caravan going north. Shall I speak to the master? You will have the protection of the caravan's guards, though they be but desert nomads.'

'That would be kind of you, sire. And will I meet the Temple's Master before I go?'

Again a hearty laugh. 'You? The Master of the Templars give an audience to a squire? I think not, shaveling. Go about your business.'

When Andrew told Tomas, the other became quite excited by the prospect of going out into the unknown. However, Andrew said he needed to do it alone. He did not want Gondemar to see Tomas just yet. So he told Tomas that he must stay in Jerusalem and await his return. Tomas was only mildly upset. After all, he told Andrew, Jerusalem was the most exciting city he had ever seen, next to Venice. It was full of knights and warriors of every kind. There would be plenty to see, plenty to do.

'We must go to the suq before you leave, Andrew,' said Tomas. 'I glimpsed it from the street. It is a wonderful place, full of spices, fabrics, brass lamps, weapons, carpets – some of them magic, no doubt – oh, just about everything you never thought of or saw before in your life. What a place! I could die here with pleasure, if I were not already immortal. Even as I led the horse down to the stables a man tried to sell me some precious stones. He told me the names: lapis lazuli – a startling blue-orange cornelian, brown jasper, garnets of dark red, smoky agate, deep-green jade and golden tiger eyes. But I had no money to buy, so he cursed me in his own tongue.

Whereupon I cursed him back, with an angel's curse, and now I feel bad for him for he will die choking on a blackened, swollen tongue, his eyes starting from his head.'

'Well, he cursed you first.'

'Yes, but he was not to know that his curse was useless, since angels are immune to Eastern magic.'

'Oh well, more fool him.'

So, no sooner was Andrew a citizen of Jerusalem than he had to leave. The black-bearded Templar had found him the promised caravan, which was some fifty camels long. The head of the caravan was a Yemeni merchant from the city of Adan which lay at the bottom of the Arabian peninsula on the corner where the Red Sea met the Indian Ocean. Adan, Andrew was told, was a city with natural walls, being enclosed by the cone of an extinct volcano. What further wonders? The merchant was carrying cloth woven on the looms of this southern land, which had once been ruled by the Queen of Sheba, back in the time of King Solomon himself.

When asked how he would pay his passage, Andrew told the merchant he would do so with his services.

'I shall be one of your protectors,' he said. 'Will that be acceptable?'

The stink of camels was overpowering and Andrew wondered if he would be able to get upwind of them on the journey.

The merchant shrugged. 'Just make sure you don't run away at the first sign of bandits.'

'Sir,' Andrew replied haughtily, 'I am bound by honour.'

The caravan set off at dawn, men swathed in robes and bearing scimitars riding horses down either side. In the centre were the camels with their drivers urging them on. The camels could not make a single step without a number of oaths being hurled at them, or so it seemed to Andrew, for the drivers never ceased their cursing for a moment. Andrew could not understand the language, of course, but it was not hard to recognise a curse by its guttural utterance. Dogs ran alongside and between the legs of the camels. Children and women, those without asses to carry them, that is, trudged behind.

Besides Andrew there were three Christian knights accompanying the caravan, also bound for Antioch. They wore black robes with white crosses, so Andrew knew they were Knights Hospitaller. There was hostility between the Hospitallers and Templars, and Andrew naturally felt partisan towards the Templars. In any case, the three knights, from some central European country, spoke another language. He felt very much alone as he rode alongside the camels which he was supposed to be guarding.

In the evening he made his own fire, but within the circle of the others. The Hospitallers did not invite him to eat their food. He warmed some bread given him by Tomas before he left. He was just about to eat it when the eldest son of the caravan leader came to the entrance of their tent and beckoned. Andrew went to him.

'My father wishes you to join us for our meal,' said the man. 'It is our way to give hospitality to the stranger in our camp.'

Andrew could smell cooked meat and his stomach growled at him to accept this fine offer.

'But you have several strangers.'

'None as strange as you,' answered the man. 'Come, we have many sweetmeats you will like.'

159

Andrew entered the tent to find the floor covered in carpets, the walls hanging with tapestries. It was like a cocoon, warm and cosy, out of the desert wind. Tea was brewing on the fire. There were platters of meat and vegetables on a cloth on the floor. Several men sat cross-legged on cushions, or on rugs, and they were eating. Old Yusuf had told Andrew that people in this region ate with their right hands, their left being used for the dirty tasks in life. Thus he sat down, not forgetting quietly to thank his host, and used his right hand to partake of the meal. The elderly leader of the caravan looked at him with approval.

As Andrew was eating, he looked across to see a youth a little younger than himself, sitting by the master of caravan. A companion of his own age! He smiled at the boy, but received a dark scowl in return. Clearly sitting down with these Arabs was not going to break down all the barriers.

That night Andrew slept against Warlock, as the steed stood nearby. It was bitterly cold for both man and beast. The water in Andrew's goatskin froze within two hours.

The next day he saw the young boy again, but once more received a contemptuous look in reply to his own enquiring one. No friends to be made there. And one of the Hospitallers reproached him in English, saying he should not have joined the 'Infidels' at their table.

'Why not?' asked Andrew. 'I was invited as a guest.'

'They are not of our thinking,' came the reply. 'You should feel shame as a Christian for entering a heathen tent.'

'It was more than I got from you,' he snapped back. 'Where was your Christian hospitality?'

'Be careful,' the knight snarled, 'or I may have to cut out that abusive tongue and feed it to the kites.'

Andrew turned away. There were three of these black-frocked pi-dogs, all brutish men with big heads and thick necks. They lived by the sword and the boot. He knew they would not think twice about murdering an unaccompanied youth, even if he was of their faith and culture. No friends to be made there, either.

Sir Gondemar, before he had left England on an early winter morning, was accosted by a youth of Cressing village.

'Sir, my name is Harold, son of the butcher.'

'Son of the . . . ? And you have the effrontery to accost a knight of the realm?'

'Sire, forgive me, but if it please you to listen? You know the harvest was not good. My own thoughts are that the Horkey Boy was bewitched and therefore the horkey branch evil . . .'

Gondemar sneered. 'Boy, it is well known you and my squire are at loggerheads. Have a care. My time is valuable.'

Harold visibly expelled air into the frosty morning, sending blooms of steam into Gondemar's face.

He said, 'I know where the witch lives.'

Gondemar arched an eyebrow. This was interesting. This was more than a squabble between village boys. Gondemar had long been concerned about the presence in the forest of two magicians. Few had gone up there to look for them, because that particular forest was well known as a haunt of dead men and monsters. Not that Gondemar was afraid of such things, but a knight would not demean himself by trudging about a woodland looking for sorcerers. Nor could he send his men-at-arms, who would run at the first snap of a twig. His men were brave enough in a physical fight, but sorcerers were terrifying.

'The witch? And the warlock?'

'Both, sire. I can lead the villagers to the hut. We can rid ourselves of these pests.'

'You can persuade your neighbours to hunt them down?'

Harold replied with obvious satisfaction, 'I've been working on them for some time now. Since the harvest was so poor last autumn, many have been starving. They need but an excuse to ignite them to action. I need the authority of one of our lords, and I come to you for that.'

Blame for a poor harvest does much to spur men to action.

'You have it. I shall speak with the prior and the lord of the village, and settle it with them.'

The prior might question the wisdom of such action, but the elderly lord of Cressing village, a king's post separate from the enclave of the Knights Templar attached to that village, was a close friend of Gondemar.

'Do it.'

Harold returned to his friends with the news. They were highly excited, almost ecstatic with the idea. To kill a warlock! It raised a fever in their brains which was fuelled by alcohol throughout the day as they drove in thick posts and gathered faggots for the fires. They were to burn a warlock and his witch wife! What brave men they thought themselves, to carry out such a deed. Perhaps half of them would be toads or snakes before the night's end, but they did not at that moment care, for strong drink had given them the courage of lions.

That night, carrying flaming brands, some forty men set off for the forest, with Harold at their head. With fast-beating

162

hearts they surrounded the hut where Grindel and Blodwyn slept and dragged the pair from their beds, swiftly binding and gagging them to prevent them from cursing their captors or casting spells.

The warlock and his wife were carried on poles, in the manner of slaughtered pigs, down to the village.

There the hapless pair were strapped to the stakes.

Harold set a torch to the dry faggots under their feet while Gondemar watched, his eyes gleaming red in the firelight that sprang up instantly. He held a scented kerchief ready to put to his nose, once the stench of burning flesh rose up into the night air. The crackle of the flames and the sizzling of skin and hair sent the villagers crazy, and they screamed with insane delight and danced wildly around the flames.

10.   CARAVAN TO ANTIOCH

They travelled a desert landscape broken only occasionally by waterholes which the Arabs called oases. The oases were pleasant areas where those strange trees grew. They were not the trees of England. They resembled the bare brown backbones of skeletons rising up in a curve towards the clouds. The scant foliage was at the very top, spread like a parasol. Andrew had heard of palms from the monks at Cressing. Friar Nottidge could read the language of the Bible and had mentioned palm trees. Andrew remembered the story about palm leaves being spread on the ground before Jesus on an ass. But he had not paid much attention at the time. There were palms which grew dates and palms which grew huge nuts. Andrew liked the fruit of both.

One day they were camped by a well, rather than an oasis, and Hassan, the younger son of the caravan leader, came leading a small herd of goats. Warlock was drinking from the well's leather bucket when Hassan tried to snatch it away. Andrew was incensed and stepped between the boy and his horse. Hassan's hand went immediately to the broad, curved dagger in his belt.

'My goats are thirsty,' the Arab boy cried. 'You are unwelcome in our land – you will wait until my goats have drunk.'

The English boy's hand went to his sword. 'No, you will wait until my steed has finished,' he snarled.

'You *Infidel*,' shouted the Arab boy, hotly. 'You will not be long in Arabia. The great Saladin will chase you all out like dogs. Even now he is lord of Damascus and Aleppo. He will sweep across from Egypt as a fierce wind and drive you all into the sea.'

Andrew had, of course, heard of Saladin, the young warrior leader of the Saracens. Indeed, he had already won many victories, had conquered several cities. Even the best Christian knights respected this Kurd who had united all Muslims against Christians. More alarming than his courage and fighting skills was the fact that Saladin was a leader who knew how to show compassion. Savagery was the order of the day, on both sides, and Tomas had said that a man great and confident enough to rise above this brutality was surely someone to be reckoned with.

'I do not care for your Saladin. I shall cut off his head.'

Hassan's eyes opened wide with disbelief at this sacrilege. He drew his dagger.

'I will make you eat those words,' he cried. 'You will die now . . .'

Suddenly a shadow fell on the boy. A hand came out and gripped his wrist, wresting free the sharp steel gambia before it was plunged into Andrew's chest.

'This knight is our guest,' said the youth who had restrained Hassan. 'You will respect our sacred laws of hospitality!'

'He is our enemy,' choked Hassan, finding himself held by his older brother.

'While he is in our camp, while he helps us repel bandits and thieves, he is our friend.'

'I hate him.'

'You will apologise for your fault, or I will take you to our father. Say you are sorry for your poor conduct.'

Hassan did not look the kind of boy who feared a beating, if that was what was threatened, but he did look the kind who did not like to fall into the disfavour of his father. Fathers are formidable creatures, whose disappointment is often felt more keenly than a swipe from a stick.

Hassan hung his head as he turned back towards Andrew. 'I'm – I'm sorry for my conduct.'

Andrew knew the words had been wrung from the boy's soul with immense effort. All his own anger was gone now. He felt sorry for young Hassan. After all, how would he have felt if some Arab boy had come to Cressing and simply took what he wanted from the walled garden without asking? He knew he would be in a rage over it. So was it not understandable that this boy was angry with him?

'I accept your apology,' he said. 'Please take the water.'

'No,' mumbled Hassan, 'you take the water first.'

'I have finished. It is yours now.'

Andrew led his horse away.

That evening Andrew foolishly wandered out into the desert. He was upset by his quarrel with Hassan and he was feeling homesick for his village and family. The girl, Angelique de Sonnac, was also on his mind. 'I suppose,' he said to himself, as he sat in the hollow of a dune, 'that slim boy with his silly velvet cap has now wormed his way into her heart.' Andrew gave a deep sigh, remembering how lovely she had looked when he last saw her. He stared out over the wilderness, feeling a little bitterness creep into his own heart. The gloaming was coming in, filling the hollows with darkness, covering the landscape with one big shadow. There were no lights out there, in the wasteland. He began to get worried, not having taken notice of where he had walked. Would he find his way back to the camp in the dark? He rose to his feet, then had to sit down again, as he felt giddy. His head swam. What had done that to him? A hotness came over him, like a fever, which might have been brought on by the water he had drunk from an unknown stream.

'Animals have been in that water,' he groaned, clutching his stomach, 'and left their dirty traces . . .'

'Sit down,' said a voice. 'I need to talk to you.'

There was a faint scent of almonds in the air.

Andrew stared about him with feverish eyes.

'Where are you?' he cried. 'Come out!'

But there was nowhere for anyone to hide. The level sands stretched beyond his hollow, empty of any creature. Then another strange thing happened, which made Andrew's flesh crawl. Scorpions and small snakes suddenly appeared all around, the former scuttling over the surface of the sand, the latter slithering out from under rocks. Surely this was the Devil's work? Andrew grew seriously afraid. Even as the creature appeared out of brightly coloured flames and a smoky haze, he was sure that it was a demon who appeared before him.

'What are you?' he cried. 'Come closer, coward, and face me if you dare.'

The being was not tall. It would have stood about a metre high if it were not sitting cross-legged. It wore no clothes. It had no hair. The ears were leaf-thin, the tips pointed. The nose sharp as a sword point. Its almond-shaped eyes were narrow in the middle, its general bodily stature quite slim and even fragile-looking. Long, thin fingers sprouted from its palms. There were long, lean, narrow feet with curled toes. But the aspect of this horrible creature which terrified Andrew the most was its insubstantial form. It was a translucent thing, with a hint of green running through a watery paleness. It was there, yet it was not there. A blink and it might disappear, into green gas, into the ether. Indeed, Andrew rubbed his eyes hard. But when he looked again it was still with him, a slight smile on the wide, crescent, lipless mouth.

'Please,' groaned Andrew, 'I have no argument with those from the kingdom of the elves. Won't you leave me alone? I'm feeling sick.'

'Elves? Those foreigners? You insult me.' The voice was husky, the words taut. 'I, sir, am a jinnee. The jinnee who comes to . . . ah, but you do not know, and I am not the one to tell you. A secret, it is. It is something I know and something for you to discover yourself. But that is of no matter at present. I come with a warning. You must be out of your bed early tomorrow. Rise before the sun. If you do not, death will come out of the east and slaughter you in your blankets. The earth beneath the tents will run red with the blood of your companions.'

'A jinnee?' cried Andrew, wildly. 'What is a jinnee?'

The creature sighed and put its face into its hands.

'Have you not heard a word I've said?'

'Yes – yes, I must rise before the day dawns.'

'Good. Now I will leave you. Look for the lights of fires to find your way back. Look for those nearest you, for other more unfriendly fires are also about.'

With that the creature vanished and the honest scorpions and virtuous snakes which had ringed Andrew, preventing his escape from the jinnee, now scuttled and slithered away to their rightful homes.

Andrew stood on the top of the dune and stared. To the west there were bright, warm-looking fires. To the east there were other less friendly looking fires. Another caravan? The jinnee had been right. He was between two groups of men. And what was this *jinnee*?

'An elf or fairy, I suppose,' he told himself, as he stumbled down the slope towards his camp, 'of this Arabian land.'

It had said it knew a secret. Was that the same secret the two dead men had withheld from Andrew? Or was this another piece of knowledge hidden from his knowing? Who knew?

He fell asleep after this, curled on a dune, and woke very late evening feeling a great deal better.

He told no one of his encounter with the jinnee. Andrew was afraid he would be laughed at, or, worse, thought of as a sorcerer. Instead, he went straight to bed and rose before first rays fell. By the light of a lamp he emerged from his tent, still unsure that the encounter with the jinnee was real and foretold the truth. Looking about him he saw that the sentries were all half asleep. The end of a long night did that to men who had had little rest. Twilight entered the world, with shadows that chased each other. It was the kind of light in which even inanimate things like rocks seemed to move. Andrew climbed to a high point. He stared out into the half-light for an hour, thinking he was being foolish and that nothing would happen, when at that point he saw them coming out of the east. He ran back to his tent and grabbed his sword, then let out a yell which made the sentries jump and sound their horns.

It was a dawn raid. A hundred riders swathed in black

came thundering on camels and horses, out of the rising sun. They waved wicked-looking scimitars which flashed in the weak light. Horns were now blaring out their warning all around the caravan camp. Andrew leapt on to the bare back of Warlock. 'Hup!' he yelled at his steed, and charged at the bandits without a second thought.

A raider swept towards him, his black robes flowing behind him. All Andrew could see were the man's narrow brown eyes. The scimitar slashed down at Andrew, narrowly missing his head. Alarmed by the nearness of the snorting dromedary, Warlock shied away, and Andrew's thrust also missed its mark. The raider saw his chance and wheeled his mount to make a second strike. Before he could do so, he was hit by an arrow, which went through his chest, the point emerging from his back. He fell from the saddle.

Andrew turned to see Hassan behind him, a bow in the boy's hands.

Then Andrew was attacked again. This time he clashed blades with his antagonist. The pair fought for a few minutes, neither wounding the other. Then Andrew's sword bit into the shoulder of the raider, a big man who yelled in pain. The raider dropped his scimitar and turned his mount to ride back out into the desert. Andrew was too exhausted to give chase. He wheeled Warlock and went back into the fray, slashing at the shadowy bandits wherever he could. The next few minutes were a haze of whirling swords, flying arrows and screams.

Not more than ten minutes after the first alarm, the last raider rode away, back into the sun. They had been beaten off, leaving wounded and dead behind them. Those who had fought against them went around congratulating each other.

The leader of the caravan personally thanked Andrew for his part in the fight, telling him he was 'a man'.

'You fought without your armour.'

Andrew said, 'I had no time to do otherwise.' He was kicking himself for not fully believing in the jinnee's warning.

The three Knights Hospitaller staggered out of their tent, bleary-eyed, and stared about them. One of them muttered something about breakfast. These three had missed the entire event. Others stared hard at them and shook their heads in disgust. How contemptible! They sneered at the yawning Hospitallers. Another Christian knight travelling with the caravan called out that it was typical of that trio: they would miss the end of the world if it did not explode loudly enough to wake them.

Andrew was quite impressed by the fight. It had been quick and without warning. He had fought instinctively, but now sat a little, thinking of how close he had been to death. Once again, as in Sherwood Forest, he found that he had not been filled with fervour during the act of war. Glory had been the last thing on his mind. A sense of survival had taken over swiftly. And, yes, he had panicked a little, when the second man had swung at him with that sharp, curved weapon favoured by the Saracens. Had it struck he would have lost a limb or even his head. How quickly the world changed from a peaceful dawn into a deadly fight for your life! One moment admiring the sunrise, the next struggling with evil black figures intent on killing you.

Later, he swallowed his pride and went to find Hassan, who was helping his older brother pack the camels.

'Hassan,' he said, humbly, 'I thank you for saving my life.'

Hassan looked up from tying a bundle.

'It was nothing.'

'Yes, it was – it was the act of an honourable man, since you hate me so much. Your Saladin would be proud of you.'

At this compliment, Hassan's eyes shone with pride. He straightened his back and looked at his brother, who nodded in confirmation of Andrew's words.

Hassan said to Andrew, 'I watched you fight, too. You fought bravely.'

'I was afraid much of the time.'

Hassan's brother said, 'We all were. A man who is not afraid of dying is a fool. You are no fool, knight.'

'And that's another thing. I'm not a knight. Not yet. I'm only a squire. I have a fine horse and armour, but I have not yet been accepted into the knighthood.'

'Well, you fought like one.'

Andrew left the two youths and went back to his post. No one had realised that it was he who had raised the alarm. The sentries had been jerked awake by his call but thought it had been one of their own who had made the cry.

Andrew wondered about the jinnee, but there were other things on his mind, too, like the depleted purse he carried. In taking Tomas with him he had spent more money than he should have. And now he was within a few days of meeting his lord and master. He had decided to tell Sir Gondemar the truth and hope for some understanding.

Two days later, just before they reached Antioch, Hassan came to him.

'I have a gift for you, Andrew.'

Andrew was a little upset by this.

'It is I who should give *you* a gift – you saved my life.'

'You are a guest in my house,' said Hassan, waving at his

father's tent behind them. 'It is right and proper. And the sentries have told us it was you who gave warning the morning we were attacked. You are obliged to eat with us, if you are invited.'

'If that is the custom, I shall be proud to do so. How is it that you speak such good English? Have you been to England?'

'No,' replied Hassan, smiling, 'but I have been tutored in your language by my teacher, who shows me the magic of algebra, our own writing and the alphabet of you Englishmen, as well as the holy words of the Koran.'

Andrew murmured something about knowing 'letters' and left it at that, feeling very humble in the presence of an educated boy.

A piece of dark red cloth, heavy with some flat, metal object, was thrust into Andrew's open hands. When he unwrapped it, he saw that it was a thick silver disc about the size of a tea saucer. The disc was made up of several heavy silver rings set within each other. The whole item was decorated with stars and moons, and the sun. It seemed you could turn the rings to match certain patterns in the night sky. Or use the sun on the centre of the object for some purpose.

'What is it, Hassan? Is it a toy?'

Hassan shook his head gravely. 'This is no toy, Andrew. This is an astrolabe.'

'Which is what?'

'Men of our faith use it to find the direction of Mecca, so that we are praying towards the Holy City.'

'I see.' Andrew thought it was of doubtful use to him, since he was, of course, a Christian.

Hassan laughed. 'But don't you see, Andrew? You can use it to find your way, if ever you become lost. What is more, it is a *magic* astrolabe. You need never be lost again. Here it is easy to wander out into the desert, or lose your way in a sandstorm. Wait until the great simoom comes! The hot, poisoned wind that brings death on its breath. If it does not choke the life from you, it separates men and flings them far apart into unknown regions. With this magic astrolabe you need never fear the simoom – you will never be lost again.'

Andrew was aghast at the value of such a thing.

'But Hassan, we are not even friends, and this must be worth a fortune.'

'Ah, we *were* not friends, but we are now. We were bound together like brothers in our fight with the raiders. We must put aside our differences.'

'Well, I think so, too, but you must not give me a gift that is worth a king's ransom. Your father and brother would not approve.'

'I have already spoken to my brother. You must take the gift, Andrew, or you will insult me and my family. Also, you must join us for our last meal before we reach Antioch. We are having a stew of sheep's eyeballs.'

Andrew smiled wryly. 'You know I hate sheep's eyeballs. We had them when I last ate with your family. No one told me what they were until I'd swallowed one, and when they did I was nearly sick.'

'I shall enjoy watching you eat them,' said his incorrigible new friend. 'You make such interesting faces when you chew them. You cannot refuse . . .'

'I know. It would be an insult.'

'Of course.'

Both boys laughed out loud.

Andrew took the treasured gift and put it in his saddle-bags. He wondered if he would ever have to use it. Of course, even putting aside its purpose, it was a gift that a prince would love. And he, Andrew of Cressing, mere squire to Sir Gondemar de Blois, had been given this wonderful instrument that showed men the way through wilderness and wild country. A magic astrolabe! The words themselves sounded exotic and marvellous. Was it the work of a sorcerer, or a holy man? Did it matter if the Devil revealed the path to life, or the Lord? Well, yes, of course it mattered, but Andrew was not going to dwell on such things. It was a present from a friend and he would treasure it for life.

When they entered Antioch, people were talking of only one thing, the recent, huge battle between the Byzantine Emperor of Constantinople, Manuel Comnenus, and the Seljuk Turks led by Kilij Arslan, the Sultan of Rum. The battle had been fought at a place called Myriocephalum, a name long enough to make Andrew's head spin, and the Seljuk Turks had won the day. Thousands of Christian knights had been slaughtered, many of them Hungarians. What was more, Andrew learned from Gareth, Gondemar had fought in the battle and had been wounded.

'Did you fight?' asked Andrew.

'I held Sir Gondemar's shield,' said Gareth, proudly. 'I was his squire.'

'But did you fight?'

'I was asked to hold the shield and I did so.'

If the other youth had expected Andrew to be jealous, he was to be disappointed. Andrew had been in a battle of his own. Admittedly, it was a tiddler of a battle compared with the one Gareth had witnessed, but at least Andrew had taken part in the fighting. All Gareth had done was hand his master his shield before *he* went into battle.

Antioch was ruled by Behemond III, also called 'The Stammerer', for obvious reasons. Sir Gondemar was staying with the ruler at his palace, being tended by Behemond's most reliable and knowledgeable Jewish physician. Sir Gondemar de Blois had friends in high places everywhere and was respected as a proud knight, though it was said he lacked a sense of humour. He sent Gareth to fetch Andrew and to bring his second squire before him.

'Go to him,' said Gareth.

Gondemar was resting on a couch covered in silk cushions. He was attended by a fine-robed physician, who was removing a bandage from his right hand when Andrew was ushered through a horseshoe-arch doorway into their presence. The room was cool, with latticework windows that allowed the breeze to enter from all the four corners of the Earth. Arabian decorations were engraved on the walls, some of them sentences in Arabic, others just curling, swirling lines.

'Well, squire, have you set things up for me in Jerusalem?'

'Yes, sire. Your chambers await you.'

'Good.'

Andrew watched his master gingerly lift one arm with the other as the bandage came off. A horrible stink filled the room. He saw the Jewish physician's eyes narrow as that man inspected the injured limb. The flesh was blackened and the shape of the hand twisted and crushed.

The healer spoke.

'Sire,' he said, 'the appendage is beyond redemption.'

Irritated, Gondemar snapped, 'And then what is to be done?'

'Surgery. It must be removed.'

Gondemar pulled his arm away from the physician.

'Are you mad?' he said. 'This is my sword hand.'

'But useless, sire, and dangerous.'

'Dangerous? How so?'

'It has become poisoned.'

Andrew recalled the words of Old Foggarty, when that man had told him about his missing arm.

Gondemar's voice became shrill. 'The hand will heal, with God's help, I know it. I am attended by false healers, squire. You see? *You see?* Sever my hand? Never. You know what they do to thieves in this godforsaken land? They cut off their right hands. What? Shall I be taken for a thief and robber, as I wander the marketplace, or travel with my fellow knights? Never, I say. I would rather die first. You,' to the physician, 'get out of my sight. Go peddle your lies elsewhere.'

The elderly bearded healer left the room, quickly, the hem of his gown swishing as he went. Sir Gondemar wrapped his own wound with his free hand. Andrew could see his master wincing as he did so, obviously in some sort of pain. Once the wound was covered, Gondemar turned his attention to his squire.

'Now, boy, where is the purse I gave you before you left – I must see to the accounts.'

Nervously, Andrew produced the money. 'Here, sire.'

'Good.' The knight began rewinding the bandage around his crushed hand. 'Go and find Gareth for me. Send him in.'

'Yes, my lord. And shall I come back, too?'

'Not until I send for you.'

'I shall pray for your recovery, sire.'

Gondemar nodded curtly.

Outside the room, the physician was waiting for Andrew.

'Young man,' said the healer, 'your master . . .'

'I know,' replied Andrew. 'I have heard of this rot which will eventually poison the heart. But what's to be done? He will not listen.'

'Then we must do it for him, or he will die within the month.'

Andrew looked helplessly at the Jewish gentleman.

'How?'

'I will have a basin of hot pitch ready. You must be the surgeon, for he will not let me near him again.'

'Sir,' said Andrew, frightened by what the healer was suggesting, 'you will have me hanged.'

'No, I will speak to the prince and explain what we are doing and why we are doing it. The prince trusts me and knows my skills are genuine. I will get his permission for the amputation before we carry it out.'

'Will it work? Shall you and I be safe?' asked Andrew.

'I believe it will.'

The plan was laid. The next day Andrew sent Gareth to Sir Gondemar to say that he, Andrew, had a message of dire import to disclose to his lord. 'But it must be told in the Courtyard of the Lions,' said Andrew, 'where the myrtle bushes and fountains will stifle the sound of my words, for the message must not be heard by anyone but Sir Gondemar.'

A short while later, Gareth came back to him and told him their lord was indeed pacing the courtyard.

'It had better be good, Andrew, for he's in a foul mood. He

calls you a thief. The purse he gave you for your travels is almost empty. He does not understand why you have spent so much money.'

'It – it was on a servant I employed. I will explain it to him.'

Gareth's eyes widened. 'You employed a *servant*?'

'Well, he's more of a friend, really. But he will be useful to Sir Gondemar, I know he will. He has many talents.'

'Good luck,' said Gareth, in a tone which suggested that Andrew was heading for disaster. 'I'll remember you in my prayers.'

Andrew left the other squire and with a heavy heart, and shaking hands, went to the Courtyard of the Lions. There he found his master pacing the edge of a rectangular pool in which there were a dozen fountains spraying water. Goldfish swam in the clearness of the man-made pond. Scented myrtle bushes followed the marble paths and added to the air of tranquillity in the courtyard. Andrew went directly to Sir Gondemar, who glared ferociously at his squire.

'What is this nonsense, boy?' roared the knight, who was wearing his white robe with its red cross. 'Out with it now!'

'Sire,' said Andrew, absolutely terrified now by what he was expected to do, 'please could I see your injury? I have heard of a cure, in England, before I left. I may be able to help.'

'Is this your important message? Eh? Why so secret? Why here in this garden? Tell me of this wonder cure, if there be one.'

'Sire, the hand. Could you hold it forth? I must see it close to. I would be loath to give you false information.'

After a long wait, with a grim look on his face, Gondemar

at last stretched out his arm. Andrew drew his sword in a flash and severed the hand at the wrist. Blood leapt from the wound, spraying the Templar's white robe with red streaks. Gondemar stared stupidly at the end of his arm, no sound leaving his lips. Then the physician rushed forth, from behind a pillar, and plunged the gory stump into a bowl of hot pitch to cauterise the wound and stop the flow of blood.

Gondemar screamed, high and loud.

'Aaaghhhhh!' he shrieked. 'Assassins! Assassins!'

He knocked the healer away heavily with his left arm, sending the Jew flying into the shallow pool. Then he kicked out savagely at Andrew with a mailed foot. His aim was poor, he missed, and the momentum caused the knight to topple over, into a myrtle bush. Andrew watched in great fear as his master struggled to his feet, waving the smoking, tar-blackened stump on his right arm. Speechless again, Gondemar then fell on his knees, seemingly searching for his missing hand. Andrew ran from the place, convinced his master was going to kill him.

Andrew collected his armour from his room, then went straight to the stables and found Warlock. He fled through the city gates as the sun found its noon. He had no faith in explanations from the prince of Antioch. Words were not going to save his life. Sir Gondemar would have him dangling from the end of a rope before any explanations or entreaties found the knight's ears. All was lost. Andrew knew that he was now on his own. His former master would no doubt attempt to hunt him down, but he was going to try to escape, back to England.

11. WALTER PUGHSON'S NIGHTMARE

Walter Pughson had given up all hope of life when they let him out into the sunlight again. The Assassins had kept him captive in a dark hole for a reason: when he was let out he had nothing but gratitude for those who released him. They were not the same men who had put him in the oubliette. They were different men, kinder of face, who seemed to sympathise with his plight, though they did not let him go home. One of those who spoke with him, while walking in beautiful gardens and courtyards, was a youth of his own age called Nazir.

Nazir told Walter, 'You are now in the castle of Alamut, which we call the eagle's nest. I am the son of the Prince of the Mountains. This garden we are in is our gift of Paradise to living men. We are favoured with a glimpse of what is to come, my friend.'

The gardens were indeed wonderful, with running fountains, beautiful trees and shrubs. Fruit dripped from heavy branches. There were camomile lawns, green as jade, and myrtle hedges scenting the air. Paths of crushed marble wound around small, shady pavilions where one could sit and rest, protected from the sun. Lovely maidens sat with baskets of dates, sherbet drinks, sweetmeats and other delights, ready to feed the stroller through these pleasant green walks.

'I know what you are,' said Walter, regaining some of his

lost confidence. 'You are the fearless killers known as the Assassins. You send out men with daggers in their hands to murder people.'

'This is true,' admitted Nazir, 'and I make no apology. This is our creed, to rid the world of high-born leaders who are not of our sect. Only a short while ago we attempted the life of Saladin himself at Aleppo. The man we sent failed in that enterprise. Saladin is a difficult man to kill.'

'Surely Saladin is one of your kind?'

'No, he is an Ayyubid, which is not of our kind. To you Christians we are all Saracens. You see one face of an enemy, but we have many faces. We too have our differences, just as you in Europe. Have you not had wars against the Franks? Against the Norsemen? Has not Angle fought against Celt, Norman against Saxon? Christians all? Harmony is not to be had in this world, my friend, even with close neighbours. *Especially* with close neighbours. Though we have a saying: *I am against my cousin, but my cousin and I are against the stranger.* So, in that respect, you are partly right, my friend.'

'Why do you keep calling me your friend? You have abducted me from my father's home. What do you want with me? Is it just sport? Why not kill me now?'

Nazir smiled at Walter. 'Because you are to become one of us, my friend, an Assassin. You are to be accorded the rare privilege of serving our cause, even though you are a despised Infidel. Welcome to my family, Walter Pughson.'

Walter did not know what to make of this. An Assassin? This was the furthest thing from his mind. He thought they might torture him. He thought they might kill him. But to make him one of them? Why, that was a worse fate than he had imagined. How could they think he would accept such an offer?

'No,' he said, firmly.

'You mean *yes*,' replied Nazir, smiling.

Walter was curious. 'Why would I mean the opposite of what I say?'

'Because you value your father's life. Pugh the swordsmith will die horribly if you do not do as we say. It's as simple as that. We can kill him easily, you know. We have poisons which will cause a man to writhe in agony for days, vomiting black bile, before finally falling into that dark chasm we know as death. A simple craftsman? It would be too easy. A child among us could do it. Why, we have murdered kings and princes, sultans and viziers, when they believed themselves absolutely safe, surrounded by thick walls and a hundred bodyguards. Your father has neither a safe house nor an army at his back.

'We always send out a single man at a time, a dagger in his hand, dressed as a merchant, a camel driver, a seller of brass lamps. If the first one fails, we send another, and another, and another, until finally the victim is killed.'

'You did not manage the Saladin.'

Nazir smiled again. 'We will. Patience, Walter, patience.'

Walter felt despair entering his heart. His adoptive father was all the world to him. He loved the old man as if he were his own father. Walter had received nothing but kindness, nothing but a good home, an apprenticeship, a loving relationship with his adoptive father.

'I have no skill in killing other men,' he said to Nazir. 'You have chosen your student badly.'

'We will teach you. We will train you. When you leave here you will be able to pick the exact spot a dagger must enter a man's chest to pierce his heart. You will have the strength and the fortitude to drive it through flesh and past bone. We will show you how to become a shadow, unseen by other men, so that you can slip into places and be invisible to other eyes. We will teach you the art of death, which you will come to know and understand better than any outside this kingdom. You, my friend, will become *me*, for the mission we choose.'

Walter, entirely distressed by this vision of terror, said helplessly: 'But if you can kill anyone you like, why do you need me?'

'Because, my friend, you are a Christian. It must be one of your kind who does the killing, so that we are not involved. Ah, I see a light in your eye! You will confess, after the murder, that you were abducted and trained by the Assassins? And who will believe you? We will deny such a claim. It has never been done before and those you tell will look to our history and say, "Not the Assassins, for who has heard of such a thing?" Now, now, don't look so dejected. You may run to us once the deed has been accomplished. You will live in this garden of delights, for the rest of your days. What? Isn't that the most wonderful reward you could ever hope for? I should say so. So let us be of good cheer, Walter Pughson, and go into this enterprise with enthusiasm. Lift your expression, become joyful. Death is a thing which comes to us all. You are merely hastening the final gift for a miserable life here on Earth.'

Walter felt utter hopelessness and despair enter his heart.

12. KING BALDWIN IV

Andrew tried to follow the coastline back to Jerusalem. He wanted to get to the port of Jaffa, where he knew he could get a ship home to England. There were other ports on the way – Tyre and Sidon being two – but he did not know if they would have any European ships in their harbours. Jaffa was the most certain to have such vessels. So it was to Jerusalem that he travelled on Warlock.

One night in the desert he was feverish with lack of food. The day had been sweltering and the night cold enough to freeze the water in his goatskins. He sat there shivering over a small fire, when a much larger fire suddenly erupted in a nearby bush. Stumbling over to this phenomenon, he warmed his hands in the blaze. It was then that, out of the flames, the same jinnee which had appeared before came to him.

'What are you doing out here, boy? You should be chasing your destiny, to become a great knight, a Templar.'

'Ah, Green One,' said Andrew, unable to keep the sadness out of his voice, 'I've thrown all that away now . . .' and he told the jinnee what he had done.

'What fools these knights are, then?' said the jinnee. 'He should have rewarded you, not threatened you. And why do you need this Sir Gondemar de Blois. Find another to help you reach your ambition! There are more powerful men than ordinary knights in the world. Dukes, earls, sultans, kings, princes. Find one, do him a service, earn a reward.'

A sandstorm was coming up and Andrew wrapped himself in a blanket, to keep the sand out of his nose, eyes, ears and mouth.

'First, I must find my way back,' he told the jinnee. 'At the moment I don't know which path to take.'

'You don't need me for that,' said the jinnee; 'you have your gift from the boy known as Hassan – the astrolabe. But I will give the gift of understanding all tongues, from all men, then you may also have the power to ask your way home.'

After the sandstorm young Andrew took out the heavy magic object and held it flat in his hand. The concentric silver circles turned of their own accord, until the pointer directed Andrew on the path to the sea. But he had wandered a long way out into the arid desert. There were mountains barring his way, with black caves that might hide bandits, and narrow passes where ambushes would be easy for hostile tribes. He set off with hope in his heart to traverse the wasteland that stood between him and the road to Jerusalem.

In one of those slim valleys of volcanic rock he was confronted by two lean, turbaned men riding asses. He drew his sword and, in a tongue previously unknown to him, warned the men that he was a ferocious fighter and ready to cut them down.

'That is unnecessary,' said one of the riders, a gaunt fellow with a white beard. 'My nephew and I are peaceful men. However, you will need the blade soon, for you will pass a great cave inside which lives a giant. The giant hates all other men of any creed or colour. A youth like you would make good eating for a hungry giant. I have heard he roasts men alive on a spit over a fire of camel dung and dried weed.'

'Thank you for your warning,' said Andrew, worried. 'I shall try to pass by the cave at night, when he's asleep.'

Andrew rode on, carefully studying each hillside cave. In the daylight the caves were sinister looking black pits in the sides of the mountains, seemingly ready to disgorge giants by the dozen, but of course in the gloaming they melted into the rockface and were hardly visible. Andrew grew tired after the long, hot day and subsequently, with the coming of the cool evening, his concentration lapsed. He became careless and dreamy as night fell and he failed to notice one huge cave in the side of a red sandstone cliff whose high, steep brow over-shadowed the goat track along which youth and steed were ambling.

Warlock stumbled on something in the dark, his hooves slipping on a mound.

'What's the matter?' muttered Andrew, annoyed at Warlock. 'Watch where you're stepping.'

The horse refused to move forward and became skittish, backing away suddenly with dancing hooves

'Lively all of a sudden, eh? I thought you were tired,' grumbled Andrew, not noticing that his voice was echoing around the canyon. 'What is it? A snake?'

He dismounted in an irritable mood and kicked at the mound on which Warlock had slipped. It rattled. 'What the Devil . . . ?'

Andrew tentatively kicked again and struck something that rolled away like a wooden ball. Just then, the moon rose over the horizon and illuminated the canyon through which they were riding. As he stared down at his feet Andrew's eyes opened wide. He was standing on a pile of long bones and the 'ball' he had kicked was a human skull. It rattled down into a heap of rib bones that looked like white cages. As Andrew's eyes ranged over the scene he could see there were bones everywhere and most of them had once belonged to men.

'Oh no . . .' he murmured.

At that precise moment a giant figure came roaring out of the cave, joyful at finding a succulent, meaty youth passing by. The giant, some three times taller than Andrew, was dressed in light armour which glistened in the moonlight. He carried a spear in his left hand and a net in his right. Bits of food and saliva had dried in his beard and made it stand out stiffly from his face. Andrew could see what looked like the tip of a man's tongue, caught in the tangle of the giant's black chin hair, and a piece of lip, the lobe of an ear. And in the giant's unwashed chest hair, crusted blood from the veins of travellers. And on his sleeves the gore of the innards of innocent passers-by, cooked to a recipe the giant's mother had left him, before she too had succumbed to his gargantuan appetite one lean winter, many years ago.

Andrew leapt from his horse. The pair confronted one another in the moonlight. The two antagonists circled, one flicking the net ready to cast it, the other with a wary eye on both his opponent's weapons.

The giant was skilful with the net. It had caught many two-legged fishes for him in the past. Here was a pale-skinned trout with soft meat on its bones. The giant could see that the fish, dance out of reach as it might, would tire before the night was through. Once the youth was tottering in exhaustion, the giant would cast his net and spear his victim through one of the holes. Food in these mountains was scarce, there being few gazelle or other game in the region. A youth like this had a soft liver, a tasty heart, sweetmeat eyes and juicy flesh on his limbs. Yes, he would even eat the offal, once he had gutted the boy. The stomach and intestines would make a good stew and the kidneys would fry in the boy's own fat for a second breakfast of the day.

Towards dawn Andrew began to weaken. The giant chased him round and round the rocks, and seemed to have unlimited energy. Then came the moment when Andrew tripped and fell among large stones. The giant rushed forward with a cry of triumph. The circular net went out, flying over the head of Andrew, floating down upon his form. He tried to scramble out of the way, disturbing more of the stones, out of which came scorpions, rats, snakes and other wildlife. These creatures had crawled there for warmth, awaiting the rising of the sun.

A solitary nightjar shot up from among the pebbles. It flew straight into the face of the giant, who screamed, dropped his spear and swatted the bird like a fly, with both hands. The net, tied to his wrist by a rope, was therefore jerked backwards and fell short of Andrew. Andrew leapt to his feet again with renewed energy. Rushing forward, he drove his sword into the leg of the giant, under the kneecap, and the great fellow fell with a cry to the earth, making the ground shudder.

Andrew then stepped forward and with a single mighty stroke cut off the giant's head. The monstrous ball of hair, bone and blood rolled down a slope and was brought to a halt by the pile of human ribs outside the cave. There it rested. Even as Andrew found Warlock and mounted again, to leave that dreadful place, the flies were settling on both body and head of the giant. Men would no more fear this cave of horror. The great cannibal was dead and would eat no more human flesh – at least, not in this world, though none know what might be in the next.

Warlock carried his master back through the mountain passes, to the sea. Once again Andrew followed the coastline, until he came at last to Jaffa. He was just about to board a boat when he remembered his faithful servant. Tomas was, of course, waiting for him in Jerusalem. Andrew told the captain of the vessel to go without him. He then mounted Warlock and rode to Jerusalem. Inside the walls he sought Tomas, who was in the lodgings they had procured.

'We must go, Tomas,' said Andrew, beating the dust of travel from his armour. 'Sir Gondemar wishes me dead.'

'What?' cried the other youth. 'But your destiny, Andrew.'

Andrew told his servant-companion all that had happened, but still Tomas believed they should stay.

'Nothing will happen to raise you up in England,' said Tomas, pronouncing the last word disdainfully. 'It is here that you will achieve your ambition. This is the land where knights are made. Think, Andrew, about what you are about to abandon.'

'But Gondemar will forever hound me, making my life miserable. That, or he'll simply kill me. He's a powerful knight.'

'Still his influence will probably reach England, too – you'll be no more free of him there than you are here. And, Andrew, England is no place for a warrior,' said Tomas, disparagingly. 'This is the land of opportunity.'

They talked a long time, into the night, even while Andrew stripped and washed in a copper bowl, then put on clean clothes and partook of food and drink. Once he was refreshed thus he began to view things differently himself. Before the morning came, he was asleep on a horsehair mattress, resolved to confront Gondemar when he came.

Two days later Andrew thought he saw Gareth in the market-place and raced from there along a narrow alleyway. When he turned the corner at the end he ran straight into someone else, sending the other person bowling. Reaching with an arm, he assisted a youth of his own age to his feet and found himself staring into the eyes of the king.

'Y-y-you – are King Baldwin,' stuttered Andrew, horrified, recognising the fifteen-year-old boy he had seen only at a distance before now. 'My liege lord, I – I am so very sorry. Forgive me for being a clumsy oaf.'

'Pinch me!' The king, dressed in clothes that would have purchased a good house and grounds, extended an arm towards Andrew. 'Go on, pinch me!'

'What?' cried the confused squire. 'I . . .'

A velvet sleeve was pulled up to the elbow. 'Pinch my arm,' came the command, again.

Andrew did as he was asked.

'Harder. Pinch it harder.'

Andrew nipped it savagely between thumbnail and finger.

The king laughed. 'See? It doesn't hurt. Neither did my fall. I can't be hurt. I have a magic shield around me.'

'A magic shield? Why, what is it?'

'It's called leprosy,' replied the king. 'If you have it, it deadens the nerves. I have it, unfortunately. But don't worry, it's not the kind you can catch. Who are you? What's your name?'

'My name is Andrew of Cressing, my lord. I was squire to the Templar Knight Sir Gondemar de Blois, but I cut off his right hand and I believe he wishes now to kill me.'

King Baldwin IV laughed uproariously.

'Are you in the habit of knocking kings off their feet and chopping bits off knights? Ah, here's my escort . . .' – several elderly nobles came running around the corner, puffing and blowing with the exertion – '. . . I thought I'd get away from them for a while. They're all old men, you see. They can't run or do anything much.' He took Andrew's hand and shook it vigorously. 'It's so good to meet someone my own age. And a warrior, too. Have you fought in any battles yet, against the Saracens?'

'Sire, not against an army, but against bandits and giants.'

'Giants? Well, there you have it over me. I've never fought with a giant. I think I should like to. Do they make a huge crash when they fall?'

'The earth shakes, my lord.'

'By God, does it indeed? You hear that, Sir Randolph? The youth has felled giants with his sword. Why don't I get the chance to do that? Where did you find one, Andrew? Nearby. Are there any left?'

'In some caves north-east of here, sire, but there are none left now. I think perhaps I might have killed the last.'

'What a pity. But if you should find some more, please let me know. Have you eaten? Do come and dine with me. Who's this?' Tomas had come around the other corner now, making it an extremely crowded place at the end of the alley. 'How white his hair is! How blue his eyes!'

'He is an angel, my liege, who fell from Heaven.'

'Indeed he looks like an angel. Does he belong to you, Andrew?'

'He is my servant and my friend.'

'Can one be both? I suppose one can, at a stretch. You and Tomas must come with me to dine at the palace. Sir Randolph, have you got your breath back?'

Sir Randolph, a nobleman with a salt-and-pepper beard, said brusquely, 'Next time, my liege, I shall leave you to find your own way back to the palace.'

'Look how he glowers at us, Andrew. He envies us our youth, you see. All is in the past for him. His name is in the history books, but he can't catch a two-year-old on those legs. They are the legs of a chicken, under that hose. No muscles left. Only skin on bone. And much the same with the rest of them. You are a Templar's squire, Andrew. You must meet someone from your Order. The Master of Solomon's Temple, Odo de St Amand – Odo, are you there? Step forward, sir, and meet one of your flock.'

The Master stepped forward, but looked anything but happy to make the acquaintance of a mere shaveling squire. He was a man of imposing presence. Every inch the warrior, Odo made men tremble with one look of his eyes. All men, that is, except the young and effervescent King Baldwin, who was afraid of no one.

Andrew bowed low to the Master, awed by this great personage. He was the first Master to be elected from among the French of Outremer and also the king's personal choice. Tomas, who somehow knew all things, had told Andrew that Odo de St Amand held several fiefs in the Kingdom of Jerusalem. He was the Kingdom's Marshal, its Castellan and Butler, and had been ambassador to Constantinople. He was a powerful man simply by position.

'Sire,' said Andrew, with Tomas kneeling beside him, 'I am

greatly honoured to meet you. I come from Cressing, from among the Templars of Essex, where your name is spoken in a reverent whisper. You are all that any knight would wish to be and I have long held you in admiration and esteem, even though I am but a lowly squire – and not even that now, since my master has dismissed me.'

'Prettily spoken, boy,' said the Master, mollified. 'But how dismissed? Have you wronged your lord?'

King Baldwin interrupted with a touch of glee in his tone, 'He cut off his master's hand.'

Odo's eyes widened. 'You severed his limb, boy?'

'Sire, the hand was diseased. It had been crushed and was black with rot. I was told by the healer that if the hand was not removed, the corruption would go to my master's heart and kill him. My master, Sir Gondemar de Blois, was of another opinion.'

'De Blois? I know him. A courageous knight. You are right in your assumption, boy. The poison would have killed him. Yet is that not his choice, rather than yours? You take too much on yourself.'

'I see that now, sire.'

'I'll wager you do, with a raging knight after your blood. Where is de Blois now?'

'In Antioch, my lord.'

'Then my advice to you, boy, is to run. Run like the wind. Run anywhere. Egypt is probably safe, now that the Caliphs have gone and Saladin rules. They say he's a compassionate man. Throw yourself on his mercy and hope he gives you leave to stay there. You will be out of reach of de Blois, who, if I know anything about him, will not rest until he has your head on the end of a lance.'

Andrew was naturally upset by this speech, but King Baldwin interrupted the interview: 'This de Blois will not harm my new young friend. I place Andrew of Cressing under *my* personal protection. Do you hear that, Odo? My personal protection.' Baldwin nodded at the Master of Solomon's Temple. 'That goes for his angel, too.' Then he added, thoughtfully, 'Though I don't suppose angels can be robbed of life, for they are creatures of a supernatural order.'

'My liege,' said Odo, 'it is wise not to interfere in quarrels of this nature . . .'

'Who said I was wise, Odo? You are always telling me how stupid I am.'

The Master looked shocked. 'No, no, my liege. God forbid. I would never call you stupid.'

'Well, you think it, anyway. Come on, I'm getting bored with all this talk. Who's hungry? I'm starving. Let's get back to the palace where we can all eat. Andrew, do you like the flat unleavened bread of the region? I adore it . . .'

Thus, Andrew was taken to the palace of a King of Outremer, and Tomas followed happily behind.

Now under the king's protection, Andrew gave up all thought of returning to England. Having met the Master of the Temple of Solomon he was once more fired with his desire for knighthood. The idea seemed remote, now that he had been dismissed as a squire, but still he held on to the idea that he was destined for greatness.

While Andrew was eating at the king's table, a craftsman came to the king. He said his name was Pugh, a swordsmith.

'I've heard of you,' King Baldwin replied. 'You make excellent swords. What do you want?'

Pugh had eyes only for the king. He seemed distracted and agitated. 'My liege, my son has disappeared.'

'Well, I don't have him.'

'Yes, I know that, my liege, but I thought perhaps in your position, with spies scattered about the countryside, you might have heard of a young boy – a youth about your own age – perhaps lost or abducted?'

'Ah, you're accusing me of spying, are you, old man?'

'Sire, of course you must keep a watch on our enemies. You must keep yourself informed of what is happening outside the city, and in other cities. I ask only that your agents keep their eyes and ears open for such a lad. His name is Walter. He is my apprentice as well as my adopted son, and may have been taken to pursue his trade by those who need weapons.'

Baldwin nodded. 'I'm sorry your son has gone from you. Did you treat him with some cruelty? Perhaps he ran away?'

'I never laid a hand on him, nor even gave him a harsh word. I love him dearly and I believe he loves me as his father. We are devoted to one another. I'm afraid for him. Perhaps he's been murdered? Men are murdered for the shirt on their backs these days. Or perhaps abducted into slavery? Or taken on board a ship against his will, to row or sail for some master who cares not where he finds his crew?'

A woman's voice, along the table to the left of the king, now interrupted: 'Perhaps he's lost his heart to a wench? Boys of that age often do. Mayhap he is in the arms of some young girl?'

Pugh replied, 'He has never spoken of such a person to me and I would have blessed any maid who captured his love.'

King Baldwin sighed. 'Well, then, swordmaker, I shall indeed speak of this matter to those who might hear something, but be aware that people vanish every day, for this or that reason, and are never heard of again. Walter de Mesnil, for one, though I fear my father – may his soul rest in peace – was responsible for that disappearance.'

'Thank you, my lord – it is all I ask.'

When Pugh had left, Andrew turned to look at the woman who had spoken and saw with amazement that she was dressed as a knight.

'Sire, who is that?' he whispered to King Baldwin. 'Is that indeed a lady?'

Baldwin laughed. 'She, my young friend, is Catherine of Tortosa, a lady knight.'

Andrew's eyes widened. 'Is there such a thing?'

'Yes, there is. Catherine is of the Knightly Order of the Hatchet. Two decades ago she and a number of other women donned armour and fought the Moors in Catalonia, when the men had been called to battle elsewhere. Catherine and her dames forced the Moors to raise the siege and afterwards were granted a Military Order of Knighthood.'

'How astonishing.'

Baldwin put an arm around Andrew's shoulder.

'Listen, lad, I have sparred with Catherine many times and have come off the worse more than once. Never underestimate anything unusual in this life. Catherine!' the king yelled down the table. 'Here's a young squire who would fence with you, if you like.'

Catherine smiled. 'He looks at me as if I were a ghost.'

'Ah, he is not used to females in armour, Catherine, but I have told him you are a formidable opponent in matters of war.'

'I am a formidable opponent in matters of war *and* love, though I have no use for young striplings. Come and see me one day, squire, and I'll show you the Catalonian defence. It's a simple move – mere women can do it – but it might save your life.'

The knights around the hall chortled uproariously and banged their goblets on the wood making such a racket that the dogs underneath the tables stirred and ran about thinking there was to be a game.

Life in Jerusalem was at first exciting, since the city was a colourful place with many Eastern mysteries. There was a great mix of people of many nations and religions. Andrew was occasionally invited to the palace to play board games and to talk with the king, though the courtiers who surrounded the monarch disapproved of this liaison. Tomas told Andrew that King Baldwin would tire of them before long and the pair would be forgotten. Andrew was inclined to agree, but for the time being was flattered and pleased to be the king's companion.

The walls of Jerusalem were confining and Andrew and Tomas found themselves riding out into the desert on many occasions. It drew these two country boys to its heart. They both found the desert haunting and eerie. Its space seemed to stretch to infinity on all sides. Its twilights seemed to promise a peaceful afterlife to the two boys.

While in the desert Tomas woke early beside an oasis one morning, when the air was still cool, and saw angels standing out on the sands. Their forms shimmered and rippled in the sunlight appearing from behind the dunes. He rubbed his eyes and stared in great satisfaction at these shining creatures who

he believed were his kin. One of the angels smiled and beckoned to him. He rose and started to walk towards the angel,
when another of its kind then shook its head and waved a
finger, indicating he should come no closer.

'Am I to advance with you, or no?' he said to these visions.
'What is it you want me to do?'

It was then that the angels seemed to diffuse into glistening
droplets of moisture then disperse like marsh mist. Tomas stood
there wondering whether he had actually seen angels or some
hallucination thrown up by the strange morning desert light.
Why would he first be invited forward, then told not to advance?
He could only think they were asking him to return home, to
his place in Heaven. When he told Andrew about it, Andrew
looked askance at his servant and said that he should not read
too much into things experienced in the desert.

'These sands have their own secrets, which are not necessarily in agreement with our own real world,' he told Tomas.

Yet shortly afterwards, Andrew had his own strangeness to
contend with when he was fetching water from a well. A giant
serpent was climbing out of the hole in the ground to confront
him. In the depths of the well, down below the serpent, Andrew
caught a fleeting glimpse of a laughing jinnee and he wondered
if this monster snake had been conjured up to test his fighting
skills. Indeed, as it poured out of the well and coiled like a
cobra with its head reared, he had to be quick to draw his
sword and defend himself. The serpent had the girth of a bull
and was over twenty metres long. When he sliced off its head,
the tail turned and he found there another set of fanged jaws.

The markings on its skin were red and green, on a black
background, and served to bewilder its opponent with their

whorls and flourishes. Though not swift in its movements, its skin was as tough as oak bark and Andrew was having great difficulty in piercing it. Even when his sword did enter flesh, the great snake seemed not to be concerned. A whole hour he battled with the beast, which grew smaller but no less dangerous, until finally it had been severed into small pieces. These pieces then formed into lizards which scuttled away, hiding under the rocks. Andrew, sweating profusely and breathing heavily, asked Tomas if the creature had not been the worst he had ever seen.

Tomas blinked and asked what monster Andrew meant?

'Why, the great serpent I've just been fighting? It had scales the size of dinner plates!'

'Oh that? I thought you were just practising with your blade. You did execute some wonderful flourishes, I have to say.'

'Flourishes?' cried an incensed Andrew. 'I was fighting for my life – and yours.'

Tomas shrugged. 'Well, Andrew, all I saw were swirls of sand rising with the breeze and you slicing your sword through them . . .'

This was on the same day of the same night that a grey wraith came to Tomas. He was awoken by this hollow creature which led him to a cave. There the wraith pointed, then entered a moonshadow and became a shadow itself. It was like pitch poured on to pitch. Tomas could no longer separate one dark patch from the other.

Tomas then turned his attention to the cave. He had never been afraid of dark places and made himself a torch before entering the place. Inside he found a large wooden casket full of rubies, emeralds and diamonds which appeared to be waiting

200

to be taken. Tomas did not touch this earthly wealth, but simply mused on it.

'A thieves' den,' muttered Tomas, 'most surely. This is their stolen treasure.'

Tomas returned to Andrew and told him what he had found.

Andrew sat up from his blanket and said, 'Are you sure this is not like those angels you saw? When we get there, these jewels and gems may disappear into vapour.'

'I'm sure these are real, even if my guide was not.'

'No figment of the mind? No fantasy thrown up by a fevered brain? We have been a long time out here in the wilderness, Tomas, and our minds are not always our own to command.'

'Not the jewels. They are real.'

Andrew went with Tomas and was astounded by what he saw. The chest itself would not budge when he tried to lift it, so full was it of gold and gemstones and silver ornaments. Feverishly, Andrew filled his pockets with the treasure until he was so weighed down he could not walk with a light tread, but clumped around with a heavy, clumsy gait. Yet still more he crammed into his breeches, into any cavity he could find among his clothing. Then he took off his sandals and tried using them as containers, filling them, oblivious to the fact that gems fell through the holes in the leather and trickled after him on the ground in a glistening line. He became like a snail leaving a trail of shining slime in his wake. He even tried filling his cheeks with diamonds, but the sharp stones cut into his gums and he had to spit them out. For a time he was one of those men suddenly turned insane by the sight of riches.

Tomas took nothing, telling Andrew he had no use for things of mundane value.

'But the gems will help you in your quest for knighthood, won't they, Andrew?'

Andrew's jaw dropped. The gold fever left him almost as quickly as it had come. With a cold, sober mind he thought about Tomas's innocent statement. He thought about knighthood and the Templars. On being reminded of his ambition to become a Templar, Andrew now realised he could take none of the treasure. He emptied his pockets again with a long drawn-out sigh, scattering the wealth on the floor of the cave.

'I can't take these,' he said, sadly. 'Templars are sworn to a vow of poverty.'

'Can't you use them until then? You're not a Templar yet, Andrew.'

'I'll take just a single one,' he said, pocketing a ruby the size of a thumb print, 'which I will give away on the eve of knighthood. The rest will still be here, should we ever want them, Tomas. For the moment we have all we need. We're fed and sheltered by the king's command. I'm blessed with a jinnee who lifts my spirits when I'm down. What more could we want at the moment? Knighthood can't be bought. It must be earned.'

13. THE RETURN OF DE BLOIS

The two youths did not always go out into the desert alone. They took to tagging on to the tail end of bands of Templars who rode out seeking battle with Saracens. In this way Andrew sought adventure, hoping to be used in such skirmishes. However, the knights scorned this boy with a sword, even though they admired the wonderful armour on his back. They sent him scurrying away when he tried to join in their battles, threatening to kill his horse if he continued to bother them.

On one such occasion the feared simoom, that fiery wind from Africa, swept over the landscape. It was called the 'wind of poison' because it sent men mad with its heat and stifling atmosphere, but it also brought sandstorms.

This particular expedition was being led by the Master himself, since it was hunting Assassins, who were thoroughly hated by the Templars. Two or three years earlier, when King Almeric ruled Jerusalem, the Assassins were allies of the king. Disregarding this, a Templar knight by the name of Walter de Mesnil attacked a party of Assassin ambassadors returning to their fortress and slaughtered them. King Almeric arrested de Mesnil, who was thrown into prison and never seen again. The quarrel between Almeric and the Templars was never healed and the Templars continued to think the Assassins vile creatures.

Now, though, the hunters were caught in one of the most

appalling sandstorms imaginable, which threatened to smother the knights. If they could not breach the simoom's fierce wall of sand, they would possibly all suffocate. Andrew went down into their camp as visibility began to disappear in the whirlwind blizzard of yellow-grained dust.

'Sire!' he yelled, as the world disintegrated and swirled about them, swallowing them. 'I can lead you out of this place.'

'How?' cried the Master, Odo de St Amand. 'How do you know the way?'

'I have an instrument.'

Andrew produced his magic astrolabe.

'Every man must cover his face with a scarf. Then get each knight to lead his mount by the bridle and grasp the tail of the horse in front. I shall take the vanguard.'

Sand was blinding eyes, stinging noses, filling mouths. It was a shrieking monster, intent on stripping the skin from the back of every man. It whirled with tremendous force, screaming into the ears of Odo, who realised that he had to trust the boy to save them from an ignominious and horrible death. Odo informed his men, calling above the wind for calm and order, while Andrew consulted his astrolabe. Then Andrew led the way, fighting against the blistering hot wind, the abrasive sand that drove into them, stinging like a thousand bees. Bit by bit they made their way forward, a line of horses and men, seeking a place where they would be safe from the killer wind.

Two men were lost that day, but that was no fault of Andrew's. They were at the tail end of the line and somehow became detached. When discovered again, after the wind had gone, they were buried under several feet of sand. They and their horses had suffocated. Their grave marker was the rein of one of their mounts, which showed above the ground only as a small loop of leather.

Andrew was called into the presence of Sir Odo.

'Well done, boy,' granted the Master. 'You have risen in my estimation.'

'Thank you, sire.'

'However, I have your own master here – the master that was – who asks that you be given to him for punishment.'

Andrew's heart sank. 'Sir Gondemar?'

'Yes, him.' Odo stroked his chin. 'I know not what to do. Gondemar is entitled to reparation . . . yes, yes, I know what you did, you did it in thought for your master's health, but he did not order you to do so – indeed, did not even request it. You acted with an independent spirit. Yet, you saved many lives in the simoom and you're a favourite of the king.' The Master came to a decision. 'I am going to have to let him whip you. What do you say to that?'

Andrew was naturally upset. 'Sire, I have done nothing wrong.'

'In your eyes, perhaps. But Gondemar wants blood.'

Andrew set his jaw and said grimly, 'Then I shall take the whipping.'

'If it was your life I was handing over, I would have let him hang you. Twenty-four strokes of the flail. Would you accept that, without running to the king and crying for revenge?'

Andrew's voice was taut firm.

'Yes, my lord.'

Sir Gondemar was called.

'Twenty-four strokes!' he shouted, when he was told. 'I may as well give the bastard a saucer of milk.'

'If you think so little of the punishment,' growled Odo, thoroughly tired of this business, 'perhaps you could show us how easily *you* could take such a number?'

Sir Gondemar's face darkened at these words. Andrew noticed that the stump of his wrist was tightly bandaged. He kept stroking it as gently as he might nurse a kitten.

'All right, but that won't be an end to it.'

Odo said, 'It will be an official end to it, de Blois – anything you do to the boy after that will be outside the law. I've told you he's the king's playmate at the moment. You would be well advised to give him the lashing and leave it at that. I went up against Baldwin's father over Walter de Mesnil, and suffered for it. I won't brook another king. Give the youth a lashing and be satisfied.'

De Blois's lips tightened. 'I shall do it myself.'

Odo sucked his breath in and shook his head firmly. 'Unprecedented for a noble. What, would you lower yourself to the level of a peasant? Where's your honour? Have some pride, man. He's a mere underling. Let your squire whip him.'

So it was done, in the ante-room of the Master's hall, in the Temple of Solomon. They tied Andrew's wrists to the arms of a heavy teak chair while Gareth stood on a stool to get more striking power at his back. Each stroke, with the lead-weighted flails, bit into Andrew's ribs, until they were raw and bleeding. Odo had told him quietly to start yelling after six strokes, to increase Gondemar de Blois's satisfaction, but he would have done so anyway. The flails hurt.

'Sorry,' Gareth whispered afterwards. 'He told me if I didn't bring a chalice of blood from your back, I would get the same.'

Andrew sighed, 'You brought a bucket.'

'I know. I'm sorry.'

Andrew felt half dead as he lay on his stomach in his quarters. Tomas carefully smeared ointment on his back, a balm made from local herbs. For the next two weeks Andrew was in pain, full of resentment towards his former master. In his private moments he swore he would get revenge on the knight, though he knew this to be impossible, for Gondemar was untouchable. He felt humiliated. All his former life he had been bullied by those stronger than himself. Since arriving in Jerusalem, however, Andrew felt he had earned respect. He deserved to be better regarded than when he was a village boy. Yes, since those days he had fought with bandits and giants. He had made friends with a king. He had actually served his aristocratic master to the best of his ability, saving him from a horrible death. How, then, did he deserve being whipped like a dog? Such punishment did not bear justification.

Happily, Gondemar had been made aware of the acquaintance of his former squire with King Baldwin and the knowledge of the whipping was kept from the king. Neither Andrew nor Gondemar stood to gain by having the boy king know of the punishment. One would have been concerned for his standing, the other would have felt mortified. So both kept the secret to themselves and others, like the Temple's Master, who also felt that it was not the sort of thing that should reach a king's ears.

When the king finally saw Andrew next he cried, 'Where have you been? Out in the desert killing giants again?'

Andrew laughed it off, replying, 'Very small giants, my lord, not much larger than dwarves. I'm saving the big ones for you, when you have the time for a wild hunt.'

Andrew was still living off the king's generosity. He had been given a room at the rear of the king's chapel, where he and Tomas slept. He ate at one of the king's tables. Not necessarily the table at which Baldwin himself ate, but there were others, for servants, for lesser gentry, for squires. At this time an opening appeared for a squire with a knight called John of Reims. Sir John's previous squire had died of a yellow disease and the king recommended Andrew to him.

John of Reims was an important Templar, a close friend of the Master and a man who took little notice of other knights. He was a man of cheerful disposition and amiable character. He said he was delighted to have Andrew as his squire, and, when told about Tomas, laughed and said, 'Two for the price of one! I am blessed.' Andrew could not have been more fortunate. Sir John and Gondemar despised each other and so it mattered not that Andrew was in the latter's disfavour. In fact, Sir John would have employed Andrew to spite the other. Thus Andrew and Tomas moved to new quarters. Andrew became just a little arrogant, being the squire of such a great knight. When he next saw Gareth he snubbed him in the passageway and Gareth believed it was because of Andrew's rise in fortune; in fact, it was simply because he had been the one who had wielded the lash.

Andrew's boots were, if anything, getting smaller.

14. ANGELIQUE

It was a bright, still, hot English summer's day. Bees were filling the garden with their buzzing. Birds were picking at early fruit. Hounds sought the deepest shade among the orchard's trees. Ducks and geese boated on pond and lake. Goats ambled around the brambles, eating anything that they found within reach.

In a large striped pavilion, erected by the lake to encourage coolness of mind if not body, Robert de Sonnac called Angelique to his side and told her that it was time he joined the crusade.

'Secular knights such as me,' he told his daughter, 'those without strong religious convictions, are expected to do our part. Also, in truth, daughter, I need to be in Outremer. King Henry is still having trouble with Prince Henry and Prince Richard.' Angelique knew that the two sons of the king had in recent years rebelled several times against their father from their base in France. 'I believe,' continued Robert, 'it to be politic not to get involved in that fight. Prince Henry will one day be king himself, or Richard if the young Henry does not survive until his father dies. Either way, princes who have been elevated to kings often have long memories. If I assist the king against his sons, when those sons become rulers they will remember it and I will suffer for it.'

'But you are expected to support the king, Father. You would support either of the princes, once they became king.'

Robert sighed. 'Well, you would think they might know that – but both Henry and Richard are not gifted with cleverness. Richard has the mind of a wild boar. His brains are in his sword hand. Henry is a little better, but has the same foul temper owned by his brother. There's not much to choose between the pair of them, when it comes to understanding the world. I think I would be better off out of the way, while King Henry deals with his offspring.'

Angelique was growing into a fine young lady. Unlike the princes, she had a good mind.

'Then there's his wife, the Queen Eleanor, who demands a divorce from the king.'

'Yes, indeed, the rebellious Eleanor, along with her favourite son, John. She, too, has been causing a great deal of trouble since her husband imprisoned her. The whole family is daggers drawn and at each other's throats. I don't wish to be pig-in-the-middle. Some knights might enjoy the intrigues and plots, hoping to further their ambitions. I wish to be well out of it all.'

Angelique put her arms around her father.

'I shall miss you, Papa.'

'And I you, child. I would take you with me, but the journey will be hard . . .'

'I can stand hardship.'

'So you can, I know, but I need you here, to manage my estates. If I am constantly worrying about you, I shall not be able to do my duty.'

'Which is it, Father? You need me here or you don't want me to be a trouble to you on your crusade?'

He smiled down at her. 'Both.'

She smiled back at him, then her face became serious again.

'And if you should see a young man . . .'

'By the name of Andrew?'

Her face lit up. 'Yes, yes, Father. Tell him to write to me, as he promised. Why has he not answered my letters, do you think?'

Robert de Sonnac turned his own face away from his daughter's gaze.

'Oh, I should think the boy has too much work. And he is unlearned, you know. He would have to get a scribe to write a letter for him and no doubt Gondemar is always out in desert places fighting the Saracens. If Gondemar is out in the thick of it, then so is young Andrew. No, he won't have time for letters, my sweet. He'll be with his master on the battle-field. Then, one can't trust couriers these days, either.'

'At least *one* of my letters must have got through.'

'Oh – oh, yes, at least one. But then, you know, so many souls die on their way to the Holy Land. We have lost hundreds of thousands of knights on the Turkana plains. Not *us* exactly, for I include all the other countries sending knights, such as Hungary, Bohemia . . .'

'Yes, yes, Father. But even so, *one* letter. Thousands of souls don't die on the ships. Some, but not thousands.'

Robert heaved a great sigh, knowing he was the one who had stopped Angelique's letters from going any further than London Bridge, and made a promise he did not intend to keep.

'I shall seek the boy out myself and give him a letter with my own hand,' he said. 'Write it today, child. Place it in my saddlebags yourself.'

Angelique's eyes lit up. 'Oh, thank you, Father.'

Robert bit his lip in anguish, knowing he was not bound for Heaven. But how could he consign his daughter to the son of a lowly farrier for the rest of her life? She might think herself in love with the young man, simply because he was her saviour. Indeed, Robert himself was eternally grateful to Andrew for rescuing his daughter from drowning, but the boy had received his reward for that service. He was the squire to a famous knight, had his own armour and horse, and had been elevated far above his station. Young Andrew had no right to expect more. Certainly not the hand of a knight's only daughter. Give it time and she would forget this fantasy, this infatuation. Angelique deserved more. A husband with wealth and position. An earl or a duke. Someone who could protect her and give her everything she deserved.

'Just put it in my saddlebag,' he murmured, 'and then I can pass it on to the boy when I see him. Oh, and your Aunt Elspeth will arrive the day after I leave. Treat her with politeness and good manners, child. I know you find her difficult, but I have appointed her your guardian in my absence. She must be shown every courtesy.'

It was Angelique's turn to sigh. 'Oh, Father.'

'Yes, I know, but I couldn't leave you alone and she has offered to come.'

'I wouldn't be alone. There's Ruben.'

'My ageing steward? As if I could leave you in *his* care, Angelique. He can hardly see the hand in front of his face. No, your Aunt Elspeth will do nicely, thank you, and you will accept it.'

Another sigh. 'Yes, Father.'

Later he said to Old Foggarty, 'On the journey, I want you to look after one of my saddlebags.'

Old Foggarty raised his eyebrows. 'Yes, master. I look after a lot of things for you.'

'Ah, hummprumph, it might be that this particular leather bag will be lost in the mountains of Italy.'

'Might it?' said Old Foggarty, wonderingly. 'Is that so?'

'It's a great possibility. The saddlebag is old, the strap is worn and might snap at any moment. It's important that *I* do not lose it, but should *you* do so, it is obviously fate.'

'Well then, sire – we must be certain not to put anything of great value in that particular piece of luggage.'

'Quite. I have one or two items which will be in that wallet, but you need not concern yourself about them.'

'Well then, sire, I won't.'

'Good.'

The two men parted while Angelique was busy at her writing desk, employing the education passed on to her by the priest of her father's chapel. Father William had taught her well, in English, French and Latin. She usually wrote letters in a mixture of all three, partly because she was still young enough to want to show off her knowledge, and partly because most everyday things were better said in English, while she liked to express her deepest feelings in the French language. Latin was reserved for a succinct phrase such as 'all other things being equal': *ceteris paribus*. She had no thought for her poor recipient, Andrew, who struggled even to remember the letters of the English alphabet. It did not cross her mind that he would have to get some stranger to read her most secret thoughts to him. His blushes were not to be saved. If the letter ever reached him, which seemed unlikely given the plot hatched by Sir Robert, Andrew would have to squirm in his seat while some crusty old sage told him some very, very personal things.

Once her father had gone, Angelique settled down to some weaving. She was making a tapestry for the hall. Into the patterns she had woven her mother's name: *Isabel*. She had done this subtly, so that it appeared to be part of a woodland glade scene, the branches entangled with the secrets of a daughter's heart. In the centre of a glade was a hart, which represented her father, seeking his mate. But the doe had gone forever, perhaps taken by hunters, and the stag was left forlorn and lost, seeing his mate's name everywhere, but never a trace of her form. It was as if the doe herself had become unravelled at the point of leaving and had left thin ribbons of her spirit in the thickets and spinneys.

Aunt Elspeth arrived the next morning.

Elspeth was a formidable dame whose ambassador husband was forever abroad. Despite the dangers, Sir John seemed to prefer disease-ridden climes and the knife-edge existence of a diplomat to his family home. Sir John was aware that the family fortune remained untouched by his wife whenever he was held to ransom by some blackguard of a distant ruler, but it did not matter, for somehow he always seemed to escape this common fate of ambassadors of Henry II, despite Elspeth's callous regard for the family coffers.

Elspeth came striding through the doorway. She wore a gown of sheep's wool, despite the warm weather. But this was not what captured Angelique's attention. That was down to the extraordinary piece of headgear. The hat, if that is what it was, seemed to be fashioned from cast-off rags of many colours. It was both shapeless and startling. It was as if some bird of paradise had been mangled by a gin trap and then rammed hard on to her skull. Angelique's mouth fell open on seeing this piece of millinery. She could not take her eyes off it. Fortunately, her aunt took this as a compliment and nodded approvingly.

'The hat was given me by my dear husband, before he left for Aragon,' said Elspeth. 'I understand it was a gift from the Satrap of Rum, for your uncle's services to that particular gentleman, may his soul rest in peace.'

'May whose soul rest in peace?' enquired a concerned Angelique, thinking her uncle had at last met with a ruler who had the gumption actually to carry out the execution of one of Henry's ambassadors. 'Uncle John . . .'

'What? No, no, child – the satrap or sultan, or whatever he was – he was beheaded by one of his own courtiers.'

'Oh.'

Then Angelique's heart sank, for who should come through the doorway next but her cousin Ezra. Her aunt's son was about three years older than Angelique. Despite being her first cousin there had been talk of a marriage with Ezra. Angelique had pleaded with her father to put all thoughts of a wedding with her cousin out of his head. Robert, seeing the distress in his daughter's eyes, had agreed to do so.

'Ah, cuz,' said Ezra, 'how are you?'

Angelique curtsied to the tall young man, now nineteen years of age. He had grown handsome in a dark way, but he had a cruel mouth and his eyes glinted too much for Angelique's taste. There was strength in his arms and shoulders, but his legs were thin and awkward looking, the toes pointing inward when he walked. He dressed reasonably well, with taste, which was extraordinary given that his mother had no dress sense whatsoever. His general stature indicated confidence. There was arrogance there too, of course, but that was not unusual in the son of an earl, even an impoverished one such as Sir John.

'I am well, sir. And you?'

He took off his heavy gauntlets and tossed them towards a servant, hitting Minstrel, Angelique's spaniel, in the process. The little dog yelped, but Ezra took no notice.

'Oh, you know, well enough. But I'm anxious to be off on the crusades. It troubles my spirit to be among silly women.'

This did not even cause his mother to raise an eyebrow.

'You – you will be leaving soon?' asked Angelique, hopefully. 'I mean, this house has nothing *but* silly women in it.'

'I don't want to let him go yet,' Elspeth answered for her son. 'I need him by me for a little longer. Once sons have left the home they seem to return only for a short while before going off again. Now, where is that doddering old fool Ruben? Ah, there you are! Show us to our chambers, steward – and arrange for my trunk to be carried in. Ezra, you did pack some clothes, did you not? Where is your box?'

'I brought nothing, Mother. London is but a stroll away. I shall buy new clothes there.'

'That's rather extravagant, Ezra.'

'I tire of my wardrobe so quickly, Mother.'

She shrugged. 'As you please.'

Angelique said, 'There's food and drink laid out in the hall, Aunt, if you need refreshments.'

'Thank you, child. I need to lie down first, for the journey has fatigued me beyond anything. Ezra, you stay and amuse your young cousin. I'm sure you have plenty of news to exchange. Go out into the garden. You won't be disturbed there.'

Alarm bells began sounding in Angelique's head immediately. Why should they *not* be disturbed? But her aunt was now gone, following the tottering Ruben along a dimly lit passageway, the long hem of her gown rustling as it dragged over the stone flags. Ezra took her hand and led her out through a back door and into the garden beyond. When they reached a garden seat she wrenched her hand from his grip. He looked at her with surprise and then pretended to mistake her meaning.

He smiled. 'Ah, you think yourself too young to be fondled by your older cousin? Well, I like holding your hand. Or sliding my arm around your waist – thus.'

She sidled away from him.

'I do not *like* being held, sir. I am a woman, grown.'

He laughed now. 'Almost. Not quite, but almost. Certainly,' he looked her up and down, 'you have the form of a woman now . . .'

She gasped indignantly at this gross breach of manners.

'. . . but still the mind of a child. Cuz, cuz, you and I do not stand on the formalities of etiquette. We know each other too well.' He tried to take her hand again, unsuccessfully, because she put her arms behind her back and locked her two sets of fingers. 'Why, we still might be married, you know. It's not settled either way, so far as I'm concerned. I mean to approach your father again, when he returns.'

'That is your right, but know this, Ezra, I have no love for you at all, beyond our blood. You are my cousin, but it ends there.'

He stared into her face and his look darkened.

'Ah, you've met someone else? What's his name?'

Minstrel, who had followed them into the garden, cocked his ears and growled at Ezra's angry tone. Ezra turned and flicked the dog's nose contemptuously with his long, pale fingers while he waited for a reply. Minstrel yelped in pain for the second time that day.

Angelique said, 'I have met no one.'

'But you have, cuz. I can see a phantom in your eyes. I might look the fool, but I know women. I've seen that ghost in maidens' eyes before. You've met someone who's stolen your heart. Yes, yes, I see the starlight leap to your eyes again! So, tell me his name. I shall meet him on the field and God shall decide who is best for you. Is it that idiot Wakefield? A duke's son would not be out of your reach. Or Guy of Castlemaine? An older man, but still with good looks. Who?'

'No one you know.'

His lip curled like a snake writhing.

'So, no one I have met. Well, I will meet him, be sure of that. And when I do . . .'

'He will strike you down.'

Ezra suddenly laughed. 'Oh, I see more in your face now – he's a boy, isn't he? A mere boy. What foolishness is this, Angelique?'

She was dismayed by his astuteness. 'How can you know?'

'I've told you, I make a study of women's features. I can read them like a parchment. You can hide nothing from me, wench. All your thoughts are written in your eyes, on your lips, your brow. I'll find this boy of yours and whip his backside before sending him home to his mother, sobbing. Make no mistake. I will discover him.'

Angelique's heart was leaden. She knew Ezra almost as well as he knew her. He would not rest now until he had uncovered her secrets. She hated him. She hated him and his mother. The pair of them were agents of the Devil, so far as she was concerned. Perhaps the time had come to run away again, to her other cousins? Or even beyond? Did she dare try to find Andrew, wherever he was? It was a thought.

Angelique left Ezra in the garden and, followed by her devoted spaniel, went to her chamber. She stayed there for the rest of the day. Her aunt came to see her before she retired for the evening, but only to ask for the key to a chest. Her sleep was troubled that night. Her dreams were full of unpleasant occurrences. She was woken in the early dawn by the growling of Minstrel. By the grey light coming through the open window she witnessed a tall, silent figure standing at the end of her bed. She sat up and gathered her bedclothes around her.

'Ezra?' she cried, alarmed. 'What are you doing in here?'

Ezra said nothing. His expression was blank. He simply stood and stared at her. He was dressed in nothing more than a satin robe. The two of them held each other's gaze for a long while. Still he did not move, neither towards the doorway, nor towards her. But there was something in his look which chilled Angelique to her soul's core. Suddenly, she knew she was but moments away from an attack.

'No,' she said calmly and evenly. 'If you do, you know my

father will hunt you down and kill you like a filthy animal.'

Ezra continued to stare at her for a short while after she had made this statement. Finally he turned, and left the room. Angelique leapt out of bed and bolted the door behind him. Her heart was thudding in her chest. She knew how close she had come to dishonour and disgrace at the hands of her ruthless cousin. Only fear for his life, the certainty of the truth of her words, had turned him from his purpose. Even the damning of his soul would not have put him off. Only the absolute conviction that he would die horribly had thwarted him. Thank God, she thought, for a father who was feared by all for his fighting prowess.

'I would like to cut out that man's tongue,' she told Minstrel, who looked up at her from the end of her bed, 'and feed it to the chickens.'

Minstrel cocked his head to one side and looked at her with the liquid-brown eyes of an adoring spaniel that he was.

PART TWO

15. THE BATTLE OF MONTGISARD

Andrew still harboured a strong resentment against his old master for the whipping. In the heat of the East wounds took a long time to heal. They festered and wept with pus for much longer than in a temperate climate. The lacerations left by the metal-tipped flails closed only slowly and subsequently the cuts in Andrew's spirit also remained open and raw for a great deal longer than they normally would have.

He had grown up used to being treated as less than nothing by his betters. Knights, priests, landlords, and officials of all kinds, felt they had the right to do as they wished with those below them. His father was at least a craftsman and not the lowest of the low. Still, it was instilled in Andrew's nature, and had been from birth, to accept punishment handed out by his overlords. Even when it was not just. So he did not swear to get even with Sir Gondemar. That was outside the scope of his imagination. But he did hate the knight with a good deal of venom. After all, Andrew had tried to help the man, saved his life, and had been given pain as a reward.

'I tell you, Tomas,' he said to his servant, 'some people should receive a whipping themselves, before handing it out to others. Then they'll know what it feels like – they should *feel* the agony – and also feel the damage it does to a man's spirit.'

Tomas applied balm to the youth's back. His hands were

soft and easy, not causing any hurt themselves to the inflamed skin. Tomas's hands were indeed the hands of an angel. His sweet nature, his gentle ways, were in sharp contrast to that of others, even Andrew. Andrew himself had a fierce temper and could verbally attack someone without just cause. Tomas would never do that. His innocent face, his deep blue eyes were completely void of malice. There was nothing but kindness in them, nothing but pity for the suffering of others. He could feel the sorrow of another man, while remaining oblivious to his own state of sadness.

'Yes, Andrew,' said Tomas, his hands sliding back and forth over the wounded back, 'men should always experience themselves what they give out to others.'

'Except hanging,' Andrew added, thoughtfully, 'for that is permanent.'

'Of course, except hanging. The hanged cannot pass on their judgement of their punishment. They learn nothing except the darkness of Purgatory, which they will never be able to describe to another man, even if they return as a spectre.'

Andrew lifted his head. 'But you, Tomas – have you seen Purgatory?'

'I may have, but I can say nothing more.'

'How so?'

'Because if I try to reveal the secrets of the afterlife, my tongue twists into a knot and robs me of speech.'

'Is it Gabriel, or Raphael – one of the archangels – who makes your tongue do that?'

'No doubt, for it is quite forbidden to reveal such a thing.'

'Some people do – they come back and brag to other men about what they have seen on the road to Heaven.'

'In which case they are lying and for that they go to the other place,' replied Tomas, primly.

'Ah, they are wafted into Hell, to burn.'

'Yes.'

'Serve them right, I say. A secret is meant to be kept.'

'I agree, Andrew.'

At that moment a breathless Gareth burst into the room. His eyes were shining and full of excitement.

Andrew glared at Gareth, the person who had actually put the red weals on his back.

'What do *you* want, Welshman?' he growled.

'Andrew,' said the agitated Gareth, 'it is war!'

Instantly Andrew forgot his wrath. 'What is?'

'The Ayyubids have attacked us.'

Andrew sat up abruptly. 'Saladin?'

'Yes. As you know, King Baldwin was planning an attack on Egypt, but Saladin has decided to strike first. He has marched into Palestine with nearly thirty thousand warriors. We are leaving Jerusalem for Ascalon. Your master, John of Reims, is going, as well as my own master. We are to be squires in the field, Andrew. Myself for the second time, of course, for I was with the Byzantines in Rum.'

'I have fought,' cried Andrew, indignantly.

'Yes, but with caravaners and such,' replied Gareth, disparagingly, 'against wild tribesmen. That's not real war, Andrew. It's not against an army.'

'If you get killed by an enemy, it doesn't matter who they are!'

'True, but you were not killed – for here you stand, arguing, as usual. Come on, make haste. Go to your master. We must leave for Ascalon. Saladin has already burned down many villages along the coast, at Lydda and Arsuf. People are fleeing everywhere. They say he is a great general, but how can he be if he is an Arab? They don't make great generals, do they, Andrew?'

'He is a Kurd, Master Gareth,' corrected Tomas, 'and there have been great generals who were not Christian-born. Julius Caesar, for one.'

'Well, he was not from Africa or Arabia,' retorted Gareth.

'No, but Hannibal was, and he made fools of the Romans.'

'Tomas is right,' said Andrew, starting to put on his armour. 'Saladin has not yet been beaten. Even the Assassins haven't managed to kill him and they've tried more than once. But if Saladin has attacked north of Ramla, he must have passed by Gaza. Didn't the Templars at Gaza stop him?'

'They let him pass by, but now regret their action.'

'I should think they do,' cried Andrew, 'for the Templars are the greatest fighters the world has ever known. They care nothing for their own lives, which are dedicated to the service of God. They are feared across the Earth for their ferociousness in battle. Not one would ever leave the field in defeat. Who would face a warrior-monk if not with a quailing heart and trembling fist?'

This speech was left to stand, unchallenged, for Andrew was merely quoting what the boys had heard many times before from the mouths of others. Tomas quietly blessed his master's sword, the wonderful Ulfberht blade. In the meantime, Gareth left to find his own master.

Once the arming of Andrew had taken place, he collected his steed from the stables and rode to the Temple of Solomon.

There a very few Templar Knights were gathered. The sixteen-year-old King Baldwin was ill with his leprosy, so he had handed over command to Raynald of Châtillon, Lord of Oultre-jordain. Raynald had recently been a prisoner in Aleppo, but was now free. He was a fierce enemy of Saladin and was a good soldier. Raynald and the king had gathered together several hundred secular knights, whose ranks would soon, hopefully, be swollen by Templars.

'How many Templars are we?' asked Andrew, joining his master.

John of Reims looked his squire up and down, seeing the magnificent armour and the wonderful war horse for the first time.

'My God,' said Sir John, casually blaspheming, 'you look more beautiful than I do. Are those inlays *real* gold? I feel rather drab in comparison.'

Andrew was suddenly embarrassingly aware of his splendid appearance. The marvellous helmet gleamed in the Eastern sun. There were bright flashes from the semi-precious stones embedded in various bits of armour. A scarf hung from his shoulders with casual élan, the pelisse of a young Greek god. The hilt of his sword with its raised letters dazzled onlookers with its splendour. Indeed, he looked a hero mounted high on the back of his charger. Had the pair been cast in polished bronze, the athletic young squire and his steed, Warlock, they would not have caused as much of a stir as they did among the Templars outside their headquarters. Gondemar de Blois glared with great ferocity, but others simply looked on, stunned by the sight.

'My lord, I'm sorry if I cause you upset,' said Andrew, humbly; 'the armour was a gift from an English knight.'

'I should have such friends,' laughed Sir John. 'Saladin will wonder which one of us to run through with his scimitar, the shield-bearer or the knight. I fancy you will make a more appealing prize than this shoddy man.'

'Sire, please don't call yourself shoddy – you are a knight everyone thinks grand.'

'Grand, am I?' John laughed again. 'I haven't two pennies to rub together, yet I ride with a youth who might own Babylon. Up, boy, up. We must join our king.'

'Is the king fighting today?' asked Andrew, anxiously. 'He doesn't look well. Is it his leprosy?'

'Sick or no, the king will fight. He has the courage of ten lions, that young regent. Troubles, he has plenty, but bravery he does not lack. On, boy, on.'

As they rode out of the city, a handful of Templar Knights and nearly four hundred secular knights, Andrew thought about the king's 'troubles'. There was no heir to his kingdom and yet he might fall any day in battle. His subjects looked to the king's sister, Sibylla, to produce an heir to the throne, but her misfortunes had continued with the death of her husband. A new husband had to be found for her, one of whom Baldwin approved, naturally. Philip of Alsace, Count of Flanders, had proposed once, but Baldwin had rejected this offer.

The office of husband for Sibylla was still open, and here was the King of Jerusalem riding out into the jaws of death. The king had said recently to Andrew, 'You would make a good husband for my sister, my friend. At least *I* like you.' Andrew had been horrified and replied, 'My liege, she is too old for me, and I too young for marriage. Also, sire, perhaps you forgot I am to be a Templar.' But Baldwin just laughed. No doubt he had been jesting.

This small army of a few hundred knights, accompanied by a few thousand infantry, marched to the town of Ascalon. There they made their camp and prepared to defend it. Baldwin had been hoping for reinforcements but the Knights Templar garrisoned at Gaza had been blockaded and could not reach the town to join with the king's forces.

Saladin's columns soon arrived to surround Ascalon and hem in Baldwin's men. The Christian army was heavily outnumbered and were hard put to defend the town against the great Muslim leader's forces. Andrew spent a miserable night or two cooking stew for his master, while sergeants, knights and men-at-arms twiddled their thumbs.

One evening a shout went up among the soldiers.

'What's happened?' cried Andrew. 'Are we attacked?'

'No,' replied his master, 'the enemy has decamped. They have abandoned us here without a siege. We are free to leave.'

Andrew asked, 'Where will we go?'

'Why,' cried Sir John, with great glee, 'we go to fight the Saracens. They leave us here thinking we dare not follow. Us? Dare not? We shall give them the surprise of their lives, lad. We shall smash them from the rear. Hark! You hear that? The Templars from Gaza have arrived. Odo de St Amand, the Grand Master, rides with us. Eighty Templars! Why, we are invincible lad, invincible.'

Eighty Templars, thought Andrew, but thirty thousand Saracens.

'Are we enough, with Hospitallers and Templars, and others?'

'If we are not,' roared Sir John, 'then we shall all die with honour, eh? Death or glory. Which is it to be? Do I care? Only a little, for one is as good as the other. Come, lad, follow the banner. Lift my shield high so that all may see my herald, my coat of arms. John of Reims is here, with Baldwin, King of Jerusalem, with Odo the Master of the Temple. If I fall today my name will forever live on after me.'

'And mine too?' cried Andrew.

'You?' Sir John laughed again, enjoying his amusement. 'Of course not. You're a bloody squire, boy – no one will remember you.'

The small army of three hundred and seventy-five of the king's knights, eighty Templars and just a few thousand infantry, set out after Saladin's much greater force. The outriders of Baldwin's army, still under the overall command of Raynald, reported that the Saracens were spreading out over the countryside, looting and pillaging villages. Others were foraging for food at some distance from the main group. Raynald was happy to tag along, out of sight of Saladin's men. The knights followed the coastline, simply keeping pace with the larger Saracen army.

When Saladin was approaching the castle of Montgisard, near Ramla, Raynald prepared to attack, telling his men they would sweep down into the shallow valley which contained the enemy and surprise them by coming out of rocks.

Andrew handed John of Reims his shield. Since he had to carry that of his master, he had no shield himself. So he drew his sword, ready to fight by Sir John's side.

'Sire,' he said, looking down at the myriad colourful Saracens on their mounts, 'which is Saladin?'

'There, lad, riding up that hill on that tall camel.'

'How can you recognise him, sire, from all the other Saracens.'

'He rides with a bodyguard of Mamluks. They are there, surrounding his person. Saladin is a great and courageous warrior, but, like all rulers he has fanatics who protect him to the last.'

Andrew stared at Saladin as the caliph formed his men into a line on the brow of a hill.

'Mamluks? What are they?'

'Why, slave troops, lad. Mostly Turks. They are slaves, yet they are not slaves, for they fight by the ruler's side and would die for him. Saladin's Mamluks would throw themselves into a fire if he asked them to.'

'What strange things happen in this world,' Andrew murmured.

The excitement was rising in his breast. He had fought before, but not in a pitched battle. Now he was going to charge into that mass of men who had flowing robes and turbans, who filled the valley and covered the hill ahead. Scimitars and swords were bared to the sun. A thousand brilliant flashes filled the day, from blades, from rings, from armour and bejewelled headdresses. A single diamond-studded sword hilt leapt to brilliance in the hands of a nearby knight. Horses whinnied, camels hooted, dogs barked. The stink of horse breath and camel sweat rode on the back of the wind. Banners flapped, flags unfurled.

A hush descended upon the scene.

Then the Bishop of Bethlehem broke from the ranks of the knights with his hand raised high. He held up a piece of the True Cross, riding forward in pomp. His robes were magnificent, their gold and silver threads flashing in the sunlight. A splendid mitre like a spear tip pierced the air above his head. Who could withstand this bearer of celestial power? Who would not shield his eyes and cower before such radiance as shone from this spiritual leader. He was their soul strength, the bishop, filling the knights with the fervour of their purpose. The bishop ensured they had the whole host of Heaven, the angels of the Lord, in their ranks.

A great, hoarse cheer went up from the throats of men ready to die for their king and country.

On the other side, Saladin's men began invoking the blessing of their Prophet, and called to Allah for victory over the detested Infidel.

Raynald of Châtillon cried, 'King Baldwin!'

The knights began their charge, hooves thundering down the slopes and along the valley, booming their battle hymns.

Andrew's heart leapt into his mouth. Automatically, he kicked the flanks of his steed. Thereupon he was swept along with the rest. Warlock felt the sudden release of tension, the snapping of the invisible bonds that had held them. The steed's eyes were wide and white, his nostrils flared, as Andrew tried to control the charge. Warlock was a war horse and he knew a battleground when it was under his hooves. This was his time. This was his place. He would carry his master, willing or no, into the thick of the fighting, for this was his *raison d'être*.

Even before the horde of charging knights struck the centre of the Saracen line, driving through it with great force and energy, the enemy had begun to break up. Saladin strove to hold his flanks, but when the hammer blow of metalled men smashed through his troops, he lost control of his army. Saladin's cavalry was exhausted by the long march from Egypt and the subsequent pillaging. They could not protect the warriors on foot from being slaughtered. Saracen foot soldiers began streaming from the field almost immediately, leaving their ruler and his Mamluks to fend for themselves.

Warlock had managed to make sure Andrew was in the thick of the fighting. The fear and trepidation Andrew had felt prior to the battle had evaporated. Now he simply fought for his life, mindlessly hacking with his sword on all sides. There was an anxiousness there, but only one of watchful care. He did not want to be surprised by a scimitar coming at him from out of the blue. Once or twice he was almost sliced by one of those wicked blades, but managed to evade the blow. He saw the king, Baldwin, not far from him, wielding a sword with great ferocity and skill. And the king looked up, saw Andrew doing likewise, and yelled encouragement.

The sound of steel blades striking metal was deafening. Swords ringing on swords, battleaxes crashing on armour, battle-hammers clanging on shields. Metal smashing metal everywhere, producing the most excruciating noise. A sound that startled the wildlife in all directions and had it running between the legs of combatants.

Sticking close to John of Reims, Andrew began to see his role as protecting his master's rear from a sneak attack. A Saracen charged from out of nowhere, but the warrior's scimitar simply snapped on striking Andrew's Ulfberht. He took great heart. His sword was one of the strongest in the world. In truth, many so-called steel blades of the Christian army were as brittle as iron. They had no ability to bend and carried many faults in the metal. Indeed, the scimitars of the Arabs were far superior to the swords of the Europeans, being made of stronger, more flexible steel, the science of which was a secret the Middle Eastern races kept close to their hearts.

As a squire Andrew was, of course, responsible for protecting Sir John. Should his master lose his sword, Andrew would be expected to give him his own. Should his master fall wounded, he was expected to stand over him and keep the Saracen from finishing him. Until then, he would fight alongside John of Reims and watch his back. Thus Andrew did his duty with all the skill instilled in him by Old Foggarty. His training was now being put to use, good or otherwise, and his life was saved many a time by Old Foggarty's voice in his head.

A Mamluk came at John of Reims from the side, while he was engaged with another of the enemy. Andrew intercepted. He slashed down on the Mamluk's scimitar, forcing it to slice into the man's saddle and bury its blade there. But the Mamluk was quick and with his left hand he drew and flung a dagger. The missile struck Andrew in the chest. The armour stood the test: the dagger glanced off and went spinning away. Andrew now thrust with his sword and took the enemy in the shoulder. A look of intense pain crossed the Mamluk's face. The point of the sword had found his shoulder joint.

The man's face was so close to Andrew's own at this point that they were looking into each other's eyes from just a few centimetres. Andrew was shocked by the hate he saw there. The eyes blazed with it. The mouth curled with it. The teeth were bared with it. Andrew drew back from this naked emotion instinctively. This gave the Mamluk time to wheel his mount and gallop away, thus saving his life, for the next thrust of Andrew's blade would surely have been through his heart.

Andrew had no time to think about this encounter before the next man was upon him, with heavy, sweeping slashes of his curved scimitar. Andrew countered this way and that with his straight sword. It was an odd fight between Saracen and knight, for the Saracens slashed with their scimitars, while the knights thrust with their swords. One tried to slice: the other tried to pierce. It was strangely unequal, like a battle between a bull and a leopard: sharp horns against razor-like claws.

Only thanks to the dancing skills of Warlock did he escape being cut in a dozen places. Warlock knew when to retreat and he did so now, turning a tight circle, so that Andrew was then behind his attacker. But the man galloped forward out of reach and was soon buried in the heaving mass of fighting men who were in such a tight knot that most of them could not free their arms to strike.

At one point Andrew found his master fighting close to the boy king. Baldwin was a brave and skilful fighter, who delighted in fierce hand-to-hand combat. The king quite often slipped his personal guard to bury himself in the thick of the battle. Naturally this concerned his followers, who tried desperately to keep the king in a ring of bold knights. Now it seemed Baldwin had broken out of the defensive circle that normally surrounded him and was wielding his sword, fending off three Saracens with flashing blades. Andrew rode forward and gave assistance to the king, felling one of his attackers and helping to drive off another. Baldwin turned his head and saw who it was who had assisted him, raised a clenched fist as a sign to thank his young friend and subject, and was then again surrounded by his bodyguards.

At first the Saracens gave as good as they got. They were a fierce fighting race who knew how to do battle, especially from the back of a horse. Their scimitars sliced with great precision: deadly weapons wielded by highly skilled warriors. Here a knight was cloven through his armoured body. There a knight was forced to retreat from blades that fell relentlessly upon his form. Saracens had not just bravery on their side, but a fervent belief that they had been wronged. These knights they fought against were invaders in a land which had long been Saracen territory.

However, Saladin's army had been caught off-guard. They were soon in disarray, having been out of battle order when the knights arrived unexpectedly. There was a weariness about them brought on by a campaign that was lasting longer than their leader had planned. Surprise is a great weapon in war and the Saracens had certainly been surprised. Gradually, the knots of fighting men broke up and swathes of exhausted Saracens began to flee. They spread wide and raced from the battleground in great panic. Knights hurtled after them, cutting them down from behind. Some individual Saracens turned again, and offered themselves to the enemy, but the majority realised the day was over for them. The battle was lost. Their great leader tried to rally his men, but they were exhausted and in disarray, unable to form a cohesive unit. For the Saracens the battle was over and their retreat turned to a desperate rout.

Then the rout of the Saracens turned into a slaughter. King

Baldwin and his knights captured the enemy baggage train. Slaves, women and goods fell into his hands. Saladin, seeing that all was lost on this day, fled for his life on the back of a racing camel, taking only a tenth of his great army with him. The rest were killed or were lost somewhere on the fringes of the region. Saladin would live to fight again, perhaps to conquer in the future, but this day was King Baldwin's.

Blood and gore stained the landscape. When it was all over, Andrew stared at the bodies of men and animals, strewn like discarded clothes upon the red rocks and sand, and felt a deep sickness in his belly. The dead were everywhere, many of them from his own side. Perhaps over a thousand or so troops lay lifeless in the dust. On the other side, more than twenty thousand, perhaps even twenty five, littered the ravines and rocky outcrops. They draped the stones of Montgisard with their bodies. They choked the passes and escape routes from that dreadful place. Faces were frozen in a look of terror, or resignation, or supplication: the faces of men who knew they were about to die. Their limbs were twisted into desperate angles and shapes. Their eyes, empty of light.

Unspeakable. Ugly. Unforgettable.

'Well done, squire,' said John of Reims, as they rode slowly back towards Ascalon. 'You performed with honour.'

Sir John's face was smeared with blood. His arm hung broken from his drooping left shoulder. Any triumph the knight had felt at the end of the battle had since drained from his expression. He looked utterly fatigued.

'Thank you, my lord,' murmured Andrew, stroking Warlock's neck, 'my horse was the better warrior.'

'So, lad, what do you think of war?'

Andrew felt a little dead inside.

'I think it a terrible thing, sire.'

'Indeed it is. A most dreadful thing. But, unfortunately, unavoidable. Would we could do without it, but we seem unable to be rid of it.'

'A man could stay in his own home, in his own land.'

'The Celts tried that, and the Romans came. Then the Angles and Saxons invaded and drove the Romanised Celts into the setting sun. Then who should come along next but the Vikings, crossing the sea in longships, slaughtering church congregations and robbing them of all they possessed. That should have been an end to it, but, of course, William the Norman crossed the water and chopped down King Harold's Anglo-Saxon army and yet again there were new rulers in the land. They all stayed in their own homes, my boy, homes they had taken from others, only to find that war will seek men out, crossing mountains and seas to get to them.'

Andrew had not the strength of mind to argue with his master, even if he could find an answer to the riddle of men and their wars.

'It seems a shame for the Celts, who were there first.'

'Ah,' said John of Reims, 'but were they? I think not. The ancient race of Celts came from lands where the sun rises earlier than in the village of Cressing, from beyond any region which now spawns Franks, or Burgundians, or you willowy English youths. Out of an area of vast plains which give rise to so many different tribes of men, deep inside the continent. There must have been men on the island of Britain before the Celts, my boy. And perhaps men before those men? Each nation grows as a people and seeks new lands throughout time.'

It was all a bit too deep for Andrew, who had seen a bloody battle and just at that moment never wanted to see another.

'So,' said Andrew, 'my first battle. I hope I may not see another one like it, with all the dead men, and those left without limbs. But if I have to, I'll fight for the king again.'

'Good lad,' replied John of Reims. 'And your actions on this field might very well reap you some reward, especially since you fought by the king's side and aided him. This was no ordinary battle, Andrew. It was one that old scribes will even now be recording on their parchments for the benefit of history. There will be rewards for those who took part. Even the meanest man-at-arms will get something.'

Andrew's eyes opened wide. 'What sort of reward? Money?'

'Money?' scoffed the knight. 'Money is for the peasants. Money simply dribbles away and leaves one with regrets. The foot soldiers will be given money. In your case I'm talking about advancement.'

He left Andrew to think about that one.

Advancement! Perhaps he would be made a sergeant-at-arms. Or even a knight? Was that too much to hope for? Perhaps hoping for the latter was a bit too much like reaching for the stars. Something, anyway. He would have to wait and see.

For the moment he was too full of different, combating emotions to think too deeply about what he might receive from his king.

Emotions?

Elation, yes, for the victory. Horror at what that victory had taken in terms of lives. Sadness for those he had known who would no longer walk the Earth. Humility when he thought of the brave deeds he had seen of men on both sides, saving comrades, protecting their lords, throwing themselves at impossible odds. There had been many men with loyal, generous hearts who had fallen in place of others.

Also he still felt amazement on recalling the spectacle of two great armies clashing together. Magnificent banners of gold, silver, red and blue flying like dragons from their poles. A moving forest of lances. Everywhere the sunlight glancing from armour, flashing on thousands of metalled men. Bright shields, glinting swords, the colourful, flowing robes of Saracen warriors. Such a spectacle! And the smell of horse sweat, dung and fear, and, above all, blood. The smell of a deluge of blood on a blistering day, in a hot valley packed with struggling men. Blood had poured on to the soil as rain, soaked it scarlet, turned the dust to slime and thence to red slush. What would not grow in that now fertile earth, watered by the lives of men?

When they returned to Jerusalem, Tomas wanted to know everything, all that had happened. Despite the fact that Andrew was bursting with knowledge, he found it difficult to share. He spoke a little about the battle, but in generalities, playing down his own role in the fighting. He was surprised to find shame in his soul, where there should have been glory. And distress where there should have been a feeling of honour. He wondered at the difference between coward and hero, thinking he could easily have been either.

Yes, there were times when he felt proud of his part, knowing he had probably saved the life of his master. Then there were those darker moments, when he recalled the suffering of the dying, the feeling of blade cutting through flesh, the look on the face of a man into whom he was driving the point of his sword. Such things, such feelings, were not easily put into words. He felt like swallowing his tongue when asked to describe his deeds. And his dreams were full of the cries of mortally wounded men, as they slipped away into oblivion.

Tomas seemed to understand Andrew's reluctance to impart his experience of the battle, which was already being spoken of as a great one, and quickly changed the talk to other subjects.

'One good thing,' said Tomas. 'I have heard that Gondemar de Blois has left Jerusalem for Antioch. I saw Gareth and spoke with him.'

'Gareth, too, was at the battle. Did he fight? I did not see him. The place was thick with men and weapons.'

'Gareth fought with his master and received a wound to his leg.'

'Good for him – to fight, I mean. Gondemar will appreciate that. Gareth is a good Welshman, a good Celt. He deserves to find improvement in his position.'

'I hear they have made him a Templar sergeant-at-arms.'

'Would that they would make me a chaplain,' said Andrew, speaking of the only other Templar rank besides knight, 'and then I could cast off this sword.'

'But you love your Ulfberht, Andrew – it is your badge.'

Andrew sighed. 'You're right as usual, Tomas. I wish you weren't, but you are. I'm not a man who can wield a pen with any feeling but boredom. Anyway, I can't even read or write properly, so they'd never make me a chaplain. Do you think they'll make me a sergeant, too?'

'You could ask for it.'

'No, I can't do that. It would be humiliating if they said no.'

The next day Andrew was summoned to the main square of Jerusalem, which was crowded with both commoners and nobles. The king was standing on a balcony, in conversation with the highest born of the land. Baldwin was dressed in his finery and so were his courtiers. The whole populace looked to be in a serious, sombre mood, yet there was an underlying excitement in the bearing of the soldiers and knights. Clearly the king was going to make a pronounce-ment, for there was a rolled-up scroll in his right hand, which he was at that moment using to emphasise a point. What was going on? Was a trial about to take place? Or perhaps the announcement of a public feast to celebrate their victory over the Saracens? Suddenly the king turned and seemed to notice how large the crowd had become and he unrolled the scroll in his hands. He was about to speak himself, but then appeared to have second thoughts and handed the parchment to the most senior of the elders standing with him. This man took the scroll with a grave bow and stepped forward to address the gathering in the square below.

'Listen,' he cried from the balcony, 'listen to the word of your king.'

He read: 'We have triumphed in battle over the Saracen. We give thanks to those who took part in that battle and praise the loyalty and bravery of all soldiers, be they men-at-arms on foot, or knights on horseback. Your king is pleased with each and every one. You have all shown great fortitude and strength in the face of superior odds. All those who took part in the fighting have our gratitude, but some were exceptional.

242

The following knights excelled themselves on the field and are to be commended individually . . .'

There followed the names of knights who were to be made earls, lords and baronets, and others with lesser noble titles. Andrew was pleased to hear that John of Reims was to receive the prize of an entire town in the land of the Franks. He knew his master had fought well and hard and deserved to be praised for his efforts.

Once this list had finished, the elder then continued.

'The following squires were seen to act with great merit and remarkable expertise, both in the defence of their knights and in the service of the king.'

The elder cleared his throat.

'Albert Silverhall.'

A ragged cheer went up in one corner of the crowd, where that squire's supporters and friends stood.

'Peter von Koln

William Rushforthe

Stuart Kilmartin . . .'

Here the scroll slipped from the fingers of the elder and it fell from the balcony down into the mud of the street. There was a scuffle as men tried to pick it up and throw it back to the flustered man, but the balcony was too high for this. The king looked a little bored and beckoned his elder to his side. He whispered into the clumsy fellow's ear and the elder nodded gravely and went back to the edge of the balcony.

'There were two more names on the list of squires, which I will now give you and you may then consider the proclamation complete.

Andrew Cressing.

Christian de Poissy.

There is the end to the king's word and God give us the grace to savour our victory without unseemly arrogance and contumely pride.'

A loud cheer went up from the square and the people began to disperse, chattering and laughing and calling to friends.

Andrew simply stood there, stunned, his heart swollen with pride.

'My name,' he said, to no one in particular. 'My name was among the chosen few picked out for commendation.'

'Good on yer, lad,' said a working man in a leather apron as he passed, slapping Andrew on the shoulder with a hand as hard as granite, 'I'm sure y'deserved it.'

16. WALTER PUGHSON RETURNS

Walter loved to walk in the gardens of Paradise and sometimes envied those who followed the path of Islam. The
Heaven of Christians was supposed to be a paradise, too, but
you could not taste of it while still on Earth. Orange and
lemon trees, date palms, myrtle bushes and green, green grass.
Water flowing everywhere, in channels, through fountains,
down stairways, into crystal pools. Green shadows. Green
light. Cool arbours with tranquil glades where one could sit
and think pleasant thoughts.

In the end he did not convert, much to the dismay of his
kidnappers, but of course he had to agree to carry out the
murder. He had no choice. His father would die if he did not
and if it was a choice between a stranger's death and the loss
of his father, there was no choice at all.

In the beginning he had told them he was a Christian and
one of God's Ten Commandments forbade him to kill. They
laughed at this and told him that when the Christian knights
and their foot soldiers took Jerusalem for the first time they
had slaughtered the whole population – Muslims and Jews
alike – without a thought for any commandment.

'But they were warriors. I am no soldier. I am an artisan,
a craftsman. I use my hands to make things.'

'You make swords. What are swords for but to kill other
men? If you made ploughshares or pens your hands would

be clean, but you make the weapons used in war. Let us not continue this nonsense. Your hands are already dirty.'

He had no argument to counter this, though he had never thought of his craft as being unclean.

They told him the name of his victim. Walter had heard of the man, but had never met him. He lived in Jerusalem but was of such high office that someone like Walter would not meet him in the ordinary way of things. Even if Walter or his father had made a sword for the man, it would doubtless have been ordered through and collected by a third person, probably a slave or servant.

'When shall I kill him?' he asked the Assassins.

'You will be told the hour. Not yet. You are now free to go back to Jerusalem. We shall send you with a guide.'

'I don't want a guide. I will find my own way back.'

'If you wish. Do you know the path?'

'I will find the path.'

In truth, Walter was sick of the company he had been keeping all these months. He wanted to be alone for a while. Not alone, as in a cell, but alone in the wilderness. There he could decide whether he was actually going to return to Jerusalem or kill himself. If he did the latter there would be no point in the Assassins murdering his father. There would be no punishment and no gain. You could do nothing to a dead man worse than he had done to himself.

They gave him food and directions, and a word to throw at any man – bandit, tribesman, wanderer – should he be accosted. The word would protect him, inform those who would attack and rob him that he had the most powerful people in the region at his back. Assassins were feared throughout Asia Minor. They were known all along the Euphrates and down to the source of the Tigris; from Philadelphia to beyond the far pale of Persia; on the distant banks of the Black Sea; on the steppes where the Mongol hordes were gathering – perhaps even to the borders of Tartary itself. No man in his senses would interfere with Walter after hearing the word.

Of course there was always the possibility of meeting a violent madman, but then that would be an accident such as falling into a lake and drowning, or dropping from a high place on to rocks. There was no common defence against lunacy.

Walter went down from the green hills to the dusty plains and arid mountains which stood between him and Jerusalem. At first the road was clear and his instructions easy to follow, but inevitably he became lost among thorny mazes and dry river beds. He grew hungry until he killed an ibex and ate a whole haunch in one sitting. He slept in hollowed places and drank from muddy pools. Rains came and further destroyed the trails he tried to follow. Finally, he sat down on a log and gave in to despair, ready to abandon his life. For over an hour he sat and stared at a leafless tree, stark against the sand.

Suddenly, a figure appeared in the branches of the tree, squatting like a fiend. It came surrounded by smokeless flames that did not seem to burn either branch or leaf. The colourful flames then fell from it, like the shell of an egg dropping away, to reveal just the being itself.

Walter jumped from his seat and pointed a shaking finger.

'Are you a demon, sir, sent to drag me to Hell?'

The face of the figure sneered.

247

'What colour am I?' it asked.

'I would say you have a sort of bluish hue, though one can see right through your form with the sun behind it.'

'Demons are red and opaque.'

'They are? I hadn't thought.'

'That's the trouble with boys: they never think things through properly. They simply clutch at the most obvious answer. What shape are my ears?'

'Pointed, like spear tips.'

'Eyes?'

'Purple.'

'And my teeth? What colour are my teeth?'

'Yellow.'

'Ah,' muttered the creature rubbing them with the long nail of one finger, 'something I ate, most probably, but they will go back to being ivory again.'

'If indeed you are no demon,' said Walter; 'pray, what are you?'

'A jinnee – have you heard of such a thing?'

'I have heard talk of jinn in the marketplace, among the nomads. Are all jinn your colour?'

'Some of us are blue, some are green.'

'And what do you want with me?'

'I would rather think it was the other way around – I'm not the one who's lost.'

Walter was both amazed and intrigued by this strange being. He had indeed heard of jinn. It would seem that such creatures were uncommon out in desert places, but would appear before men in certain circumstances. However, he had also heard that a jinnee would only show himself to a special mortal, one already touched by magic. So far as Walter knew, he had never been near a magician or his works. Walter had led an ordinary life, full of hard work and little else. His adopter-father was a practical man, with little use for the supernatural elements of the universe. Yet here was this ugly being, talking to him, offering to help him.

'Why me? What have I done to deserve your assistance?' he asked the jinnee.

'You don't know?' cried the jinnee in surprise. 'Well, I'm astonished.'

'So what is it about me?'

The jinnee folded its arms. 'Not for me to tell you.'

'All right. But you don't mind showing me the way out of these mountains?'

'Not at all. That's what I'm here for.'

And with a rustle the jinnee flew down from the tree and landed close to Walter. Walter watched and listened as the jinnee drew a map in the sand with a twig. When the jinnee had finished he thanked the creature and asked him if he was going to accompany him further.

'No, this is my home, between that tree and that far rock.'

'Do you never move from here?'

'Oh yes, in the season of winds.'

'And where do you go?'

'Wherever I am taken.'

They parted company, with Walter feeling more cheerful than he had been for a long time. The jinnee had not only given him the path, but had injected an unfamiliar joy into his spirit. It was nothing like anything Walter had experienced before. He knew the pleasure of singing hymns, a sort of sacred happiness. He knew the felicity of making a blade that was near perfect. He knew the joy of being aware that he was loved by his adopter-father. But this was different from anything he had felt before. It was a kind of infusion, as if Walter had drunk of a cup of happiness tea which had spread to every part of his body, even into his very soul.

He was stopped by bandits that night, while travelling through a narrow pass. He flung the secret word at them and they melted away into the darkness with groans of terror. One of them even left a bag of dates behind. Walter ate these with great relish for breakfast the following day.

Finally, one happy day, he came to the gates of Jerusalem. He made his way through the throng to his father's workshop, and entered.

On seeing him again, his father went pale and dropped a pair of metal tongs, which clanged and bounced on the stone floor.

'Walter, my son, is it you?'

'Yes, Father.'

'Where have you been?'

Walter had thought about this moment ever since his release from the Assassins' fortress. A dozen excuses had been whirling around in his head. The one he favoured most was of having been enslaved by a sea captain and forced to row his ship. But now that he was faced with his father, he found he could not lie. At least, not about where he had been imprisoned.

'I was taken, Father. The Assassins took me. They carried me off to their castle.' Walter now broke down and wept, remembering all the trials he had been through. 'They cast me in a dungeon and I lived on scraps and water running down the walls.'

Pugh took him by the shoulders, one hand on each, and looked his son up and down, searching for injuries.

'Did they beat you, my son? Did they torture you? How did you escape? Why did they take you?'

'I know not why I was taken, for, in the end, they simply let me go. I fear they may have had some use for me, but for some reason that use became unnecessary. Perhaps they wanted me for a messenger, or to make a sword, I never found out.'

'But they did you no harm?'

'No real physical harm, Father, but . . .'

Pugh hugged his adopted son to him. 'Yes, yes, the mental torture must have been unbearable. To be thrown in a dungeon! Oh, my poor son. I am aware you are almost a man now, but to me you will always be a boy. I expect you thought you were going to die, that we would never see each other again. It's understandable that you should be so damaged in your head. Cry, yes, weep. Do not think it unmanly in front of your own father. He understands. No man's spirit is unassailable. To be tortured mentally is as terrible as to suffer physically. I understand.' He hugged him hard.

Walter pulled away with a feeling of guilt. He hated deceiving this kind old man, yet he could not tell the sword-maker the truth. It would kill him. Literally. For he knew his father would not let him murder on his account. He would say, 'Damn the Assassins, let them try for me', and would not let Walter go through with his undertaking.

So he told his father nothing about the task the Assassins

had given him, and hoped they never called on him to carry out the deed. After all, the man they wanted dead might die of disease or old age before his time, or be killed in war, or be struck down by another in the street. Anything could happen, given the passage of time.

'Well now, Father, I am home.' He took off his dusty tunic. 'And willing to get down to work. I have missed my place at the furnace. Look how you have neglected the bellows. Here, let me . . .' He bent his purpose to the leather bellows and soon had the heart of the fire to a searing whiteness again. 'Now, let us put this event behind us. What's for supper?'

The old man stared hard at him for a few minutes, then said, 'Red snapper fish – poached. You like that.'

'I love it, Father. I dreamed of poached fish in that horrible fortress. They had nothing there but dried goat's meat.'

'Then you shall have some lobster, too, and clams, and big prawns sent up from the Red Sea . . .'

Walter laughed, his tears drying on his face.

'Stop it, Father. You feed me too much. Look, my hands are straying towards that half-finished sword. May I continue with it? Please? I have a yearning in me to work.'

Pugh smiled. 'Go ahead, my boy. I'm going out to buy bread. I'm famished myself. I've hardly eaten since you left, I was so worried. Now you are home, my belly is sending urgent messages to my mouth. Bread, and fruit, and sweetmeats. Yes, you finish the blade.'

Once his father had gone, Walter put on the large, worn leather apron. Then he inspected the unfinished work. The making of a single sword was not a simple task. A sword was not fashioned out of just one piece of metal. First a billet of iron was cut into strips and these strips welded into a bundle. The bundle was then twisted into a spiral rod and beaten flat. Three of these rods were hammered into patterned lengths. The swordsmith then welded all three to an iron core. This long, broad length of iron he at last beat into the shape of a sword. Finally, steel strips were added to the weapon for the cutting edges before the completed blade was ground and polished.

His father had reached the part where spiralled iron rods had been flattened. Walter could already see that these strips with their leafy patterns would eventually become a handsome blade. He took up the hammer. It felt heavy and easy in his hand. A surge of creativity went through his body. This was what he loved, the creation of a thing of beauty from raw metal. There was the ring of hammer on metal as hammer met coiled iron upon the hard, flat table of the anvil.

Yes, he recalled the words of the Assassins, it was a *deadly* work of art, to be sure, but that was an aside to the craftsman. What counted with the artisan was whether the finished object was strong, well balanced, well shaped and had a pattern on the blade that caused the beholder's spirit to soar. Its eventual owner needed to be proud of the finished article and to view it as one might view a bronze statue, or a wonderful tapestry, or a painting by a genius. Swordmakers could be geniuses, too, in their given field.

The hammer struck the iron rods against the anvil with a ring that might have come from a church bell.

17. THE SAKER FALCON

Now that Andrew was squire to John of Reims, he no longer slept in the king's chapel. Instead, he was expected to room in the quarters of his master, so that he could be on call at any time. Sir John, however, was a self-contained man, who required little from his servants. He would wash himself, dress himself and take himself off to eat. He even liked to groom his own horse, a huge black beast called Samarkand, which savagely bit anyone else who tried to approach it.

Andrew was expected to look after his master's armour, keep it clean and polish those parts which needed such attention. Sir John continued to rib his squire about their respective suits of armour, asking if a lowly knight such as he could sometimes clean the armour owned by his squire. Andrew was highly embarrassed by this running joke, but this appeared only to encourage his master.

One morning in early December, Andrew rose and drank the water from the jug beside his bed. It was icy cold and hurt his throat. By the time Tomas came back from the market he was dressed and stamping around his room in the palace, the stones of which never seemed to hold any warmth. During the summer months it was pleasantly cool in that room, but as soon the winter suns arrived, the room turned surprisingly cold, the chill capable of penetrating a man's bones. There was no place for a fire so thus it remained until the summer returned.

'What have you bought, Tomas?' asked Andrew. 'I see some goose eggs. Are they still warm?'

'Hard-boiled. And bread straight from the walls of the oven. It was so hot I could hardly carry it.'

The pair set to the breakfast. Andrew ate five of the goose eggs, with Tomas looking on round-eyed.

'You will suffer for that later, Andrew.'

'Oh, you always spoil my indulgences, Tomas. It's no wonder you're an angel.'

'Well, eat some watercress as well. Green things are good for the digestion.'

'Says who?'

'All the old Greek philosophers.'

'I suppose they lived to be a hundred.'

'Some of them, though others killed themselves before they were able. I told you – Socrates?'

'You said he had to, for he was in prison.'

'True.'

'And what was the one called who lived in a barrel?'

'Diogenes.'

'Yes, I like that story where he told the king to get out of the way of the sun which was warming his skin.'

A shiver went through Andrew at the thought of the sun. How he wished it were summer again. He had forgotten how he hated the heat of the summer months.

Andrew settled down to cleaning the dried black blood from his master's armour. It was blood shed at the Battle of Montgisard and Andrew was not sure whether it belonged to Sir John, or someone Sir John had dispatched to the next life. He found it strange to think there was no difference between a Saracen's blood and the noble Christian blood of his master. At least, if there was a difference, it was not a visible one. They both started out red and both dried to a blackish consistency difficult to get out of the creases and joints of the armour. Put together, they were one and the same, which made all men alike under the skin.

He worked diligently for over two hours, with Tomas helping him, when something happened, a slow rumble from Andrew's stomach. He clutched his abdomen and looked at Tomas.

'My bowels! I think they're moving.'

'You would be very fortunate to have a movement after eating five hard-boiled goose eggs.'

'Ah, you're right, Tomas. It feels as if I have a large lump of clay in there. It simply shifted its weight, like a movement of the Earth. In fact,' he ran his hands over his belly, which was as tight as a drum, 'I fear I shall never be at stool again – not for a long time, in any event. And when I do, I expect it to be painful. Oh, why did you let me eat so many eggs, Tomas?'

'I did try to stop you, but you wouldn't listen.'

'You must *make* me listen. I think you a fool, but I'm an even bigger fool. I always am when it comes to food. Give me some of that mustard and cress. I need greens to shift things now. Yes, a whole bunch, if you please, Tomas. And another handful. Yes, yes. Why do you look at me like that?'

'Perhaps you are overdoing it in the other direction?'

'Am I, by God. You seem to be the expert on my stomach. How then do I manage it? I have eaten too much of one thing, and now too much of another. It's beginning to hurt. See how my gut has expanded? Tomas, what should I do? Is there any medicine?'

256

'For that ailment, yes, but you must not take too much of it – wait while I get my leather bag. Look, do not stray too far from a garderobe after I give you this.' Tomas was speaking of the palace lavatories. 'Here, swallow a spoonful – that's it. Now, be ready to visit the garderobe at any time in an hour or so. This is a strong mixture of hazelwort and some Eastern herb. What, now? So soon? Andrew, your body reacts to things at such an alarming pace. Are you sure . . . ?'

Andrew had already left the room at full speed. John of Reims was in the passageway as Andrew sped past him. Sir John raised a finger, but if he wanted Andrew for anything urgent he was out of luck. There was no stopping the youth. However, when the squire reached the garderobe – there was only one in this part of the palace – he found the door securely locked from the inside.

Andrew hammered on the thick wooden panelling with his fist.

'Open up! I need . . . I must come in. Open, I say.'

'I am at stool,' a voice grumbled in a low, exasperated tone, muffled by the thick door. 'By heaven, is there no peace?'

'Let me in, I say,' cried Andrew, not caring whether the king himself was inside. 'I have a great urgency.'

'Go away,' growled the voice.

Andrew became quite angry. 'There are three seats in there – are they all occupied? Are you too high-born to share the garderobe with another?'

'Not so much high-born as born different,' came the muted answer. 'Find another place to perform your ablutions.'

'What are you then, a dwarf? A cripple? Do you have twelve fingers? It matters not to me, in my condition. I must have one of the spare seats. I must, I tell you. There will be a most embarrassing accident, if not . . .'

The door suddenly flew open. Catherine of Tortosa, the lady knight, stood in the opening. Her long black hair hung loosely down past her shoulders. Her clothes were in some disarray. She wrinkled her hawk-beak nose and twisted her mouth as she stared at the squire, who was hopping about on one leg.

'Come in then, boy, if it's that bad, but I have not yet finished myself. Let's have a chat, shall we, while we are close neighbours? Why, there's barely space to run a knife between sitters, especially one with hips the size of mine. It's the goat meat that does it – I can't resist the fatty bits – but I digress – do come in, boy, join me . . .'

Andrew ran for his life. He managed to make the dry ditch running around the palace before his bowels exploded. It felt like the release of a flock of starlings. When he looked up, however, there were common men-at-arms leaning over the battlements, grinning down at him. He shook his fist at them and their expressions changed.

'Ho, it's like that, is it?' yelled one. 'Well, you come up here, boy, and I won't wave *my* fist at you, I'll let you have it full on the jaw.'

'I'm a squire . . .' began Andrew, haughtily, trying to do up his breeches.

'You're a bloody squirt, that's what you are,' cried the soldier above. 'I don't care if your father's the Sultan of Greater Mesopotamia, you don't shake your fist at me. If you were a man I'd come down there and stuff you full of stones.'

Andrew decided that humility was the best option here and

he slunk away, hoping he would not be recognised. Someone was still shouting from the battlements. It sounded like Tomas, but Andrew did not want to speak to anyone at that time, even his own personal angel. He wished to be left alone.

Andrew wandered down to the suq, feeling he wanted to be lost in the bustle of the crowds. He loved the marketplace of Jerusalem, so different from his own village market. Here there were goods that came from as far away as Tartary and India and the African south. Brass tea kettles, silk carpets, jewelled ornaments, richly coloured fabrics, ornate daggers, small, beautifully shaped bows made for horsemen (quite unlike the roughly hewn bows of England), tapestries, hookahs, ocean shells, black ebony carvings of strange figures, brown-wood carvings of elephants and fish, ivory, jade, precious stones, oh so many different and varied items as to make a young man from a small English village blink with astonishment.

He stopped and took tea in a huge tent that had been erected by the city wall. Someone, a European, was playing a lyre, while a black African picked up the rondeau on his flute. A pleasant atmosphere pervaded the whole scene. Despite the recent battle, normal trading had resumed again. Battles were many and often in this region and if life were to pause for an aftermath, it would never begin again. Beneath the surface feelings might seethe and bubble, but until there was one final battle which would settle all accounts for good, ordinary working-day life would continue.

Sipping his tea Andrew found he was looking across some tables at an Arab girl (or so she seemed to him) whose eyes were the largest he had ever beheld. Covered as she was by her clothing, only her eyes were visible in the narrow opening between the head covering and her veil. But they were the most beautiful eyes. The liquid brown of forest pools. They regarded him steadily, like the eyes of a doe about to break and run. A sudden great yearning coursed through the young man. Oh, what hidden loveliness went with those eyes. He could only guess, but he allowed his imagination full rein. This girl was, he believed, the most beautiful he had ever encountered. Of course she had to be with eyes like that. His heart was lost. His heart was as butter melting in the sun. His mind was stunned by this vision of absolute beauty. Those eyes would trouble his dreams for ever and a day . . .

He was suddenly, and quiet rudely, interrupted in his gaze and reverie by an Arab boy, who came up to him and tugged on his collar to attract his attention. Intolerable! Without so much as a by-your-leave, or excuse me! He glared at the boy, whose face was half covered by his headdress.

'Don't you recognise me?' cried the boy, now pulling aside his head covering. 'It's me, Hassan!'

Andrew's heart stopped melting immediately. A quick glance across the tables showed him the girl had gone anyway. He turned back to Hassan.

'My friend,' he said, shaking the boy's hand with enthusiasm, 'your generous gift saved my life more than once.'

'Ah, the astrolabe? I am pleased for it.'

They looked each other up and down, laughed, delighted to be together again. There is nothing quite like the friendship that comes out of first being enemies. The bond seems to go much deeper more quickly than when two people like each other from the start. Certainly these two youths were quite in tune with one another. There was a warmth that flowed in both directions. Suddenly, though, Hassan's expression changed and his face took on a pinched look.

'Were you in the battle against Lord Saladin?'

Andrew felt the closing down of the shutters.

'Yes – I fought against your hero.'

Hassan said, 'It was a great victory for Ayyub's son, the great Saladin.'

Andrew was aware that stories were now circulating, no doubt fostered by Saladin's vizier, that the Saracens had in fact won the day.

'What nonsense,' he fired back, incensed. 'He only escaped with one-tenth of his army. If he had not been riding a racing camel his head would be on our battlements now.'

Andrew recalled how proud he had been of the Templars in the battle. Knights from every European region – Nordmark, Pomerania, Poland, Italy, Bavaria, Burgundy, Austria, Carinthia, England – many more. He had seen them fight with all the fury of oath-bound warrior-monks in their white mantles with the blood-red crosses on their fronts. How could this boy now say that they had been defeated? It was a monstrous lie and one he was bound to refute.

'Saladin will never be beaten,' cried Hassan, his own temper at a great height. 'Saladin is king of all these lands.'

'Don't say that, or I will have to kill you,' cried Andrew, drawing his dagger.

'Not if I kill you first,' yelled Hassan, whipping out his wide-bladed, curved gambia. 'This is razor sharp.'

'So is mine,' shouted Andrew. 'It can split a hair.'

Around the two boys the local population were going about their business. No one was mindful of them. They had not aroused any looks with their attention-seeking behaviour. In truth, no one really cared if they killed one another. No one had the time or the energy to enquire about their dispute. They were simply two youths, one Christian, one Muslim, who were arguing over an event that was already history.

'This knife,' cried Hassan, 'was made in the city of Aleppo and is the best knife in the world.'

'This dagger is made of the finest metal money can buy in a place called Toledo in a land called Iberia.'

'Ha, Iberia is ruled by the Moors.'

'Not all of it. And they will be driven out.'

'So you say.'

'Yes, so I say.'

The youths stood simmering for a while, until finally Andrew sheathed his dagger. Hassan then did likewise with his gambia. All the fire went out of them. They became embarrassed then, looking at each other, then not looking at each other, in silent turns. Finally, Hassan spoke again.

'I have brought you another gift.'

'Oh, please don't say so,' said Andrew, feeling awkward, 'for I have nothing for you at all – not yet – though I hope to have something for you in the future.'

'Well, I have it, nearby. I caught it myself, when it was a baby, and trained it myself. Will you come with me? It is in one of the passageways.'

Despite their heated exchange of only moments earlier, though it never would have ended in bloodshed, Andrew completely trusted that no harm would come to him if he went with Hassan. He had no fear that he would be assaulted in any way. Many men would have thought, 'Ah, this boy is going to have me beaten or killed for what I said about his hero', but not Andrew. This was not foolishness on his part, for he was certain there was no deep malice in Hassan for him. The Arab boy might hate his race, his creed, but not him personally. Their understanding of each other was unique and went to the core of their spiritual beings.

'All right. Let's go.'

On the way to the alley, they passed an elderly beggar woman who asked for a coin. Hassan gave her a piece of silver. It was one of the obligations of a Muslim to treat a beggar with respect and generosity. The old woman then clutched at Andrew's robe and held him there, saying, 'I am a soothsayer. Do you wish to know your future, sir?'

'I know *my* future,' replied Andrew, 'what about you, Hassan, do you want to know yours?'

'Not mine, but that of Saladin.'

'Saladin,' said the soothsayer, 'will rule all Arabia and will drive the Infidels from the land.'

Andrew did not give it voice, but he thought, yes – you would say that, you are of the same clan.

Instead, he asked, 'But what of the Battle of Montgisard? Who won that battle, soothsayer?'

'Why, Baldwin, the leper king, of course.'

Andrew was genuinely surprised to hear the local soothsayer speak the truth about the battle. Hassan threw the old woman a black look, but Andrew told his friend, 'You can't have it both ways, Hassan. If she is telling the truth about the future, then you have to accept she is telling the truth about the past.'

Hassan took a deep breath, and sighed, before admitting,

'There is talk that the battle was lost to the Ayyubids, won by the knights you love so much. But mark what she says. Saladin will triumph in the end. You will go home, Andrew.'

'By then I shall probably be ready to go.'

They entered the alley, arm in arm, Hassan no doubt offering his in protection to his friend. There were low elements in the backstreets and passageways of Jerusalem, as in any city, and those who were known were often safer than strangers who wandered down them. Should they be accosted, Hassan was showing that they would fight together against any common foe.

Andrew was taken he knew not where, through a maze of tight alleys and winding passages, until they came to a thick, nail-studded door, which the boy simply pushed open and entered. Beyond the door was one of those hidden courtyards which astonish the visitor, with pools, a fountain, shrubbery and carved archways. Hassan greeted one or two people who happened to be in the courtyard of the house at the time, but did not explain why he had brought someone back with him.

'I must pay my respects to your mother, father and brother,' said Andrew, 'before I leave. May I?'

'Of course, but I have to show you your gift first, for it is burning my spirit away inside me.'

The boy was obviously extremely excited.

On the far side of the courtyard was a window niche covered by a curtain. Hassan went to this curtain and drew it back, to reveal a beautiful falcon in a large cage. The falcon turned its head towards the light and stared at Andrew. Andrew was assailed by the same kind of feeling he had experienced on first seeing the girl with the liquid-brown eyes.

'Oh, what a wonderful creature. Is he really mine? A gift for me?'

'Yes, Andrew. He is a saker. Do you know saker falcons? They are the best falcons in the world.'

Andrew thought about the peregrines and goshawks of England, but fortunately bit his tongue.

'I thought of you, Andrew, when I raised this bird. I knew you would like him. He is yours to keep. He will make a good hunter, they always do, saker birds. He swoops like a falling star and always brings down his prey. Come, we will go out into the desert and I will show you . . .'

Andrew had a lifetime's affinity with birds, especially birds of prey such as this one. Indeed, the barn owl had saved his life outside the wood, just before he had met the dead men. There had been other raptors which had helped Andrew as a young boy, when he was being bullied. He guessed it was something to do with his godparents, the warlock and his wife. Now, as he stared into this bird's eyes, there was an instant rapport between them. If it was not magical, it was something quite unusual, this feeling of sympathy between man and bird.

Andrew reached forward and opened the cage.

Hassan stepped forward, alarmed. 'Andrew, be careful, this is a wild creature – yes, it knows me, but . . .'

The saker went straight to Andrew's wrist, its talons gripping lightly.

Hassan was astounded. 'Now, what's this? You are a stranger to the bird. When my brother tried to handle him – well, he was badly clawed. He still bears the scars.' Andrew detected a mildly jealous note in Hassan's tone. After all, this was *his* bird, caught and trained by him, even though intended as a present for Andrew. Yet it had gone to a stranger's wrist rather than to his and seemed more comfortable there. Hassan had every right to be put out by the bird's behaviour.

'Please don't be upset, Hassan,' said Andrew. 'It's not that he prefers me to you. I had a strange birth and several things were gifted to me by the midwife, whose husband is a magician – one was to be a brother of birds of prey, like this one. If I had not been so gifted, it would not happen, but the bird is drawn to me, as I am to him. It can't help itself.'

This explanation mollified Hassan a little.

'Ah, magic. Who can resist magic? So, Andrew, what are your other magical gifts?'

'I can swim.'

'So can I – that's not magic.'

'But I can swim better than any man I know. I have webbed toes, like a duck's.'

This was said in all seriousness, but Hassan laughed out loud.

'So, my friend, you are half-duck? I knew there was something special about you. Can you waddle, too? Can you quack? Show me.'

Andrew did not rise to the bait. Instead he put the bird carefully back into its cage and asked if he might now pay his compliments to Hassan's parents and brother. Once this was done satisfactorily, the boys went out to take sport with the falcon. It was a magnificent day, for both of them. They watched the bird soaring and swooping, the wind rippling through its feathers. It was indeed a beautiful raptor. They did not send him up after any prey, although they saw a large purple heron flap off from the edge of a swamp. They were a little afraid of losing control of the saker at that point in time.

Afterwards, they went back to Hassan's house to eat.

'One thing I have to tell you,' said Andrew. 'I hope you won't be angry, but I have to leave the bird here with you, to take out when I visit.'

'Why is that?' asked his friend.

'Because Templars are not permitted hunting hawks. It's considered frivolous to own a falcon and to hunt with it. I wish to be a Knight Templar and if I owned a bird like this it might go against me if and when I have the opportunity to be considered for knighthood.'

'I would rather you did not become a Templar, for I believe them to be the very Devil's spawn.'

'Alas, we must always disagree when it comes to Templars and Saracens, for we come from different lands. We must not let such differences come between us as friends, though.'

'It's extremely difficult.'

'Yes,' replied Andrew, 'the most difficult thing in the world – but if we cannot, we must part now and never meet again.'

Hassan thought for a while about this and finally replied, 'While we can be friends, I think we should try. Perhaps some day we will fight against each other, like two brothers from the same family sometimes choose different sides. Then, perhaps, it will become impossible to remain friends. But for now, let us hold friendship higher than our differences.'

Andrew smiled and clasped Hassan's hand.

'I agree,' he said.

18.   THE PROPHECY FULFILLED

On returning to his lodgings later that day, Andrew found Tomas in a state of great agitation.

'The king wishes to see you,' said Tomas. 'I tried to call you earlier, but you rushed off into the crowd.'

Andrew was annoyed.

'He wants to make fun of me,' he said.

Tomas raised his eyebrows. 'Make fun of you? How? Why?'

'Because I asked to share a garderobe with Lady Catherine, the female knight.'

Tomas raised his eyebrows even further.

'You wanted to go relieve yourself in the presence of Lady Catherine?'

Andrew shook his head. 'I didn't *want* to, I had to. That is to say, I needed to go – badly – you will remember the medicine you gave me to shift the goose eggs? I was desperate for the garderobe. When I got there, it was occupied. I hammered on the door with my fist and someone answered, I knew not who, for the voice was muffled by the thickness of the door, and so demanded entrance. I had no idea Lady Catherine was the person behind that door. She mocked me . . . '

'As one would,' murmured Tomas, a ghost of a smile playing on his lips.

'Are you laughing at me, too?' cried Andrew. 'This is too much to bear.'

'Oh, calm yourself, Andrew. It is but a small thing and will amuse people for a while, but they will soon forget it, believe me.'

Andrew's looks darkened. 'I refuse to be mocked further, even by a king.'

'But you must go,' said Tomas, now anxious. 'The king commands it. A number of squires were called to the king and you were one of them. All the others were here and able to answer the king's bidding immediately.'

Andrew debated with himself for a while, then decided that Tomas was right. One could not ignore a summons by Baldwin. The boy king was as touchy as anyone about rank and obedience. Even a noble would think twice about ignoring such a command. One whipping was enough. His back was still scarred from Gondemar's punishment.

Andrew summoned his mental reserves and set out for the Great Hall, where the king held court.

There was feasting in progress as Andrew entered. A huge log fire warmed the back of the leper king, who was still a pasty hue despite the best physicians attending him. He saw Andrew enter the hall and with his eating knife waved him to come forward. On the king's left sat John of Reims and on his right was the eighth Master of the Temple, Odo de St Amand. Both seemed surprised at Andrew's entrance.

The atmosphere was convivial in the hall and many knights were calling to each other across the floor, simply conversing about the day's events. There was laughter from one corner which Andrew quickly realised was directed at him as he recognised one who had been peering at him over the battlements while Andrew was going about his emergency business.

The knight pointed at him and said something to his companions, all of whom turned to look and snigger at the youth's approach.

Once Andrew was in front of the king's table, King Baldwin stood up and raised a hand.

The hall went silent immediately.

'Ah-ha,' said the king, darkly, 'you deign to answer my call.'

Andrew went down on one knee. 'Forgive me, my liege, I was not here at the time, but in the marketplace . . .'

'Never mind all that, you're here now.'

'Yes, your majesty.'

Baldwin nodded.

'Gentle knights,' said the young king, turning this way and that, and now smiling, 'I have an important proclamation to make. But first, a joke . . .'

Here it comes, thought Andrew, the king's jest. Now, don't get angry, don't get upset. Take it on the chin. He sneaked a look at Lady Catherine and saw that she wore a bland expression. She seemed more interested in her neighbour, a handsome Galician knight, and was whispering in his ear.

The king began and everyone became more attentive.

'Every week, one long summer, two philosophers met for a competition, which the scholar called Primus always won. On the last week of that summer the pair were swimming across the Hellespont and Primus was, as usual, ahead of Caspian. Caspian called to his opponent, saying, "How is it, Primus, that I can never beat you at anything?" Primus replied, "Well, as you know, Caspian, I speak forty-seven different languages fluently. My secret is that I always think in the language of a people best at something. The Persians are the best at sword fighting, so when I fence I think in Persian. The Parthians ride horses better than any race on Earth, so when I race horses I always think in Parthian. And so on.

"Now, the pearl fishers of the Maldive Islands are the most supreme of swimmers, so today I am thinking in Urdu."

'Caspian acknowledged this wonderful method which Primus had developed, then added, "But Primus, Urdu is the one language you have never learned . . ."

'Primus frowned, gave Caspian a confused look of despair, and promptly sank to the bottom of the sea.'

The king ended his joke and beamed, holding up his hands to show he was waiting for a response.

The hall erupted in cheers and laughter.

'This,' said the king, when the noise had died down, 'is an illustration of the folly of arrogance.'

Andrew said thoughtfully, 'Yes, I see that, my liege – but would it not have been an even better joke if Primus had *thought* the Maldivian people spoke Urdu, but in fact they spoke some other language, like Hindu or Genoese?'

Several of the company gasped at this breach of manners. The king looked at Andrew askance and took a long time to answer him.

'But my uneducated Andrew,' said the king at last, smiling at him, 'they *do* speak Urdu in the Maldives.'

Guffaws broke out all over the hall again, men hammering the tables with their fists, probably more at Andrew's puzzled expression than anything the king had said.

When the laughter had died down again, the king once more held up a hand to show that he wanted no interruption.

271

'Andrew of Cressing,' said the king, in the voice of authority, 'do you attend me?'

It was only at this point that Andrew noticed five or six other young men standing by, looking intensely pleased with themselves, yet apparently sombre as if enjoying a great occasion in their lives. This was unusual enough to make Andrew wonder what was going on. Was it a ceremony of some kind? Was he going to be challenged by one or all of these men? Why did the king sound so stern?

'Andrew of Cressing, I asked if you were attending me?'

Andrew's attention snapped back to the king.

'Yes, my liege. Very closely.'

'Then answer this question – do you wish to be a knight of the realm?'

Andrew's heart stopped. He noticed that Odo de St Amand, standing behind the king, was frowning. Was that in disapproval?

'Yes, your majesty – more than anything in the world.'

'Then so be it. Perform your vigil in my chapel this very eve and you will be knighted come morn.'

A loud buzz went around the hall. Catherine of Tortosa clapped her hands, but there were others whose faces registered disapproval. Some were muttering to their neighbours and only ceased when the king glared round at the general gathering.

'Is there some dissent here? If so, I wish to hear it.'

There was no answer to this question. Knights looked away, embarrassed at being stared down by the boy king. Others tried to look innocent. Others genuinely did not care that Andrew would be knighted. One or two were actually pleased

272

for him. He was a popular youth and the only objection to his knighthood was probably that he was a relatively new squire. Knights, like any other group, rather resented newcomers to their ranks, especially young men in bright golden armour.

Andrew himself almost fainted with joy.

Odo was not so faint-hearted as many in the room. He had more rank, to begin with. He now leapt to his feet and turned to address the king.

'Your majesty, he is but a boy!' protested the Master of the Temple. 'Too young to be a knight, surely?'

'Master Odo de St Amand,' said the king, with quiet patience, 'I am of the same age – and yet a king.'

Odo looked suitably abashed, but muttered, 'It is different for royal personages; they are born to the monarchy.'

'This youth,' said Baldwin, 'performed on the battlefield at Montgisard as bravely and skilfully as any knight at these tables. I saw it for myself. In fact, he came to my personal assistance when three ferocious Saracens attacked me, while my personal guard was elsewhere . . .' – this was a little unfair on his bodyguard, since the king, in his enthusiasm, had broken clear of his protective ring of knights – '. . . and together we slew two of them and drove a third back to his master's side. No one showed more courage when faced by the Saracens than this youth.'

The king then turned to John of Reims. 'I hate to rob you of a squire, Sir John, but I'm sure you'll agree with me when I say that Andrew of Cressing will make an honourable and impressive knight.'

Put that way, John of Reims could hardly disagree without appearing to question the king's word.

'Without doubt, my liege. I gladly renounce my rights over the youth.'

The king looked at Andrew and smiled.

'Go then, young friend, and find the chapel within which you must commune with your God. If you find faults within yourself, you must confess them and ask for them to be absolved. Search your soul deeply, for any reason why you should not be elevated to the knighthood. I can find no error in your outward behaviour. It is most commendable. In the morning I shall send for you while the court is gathered. You also,' continued the king, speaking now to the other young men who were standing waiting, 'have proved yourselves worthy. Go to your personal vigils and know that tomorrow you shall all be knights of the realm.'

Andrew and the other chosen squires bowed low. Andrew's heart was now racing like a cheetah's after a hunt: beating so fast, in fact, that he thought it would fail him. He backed away from the king's table as if in a dream. Odo was still standing. Before Andrew reached the doorway to the hall and turned to leave, Odo's voice boomed out:

'Do not think that because our gracious and generous king has seen fit to honour you with his gift of knighthood that you will ever become a Templar!'

Andrew turned to face the hall and the Master, and then looked at the king.

King Baldwin remained silent.

Odo proclaimed grimly. 'The king is, of course, the king – but the Temple is my responsibility. If I deny you membership of the Temple then even the highest authority in the land cannot help you – though, of course,' he smiled silkily at the youthful monarch, 'I am always ready to listen to the advice of my liege lord.'

Baldwin spoke out again.

'I shall do my best to persuade this stubborn man, Andrew of Cressing,' said the king, 'but it's true he commands the Temple of Solomon, through the authority of the Pope. The Church is a bothersome estate and I wish it were under my jurisdiction. Unhappily, it's not. For mine own part, I would have nothing to do with these puritanical warrior-monks, for where would you get your fun if you became one of them? They wear the cross as if they had died on it. Ah, you look shocked, Odo, but it's true. Renunciation is your watchword. You are mean and niggardly with your own lives, your own selves. You make vows of poverty, chastity and all things cheerless – who would want to dedicate themselves to misery? Not I, for one. Think long and hard, Andrew of Cressing, before you throw in your lot with a set of savage, bloodthirsty fellows who love nothing better than hacking men to pieces in the name of God's Grace, and afterwards feeling purified of soul. There is something not quite savoury about a brotherhood of saints who are forever up to their elbows in blood.'

Andrew bowed again and left the hall.

As the doors closed behind him, the king called out jocularly, 'And I'd rather you used my garderobe next time, than pester poor Lady Catherine while she is about her private ablutions!' A roar of laughter swept around the tables, muted by the walls of the hall, but Andrew did not care.

He was walking on clouds. His spirit was soaring like a saker falcon. A knight! He was to be made a knight of the realm! This was only one of the steps towards becoming a

Templar. The Templars were like a club within a club. Once he was a knight, no one could take that from him, but the Templars were an elite group within the world of knighthood to which you had to be invited. They had their own strict set of rules quite apart from ordinary knights and, in truth, they looked down on the secular knights, those who belonged to no special order like the Templars, who wore their distinctive red crosses, or the Hospitallers, with their black eight-pointed crosses. These two groups were indeed the most exclusive clubs in the kingdom. *Any* kingdom.

So, perhaps not a Templar, but a knight of the realm nonetheless. That was golden. That was worth thrones, cities, powers. That was *almost* the peak of the mountain. A kind of holy ledge to be reached before the peak could be scaled.

He could not wait to tell Tomas, his – yes, his squire. *His* squire.

There are only a few ways to reach a state of ecstasy: Andrew had found one of the rarer paths.

19. ANGELIQUE AND THE PLAYERS

Angelique was imagining how the world would view her if Ezra had carried out his plan to bed her. She would walk into a room of her father's friends and the looks of those in there would change from gaiety to sour disapproval. She would see that the older women despised her. The younger women would look away, their faces red with embarrassment, horrified by the fact that there was a maid in their presence who had lost her virginity out of wedlock. They would regard her as being in perpetual sin, would make snide remarks about her behind her back, perhaps even to her face, and regard her as a loathsome creature not fit even to be a scullery maid. Angelique would run from the room in tears, completely distraught by her reception.

One or more of the men would follow her out, pretending a wish to comfort her in her distress, but actually regarding her as fair game now that she had been disgraced. The fact that a crime had been committed against her person would only excite them to more unwelcome advances. They would try to get her alone, tell her that they knew she wanted them, ignore any resistance as playfulness on her part, and attempt to take her again.

Much of this would occur even if Ezra married her, for he was the kind of man who would brag about his 'conquest' and thus she would be treated with contempt, even by her own servants. Many saw it as the woman's fault if she were raped. They would say she had egged Ezra on, incited him to the act. Angelique had heard of women who had been taken by force, had been thrown aside as used goods afterwards, abandoned by even their own fathers and families, and had committed suicide, convinced by others that theirs was a shame they should not live with. Without a male protector Angelique was vulnerable and Ezra knew it. Yes, Robert would kill him if he found out what was happening, and might even do so after the crime had been committed, but Ezra was an impetuous and rash lout and disregarded probable consequences.

Angelique was under no illusions: in the eyes of most of the world it would be *her* fault if she were raped by Ezra, not his.

Angelique complained bitterly to her aunt that Ezra was exceeding the bounds of propriety. She told her aunt that her son had visited her bedchamber, certainly without invitation, for what young woman would invite a man into her boudoir? Not only had he been in her room, he had entered during the night hours, like a thief.

'Oh, he probably mistook your room for his,' said her aunt, with a wave of her hand. 'After all, he is a stranger in this house. You know Ezra would never harm you.'

'I know nothing of the sort,' replied Angelique, 'and if my father were here Ezra would have got a whipping.'

Her aunt's face darkened at this remark.

'You forget yourself, child. I am your guardian while your father is away. You will listen to me when I speak and take heed of what I am saying. Ezra is my son. He tells me you continually tease him with your – your charms. If I see anything, it is that you're a hussy, young lady, and need handling.'

'I – tease – *him*? Oh, it's too much, Aunt. You go too far, both of you. You'll suffer for it when my father returns.'

'And when will that be?' cried the aunt, haughtily. 'If he returns at all. Many men die on the crusades. Thousands never return at all. You would be well advised to treat me civilly, child, for if he does not come home you will have nothing. Ezra will inherit the estates and he and I will then decide whether to let you stay or not.'

'How dare you!' cried Angelique. 'This is my home, not yours . . .'

Her speech was terminated abruptly by a stinging slap from her aunt. She turned and ran from the room before she burst into tears. It was difficult for her to know which was upper-most in her mind: her anger, or her feeling of humiliation. When she stared at herself in the mirror, there was a red weal on her cheek. Her heart was full of bitterness and for a moment she blamed her father for leaving her in the clutches of two such ugly relatives. But then she remembered her father had told her that only her aunt had been invited. Her cousin Ezra, whom her father held in contempt, had never been asked to visit or to attend any family functions.

Angelique was now properly frightened. If her cousin violated her, as she was sure he intended to do, she would be considered worthless as a wife. She would never be able to marry into her own class. She was aware, of course, what such an act entailed, but how it would affect her mentally could only be imagined. The thought of rape was revolting and terrifying, and a lump formed in her stomach when she pictured it, but she somehow knew that if it actually happened it would be a hundred times worse than she imagined.

She locked her door at night now, but, with her aunt almost sanctioning her son's behaviour, who was to say that Ezra would not force the door when he had had too much wine?

The day following her encounter with her Aunt Elspeth, Angelique was walking Minstrel in the frost-covered gardens of the house. A weak sun was causing purple-headed, hoar-sprinkled thistles to glisten like jewels. But Angelique was too depressed to appreciate the fairy-like beauty of the morning. Then the little dog started barking, yapping at some strangers who were passing on the road which led past the house.

The group of young men, for that was what they were, suddenly checked in their stride, then turned and approached the house. They entered the gate with the jaunty air of devil-may-care youths out looking for adventure. One of the gardeners tried to drive them away, using his hoe as a weapon, but Angelique called to them. There were four of them and they doffed their caps when they reached her.

'Excuse me, my lady,' said the fair-haired one who seemed to be their leader, the one with a warm, winning smile, 'are you the daughter of Sir Robert de Sonnac?'

'Yes, I am.'

His smile grew broader, though his friends looked a little nervous at his boldness.

'Forgive me, mistress, then you are Angelique, who was rescued from the River Thames by my friend Andrew.'

Angelique's heart leapt. 'You know Andrew? How is he? Is he here in England?'

'Alas, I know not, for he has gone to the crusades and we have had no word of him.'

Her disappointment was crushing. From elation to the depths of despair in thirty seconds. It was almost too much to bear. But then she rallied, seeing she was upsetting the youths who stood before her. They looked concerned and she thought perhaps she had turned pale. Indeed, she felt somewhat shaky on her legs.

'Oh, it's of no consequence,' she said. 'But Andrew's friends? You must be the players he travelled with? You must be Patrick, surely? And the big youth, Toby. And which is Arthur out of the two who are left?'

'I am,' replied Arthur, stepping forward. 'This is Peter, who has just joined our merry crew.'

Peter, a thin, reedy youth, bowed like a stalk of corn bending in the wind.

'Well, I am most pleased to meet you all, but you know my aunt will not invite you into the house. If it's food you want, I shall fetch you some from the kitchens.'

There were two men, Ezra's servants, whom Ezra had posted constantly to watch Angelique from the doorways of the house. It was their duty to report to Ezra anything untoward to do with his cousin. These men would stop Angelique leaving the garden and venturing forth along the road, should she attempt to do so. Once or twice she had tested them and they always came running after her and took her back. One of them now began to walk towards the group, no doubt to find out what these youths wanted in the house of Robert de Sonnac.

'No, no – we like to earn our bread,' replied Patrick. 'The truth is, London is not what it was. The crusades have sucked the life out of the city. We find it hard to make an honest coin. So we have taken to visiting the great houses and estates that surround the city, to give private audiences a chance to see us strut our stuff. We came to you especially, since Andrew described the house to us, wondering if you and your father would like to watch us perform *The Tragedy of Dido.*'

Angelique felt a pang of sorrow pass through her.

'My – my father is not here at present. He has gone to Jerusalem. My aunt is in charge – and I have a cousin – oh, I *would* like to see your play acting. It would brighten a dismal winter for me. I shall go and find my aunt.'

'What's this?' asked Ezra's servant, arriving. 'What do you churls want here?'

'It's all right, Carter,' said Angelique, walking away, 'I'm going to see my aunt to ask if these youths may put on a play for us.'

'Players?' cried Aunt Elspeth some minutes later, as Angelique pleaded with her. 'What nonsense!'

But just at that moment Ezra entered the room with a fowling bow over one shoulder and a brace of pheasants in the other hand. He was dressed for fowling in breeches and boots, and a leathern jerkin. His face was pinched with the cold, but, instead of heading for the fire, he went straight to his mother.

'Players? What's this?'

'Oh, Ezra,' said Angelique, placing her fingertips lightly on her cousin's arm, 'there are some strolling actors at the door, wishing to give us a private performance of *The Tragedy of Dido.* Wouldn't you like to see them?'

Ezra, like a great many young men, enjoyed anything theatrical in a world of mundane pleasures.

'It sounds an excellent scheme,' he cried. 'A play? By heavens, it's a long time since we had anything jolly around here, with you, Angelique, looking like a wounded hind most of the time, and you, Mother, with all your housekeeping, making sure the servants are at their work and that old goat of a steward at the management of the property. Why, it would give us all some relief from the tedium.' He leered at Angelique. 'It is a romance, is it not? This play?'

She knew what Ezra was thinking: that watching a play might loosen her morals. Many young women might be carried away by the heady excitement of watching a romantic drama performed in front of them. There was so little in the way of entertainment for girls of Angelique's age that anything, anything at all, was something quite wonderful. Afterwards she might be tempted to exceed the bounds of proper conduct. No doubt this was foremost in Ezra's mind.

'Do they play anything?' asked Ezra. 'I like to hear the lute played well.'

'I did notice one of them had such a musical instrument, Ezra.' Her fingers were still on his arm. 'I too like to hear music – love songs, especially.'

'Mother,' said Ezra, firmly, 'you must allow it. Please?'

Elspeth's face twisted into something which could loosely be interpreted as a smile.

'Oh, my son, you know I can never deny you anything. Of course we shall have the play. We'll tell the players they can stay in the kitchen until we have supped, then join us afterwards. They'll have to walk back to London in darkness, of course, but I'm sure they're used to such exercise. Now, Ezra, you smell dreadfully of killing things. Go and bathe, and dress. Get rid of that horrible leather thing you wear and take that hunting weapon out of my chambers . . .'

Your chambers? thought Angelique. This is my father's house! But she said nothing, for a plan was forming in her mind. It was a dangerous plan, a frail plan, but it just might work with the help of the players.

'I shall tell them they can stay,' said Angelique, gaily, and left the room with Minstrel padding along at her heels before she could be stopped by her aunt, who would think it unbecoming of a young girl to speak with male strangers. Later she would no doubt take Angelique to task for her behaviour, but by then it would be too late.

Angelique found the youths and spoke with them at length. The new player, Peter, was frightened by her plan. He said it would never work. He, for one, could not do what she wanted. Since Peter had a large part to play in it, this was something of a setback for Angelique. However, Toby stepped forward and offered to play the part instead of Peter.

'I don't mind,' said the amiable youth, 'for Andrew's sake.'

Patrick said to Angelique, 'You realise what you're asking?'

'I know,' said Angelique. 'It's highly dangerous. You'll be branded as criminals. They will hunt you in this part of England and you'll have to leave for foreign places.'

'Scotland, possibly. Or Ireland. Even the West Country would be too near. It's a great deal to ask of us. A great deal. Andrew was a friend, but even he would think we were being foolish if we went through with this plan of yours. If we're caught, we'll be imprisoned – probably executed.'

'It is a lot to ask but . . .' She explained Ezra's behaviour.

'If I do not rid myself of him, I will surely end in circumstances that will destroy me.'

'But what do we get out of it?' asked Arthur. 'I mean, I
sympathise with this lady, but we'll be risking all for nothing.'

'Not for nothing,' said Toby, 'for honour, Arthur.'

'And what is honour to me? I'm not a knight. I'm a boy
from the house of a serf. I don't want to work in the fields,
so I travel the roads and take my chances there. But honour?
You can't eat honour, you can't drink it, and it doesn't shelter
you from the rain, or give you a warm bed. No, no, I can't
do this, fellows. You'll have to do it without me.'

'And without me,' added Peter.

'I shall give you money,' said Angelique, quickly. 'Enough
to get you to Ireland and to live for at least two years there
in comfort. Please say yes. My aunt will come looking for me
soon and I must not be caught in a deep discussion with you
– she will suspect there is some sort of plot against her.'

'Which there is,' said Peter, 'and against her son.'

'How much money?' asked Arthur. 'Enough for all four of
us to do the things you mentioned.'

'More if I can get it. At least that much.'

He gave a great heave of breath and said, 'All right – I'll
do it. Patrick?'

'Yes – I've always wanted to go to the Emerald Isle.'

'Not me,' muttered Peter. 'I'm leaving now.'

Toby gripped the youth by the arm.

'You're staying,' he said, through gritted teeth, 'or I break
your head with the nearest rock.'

Toby was big enough to be obeyed, given that he looked
determined to carry out his threat.

'But I don't want to.'

'You're going to. Settle to that. Any more arguments and I'll knock you down now. This lady is in need of our help. She is troubled beyond anything and she is Andrew's friend. We are going to do the deed, Peter.'

Peter went into a sulk.

Patrick said, 'Off you go then, mistress. It is a most heinous crime, but we'll do it. God have mercy on us and give us the fortune to carry it through.'

'One last thing,' she said. 'Can you tumble? Any of you? If my cousin should think of changing his mind, it would be good if I could offer him some acrobats.'

'Yes,' replied Arthur, 'at least, Patrick and I are accomplished tumblers. Toby is learning fast. It's what we fall back on if the play is going badly. And, of course, there's always room for a few somersaults, cartwheels and leapfrogs in a comedy. Yes, we can put on a good show.'

'Good!'

Angelique left them and went to her chambers. Her heart was beating in her breast like that of a deer on hearing the hunting horn. She went to a chest in the corner of the room and unlocked it with a key. Then she took out some clothes and laid them on her bed. Once that was done she went looking for her father's frail and elderly steward. She found him at the rear of the house and told him that she wanted money. A great deal of it. When he asked what for, she told him she could not tell him.

'It is to protect my honour as a maid,' she said, 'and you know my father would approve of such a thing.'

'There are things going on in this house,' he said, his thin, gnarled fingers forming a fist, 'which would make the master angry enough to kill. But I am a miserable man now, in my eightieth year, and I do not have the strength or fortitude to resist the evil that stalks my master's dwelling.'

'I know – but your duty is to assist me in protecting myself – they will not harm you afterwards, for how will they ever know you gave me money?'

The steward rose, awkwardly, and hobbled to a cask, from which he removed a purse. He handed it to Angelique.

'I care not whether they harm me, or do not harm me, for I have only a summer or two left in my pocket. What does it matter if they take me from this world tonight? I am due to leave in the morning anyway. Here, child, do whatever it is that you want to do, and tell my master it was out of love.'

She hugged him, saying, 'Oh, you are such a man – *such* a man. There's courage all around me today.'

A thin, wintry smile came to his lips and a dim light to his rheumy eyes.

'I would do it all again for another of those hugs – I would, indeed, even if I was burned at the stake for it afterwards.'

She left him then and went to dine with her cousin and aunt.

Her aunt was as frosty as ever during the meal, but her cousin Ezra was full of light-hearted chatter. She looked at him once or twice during the meal, but she was careful not to overdo it in case he suspected something was amiss. Just enough to get him wondering whether he was at last breaking down some barriers. After all, entertainment was a thing all women enjoyed, he knew that. He had seen many ladies flirting even with their husbands in order to be taken to some place where there would be minstrels, or dancing, or tumblers, or players. Women loved occasions to dress up and show off their charms, while enjoying being entertained.

Angelique managed to see the players once more, before the evening performance. They quickly went over her plan, improved upon it a little. Patrick added one thing – a trick he used in some plays – which would help their escape. This addition met with the full approval of Angelique, who knew some things about Ezra which fitted with it.

'Ezra is afraid of unnatural things,' said Angelique. 'I have seen him start out of his skin at a mere owl's hoot. He'll not follow us in the dark. He is afraid of the dark.'

The plan was complicated, but Patrick decided that if it did go wrong they would fight their way out. As did all youths, they carried daggers, which they could use with some skill. One thing was certain, said Toby: they could not leave Angelique in the hands of her devious cousin. Ezra was the sort of man who might chastise himself the morning after an evening's wickedness, but, once the drink took hold that evening, he would repeat his depravities again and again.

Angelique closed her eyes and tried to imagine that Andrew was listening to her.

'If you can hear me, Andrew of Cressing, my saviour and my friend, please pray for me and help me if you can.'

A petition that did not reach the ears of the youth for whom it was intended, but when the boy's name went out on the wind, it found the ears of others who knew him.

The hall was lit with candles when Angelique came down in a full, pure-white dress. Ezra was speaking with Patrick, who was tugging his forelock and saying, 'We must use this door as our stage door, if you please, your worship . . .'

'Just call me sire. Yes, that will be fine,' Ezra's eyes were locked on Angelique as she floated past him, 'but be sure the door to the passageway behind is closed, or the candles will be snuffed out by the draught and leave us in darkness.'

'Yes, sire, the mistress did mention that.'

'Good, good. Well, my mother and cousin are in their places – be good enough to begin the play.'

The players began to strut the stage, which was merely a floor space in front of the fire. The audience settled down to watch the performance. Ezra was drinking mead from a goblet at first, but soon discarded the vessel and drank straight from the jug. 'Oh, Aeneas, my hero,' trilled Toby in a falsetto voice, 'how I do love thee . . .'

Ezra leaned over and placed his mouth against Angelique's ear, leaving it wet with the tip of his nose and his lips. 'Don't you think they would have been better using the skinny boy for the female, rather than that big oaf?' he whispered hoarsely, slurring his speech slightly.

Angelique did not shy away from her cousin on this occasion.

'Oh, perhaps the thin youth has not the voice for a lady?'

'Methinks the big one does not, either – but are you comfortable, my sweet?'

Ezra surreptitiously gripped her thigh with his large hand and squeezed it through the layers of fabric. His mother was sitting on the far side of him, so was unable to see this movement. In any event, she was staring straight ahead, her hatchet face catching the light from the candles and revealing all the cruel lines in it. On the stage, the players were going through their script with all the enthusiasm of those undertaking a large public performance. Angelique was a little afraid they had forgotten the main object of the evening's show, and her head was full of all the things that could go wrong with the plan, leaving tragedy in its wake.

'I'm quite comfortable, thank you.'

She left Ezra's hand where it was on her thigh and waited patiently for the one line in the play which was the trigger for quick action on her part. She knew that Ezra's two henchmen were posted outside, one at the back door, one at the front. It was going to be a tricky exit for all of them, but she knew that players were always ready with their fast changes. It was what they did; it was their profession. They were so swift at such things that they bemused the audience, catching it unawares. Some players were so good at illusion they were in danger of being regarded as magicians and were burned for their talent.

Towards the end of the play Peter played a love song on his lute, during which Angelique let out one or two false sighs. She noticed that there were actually tears in Ezra's eyes during this musical performance, and she was astonished. How could such an oaf as her cousin be moved by a sugary love song? It was pure mawkishness and she felt that it hardened the strength of his villainy, rather than softened it.

In the final scene Aeneas was sitting on a stool, delivering a soliloquy in the cabin of his ship as he sailed away from Carthage.

'I must leave the lovely Dido on the shore, for I love her not now the wind has changed —' his voice suddenly rose to a thin shriek as he half stood from his seat, '– but oh, oh, ye gods of Olympus, what evil thing is this that enters this dark place? Oh, how he stares at me so dreadfully, like the horrific fiend he is, the gods help me . . . am I doomed to treat him as brother, this *thing*?'

Aeneas cried in such sinister tones that even the hairs on Angelique's neck stood on end. Watching, in the candlelight, in the firelight, one might have believed that Patrick had indeed seen something dreadful in the half-darkness. His eyes were starting from his head. He looked absolutely terrified as he froze on his stool and his breath came out in gasps.

Alarmed, Ezra gripped Angelique's leg harder and stiffened in his seat.

'What has he seen?' he hissed. 'What is it?'

At that moment someone threw open the door to the outer passageway which extinguished all the candles in the room. Only the firelight now illuminated the hall. Aeneas spun round on his stool and Satan appeared for a few moments, grinning and demonic. It was long enough for the foul creature to cast an evil stare over the audience. Then Aeneas came back, very briefly, his face wearing a terrified expression.

Then, spinning back into view, the red-horned, goat-eyed Devil reappeared. This time he had a hideous winged imp on his head like a demonic hat. With a leer the ghastly imp took off and flew across the room like a hawk. It went straight for Ezra's face, and clung to his lips for a moment with its claws. Ezra screamed and knocked the creature off with his hands. He then tried to stamp it into the ground. Angelique looked down and saw nothing there. Nothing at all.

It all happened with blurring swiftness. The light from the

flickering fire warped the shapes of ordinary objects which then appeared to move. When the flames danced, so did the shadows. Some things were there and some were not. Everything seemed delicate and flimsy and quite unreal. The minds of the audience jumped this way and that, trying to find a footing in this insubstantial atmosphere. Fear of the grotesque and unnatural coursed through Ezra and his mother like a foul wind sweeping from a deep, dark kingdom.

Aunt Elspeth stood up, shrieking, then thrust a bony fist into her mouth to stop her fear from spilling over into madness.

Ezra thrashed his arms about him as if fighting off invisible demons.

Angelique leapt from her seat and ran for the stage door, into the passageway where the players were waiting. She swiftly removed her dress in the darkness. Underneath she wore her boy's clothes, those she had worn to fool Andrew when she had wanted to watch him without him knowing it was her. She rammed a velvet cap on her head and stuffed her curls beneath its brim. Four players then walked swiftly to the outer door, where the servant Carter was looking confused.

'What was that yell?' he asked in the dimness of the exit. 'I heard cries.'

His eyes ran over the group of players, seeing only four young men in the half-light.

'Oh,' said Patrick, airily, 'that was the finale of the play – most exciting – packed with high drama, my friend – but did you not hear the applause that followed?'

The four youths then swept past the servant and into the garden. Once out of his sight they broke into a run. There was no moon, but the stars were out and gave them enough light to make good their escape. At the crossroads, they paused, waiting for the fifth member of their party.

Back at the house, there was, naturally enough, some disorder. In the flickering light provided by the hall fire Ezra had seen Angelique's white dress disappearing up the stairway. It took him some little while to recover his wits. He had been thoroughly frightened by the last scene in the play. He began to suspect witchcraft. No doubt, he thought, Angelique had also been scared out of her mind. This was an opportunity. This was the time to strike. He would go to her and comfort her in her bed. Although he himself was still shaken by the experience he could not let this moment pass by.

Ezra quickly took his mother and left her in the hands of her maid-companion. Then he followed Angelique up to her chambers. As he took the stairs he made a vow to have the players flogged, at the very least, when he caught them. Angelique was his first priority, though. The drink had stirred his lust and, though the night's experience had rattled him somewhat, there was still a burning fire in his loins.

He opened the door to Angelique's chamber, saying, 'Do not be frightened, my sweet – I'm here to hold you. . .'

'Are you, by God,' said the gruff voice of the large figure in a white muslin dress, 'well this ought to hold *you*.'

A fist struck him hard on the temple before glancing away.

Ezra was stunned but not down and out. He yelled, 'Help ho, here – in the mistress's bedroom.'

Toby hit him again and this time the villain's knees buckled and he folded to the floor. Then the door was flung open and two of Ezra's men came into the room, both burly fellows with wide shoulders and thick fists. They set upon Toby, beating him at first, then dragging him to the floor, holding him down. It was now Toby who yelled for help, calling for his friends to come to his aid. It seemed an age as Toby struggled with his assailants, trying to get free. One of them was shouting at him, 'Oh, want to escape, do we? Well, take this for your trouble and keep still, damn you.' A fist slammed into his ribs and caused him to groan.

Behind the men the window was already open, ready for Toby's escape. Through this opening came the figures of Patrick and Arthur. They virtually flew into the room out of the night like bats in human form. Patrick pressed a knife to the neck of the man who held Toby's arm, pricking it threateningly.

'Leave him be, or I stab you!' cried Patrick. 'Get up. Now!'

The man did as he was told, his hands held up in the air in supplication. This freed one of Toby's arms. Toby struck out at the jaw of the other man, feeling it crunch beneath his knuckles. This second manservant was not about to give up, however, and rolled away, knocking Arthur from his feet in the process. He grabbed Arthur and threatened to strangle him if the others did not give up the fight.

'Put down your knife,' yelled the man. 'Stand aside from my master.'

Ezra was coming to now, moaning into the floorboards.

Arthur, up on tiptoe and almost off his feet as the man strangling him lifted his whole body weight off the floor, kicked backwards in his fright. A man whose air supply has been staunched often panics and lashes out blindly in this way. Arthur's heel caught his assailant on the shin. The man screamed in pain and Arthur was able to rip himself away from the deadly grip. Arthur picked up a heavy stool then and struck his opponent on the top of his head with it. The man's eyes rolled and he dropped like lead to the floor with a loud thump.

'Don't move,' said Patrick to the man on the end of his dagger, 'or I *will* use this knife. Now, do you want us to knock you senseless, too, or will you lie down and be bound?'

The man agreed to be tied up. The players had just finished binding the two servants when their master staggered to his feet. Toby said, 'I'll deal with this', and once more administered a blow which left Ezra without consciousness.

Toby quickly shucked off the white dress and stared down at the inert body of Angelique's cousin.

'Sleep well, foul libertine, for the morn will bring sorrow to your breast.'

With that quote from some play or another, all three players left the house by the window, dropping twenty feet into the garden below. They were well used to jumping from the high windows of inns when they had no money to pay for their night's lodgings. They knew how to take such a fall and rolled with the impact. Sustaining no injuries, they stole away across the lawns and vegetable plots and then hurried along the dirt road to where the other two were waiting for them.

'Are you all right?' cried Angelique. 'What happened?'

'A little bit of trouble, but we managed it,' Patrick replied. 'Come on, we must get moving now. Put some miles in while it's still dark.'

Toby rubbed his bruises, but he smiled. 'Ireland, is it?'

'Change of plan,' said Patrick. 'Better to head for the nearest port, which is Dover. Have we enough money to get to France, mistress?'

'Enough and more,' replied Angelique. 'Come, boys, let's be on our way. We need to purchase a waggon, then take the lesser used lanes to the coast.'

'I don't like it,' whined Peter. 'I really don't like it. I never wanted to be part of this. If he catches us, you'll tell him that, won't you? I don't want to hang. He's sure to accuse us of abducting this girl. The daughter of a lord? And to strike the master of the house? Why, we'll be executed for certain. You will tell them it was not my fault, won't you?'

'Have no fear, trembling one,' replied Patrick, striding out, 'we'll say you are deaf and blind and know nothing of the night's events. They'll believe us, after tonight's performance, for anyone would accept that you are thus afflicted after watching your acting this past evening . . .'

The others laughed seeing Patrick's back, which was an image of the Devil. His costume from the front was that of a Trojan hero, but the back half was a diabolical creature the mask of which covered the back of Patrick's head. He had carefully faced the audience for the last scene of the play. Then, when the time came for it, he had spun on his stool. In an instant he was the Devil. To the audience it would seem as if he had been transformed. He could switch from Aeneas to Satan in a flash. It was a simple trick, but an effective one.

The firelight had given the final touch to the scene.

'How clever of you, Patrick,' said Angelique, 'but your best trick was the imp you wore like a hat.'

Patrick frowned. 'Hat? Imp? I wore no hat.'

'The imp that flew as a falcon into my cousin's face,' she said. Then she laughed on seeing his puzzled expression, nodding sagely. 'Oh, I see, it's a stage secret, is it? No, no, you need not tell me how it was done. I respect your artistic code.'

'You're talking to me in riddles, mistress,' he said, but the subject could not be pursued, for they had to be on the road and had no time for discussing such things.

They made for London, knowing they could hire fast horses and waggon there. They needed to walk quickly because of the bitter cold. There was a freezing wind coming from the north and it was the dead of winter. If one stood for too long one would fall into a deep chill. They constantly flapped their arms around their bodies, therefore, trying to beat off the shivers that reached right down into the marrow of their bones.

20. THE AFTERMATH

Ezra woke with an agonising headache sometime in the middle of the night. He splashed water on his face and went to look for his servants. They had all gone to bed, but he roused them and questioned them. Ezra now realised what had happened. He began venting his fury on the servants, hitting them with kitchen utensils. Then, when they were down on the floor, he kicked them savagely until they begged for mercy.

Minstrel, the spaniel, came to investigate the noise, probably hoping to find its mistress. Ezra broke the dog's neck with the heel of his boot. A sharp yelp and the little creature was dead.

'That'll do, for a start,' said Ezra.

Then something occurred to him and he went looking for the elderly steward. Ezra found the old man in his bed and wrenched him out. He shook the steward violently, making his head jerk backwards and forwards. A set of wooden teeth was knocked from the bedside table. Ezra furiously stamped them into matchwood under the steward's eyes.

'It was you, wasn't it? You threw open the passageway door so that the candles would go out!'

'Sire, I . . .'

'Wrong answer,' screamed Ezra, shaking the steward again until his elderly head whipped back and forth on his scrawny neck. 'You aided the abduction of your master's daughter.'

'No, sire, I . . .'

'Shut up! Shut up!' Ezra made a decision. He said calmly, 'You are dismissed. Leave the house.'

The trembling eighty-year-old steward, dressed only in a thin nightshirt, looked utterly bewildered.

'Sire, I have been here since a boy. All my life. The master would never allow such a thing.'

'The master is not here,' Ezra replied. 'I am the master until he returns. You have committed a crime, a heinous, serious crime. I should hang you, but because of your good service over the years I shall let you go. Leave the house instantly. Take nothing with you. Go, now, at once. *Go.*'

The steward found himself being frog-marched to the outer door and pushed roughly out on to the path. Overhead the stars twinkled, piercing the blackness with their thin lights. The old man looked back at the house, his brain still somewhat befuddled. He thought about going to the stables and sleeping with the horses, but knew that when he was found he would only be sent away again. In the daylight that would be a great humiliation, for all the house servants, and those in the stables and fields, would see the high-toned steward brought down to below their level and cast out in just his nightshirt. They would laugh at him, if not outwardly, inside. He could not bear it. Better to leave in the night, while the darkness smothered his shame.

He began walking towards London, the cold flints cutting into his bare feet, turning them red and raw.

The following morning, as soon as it was light, Ezra had his horse saddled. His two men, also on fast mounts, would accompany him. Carter asked if he should bring his hunting bow, but Ezra told him no.

'When I kill each of them, I want to do it so that I can feel their dying breath on my cheek,' said Ezra. 'An arrow from a distance won't do it for me. I need to see their expressions. I want the wench to watch them die one by one.'

Ezra was more concerned about the direction they might take. Surely they would not go south? That was a journey fraught with danger for runaways. There were more castles and keeps in the south than in the east. And westwards would stretch their journey to one or two days, even more. It seemed likely that they would travel east. Just in case, he sent three men south and two men west, with instructions to capture the players alive and bring them back to London.

His mother was of the same opinion with regard to the direction they would travel.

'They will go towards the east coast,' his mother said, 'perhaps south of the river, perhaps on the north side.'

Ezra chose to go towards Dover on the south bank of the Thames estuary. He chose it because it was the easiest route for the runaways. He felt sure they would be in a panic and would want to get to the coast quickly. There was, of course, the possibility that they might have gone north and were not intending to leave the country. However, he did not think they would have the courage to remain in England, knowing he would not rest until he found them. Angelique would be sure to persuade them to cross the Channel. Her father was on the other side and she would want to meet up with him.

Ezra was only mildly concerned by what Angelique would say to her father, if she managed to find him. She would, of course, accuse Ezra of several crimes regarding her person. But his saving grace was that he had not actually touched her. She may have felt threatened – indeed, it would be strange if she had not – but, so far as Sir Robert was concerned, Ezra could accuse Angelique of having too wild an imagination. His mother would certainly reinforce that view. Angelique had imagined it all, or fabricated it in the hope that her father would return home that much sooner.

Sir Robert would be told that Ezra had been suspicious of the four players the instant he set eyes on them. 'They appeared to be wayward youths, Sir Robert,' he would say, 'but since Angelique was so unhappy my mother and I thought they might drive away her blue devils.'

Ezra had not sent them away because Angelique had protested that they were honest players simply trying to earn their bread. In the event, they had abducted her. It mattered not that Angelique went willingly. They were grown men and were responsible for the welfare of the daughter of a lord. They should have refused to listen to Angelique and informed Elspeth of her plans. The fault, the blame, always lay with the man, for a girl was a weak vessel and easily led.

Ezra rode out with his two servants, satisfied with the story he would tell his uncle.

Four miles out from the house, the three riders came across the frozen body of the steward, who had no doubt walked until he dropped. He had obviously died of the cold, lying on his back looking up at the distant stars. Ezra rode past the corpse without even looking down into the man's misty eyes. He had seen dead old men before now, vagabonds and vagrants, mouths wide open and decorating the roadside with their remains, sometimes clogging important drainage ditches. This one, with his nightshirt up under his armpits and showing his naked torso, was as worthless as the rest of them. Ezra believed pity should be reserved for one's horses and favourite hounds only. Pity was a rare commodity.

It took all day with a change of horses to reach Dover. When he could, Ezra described the five escapees to tavern keepers and villagers. Everyone shook their heads. They had not seen any group of young people matching his description. Finally, Ezra realised he had taken the wrong road. He cursed and took lodgings for the night, before setting out with his men the following morning, to the nearest ferry point across the Thames. When he did get across he headed for Leigh, the small port on the northern bank of the Thames estuary.

On the way to Leigh, Ezra had more luck. He was now receiving nods to his questions and pointing fingers. It was a race against time. The harbour at Leigh did not have any large ships due to the shallowness of the water at low tide. The tide there went out a long way, leaving on rays of water for boats with shallow draughts to get in and out. The rest was mud for over a mile. When Ezra reached the clifftops the tide was half out, flowing swiftly over the mudbanks.

'Hold the horses!' he ordered his men.

He strode to the edge of the cliff and looked down. At first the winter sun on the water blinded him like a shining sheet of silver. He shaded his eyes, surveying the river. Finally he saw them, in a black skiff, heading out along a ray. They were too far from the shore to reach now. There were only four of them, though, staring back up at him from the deckless craft. Four? Where was the fifth? Ezra surveyed the cliffs and there, yes, there stood the thin youth, the boy who had played the lute. Badly, as Ezra recalled correctly. The whelp was also standing, watching the same craft make its way eastwards, down towards the mouth of the river.

'Got away,' snarled Ezra, slapping his knee with his cap. 'Damn my eyes and liver.'

Only now did he regret that he had told Carter to leave the bow back at the house.

But there was nothing for it. He could not go chasing them in a similar boat. Even if he caught up with them, which was highly unlikely, what could he do? They would surely defend themselves and boarding such a small craft would be almost impossible. Besides, Ezra did not like being on the water. He could not swim and he was usually ill. All he could hope for was that they came to a fearsome end, out there on the sea, or perhaps when they landed in France? There were many dangers in foreign lands. He hoped they would die.

'Now, my young lute player,' he muttered to himself, making his way along the cliff to where the willowy youth stood. 'Let's show them what they can expect if they ever return to these shores.'

'Oh – oh,' cried the lute player, as Ezra approached. He held his hands out, palms up. 'Truly sire, I had nothing to do with this. They made me. I said you would be angry. I told them it was a bad thing to do. But they would not listen.'

Ezra smiled at the boy. 'What's your name?'

'Peter, sire. I'm truly sorry they were so – that they flagrantly disobeyed you.'

'I was actually struck,' said Ezra, looking aggrieved and pointing to his chin, 'here, on the jaw.'

'Monstrous,' Peter exclaimed. 'It was that Toby who did it – he was boasting about it to everyone.'

'Was he, by God?'

'Yes, sire – I took him to task for it, you can be sure,' said Peter, earnestly. 'I told him it was nothing to boast about. It was surely a hanging offence to strike a lord. I'm right, aren't I, sire? He could be brought to the gallows for such a crime.'

'He could indeed, Peter. You did well to warn him. I appreciate that. Are they looking? Can they see us standing here, do you think? The tide is taking them swiftly away, but they can't be more than a hundred metres from the shore.'

'Well, sire, I see them clearly, so they must be able to see us just as well.'

'Indeed, I would say so too. Wave to them, Peter.'

Peter frowned. 'What?'

'Give them a little wave, adieu. After all, they may never return. They may meet some ghastly end in a foreign land.'

'Surely, sire, they deserve to?'

'Indeed, but let's not be churlish – let's give them a signal that we do not wish them so great a harm.'

Peter still seemed unsure, but he lifted his arm and waved to the four in the skiff. One of them waved back.

'Who was that?'

'Arthur, I think – he was my friend.'

'Is his eyesight good?'

'Very good, I think, sire.'

'Excellent, then he'll see this . . .'

Ezra had taken out his dagger without Peter noticing and now he drove it through the back of the boy's neck. The blade came out of Peter's mouth, red with blood. The boy gagged, choking on his own blood. Then Ezra withdrew the blade and gave Peter a little push. Peter went spinning

304

somersaulting, over the cliff edge to fall to the harbour below. The body struck a mast which snapped with the weight. Both mast and corpse landed on the deck of a fishing smack, narrowly missing a sailor who was mending his nets.

'Farewell, young actor,' murmured Ezra, waving to those on the deck of the skiff. 'You played your part well.'

Then he turned and walked back to where his men were holding the mounts.

On the skiff, the little group was stunned.

'He threw Peter over the cliff,' cried Arthur. 'Peter was the only one who refused to go along with the plan.'

Patrick said, 'Ezra's sending us a message. If he will do that to Peter, an innocent, what will he do to the guilty ones?'

Angelique asked, 'Why did Peter stick out his tongue at us, before he fell?'

Toby grimaced. 'That wasn't his tongue. Did you not see the flash of the blade?'

'Oh,' cried Angelique, and was promptly sick over the side of the boat.

'What's to do?' said the captain of the skiff. 'Are we to France, or no?'

'Yes, to France,' Patrick ordered. 'The sooner we get there, the better.'

Everyone settled down in the skiff in gloomy silence. When they left the estuary and hit the Channel, every member of the group was seasick. There was no storm but the sea was choppy and the boat quite small. It had a captain and one crew member. The two men were good sailors, of course, but the passengers spent much of their time hanging over the gunwales, feeding the fishes. When they hit a squall, much further out, all four young people believed they were going to die.

The squall threw them off course and the small craft was blown southwards, down into the Bay of Biscay, not a stretch of water which men love. It seemed they would end up in northern Iberia if the wind did not turn. Indeed, it was two nights before they sighted land again. The captain was sure it was the coastline of the Kingdom of Navarre. He had no notion of landing there and made an effort to sail the craft northwards again. They made little headway and found themselves being swept westwards along the coast.

'We shall make a landfall in Galicia,' he told the group. 'The Moors have not reached so far north. We shall be safe there, I hope, though I have heard it is a country of witches and wolf-men, and other such creatures. So long as you're not afraid of strange beings and dark magic, Galicia will be a good place to start your journey. Get you ready to assist . . .'

While he was explaining what he wanted them to do, another craft approached remarkably swiftly from the southwest. It seemed to be heading directly for them. Patrick saw it first and pointed.

'What boat is that?' he asked. 'Who are they?'

The vessel was crammed with men in strange, baggy clothes: billowing pantaloons and loose coats. Colourful scarves were wrapped around their heads. They were dark of face and some had swords in their clenched teeth, while hanging on to the rigging with both hands. They looked a wild-eyed mob of men and their captain seemed intent on ramming the skiff. It bore down on the English vessel with great speed and was indeed a much sleeker and swifter craft than the small skiff.

'Christ save us,' cried the captain of the skiff in despair. 'Corsairs.'

'Corsairs?' asked Angelique. 'What are they?'

'Barbary pirates. We are lost.'

'Can we not try to outrun them?' yelled Patrick. 'Quick, man, we'll help with more sail.'

'Outrun a xebec?' said the captain, in a defeatist tone. 'There's no hope of that.'

Within the next few minutes the pirates were upon them and had taken the craft. There was no fighting. The Corsairs did not want dead men, they wanted live ones, for the slave markets in Algeria and Morocco. The crew and passengers of the skiff were bundled aboard the xebec. The pirates then took axes and hacked through the hull to sink the skiff. They then set sail for open waters. The captives were put in chains. They huddled together in the centre of the craft. Angelique, still dressed as a boy, was treated in the same manner as the others. No one guessed she was of a different sex.

Angelique felt sick and wretched. She had escaped the clutches of her vile cousin, only to find herself in worse straits. If ever these pirates found out her secret, she was lost forever. She wept a little, as did Arthur, suffering the jeers of the pirate crew, who simply taunted the four captives. Then she tried to rally her spirits, but that was difficult. She could not shake off the feeling that her life was at an end and she would never see her dear father again. Had she been stupid in leaving the house? No, she could not think that. If her cousin had violated her, as he clearly intended to do, she would have been lost then, too. At least for the time being she could hold up her head and feel she was as good as any other woman on Earth.

The mournful group was carried south and later entered the Mediterranean. However, instead of heading towards Africa and the slave markets of Morocco, the captain of the xebec, a huge man with a bushy copper beard and a massive turban on his head, sailed the craft to the Kingdom of Granada, where the Moors held sway. The pirates first sold the captain and the mate of the skiff to a passing trader vessel that wanted experienced seamen for a long voyage to the top of the world.

One of the pirates then spoke to the players in halting Norman French, telling them there was a sultan who would pay a good price for slaves to build his new palace.

'My master take you to place call Salobrena – they build big palace there. You build for the sultan. He make you build for him.' The pirate had remarkably large white teeth which he bared often when smiling at the captives. 'You will not like. No, no. You make a hurt back with the stones to carry. If you not carry, they whip you. They whip you anyways, if you carry or not, eh? You like breads? I get you some breads. Here, you drink this waters. Good for you. You like me, eh? I good to you. My name Messaoud.'

In fact, Messaoud was the only pirate who even bothered to acknowledge their existence. All the others ignored them completely. Just before they came to the harbour, where they were to land, the captain of the xebec put on a magnificent red robe, covered in a pattern of gold crescent moons and suns, and greased his beard, and put on a fresh blue turban.

Around his waist he wore a scarlet sash through which he slipped his curved scimitar. Once he had finished dressing and attended to his toilet, he looked magnificent.

'He want to look better than sultan,' whispered Messaoud, to the captives. 'He is very silly captain. Sultan will think captain has much money and not give much for you.'

Only Arthur and Angelique spoke Norman French and they passed this on to the others.

'What do we care how much the sultan pays for us,' said Toby. 'We've been enslaved anyway.'

'Why,' said Angelique, 'if you cost a lot of money he'll be more careful of your life, won't he? If he pays only pennies for you, you'll not be worth looking after. Think about it: the more expensive you are, the more you're worth to him.'

'But what can we do?' asked Patrick. 'The captain won't listen to us.'

When it came time for the bargaining, the captain and the sultan, who was dressed in gold and silver cloth and far outshone the leader of the pirates, started haggling over the price of these pale northerners. Angelique and her companions were standing to one side, while the two men spoke of them as if they were carved pieces of wood, not people. Messaoud stood near them, translating in a low voice.

'They do not look as strong as my blacks,' said the sultan, a man with heavily hooded eyes and sleek lips. 'Look at the large muscles of my African slaves. These skinny white specimens could not do half the work of blacks.'

The captain replied, 'Yes, but they have knowledge of building – I have it on good authority from Messaoud that they were all builders in their own land.'

The group all looked at Messaoud, who shrugged as he translated this for them.

'Make the price go up,' he said. 'Very good for you.'

'Ten pieces of silver for each of them,' said the sultan.

'Fifteen,' countered the captain.

'Twelve.'

'Twelve and a roast ox for my men.'

'Agreed . . .'

'NO!' yelled Angelique, making everyone jump, including the sultan, whose hand went to his sword. 'We are worth far more than twelve pieces of silver.'

Messaoud hastily translated.

'How so?' asked the sultan, sneering. 'You are but halflings.'

'We are *artists*,' replied Angelique, 'we are divine actors, who have entertained kings with our plays. The Four Splendid Ones – have you not heard of us, even here in these far-off regions? Our fame is widespread. Why, we are all accomplished acrobats. Our show is spectacular.'

The boys all had their mouths open as Angelique announced this and asked Messaoud to tell his masters.

'The Four Splendid Ones? I have never heard of you,' cried the sultan. 'What foolery is this?'

'Of course, you are not one of the kings of Europe,' replied Angelique, 'so how could I expect you to be cultured? You are a mere sultan of a second-rate kingdom down the bottom of a country no one has ever heard of. Now, if you were the King of Aquitaine, then you *would* know of our fame.'

On hearing this, the pirate captain drew his scimitar, enraged at such effrontery. But the sultan stayed his hand.

'Let me see you do a trick,' said the sultan to Angelique. 'Amaze me.'

Angelique was caught off-guard and did not know what to do. For a moment it seemed that all was lost and she would be put to the sword. But then Patrick did a cartwheel, his chains clanking on the stone floor, and then a complete handspring, and finally a spinning somersault, to land himself next to a log fire. Then he picked up one of the brands and put the lighted end in his mouth, swallowing the flame. The smoking stick was then removed from his mouth and with a spinning whirl through the air it caught fire again. He tossed it back into the fire, where it sizzled with his saliva.

'Tra-la!' cried Patrick, and bowed low.

Messaoud clapped until he caught a black look from his master.

The sultan seemed only slightly impressed.

'What else?' he said.

Arthur did some acrobatics, then from the lining of his coat took a tin whistle and played 'The Somerset Wassail', while Patrick and Toby sang the words:

> Wassail and wassail
> All o-over the town,
> The cup it is white
> And the a-ale it is brown,
> The cup is made
> Of the good ashen tree . . .

'Ah – drinking song,' smiled Messaoud, showing those long white teeth. 'Very good. North peoples good at drinking song.

North peoples good at drinking.' He laughed and then wiped the smile off his face as again the captain glowered at him.

'More?' demanded the sultan.

Angelique said quickly, 'I can sing like a girl.'

She then lifted her head and sang in clear high notes:

> Ours is the more or less is,
> But changeless all the days.
> God revives and blesses
> Like the sunlight rays.
> All Mankind is risen
> The Easter bells do ring
> While from out their prison
> Creep the flowers of Spring.

The sultan's eyebrows were raised.

'Remarkable,' he said, through Messaoud, 'he sings just as sweetly as any girl.'

Messaoud asked the group. 'Is that religious song?'

'Yes. It's "The Easter Carol",' replied Angelique, without thinking.

'Ah – not good. We tell the sultan it is about a poor goatboy who loves a princess who can never be his and is telling this to stars and moons, and wind in desert.'

Patrick, Toby and Arthur then did a country dance, to the tune of Arthur playing on his tin whistle. It was a sort of jig, which seemed to impress the sultan more than anything else. He hopped from one foot to the other himself while this dance was in motion and clapped his hands at the end.

After this had been relayed the sultan made a decision.

'Fifteen pieces of silver for three of them, ten for the large youth. These three help with work inside the palace. The big one works with the other slaves on the building of the walls.'

'Oh, Toby,' cried Angelique, her heart full of compassion for the big youth. 'They will work you to death out there in the hot sun.'

Toby shrugged. 'I'll be all right. Don't worry about me. I'm used to hard work.'

But he looked crestfallen. He would be sleeping in cramped, stinking conditions with the rest of the slaves, both black and white. There were overseers with whips out there, lashing the slaves with complete abandon, whether the slaves were working hard or not. It looked like hell on earth and would no doubt bring any young man to his knees quickly, strong or not.

Messaoud told the group the blacks had been taken from their villages in Africa while the whites had been sailors ship-wrecked on the African shores or seamen taken from ships which had been attacked by corsairs. The suffering of both was pitiful to see, though the blacks had been through it for longer than ever the whites had.

There were many, many more blacks than whites. The whites tended to die first, mostly of sunstroke and heat exhaustion. The blacks lasted longer and when they died it was usually of too much melancholy: their hearts simply overflowed with sorrow which filled their veins and they died with a sigh on their lips. Messaoud asked the group if there were slaves in England and Patrick said yes, but very few foreign slaves: mostly they were people of their own race and creed, which surprised the pirate.

The Barbary pirate captain collected his money and was about to leave with Messaoud when the sultan demanded that Messaoud remain with him as translator.

Messaoud shrugged and agreed – not that he had any real choice in the matter.

'Good,' said Messaoud, 'now sultan asks one last thing – does any want to become Muslim man?'

The group all shook their heads in answer to this question.

'. . . or perhaps eunuch?'

'What?' asked Patrick.

Messaoud smiled. 'If someone wishes to become eunuch they can work in harem, guarding sultan's wives.'

The three boys looked at Angelique.

Angelique could not help but burst out laughing

21. THE KNIGHT

'So, Tomas, you are to be my squire,' said Andrew, still bubbling with joy.

Tomas blinked. 'What does a squire have to do? I have not been attentive of your duties in the past.'

'Come, Tomas, you have seen what I do for John of Reims. I serve him his meals, I care for his horse, I clean his weapons. I also assist him on the battlefield, don't I? I have to protect him against any sneak attack from behind, or from the side, and give him any weapons he calls for. I hold his shield when he's not using it, handing it to him when he does.'

'I would have to kill people?'

'Yes, Tomas, you would.'

'Andrew – yet I must call you *sire* now – what am I at present?'

'You are more like a page, Tomas.'

'Then, sire, I wish to remain a page. I have no heart for violence. I have no wish to raise a sword against another man. I am an angel of the Lord. Bloodshed is abhorrent to me, sire. I could not kill a man, indeed I could not *hurt* a man.'

'Hmmm. A squire has to be able to fight, Tomas. Even as a page you should learn things like that. I've actually been neglecting your training until now. You know the *quintain* that I use? The wooden dummy that spins on its pole when struck with a weapon? I should have taught you to do that a long while ago, then perhaps you wouldn't be so – so backward in such things. I could still teach you. You have to learn to skip out of the way of the dummy when it swings round with its mace and chain . . .'

'You misunderstand me, Andrew – sire. I could not hurt anyone. I am an angel.'

'There are angels, even archangels, who use a fiery sword to kill demons and men. What about the Angel of Death, Tomas, who slaughtered all the Egyptian firstborn?'

'I am not one of those angels.' The boy hung his head. 'I am no Archangel Michael, or even a fiery-sword cherub. I am a failure to you, sire. I should go away.'

'Nonsense,' said Andrew, putting an arm around the white-haired youth's shoulders and looking him directly in his startling blue eyes, 'you are my friend and companion. If you can't be a page or squire, that's what you will be. You can sew, can't you? Mend my clothes? You can sing like no man I have ever heard – oh, you sing like a girl, Tomas. I can't think how life would be better without you. It would be extremely dull. I know, I have it – instead of being the guardian of my body, you can be the guardian of my soul. How's that? You must watch over my soul and let no harm come to it, eh?'

Tomas's head came up and his eyes sparkled. 'Oh, how I love thee, Andrew – it is just what I should be doing.'

'Exactly as I thought. I knew we could find the right work for you, Tomas.'

'But what about your pageboy, and your squire.'

'Oh, I can do without pages and squires,' cried Andrew, airily. 'With God and magic at my back, what need have I of others? Anyway, many of the Templars see to themselves. Most are so poor they have no money to keep a squire. And, believe me, Tomas, I have every intention of becoming a Templar, whatever Odo says.'

'You should send him a gift, Andrew. The ruby. Make a present to him of the ruby we found in the desert.'

Andrew stared at his friend.

'Sometimes I believe you are a genius, Tomas – how brilliant! Yes, I shall give him the ruby, but not immediately, for he might take it now and still not make me a Templar. He's just made a statement in front of the king and others, so he won't want to go back on that yet. Later, when things have settled down. After I have been a secular knight for a while.'

That evening Andrew bathed carefully. Tomas dressed him in a white tunic and red robes, then Andrew went to the king's chapel and knelt there to perform his all-night vigil. Hour on hour he prayed that he would be chivalrous and have honour uppermost in his mind. He vowed to protect the weak against the strong. He prayed for the purification of his soul and all those aspects of the vigil that had been told to him as a young boy by the redoubtable Friar Nottidge.

Just before midnight the chaplain came into the chapel and, taking Andrew's sword, blessed it and placed it on the altar.

Throughout the night and into dawn Andrew often thought of his mother and father, and his sisters, and prayed for them, too. He found it hard to believe that in a few hours he would have achieved his ambition of becoming a knight, the thought that had been uppermost in his mind since meeting with the two dead men. Even as a small child he had looked at the knights and thought how wonderful it must be to be of their number. He had achieved the impossible: of becoming a knight even though he was himself of humble birth. His heart filled to overflowing with emotion and several times he broke down and wept, both for joy and for the sadness of having a goal which had been reached, for now he would have to find another. Man was not happy, he decided, unless searching for something which seemed quite out of reach.

He might have fallen asleep had not a cock crowed just as the sun rose over the lip of the Earth. Then cocks crowed one after the other, their calls spreading out over the sleeping city of Jerusalem. The roosters woke the dogs, which woke the geese, which woke the asses, which woke the men and women, until only the imperturbable cats remained with their eyes closed.

The cats simply ignored the noise. So it was a new day? Was that a miracle or a commonplace occurrence? It might have been either, for a new morning arrived every twenty-four hours without fail – and yet indeed one day the sun would *not* rise – only God or Allah knew when that would be – and men would no longer stir in their beds and awake to its light.

Inside the chapel, with the sun's rays striking and penetrating the window over the altar, with the light a strange intense yellow, a figure appeared and seemed to wave a hand over Andrew's head, as if blessing him. He could not look at the figure directly, for the light was too bright, but he thought he could see wings on the creature. Was this the Archangel Michael, a warrior from Heaven, come to welcome Andrew to the host of Christian knights? Or was it simply a trick of the sunlight on the window, with its warped glass?

'Are you ready for your confession?'

The priest had returned to perform Andrew's last rite as a common man.

'Yes.'

And so Andrew confessed all those faults and sins which he had gathered to his breast in his short life. None were huge, but then some were not trivial. But a knight needed to be pure in order to perform acts of valour, or those acts might turn sour on him and turn to sins rather than good deeds.

After this Andrew went to bathe yet again, feeling absolutely drained, spiritually.

From there he went to the open-air ceremony where the king's tent had been erected on a grassy bank. The king was waiting in front of his tent, attended by nobility including Master Odo and John of Reims. Three squires were being dubbed knights that morning. Andrew was the last to go forward and kneel before his liege, King Baldwin IV.

The king looked unwell. His leprosy left him feeling weak on some mornings, but he smiled as Andrew looked up into his face. And then he nodded, giving him one of those looks which said, 'You and I are young blades, and we can show these stern old devils a thing or two.'

'Andrew of Cressing,' said the king, in a loud and clear voice, 'arise Sir Andrew, knight of the realm.'

Baldwin then struck Andrew forcefully on the chest with his mailed fist, a requirement of the ceremony. It was one of the rites the king had to perform in making a knight. The blow knocked Andrew over backwards on to the grass.

The king laughed and cried out, 'I told you one of them would fall – thank you, Sir Andrew, for not making me out to be a liar and winning me two gold crowns from Odo.'

'Oh, sire,' said Odo. 'You and Sir Andrew were in on this together.'

'Not so, Master of the Temple,' said the king, looking hurt. 'I have not seen him since the banquet.'

'Forgive me, my liege,' said Odo, hastily, 'of course you would not do such a thing.'

'Where's the fun in cheating?' added the king. 'I have no need of money – only of beating you at something.'

Two of the squires had managed to steady themselves after the king's buffeting, but Andrew had been overawed by the occasion and was slightly off-guard. He was a little chagrined, but pleased that the king had won his wager and was therefore happy with the morning. They all went off to have a good breakfast at the king's table.

Once more Andrew's heart was full of joy. He could not believe he was really there, sitting with the other knights, ordering the servants here and there, telling jokes, the dogs lying on his feet for warmth under the table. It was all so wonderful. The world was suddenly his for the taking. There was no one higher, only the king himself, and Andrew adored the king, and was himself clearly loved in return. This was his happiest moment. Only one goal remained. To become a Templar. Yet, even if that did not happen, he was still a knight, if only – in the eyes of some – a lesser one.

Even Odo had called him 'Sir Andrew' after the ceremony!

Two days later the king asked Andrew to assist in guarding

a caravan bound for Antioch, a duty Andrew grasped with both hands.

'Indeed, sire, nothing gives me greater pleasure than to serve you.'

'You speak of serving me? Oh, don't be boring, Andrew,' said Baldwin. 'I didn't make you a knight so that we could dispense with all our fun. You and I will go hunting wild pig when you return. I'll look forward to it.'

'And I, sire.'

The king clapped him on the shoulder.

'We could have been brothers, you and me – what about your father? Does he serve in Outremer, or is he still in England? He'll be proud of your progress, I don't doubt.'

'He – he remains at Cressing, my liege.'

'Ah, a man with his heart at home. Well, we can't all have a life of furious excitement, can we? Now you and I, Andrew, we are adventurers. Not for us the hall fire and the dogs around our feet. We like to be in a battle, or on the wild hunt, the wind flowing through the manes of our mounts. Be sure to tell your father he has a fine son and that the knighthood of the family is maintained with great pride. Shall I write to him?'

Andrew's heart sank, for clearly the king thought him of noble blood. He had not even asked the question of himself before now, but suddenly he knew it would make a difference to others' perception of him. Not wanting to disappoint the king, he did not put him right.

'No – no, my lord, he has never learned to read – I myself cannot read or write. It's all action with our family.'

'Ah, you should learn, Andrew. If you don't, your enemies

will have it over you. Learn to read, or secret messages will be passed under your nose and plots will form around you. Learn to understand the words that might otherwise result in your downfall. I know it sounds boring, to be a scholar, but it is one of those necessary things in life. I'll send you my tutor, Septimus Silke. He's a tedious old fart, but he's a good teacher. He used to belong to King Henry, but upset him by saying that Henry was mangling the beautiful language of Latin. He's a clever man.' The king laughed. 'He had to be, to get anything into the head of this dunce.' He tapped his own skull with his knuckles.

'Thank you, my liege, I appreciate your advice.'

'Till the hunting, then? Adieu, my friend. Oh, I almost forgot,' the king reached inside a bag he was carrying, 'these are for you. A gift from me, on your becoming one of my knights.'

He held out a pair of golden spurs.

'Oh, my liege!' cried Andrew.

'Take them. I know you want to be a Templar. Templars make a vow of poverty. But these are part of your armoury, so can't be counted as personal wealth. Go on, take them.'

'I don't know what to say,' said Andrew, overwhelmed, 'except thank you, from the bottom of my heart.'

'Pah!' cried the king, walking away. 'You're getting sentimental again, Andrew – it's something to watch out for.'

Andrew went next to find Hassan. He did not tell his Muslim friend that he had been made a knight. There was a feeling in him that Hassan would not be impressed. In fact, he would probably be the opposite considering how the Arab boy reviled Christian knights. They both did well to keep this kind of thing a secret from each other. Instead, Andrew told Hassan that he was going to escort another caravan north-wards and wanted to hunt with the bird before he left.

'Good. I begin to wonder when you will come again. My English rusts like an old sword if you are away too long.'

'Certainly your English has improved tenfold since I've known you. Your accent is still strong, but the words come out well. Do you have a tutor?'

'My father employs a teacher of English, but he is not of your country. I think he is from Byzantium.'

'Am I the only Englishman you speak to?'

'Yes.'

That was good. It was unlikely, then, that Hassan would find out about his knighthood. Of course, there were Arab speakers who knew of the ceremony: cooks, servants, sweepers, advisers to the king, sheiks who had a grudge against Saladin, others. But Hassan's father was a Bedouin merchant, not nobility or royalty, and the boy did not mix with locals in the way a city boy would. They were a family who were here one day and gone the next, down to the Yemen, on to Damascus, over the islands in the Gulf.

'Well, then, we will talk today. Where is the bird, the saker falcon? I have been dying to see him again.'

The two young men went to the creature's stand, which was in the courtyard of the rented house. The saker seemed to sense he was going out to hunt, for he began a sort of dance on his stand as the two youths approached. Andrew had a leather glove on and he took the bird and held it by its jesses, which were the leather thongs attached to the falcon's legs. It stayed there, happy to be gripping its master.

'I have been sewing one of its broken feathers,' said Hassan, 'for it had cracked in two.'

'Yes? We call that *imping*,' replied Andrew, who had often watched falconers at Cressing, 'but he seems to be in yarak – I mean, keen to go on the hunt.'

'I know what yarak means – it is one of our terms, too.'

The youths went out and spent a happy day together with the hawk, which brought down two large waders which would go in the pot when Hassan took them home. The falcon was a bird that needed constant attention and Andrew gave it willingly. The knight never felt more human than when he was tending to some creature or other, and this falcon was perfect. He longed to take it back to the palace, to show Tomas, but there was this problem of frivolity. He would not be taken seriously by the Master of the Templars if caught with a hunting bird, even though he was not yet a Templar.

The following day, Andrew left with the caravan for Antioch. He was not escorting goods this time, only the Bishop of Bethlehem, who needed protection for the journey. The bishop, of course, took a great deal of baggage with him: silken robes, velvet cushions, cotton sheets, woollen blankets, hats, two great trunks of shoes, chalices for administering mass, crosses of various sorts, altar cloths, several crosiers with gold or silver heads, books of many colours and thicknesses, silken cords, leather saddles, much, much more. These items went everywhere with the bishop. He needed all of them as much as he needed a single pillow. They made him feel secure. They made him feel he was worth something. If they were not with him, he felt naked and poor, and no bishop wanted to feel either of those things. Bishops were almost kings, in the power that they wielded; and who took notice of a poor, naked man travelling without the symbols of his holy puissance?

'Is your father rich, Andrew?' enquired the bishop as Andrew rode beside the great man's palanquin, a large platform with extended poles carried by eight men on which the bishop lay among his soft cushions. Above the palanquin was a huge striped parasol shading his grace's hallowed white skin from the harsh sunlight. 'You were born in north Essex I am told. That is wool country. I have seen some of the churches there, and just over the border in Suffolk. They are as big as cathedrals. All built by wool merchants to purchase a fast road to Heaven. None so rich as a wool merchant, I know.'

'Indeed they are large churches, your grace, but my father is in metal, not wool.'

'Ah, metal? What, gold? Silver? Perhaps he is an alchemist and is engaged in turning base metals into precious ones? Eh? The philosopher's stone? Has he found the elixir of life everlasting? What I would give for such a thing – to live forever . . .'

'But your grace, isn't that what you offer us? Life everlasting, through our Lord?'

'Oh, that,' the bishop waved a hand as if brushing away a fly. 'I mean *real* life, not some ethereal thing.'

'No, your grace, my father – my father deals in iron.'

'Iron?' the bishop wrinkled his fat brow. 'Iron? Is there money in iron? I shouldn't have guessed it. Weapons, of course, but iron weapons are reasonably cheap. Horseshoes? Not much money in that. Prison bars, perhaps? Ah, wheel hoops? Well, there it is, I suppose. Iron. Next time I'm in

England I will have a word with your father, if I may, and discover his secret of making a fortune out of iron.'

Of course Andrew had not mentioned any fortune; the bishop had taken that belief upon himself. Andrew felt guilty for disguising the truth about his parents, but he did not want to be reviled for being of lowly birth. Perhaps later, when he knew everyone of his own status well enough and could announce the truth of his birth, conscious that it would raise a laugh among his new companions? Ho, they would say, you kept that close to your chest, Sir Andrew of Cressing, did you not? What a great joke.

Sir Andrew. It was still so new to him it raised a light in his heart. Sir Andrew of Cressing. He thought of something: he would need a crest, would he not? A coat of arms? They would expect him to have one already. He thought about this and decided a plain white shield with a scarlet falcon in flight as the only symbol, right in the centre of the shield.

'Of course,' he murmured to himself, 'I could have the falcon flanked by two dead men, one on either side. One bearing an axe, his murder weapon, the other with half a skull missing. Perhaps a broken gravestone somewhere?'

He laughed out loud, startling Warlock, who tossed his head at this breach of etiquette. A knight was expected to be solemn and to go about his duties with earnest sobriety. Such behaviour brought the wrong attention to his warhorse, who was now painfully aware of his high status among equines.

Fortunately, there were no serious attacks on the way to Antioch.

The hazards were there, of course. Supernatural fiends of various kinds were always ready to invade the world of men, happy to disembowel or rip head from body. Wild beasts had to be kept at bay: there was a man-eating lion that was supposed to be particularly fond of human livers. And, of course, the wandering bands of Saladin's Saracens. Yet also savage tribes who recognised no religion, no king, no sultan: tribes which were steeped in a pagan religion called *animism*, where rocks, caves and trees were worshipped and needed human sacrifices from time to time.

These dangers all lurked in the wilderness, ready to surge or creep towards the coast, and attack any unwary caravan that might be going on its way.

There was one other great danger, which Andrew had so far not come across. This had come about as a result of Walter de Mesnil's murder of the Assassin ambassadors. Yes, Walter himself had undoubtedly been executed in secret, for nothing was ever heard of him again after his capture. But the band of knights who had been with him on his murder mission had turned rogue. They were now outlaws, living by raiding and plundering villages and camps. They dare not return to their kingdoms of Antioch or Jerusalem, or go home to their old countries, for they were wanted men. There was a price on their heads. They had followed a false knight, in Walter de Mesnil, and now they were paying for their folly.

In turn, however, they were feared. There were some forty of them, rogue knights who roamed the wilderness preying on Christian, Muslim and pagan alike. Known now as the *Chevaliers Noirs*, they knew no masters except silver and gold. They took from pilgrims on their way to Jerusalem, stripped them, left them with nothing. Men died of sunstroke, starvation, thirst, and these knights cared nought, though their victims were their own countrymen. They slaughtered children and women without compunction. These rogues had chosen evil over good. Their souls were lost and they lived only for earthly possessions. In truth, they were worse than a horde of demons straight from Hell.

However, on this occasion, Andrew's caravan arrived with its bishop alive and intact. The bishop then invited all the knights to dine with him that evening, at his friend the Bishop of Antioch's palace. Andrew went to seek quarters in the heart of the city, and a stable for Warlock.

That evening he dressed in his finest and made his way to the bishop's palace. The table was already well attended by his fellow knights, for they were hungry after the day's journey. There were capons aplenty, grapes, dates and many other meats and fruits. Andrew sat down next to another young man recently raised to knighthood, Sir Alexander.

'Tuck in,' said Alexander, 'before those old pigs eat everything they can get their hands on.'

He nodded down the table at the long-established knights, both visitors and residents. Andrew stared down the table and his heart gave a jump. There at the far end sat Sir Gondemar de Blois, who just happened to look up at the same time. Their eyes met. Gondemar seemed to choke on his food. He stood up and yelled at the top of his voice:

'What is that whelp doing at this table?'

No one knew who he meant at first and everyone was looking this way and that, even at close neighbours. However, the Bishop of Bethlehem seemed to be aware of the situation.

'Sir Gondemar,' said the bishop, 'you must not refer to a fellow knight as a whelp.'

Gondemar's eyes almost started out of his head.

'That – that boy, a *knight*?'

Andrew was quite nervous, since everyone was now looking at him. He felt he ought to do something to assert himself and protect his honour. He stood up and said, 'Yes, Sir Gondemar, I – a knight. I was given the privilege of my position by King Baldwin. It is true there is bad blood between us, but that's of your making, not mine. I sought to help my master when he was in danger of death . . .'

'YOU CUT OFF MY HAND, YOU SWINE!' screamed Gondemar, waving his stump for all to see. 'YOU CUT OFF MY RIGHT HAND!'

'Sir Gondemar, you would have died – the physician . . .'

'The healer was in league with you, you pox.'

The Bishop of Antioch said, 'Sir Gondemar, curb your language, if you please. You are at *my* table. Can you not form a sentence without calling this knight a name? For shame, sir, for shame.'

'And you can shut your mouth, Bishop,' snarled the knight, forgetting all his manners. 'This is between men. Women in men's robes need not interfere.'

'How dare you!' cried the bishop.

'I dare. I dare,' spat Gondemar, 'and what's more – no, enough of this foolery. I will have my satisfaction. The cur is now a knight, therefore I *can* have an end.'

He got up and strode the length of the table. When he reached Andrew he took one of his gauntlets out of his belt with his good left hand and struck Andrew across the face with it, causing blood to flow down his cheek. Andrew's heart was in his boots, but he maintained a straight face.

'I accept,' he said, in a low voice.

'What?' cried Gondemar, as if no one had heard. 'What was that, whelp?'

'I ACCEPT.'

'Good. Tomorrow at dawn. Outside the city gates.'

Gondemar then marched from the hall, leaving a healthy buzz of excitement behind him.

Andrew resumed his seat, drowning in misery.

'So,' said Alexander, after a while, 'mind if I watch?'

'Be my guest. In fact,' Andrew addressed the whole table, 'you can all come if you want. It's all the same to me.'

The two bishops shook their heads.

'Not I,' said the Bishop of Bethlehem.

'Nor I,' said the Bishop of Antioch. 'We are men of the cloth. Violence is only really acceptable in war, in defence of our king and our God. To kill one another is not only foolish it's wasteful. We need all the knights we can get to fight Saladin. He will be back, of that you can be sure. He will be back with an even bigger army of Saracens.'

Andrew slept fitfully but woke ready for the challenges of the day. His jinnee came to him in the early hours. It was the first time the unnatural creature had appeared outside the desert region where Andrew had first encountered him.

'Ah – you have come to help me,' said Andrew.

The jinnee shook its head. 'No, no – not man against man. Man against Nature, or against some creature of my own world, like a giant or poisonous gnome, but against your own kind you must fend for yourself. I came only to comfort you, like a priest, or a parent.'

'Oh, well, that's something.'

330

'Something? It is everything. Confidence is the best weapon against a raging enemy. To remain calm and confident. Remember, Andrew of Cressing, this Templar has only one hand. You took the other. It was his main weapon hand. He has taught himself since to use the other, but it is not his best fighting arm. Remember that.'

'Yes, of course,' said Andrew, 'but even if I win I would find it difficult to kill him. He is a former master.'

'As to that, you should cut off his head at the first opportunity,' said the jinnee, glowing green as he spoke. 'Cut off his head and ram it on a pointed stake.'

'Is that what you think?'

'It's what I advise.'

'Thank you – we shall see. I might have the anger to behead him. At the moment there's not enough rage in me, but once he strikes me it'll come soon enough I expect. Perhaps I should never have come here, to Antioch.'

'He would have caught up with you at some time. You're his main enemy now. He hates you. He lives to see you die.'

'I only meant well.'

The jinnee gave Andrew a horrible grimace.

'Those who mean well must answer for their deeds just as much as those who mean evil.'

'Of course.'

The jinnee left and Andrew was able to get a little sleep before cockcrow. When the day dawned, he got up and put on his own armour, having no squire or page to assist him. When he looked at himself in the mirror he was quite taken aback by the splendour of himself in Helmschmid of Austria's beautiful creation. The sunlight through an arrowloop struck his breastplate and emblazoned his chest. Ulfberht sword, armour, helmet, golden spurs, shield – he had painted a falcon on the white shield himself one evening on the journey to Antioch. Andrew of Cressing was armed. The young hero was armed. He would go to the fight, perhaps to his death, looking like a prince.

He rode to the gates and beyond. There he found Gondemar waiting impatiently. Gondemar was armed with a lance.

'No lances today, Gondemar,' said Andrew, drawing up alongside his adversary. 'We fight with swords.'

There was a crowd of knights watching. Some of them had been drinking wine all night long.

'You are the challenger, Gondemar,' cried a voice from the heart of them. 'The man you challenged is entitled to choose the weapons.'

'Swords it is, then,' snarled Gondemar, dropping the lance to the ground. 'Are you ready, whelp?'

'I am.'

With that Gondemar struck him a blow across the face, while his visor was still open. Andrew fell from the saddle down into the dust, landing heavily in his armour. He rolled to one side, blood pouring from his mouth. When he looked up, Gondemar was drawing his sword awkwardly from its scabbard. Andrew rolled away again, avoiding the hooves of Gondemar's charger, as the other knight reared his mount.

Andrew struggled to his feet. It was difficult in heavy armour. He managed to get to his knees when Gondemar charged his steed at Andrew, knocking him over again. Once more the youth attempted to rise. Gondemar came galloping towards him with his sword swishing the air, no doubt hoping to decapitate the young man.

This time the blade struck Andrew's helmet. It glanced off it, shearing the feathers that crowned the helmet. They fluttered down as if from the tail of a bird and Gondemar gave a shout of glee. For some reason the Templar believed he had wounded his foe. But feathers are not fingers. This time, with great effort, Andrew managed to rise to his feet. He stood there swaying as Gondemar wheeled his horse and came charging back, swinging his sword in a murderous circle.

All the other knights were silent. They believed the *coup de grâce* was about to be administered. Gondemar came up alongside Andrew and brought the blade of his sword down, probably hoping to split his opponent's helmet. But he was using his left arm, which would never be as strong as his right had been. The blow was weak, therefore, somewhat ineffectual.

Both Andrew's hands went up to protect his head and somehow he managed to grasp the sword blade with his thick leather gauntlets. He held on and then wrenched the other knight from the saddle. Gondemar came down hard on the packed earth. He lay there stunned, looking up at the sky. Andrew could not see his expression because the knight's visor was down. Andrew had his foe's sword in his hands.

The other knights stepped forward now.

Andrew stood astride Gondemar. He held Gondemar's sword by the arms of its crossed hilt, one hand on either spur, the point aimed downwards.

'Yield!' he cried.

'Never!' croaked Gondemar. 'Kill me.'

Andrew put the point of the blade to the slit in Gondemar's helmet. One thrust and the felled knight would be pierced through the eye.

'Yield!' cried Andrew again, desperately.

'Never, never, never.'

'Then live,' said Andrew, wearily, throwing the sword aside. 'I am done with you.'

The other knights seemed to let out a general sigh. They had been waiting for blood. It was not forthcoming.

Andrew found Warlock standing a few yards away. He took the reins of his mount and led him back through the gates into the streets of the city. Andrew wanted to get away from Gondemar as quickly as possible, but was unable to ride. He needed a stool or steps to remount his horse. Since he carried neither with him he was obliged to walk. It was a humiliating thing, but all knights had the same problem when they were unhorsed on the field.

Not wishing to stay in Antioch after this incident, Andrew made preparations to ride out for Jerusalem later that morning.

22. THE GOAT-OGRE

Just as Andrew was ready to go a pageboy came to him and told him that he was wanted at the city gate.

Not another duel? he thought wearily. When will this man leave me alone?

But when Andrew reached the gate he found an elegant looking citizen from a more eastern city standing there, a man of some fifty years. He was well dressed in the style of a Persian. The man seemed agitated and asked Andrew to join him in a coffee tent. When they were seated he told Andrew in good English why he wanted to see him.

'You are a friend of the family . . . ?' and he gave him Hassan's surname.

'Yes, I know them,' replied Andrew, cautiously. 'I visit them for tea when I am in Jerusalem.'

'I tell you the name, so that you know you can trust me. I am in deep trouble, sir. My daughter has been villainously abducted, along with her slave. I am told you are a gracious and bold knight, who might help someone like me.'

Andrew said, 'Can you not hire men of your own nation? They would know better than I where to find a taken maid.'

'I have tried this without success. You are a nobleman, sir, a knight. Is it not your duty to assist maidens in distress? I have heard this from other men.'

It was true that if petitioned, even by a stranger, a knight was duty-bound to go to the assistance of a lady in trouble. True, this man was not a Christian, but Andrew felt the words he had spoken keenly. Would it be dishonourable of him to turn the man away without offering his help? He thought so. The distraught father seemed to be at his wit's end. He had let his coffee grow cold in front of him, and had not taken even a single sip. Andrew did not like coffee so had not touched his either. The coffee seller was giving them dark looks, suspecting they did not like his wares.

'What makes you think I shall be successful?'

'Why, I am told,' said the man, leaning forward now and lowering his voice, 'you have *magic* on your side.'

Andrew sat bolt upright. This was exceptionally dangerous. A knight, especially a warrior-monk, accused of using magic could be ostracised, perhaps even tortured and executed. It was tantamount to dealing with the Devil. You did not have to be an old woman in an Essex village to be accused of being a witch. There were ambitious clerics and priests who used such information to further their careers. Exposing a witch helped the clergy jump a few ranks in the Church.

'Who told you that?'

The older man smiled and now took a sip of his cold coffee, much to the relief of the vendor.

'There are those who do not need to be told – they can see it in a man.'

Tomas knew Andrew was magical, of course, but then Tomas was magical himself. The secret was kept between the two of them. If Gondemar got hold of it that would be the end of Andrew's life as a knight. Perhaps the end of all?

'Who knows about such things?' asked Andrew. 'If I am to assist you in finding your daughter . . .'

'None who are your enemies. Rest easy. But, my daughter, Yasmin – yes, she is out there in the wilderness somewhere. There has been no call for a ransom, so I can only think those who have her do not want money. Perhaps they do not want anything from me? Perhaps they just want my sweet, beautiful Yasmin, because she is a lovely girl?'

'And the name of the slave? What is his name?'

'She – her name is Wadi. She was found on a dry river bed and is so called. But she is of no consequence. An African girl with no breeding or manners, very bad-tempered. We bought her in the marketplace for a few small coins.'

'But they are together?'

'The slave was not taken in the first instance, but followed the footprints of the abductor to find her mistress.'

'Tell me the region where you believe they are being held.'

The older man described the area where the girls had been abducted. It was a wild place east of Damascus, where there roamed some fierce, unruly tribes. Andrew assured the older man he would ride inland at that point and search for his daughter and her slave.

'If I find them, I will take them on to Jerusalem, for I cannot return to Antioch.'

'Because of the other knight? The one you vanquished this morning?'

'News travels quickly.'

The man knitted his fingers together and spoke in a low voice. 'I could have him killed for you. It would be a simple matter. It need not concern you.'

Andrew was shocked at the idea.

'No, no. I could have killed him myself, this very day, but it would serve me nothing. He is a man with viper venom in his veins, more to be pitied, really. No, I wish to return to Jerusalem for other reasons. My falcon is there. My king is there. My friends are there. I miss them all.'

'In that order?'

Andrew laughed. 'Yes, I suppose so.'

'If you find my Yasmin, I will pay you well.'

'I can accept no money. I wish to be a Templar and will have to renounce all my wealth if I am so fortunate as to become one.'

'Ah, you want to be one of the slaughterers.'

Andrew stiffened.

'Templars are knights of great courage and conviction. They are holy warriors of the Lord. Monks in armour. They do not leave the battlefield unless the day is won. If that makes them slaughterers, so be it.'

'I meant no disrespect. I merely repeat what is said.'

'They are savage fighters, I will agree, but if one is going to fight why not put the fear of death into the enemy by being the most dreaded creature on the field?'

'Most assuredly. But you must name a price, if you find my daughter. I must give you *something*.'

'I'll think about that, if I'm successful.'

Andrew left Antioch. Once out in the wilderness he lit a fire and summoned his jinnee from the flames. Andrew asked him about the girls. The jinnee told him they had been taken, not by men, but by a mountain ogre – part-goat, part-crocodile, part-human.

'As you know,' said the jinnee, 'goats eat everything and anything, but they tire of dry weeds and thorn bushes. Every so often this ogre will dare to creep into a nomads' camp and steal a child, or a grown woman. Children are tender and women are generally juicier than men, having less muscle on them. The ogre roasts them under a full moon, catching the melted fat in a stolen pan to drink later on, when all the flesh has gone and the bones have been cracked open for the marrow.'

'What part is goat?'

'The head and the hind legs, and the stomach. The heart is that of a man. The arms and torso are also human.'

'Which part is crocodile?'

'The skin. It is armoured like that of a crocodile. A hideous, scaly creature in all. And dangerous. It has a goat's brain, which is wickedly sly. You must not look it in the eyes, for those goaty eyes will send you to sleep. They are yellowed eyes, with black slits for pupils like scars across its irises. As I said, it likes children and women, but it will eat men if they cause it any trouble – or there is nothing else.'

'As you say, it will eat anything, like any common goat. The world is its larder.'

'Yes.'

Andrew asked, 'How will I kill it?'

'Not through the heart, for there the amphibian skin is so thick and tough that even a sharp sword point will not penetrate. You must go for the stomach, which is the weakest area, where the skin is like the underbelly of a crocodile. However, it seldom walks upright. Usually it's down on all fours. You will need to get it to stand on its hind legs if you are to have a chance. When the time comes I shall give you the power of the ogre's speech, so that you will know his language, though I myself cannot be there to intervene in the battle.'

'I understand and thank you, jinnee. Have you any other news for me?'

Andrew hoped to be told he was definitely going to be a Templar one day.

'No, no – except that your other self has met with my other self in a place not far from here.'

'What? What is this riddle, jinnee?'

The jinnee squatted and made ready to leap away into the night, like a coiled spring given release.

'I have said all there is to be said.'

'It doesn't make sense – my *other* self? What is that? My spirit? My soul? Can it leave my body, my soul, and seek your own in the spirit world? Does a jinnee have a soul to seek? This is one of those puzzles that makes my head spin.'

But the jinnee had leapt off, like a cricket in the grasses, and was soon somewhere else, remarkably quickly.

Andrew continued his journey until it was time to strike inland. His magic astrolabe, with its stars and crescent moons, gave him the direction to the place where the goat-ogre's cave was situated. The way was long and arduous. Tracks were poor, disappearing in places into plain, dusty rockland or sandy river beds that wandered away into even more arid regions where the cracked earth would not even support the occasional dwarf tree or shrivelled shrub. Snakes lay in his path, gathering energy from the sun to strike at unwary travellers. Scorpions scuttled into fissures in the ground, their breeding places. The whole landscape crawled with dangerous creatures, from poisonous spiders to deadly millipedes that crept into the crevices of a man's armour and threatened to sting or bite. Weary, weary, he became, his head hanging down, his back bent, his very soul drooping within him.

Many times he was lost, but recovered his way again with the help of the magic astrolabe. This desert world threw up visions, though, which led him from his true path. Some might call them mirages, pictures from a fevered brain, but others might allocate them to the spirit of the landscape creating phantasmagorias to lead him astray on purpose. Deserts sometimes do that. They are living entities that take a man and offer him Fata Morgana as real things, fooling him, turning his brain into a whirl of truths and untruths until he does not know the difference between them. He sleeps with fevered dreams and awakes in desolate places, bleak and bone-scattered, not a bird to be seen in the sky, not a sound that is other than a slither or a scuttle. His throat is eternally parched, his mind hammers in his head, his eyes continually sore with hot winds and blown sands, and his whole body sapped, weak with exhaustion and sickness.

Finally, Andrew came to a region which the astrolabe told him was the home of the ogre. He found a stream running with clear water and allowed Warlock to drink. Then he quenched his own thirst. That day he slept the sleep of a dead man, careless of whether he would be found by the ogre, and was thankful to wake in a cool evening still undiscovered, alive and breathing. He chastised himself for his carelessness and remained hidden in some rocks, now fearful of being found by the ogre before he was ready to take on the task of killing the creature. When night came the moon rose over the craggy fastness of that rocky region. He left Warlock and his armour down below, to climb up a hillside to the place where the ogre lived. As he approached he saw a big fire burning, a figure sitting hunched over it.

The ogre saw Andrew coming and went down on all fours. It was indeed an ugly creature. Its skin was corrugated, just like a crocodile's. Its head was that of a monstrous goat with two long, ridged, curving horns, one broken at the tip. There were two hairy hind legs, with thick hooves for feet, and a torso and arms that would have been human had they not been covered in that ugly amphibian's hide. It was a heavily muscled creature, all lumps and bumps along its back, with a glare that might melt a knight's armour from his body.

Andrew did not look the ogre in the eyes, but kept his gaze on the creature's body.

'What do you want?' growled the goat-ogre, its stinking breath enveloping Andrew in a wave. 'You can't have my dinner.'

The ogre's head moved and Andrew looked over the creature's shoulder to see two girls. One of them, the fat, lighter-skinned girl, was trembling violently. The other, jet-black in complexion, had a slightly defiant look.

The Arab girl shrieked, 'He's going to eat us!'

'Quiet, you silly fool,' said the black girl. 'He's not taken a bite yet – when he does I'll cause a great fuss. See if he likes his supper kicking and screaming in his mouth . . .'

Andrew ignored the girls.

'I wondered if I might join you?' he said to the ogre. 'I hate dining alone.'

'You want to share my food?' thundered the ogre. 'What kind of guest invites himself?'

342

'Oh, I've brought some things.' Andrew showed the ogre. 'Some oregano and rosemary, cinnamon bark, dried wild parsley, turmeric – oh, and a little fennel root to help spice the meat up. Also I'm quite good at gravy. Have you ever tasted thick English gravy? It's the best in the world. It'll have your saliva flowing like a river down your goatee beard.'

The ogre advanced a few paces on his hooves and knuckles, his eyes burning.

'Are you making fun of me?'

Andrew looked shocked. 'What? Now why would I do that? I'm a hungry man. Have you ever been so hungry you could eat a fat Persian? I couldn't care less where the meat comes from – oh, and I have some vegetables here, too', and he removed a bunch of greens from his pocket. 'You'll like this. It comes from the Yemen. Qat grass. Very pleasant.'

'Qat grass?'

'Yes. Marvellous stuff. Here, have some to chew while I get going on the gravy – which of the wenches is first in the pot?' Andrew beamed at the girls. 'The fat one? Very juicy. Or the other. Not so plump but quite delicious to look at. Good presentation always seems to make the food taste better.'

Andrew tossed some of the qat to the goat-ogre and went up to the girls, staring down at them.

Yasmin wailed, but Wadi spat towards Andrew and cried, 'You fiend – you're worse than this animal – at least he hasn't the brains to know right from wrong. You cannibal.'

Goats eat anything and everything, at any time.

With the qat grass in its scaly hands, the goat-ogre could not resist putting it in its mouth and tasting it. The qat had a strange metallic taste and the ogre winced a little at first.

But the more it chewed the weed, the better it seemed to taste. Before long a calm, happy feeling spread through the ogre like a trickling of warm water. The ogre decided it really was pleasant stuff, this qat. It sharpened the mind and gave the thoughts free rein. The ogre hummed as it chewed.

'Ah,' cried Andrew, still keeping his gaze averted from the eyes of the beast, 'you like it, eh? Me too.' Andrew popped some of the greens into his own mouth. 'I bet you thought I was trying to poison you, didn't you?'

The ogre stopped chewing for a moment and stared at Andrew with a nasty expression.

'Well, if I had,' said Andrew, 'you'd be feeling ill, or be dead by now, so you can rest assured the qat is harmless. How are you feeling?'

'All – all sort of dreamy,' murmured the ogre. 'I like this qat – it makes soft pictures in my head.'

'Quite so. Makes you want to dance as well, eh? It does that with me.' Andrew did a little jig, and staring up at the sky he howled at the moon like a wolf. 'Look at that wonderful disc of light! Have you seen a moon as big and as bright as that lately? Such a beautiful sight, a full moon.'

The ogre looked up at the moon swimming through some light, fluffy clouds.

'Beautiful,' it said. 'Yes.'

'Dance with me,' cried Andrew, whirling around with one arm out. 'Come on, enjoy the moonlight. This is a time to be jolly! Oh, how I love to dance. Look at my feet, tripping away, away, away.'

Andrew then began to sing a melody which had been popular among the villagers at Cressing.

The ogre started rocking on his hooves and hands, jumping backwards and forwards to the tune.

'Say, do you know this step?' Andrew said. 'Look, I'll show you . . .'

Andrew performed a little hop, skip and jump, two sideways, two to the front, one to the back.

'Looks complicated, but it's quite easy really.'

The ogre tried it on all fours and failed.

'No, no, here, give me your hands . . .', the ogre had to get up on his hind legs to do this, but he remained bent right over, almost doubled-up, '. . . that's it, hold on to me like a dancer holds, an arm around my shoulders. You've got it. Are you sure you've never done this before? You have a natural rhythm, you really do. It must be in your blood. Never? Well you, astound me. Now then, follow my steps as I do them, skip to the side, step to the front – that's it.'

The goat-ogre was enjoying itself. It grunted in pleasure, still chewing on the qat. Its clumsy hooves clattered on the stones and rocks, but Andrew kept telling it that its dance was perfect, was worthy of a prince. The heavy goat head bobbed on the thick human shoulders and the hairy goat hips swayed this way and that, all out of time with the music.

'You're both mad,' muttered Wadi. 'Lunatics.'

'Why,' cried Andrew at the girl, 'that's what the moon is for – a little lunacy. That's what it creates. Lunar madness. How's the qat, ogre? Want some more? I have a pocketful.'

The ogre nodded, taking some more of the green weed into its mouth from Andrew's hand. Andrew held on to the scaly fingers and gently urged the ogre into gliding round and round the fire. Andrew's feet were skipping back and forth now,

345

tripping lightly on the ground. He was laughing and giggling with glee. His free hand floated above his head, keeping time with the cadence of his song.

'Oh spring is here, fa-la-la-la, and the flowers are leaping from their bed – oh come with me, my love, my dear, and let us all our cares to shed . . .'

The ogre was now almost right up on its hind legs, dancing with Andrew, holding Andrew's left hand in its own cold-blooded claw.

Andrew whirled the creature round and round, singing lustily at the top of his voice. The ogre began laughing in a grotesque voice, its harsh, guttural tones echoing among the crags. Andrew yelled high and loud, like a Pict drunk on wine, alternately hugging the goat-ogre to his breast, then pushing it away and rocking his head and kicking out his feet. The ogre was quite upright now, oblivious to any danger.

'Oh what fun, what fun,' shrieked Andrew. 'Oh, my nose is running with the excitement . . .'

He let his right hand drop below, seemingly for a kerchief. Instead it flashed to his belt. He grasped his dagger. In an instant the blade of that weapon was drawn and buried deep in the ogre's stomach. Andrew leapt away from the fiend now, leaving the dagger where it was.

The ogre doubled up in agony, going back down on all fours again.

'You tricked me!' it screamed as it pulled the weapon out from its gut. 'I'll kill you.'

But the young knight had picked up a large rock and he struck the beast on the head with it. One of the horns broke with the force of the blow. Now Wadi was on her feet, helping

Andrew. She had taken a log from the fire and was beating the ogre's brains out. Within a few minutes the ugly goat-ogre lay on the ground, its skull wide open. It was dead.

Andrew's legs were shaking like poplar leaves in a stiff breeze. He stood trembling, mentally exhausted. The qat grass, which he had chewed just as heartily as the ogre, had made his mind spin and had caused him to feel sick. His body was not used to the strange drug and now that the fight was over his body felt the influence. His mind was in a whirl of relief, too, for the creature was dead. The battle had taken all Andrew's reserves of courage. He was fatigued beyond belief and his stomach churned. Also, another minute of that absurd, grotesque dance and he might have thrown up.

'You – you've saved me,' cried Yasmin. 'I thought you were a fool, but you came to save me.'

'Us,' murmured Wadi. 'Save *us*.'

It took some while for Andrew to recover his wits. The drama had sapped all his reserves of strength. While he was thus coming round, Wadi had cut off the goat head of the ogre and had rammed a wooden spit through it. It now roasted over the fire. She then proceeded to joint the creature, taking one of its goat legs and roasting that too. By the time Andrew had come to his senses, there was tender meat to be had. He ate some of the haunch while Wadi had some cheek. Yasmin, as was her wont, preferred the eyes of the roasted head. She squashed them with her teeth as if they were grapes.

'Mmmm – good,' said Andrew. 'But we must be on our way. We're in one of those pockets in the hills where strange beings are not rare. Now that we've dispensed with this one, perhaps another might come along. Better we start walking, even though it's cold and dark out there.'

'Hold my hand,' said Yasmin, slipping her plump fingers into his palm, 'I'm only a girl, you know.'

'I'm a girl, too,' muttered Wadi, 'but not *only*.'

Wadi then asked, 'What was that grass you gave it – the qat grass?'

'It comes from the Yemen. When you chew it and swallow the juices it sends you into a sort of trance, or dream. I don't know exactly. I didn't chew mine, I just tucked it into the side of my cheek with my tongue. I spat it out afterwards. I know the camel drivers like it. It probably makes the days go faster when you're crossing the empty quarters of the desert.'

They found Warlock grazing on the stiff desert grasses and Andrew collected his armour and loaded it on the horse. They began walking westwards, towards the sea. Yasmin clung on to his arm, chattering and laughing. Wadi walked on the other side of Warlock, her face hidden from the pair.

Truth be known, Andrew was not in the least interested in Yasmin. But he was entirely smitten with Wadi. The African girl had one of those jet-black faces with classical beauty evident in every curve and hollow. Andrew wanted to take that face and kiss it until his lips were sore. Her eyes came from the depths of the dark continent: ebony, black marble, black pearls. Her teeth were ivory. Her lips looked as soft as peaches, her hair crinkled tresses of darkness that fell from the night.

He groaned inwardly at the passion that was aroused within him, the yearning for the unattainable.

At this time Andrew could see only Wadi's hand on the

nape of Warlock's neck, and he saw that the moons of her fingernails were perfect crescents. He placed his free hand up on that same curving ridge of horse and idly let his hand slip along that curve until it − by accident − touched her fingers. Wadi's hand was removed instantly, leaving Andrew bereft.

By the time the trio reached Jerusalem, Yasmin was deeply in love with Andrew, and would not stop clinging to him, hanging on him like a vine with overripe grapes. Andrew was completely stricken by Wadi's beauty and his brain swam with images that would have made even a rake blush. Wadi, for her part, was in love with Andrew's horse and wanted him for her own, or one just like him, so that she could ride on the back of the wind.

'You found my lovely daughter,' cried the Persian, on seeing them. Then his expression changed to a darker hue. 'But what is this? You have violated her?'

'No, no, of course not,' stuttered Andrew. 'She is merely infatuated with me because I saved her life. It happened once before, with another girl. Yasmin was the captive of a fiend, which I slew with the help of the African princess . . .'

'Slave,' corrected Wadi, stroking Warlock. 'Just another black slave.'

'Are you sure you have not touched her, my Yasmin?'

'No Father,' cried the girl, 'he has been the perfect gentleman − more's the pity.'

'I am to be a Templar one day,' announced Andrew, 'and must therefore be chaste.'

'Oh, good,' muttered Wadi. 'That's a relief to hear.'

Andrew gave Wadi a hurt look.

'Well, then,' said the Persian, 'you deserve my thanks, young knight. Now, what shall be your reward? You said you could not take money? I assume that means jewels and other valuables also. What else is there that will repay you?'

Andrew swallowed hard. 'I want – I want the slave girl.'

'Wadi?' cried Yasmin. She gave Wadi a look of utter hatred. 'So, you've been sneaking behind my back, giving your favours to this – this two-faced Infidel.'

'Nothing of the sort,' replied Andrew. 'We're just good friends.'

'Not even that,' muttered Wadi.

The Persian said, 'Take the slave. I can't thank you enough for restoring my daughter to my side. May Allah's blessing go with you. Come, child, we must return to Babylon, where your mother awaits. Remember, you are to marry Ceniri in the spring . . .'

Yasmin was dragged off by her father, leaving Andrew standing awkwardly with Wadi.

Wadi flashed Andrew a look that crackled with lightning and had thunder close behind in its clouds.

'So, you are going to do with me as you've been wanting to do, ever since we met? Well, I'm your property now. I can say nothing. I must simply do what you order. Where shall I go, master? To your room in the palace? Is that it?'

'Go – home.'

'What?'

'Go to your home, wherever that may be. You are a free woman.'

This took all the fire out of Wadi's eyes. She stared at Andrew, probably suspecting a trick. Andrew returned he look with a liquid heart, yearning to hear her say she wanted to stay by his side forever, knowing she would not.

'I can go?'

'Anywhere you please – but,' he smiled wistfully, 'you can't take my horse. He belongs to me. I am as fond of him as you seem to be.'

She giggled now and her face broke into tiny creases that melted every bone in Andrew's body.

'You are not what I thought – you are a nice boy.'

'Man. I'm a knight, full-grown.'

'Almost, yes. But – thank you, Andrew.'

She went up on tiptoe and kissed his cheek.

Then she looked stricken. 'But how am I to get home? My people live in the heart of the land beyond the Nile – deeper down even than that – beyond the shores of the Red Sea. Towards the great ocean on the far side of the world. I was taken by slave traders, and brought here.'

Andrew gave her two gold coins.

'That should get you back. Here,' he gave her the dagger with which he had killed the goat-ogre, 'take this, too. You will need to protect yourself. If any man tries to enslave you on your passage home, tell him the – the best friend of King Baldwin of Jerusalem will cut out his heart if he so much as lays one finger on you. Buy yourself a bodyguard. Find one of your own people you can trust. Good luck, Wadi.'

'Good luck to you, too, Andrew – may you enter the temple you so desire to see.'

'The Temple of Solomon? I hope I will.'

'You will. And my name is Ulmurra – it means She-of-the-Leopard-Eyes.'

'Yes, you do have the eyes of a cat.'

Ulmurra walked away, her beautiful head held high. She did not turn her head to look at him before she rounded the corner of the suq. He saw that she was assuredly not in love with him. Only those who are walking away from someone they love turn at the last moment to capture that final, cherished picture.

Andrew was heartbroken. How could she not love him? Was he not good looking? Was he not a knight of the realm? Could he not give her a life of good fortune and happiness?

But love does not care for these things – it is only concerned with this mysterious and unfathomable, aching desire which no man can devise or design – a feeling formed out of nothing at all.

23. WELCOME TO SOLOMON'S TEMPLE

Feeling drained by his experiences, Andrew made his way to the palace stables with Warlock in tow. Both horse and rider were fatigued beyond measure. Andrew ached in every joint and he was sure that Warlock must feel the same. A rubdown with oil, some hay and a stall to eat it in would be most welcome to the steed, Andrew was sure.

'Hello, Andrew,' said a stableboy, carrying a bucket of dung in one hand. 'Shall I take Warlock from you?'

'You must call me *sire* now,' ordered Andrew, 'for I am a knight, not a common squire.'

'Oh.' The stableboy, who had previously been used to chatting with Andrew about this and that, looked a little hurt. 'All right, then, sire. But Warlock has the grey dust of ages on his coat. Where have you been riding him? And the sweat is on him – he has been carrying this armour a long ways?'

'This is not the business of a stableboy,' said Andrew, somewhat haughtily. 'It is your business just to tend to the horse and not ask questions.'

Andrew left the boy and walked away, but he had not gone ten paces before he exhaled with a loud sigh. He was trying to be a knight and knights were arrogant people who treated their servants like dirt. But Andrew used to *be* one of those servants and knew what it felt like to be on the receiving end of such arrogance. He walked back to the stableboy and said,

'Forgive my snappish mood, Peter – I'm trying to do what's expected of my station, but it's not . . . look, just forget what I said.'

'No,' said Peter, 'you're right – I shouldn't call you "Andrew" for the other knights will despise you for it.'

'Well, I wish that we will secretly remain friends. It's so difficult, all this pretending to be a noble.'

'Pretending, sire?'

'Well, *being* a noble.'

He then went off to find Tomas.

Tomas was delighted to see him and he at least made no mistake.

'Sire, I have missed your company.' He embraced Andrew, and began to remove those pieces of armour that had not already been shed. 'Shall I fetch water for a bath? Of course I must. You are weary and dirty. Have your adventures been many, sire? Please tell me all, for I am attentive.'

Andrew fell into a chair and allowed himself to be coddled and treated like a child. While the bath was being prepared he recounted the story of his journey and some of the incidents and accidents that had happened on the way. He did not tell Tomas that he had fallen for a slave girl with the eyes of a leopard, though he did speak of saving two maidens from the clutches of a man-eating ogre, who was now dead and gone to goat hell.

'Sire, you have been through much,' Tomas said. 'May I massage your brow? I'm sure I can make the tension in your body go away.'

'Yes please, Tomas.'

Tomas stood behind his friend and his long, soft fingers –

the fingers of an angel – made small circles on Andrew's temple. It was most soothing. Soon much of the agitation and stress of the last few days had left Andrew's mind. He began to relax and forget all his troubles with Gondemar. He wished the other knight to Hell, along with the goat-ogre, but his worries about the man evaporated under the magical fingers of his companion. Tomas's long, silky curls fell over his face and brushed his cheeks as the young man bent to his task. Soon Andrew had fallen into a deep sleep in his chair.

Andrew awoke to find that Tomas had wrapped a blanket around him and had drawn him a hot bath. Dreamily he climbed out of the chair and undressed, then stepped into the bath. How good it felt. He could have stayed there all day if the hot water had kept coming. While he bathed Tomas commiserated with him over his troubles with Gondemar.

'All you ever wished to do was save the knight's life,' said Tomas. 'No wonder you're angry at your treatment in his hands, sire.'

'Should I have killed him while I had the chance?'

'That's not the question, sire?'

'What is?'

'*Could* you have killed him.'

Andrew mused on this for a moment, then said, 'No', miserably. 'Tomas, I find it one thing to kill a stranger in battle, an enemy whose face I do not recognise, but when it comes to a man I know – a knight I once respected – my hand will not follow my head. I find it answering my heart and my heart does not have enough bitterness in it, despite the whipping and the insults. Despite all, I can't bring myself to kill a knight of my own creed . . .'

'Oh, and as to that, sire – why, that smelly Frenchman wants to see you.'

'Frenchman?'

'The Odious de St Amand – the bulky man.'

'Why didn't you say so?' Andrew leapt from the bath, spraying water all over the floor. 'Quickly, Tomas – a decent garb. Am I in trouble?' He thought about his single combat with Sir Gondemar. Everything had been in order there. No rules had been broken so far as Andrew was aware. 'If not in trouble, perhaps something to my advantage? And you mustn't use that joke name for Sir Odo, no matter how clever we thought it the first time you used it. He might get to hear.'

Tomas gave his companion a secret smile. 'I gave him the ruby, sire.'

Andrew stopped pulling on his padded jackets.

'You did what?'

'The ruby – I have given it to the odious one.'

Andrew's heart was beating fast.

'And what did he say?'

'Nothing. He took it and stroked it as if it were a small kitten. Then he slipped it into his pocket and walked away. He did not even thank me for it, sire, which I thought bad manners indeed. Sire, it was what we planned to do, wasn't it? The ruby meant nothing to us, after all. It was a means to an end.'

'Yes, it was. But I wish . . . never mind. I'll go and find him.'

Once he was presentable, Andrew left his room and walked the passageways to the palace gates. As he approached the gates another young man was coming in. The youth was somewhere around Andrew's age. The young man had a longish object wrapped in cloth and he stared at Andrew a little too long as he passed.

'Something the matter, boy?' asked Andrew, irritated by this lack of decorum. 'What's wrong?'

'Nothing really,' replied the youth, looking round. 'This is my first time at the palace – I'm unsure of where to go.'

'Just a minute!'

The youth turned and faced Andrew, probably hoping to receive some guidance on which way to go in the maze of passageways.

'Nothing really, *sire*. You are addressing a knight of King Baldwin of Jerusalem.'

'I beg pardon, sire. I did not know. You seem so young.'

'My age has nothing to do with you.' Andrew peered at the youth. 'What's your name?'

'Walter – sire. Walter Pughson. I am the son of the swordsmith, Pugh of Middle Wallop.'

Andrew burst out laughing. 'Where?'

Walter sighed. 'Why does everyone always laugh? Middle Wallop is a perfectly respectable village in the south of England. Have you not heard of it, sire?'

'No, I haven't. And don't give me that weary look, swordmaker's assistant, or I'll wipe it off your face for you. You seem strange. Can you tell me why?'

'No, sire, I don't feel strange.'

'I mean you have a strange way about you. I feel I've seen you before somewhere. Have you ever been to Cressing in Essex?'

'Not to my knowledge, my lord.'

357

'Well, I'd rather you didn't walk about looking strange. Try not to. Where are you going?'

Walter held up the object in his hands.

'I'm delivering a sword to Sir Gondemar de Blois.'

Andrew's blood ran cold and it must have shown in his face for the boy stepped forward.

'Sire, you look ill – are you about to swoon?'

'He is here? Sir Gondemar?'

'No, sire, he's coming from Antioch at some time – I know not when, but his squire is here ahead of him. The sword was ordered by the squire.'

'Gareth?'

'Yes, that will be his name.'

Andrew mused, 'No wonder Gareth was not there at the single combat.'

Walter asked again, 'Are you well, sire. Do you need assistance? Shall I call someone?'

'No, no,' muttered Andrew, 'you get about your strange ways, boy.'

With that he left the youth and continued on his way to the Temple of Solomon.

When he reached the temple, he sought permission to enter from one of the sergeants-at-arms.

'I am here at the request of the Master of the Temple,' he said.

'I'll take you to him.'

Odo de St Amand was in his study, poring over manuscripts. He looked up when Andrew was shown into the room and motioned the youth to sit in a chair until he was ready for him. Andrew felt peeved, but did as he was told. Odo was obviously deep in some problem. After reading this parchment and that, Odo said, 'Letters from the Pope.'

'Oh,' said Andrew, not knowing what to reply. 'But that, sire – what is that?'

'This?' Odo held up a chart written in coloured inks. Andrew saw squiggles all over the parchment, some large sweeping ones, some smaller ones. It did not look like writing, although there was also writing on the parchment, too. 'This is a map. It was drawn by an ancient philosopher called Ptolemy.'

Andrew dimly remembered a conversation with one-armed Old Foggarty.

'What does it do, sire?'

'Do? It does nothing. But see these drawings?'

'They look like rain puddles, sire.'

'They are regions, countries, areas. This is a drawing of the world with the mountains and hills made flat. A map of the world inside its edges – the world so much as we know of it. Here is Egypt,' he pointed, 'and here Cyprus, and there England. If you were a bird and flew high up, these are the shapes you would see below.'

Andrew peered at the 'map' and frowned.

'Surely, sire, that can't be England. It is too small for our great country.'

The French Master of the Temple laughed.

'England? In the grand scheme of things it is but a village. See, here are all the great kingdoms of France. If you wanted to live in a big country you should have been born French. Or Persian. Or Iberian, though the Iberians have no country to call their own at the moment, now that the Moors have taken much of their land.'

'Well, sire, I think of England as great.'

'I think of England as a colony of France, but we all have our different perceptions, Sir Andrew.'

That was twice. Twice the Master had called him 'Sir Andrew'. It sounded good. Andrew was a little irritated by Odo's put-down of his country of birth, but he was also eager to find out why the Master wanted to see him.

'Sir Odo, my – my page said you wanted to see me.'

Odo rolled up the chart in his hand and tied the tube with a red ribbon.

'Indeed I do. You will be delighted to hear I have changed my mind about your desire to be a Templar. The Temple of Solomon will receive you into its bosom.'

Odo looked a little shifty as he said these words, as if there were some secret guilt which had assisted him in reversing his earlier decision. Andrew wondered what had happened to bring this about, but he was so delighted by the news that he shrugged it off. What did it matter that Odo seemed guileful? He had at last attained his greatest ambition: to become a Knight Templar.

'Oh, Master – I am joyful,' cried Andrew, leaping from his seat. 'Of all that is wonderful, I am to be a Templar?'

Odo clearly did not share Andrew's great joy, for he merely nodded and said, 'You must be prepared for a life of chastity and poverty. Are you ready for such a commitment? There are rules you must follow. The worst of all crimes is desertion from the field of battle. If you ever leave the battlefield while a struggle is in progress, you will be cast out of the Order with ignominy. You understand?'

'That, Master, is something I would never do.'

Odo nodded. 'No, I don't believe you would. But, you must also conduct yourself with dignity and honour. There are secular knights who have frivolous pursuits – such as hunting with hawks – you must never indulge in such idle games. This is a great honour, to be accepted into the Order, and you must not besmirch it. Drinking, carousing, causing havoc in the marketplace, all these are forbidden to a Knight Templar. You will be a warrior-monk, one of God's soldiers, sworn to protect the pilgrims in or on their way to the Holy Land.

'Our enemies are the king's enemies. This temple is our sanctuary and our place of prayer. Also you will know that we are not the only order of warrior-monks on these crusades. There are the Knights Hospitaller, the Knights of St John. You will treat them with civility, but not with deference. If ever we beat the Saracen and have no real enemies, we might then be free to turn on the Hospitallers. Personally I despise them as much as they despise us. Jealousy exists between us, and enmity, and one day there will have to be a reckoning.'

'Yes, Master.'

Andrew went straight to see Tomas. When Andrew told his friend the news, Tomas suddenly took on a similar look to that which had been on Odo's face. Was there a conspiracy here? Perhaps it was all a joke?

'Tomas, did you know about this?'

'Oh,' Tomas waved vaguely skywards, the guilt in his expression seeming to deepen, 'I had heard a whisper of a rumour – but master, you must be joyful. It's what you always wanted.'

'You haven't done anything bad?'

'Master, do you want to be a Templar?'

361

'Yes, of course.'

'Then ask no more questions.'

And so Andrew prepared himself for a second vigil, similar to the one he had taken in order to be a knight. This one, so far as he was concerned, was far more important. His vows as a Templar were sacrosanct. Kneeling at the altar rail in the chapel, he searched his heart and mind for any defects in his character. There were many, of course. They had to be expunged from his spirit with fervent promises. He told himself that he would be the most devout and obedient of all Templars anywhere. This was the most important moment of his life. His ambition to become a Knight Templar was about to be fulfilled and Andrew of Cressing raised up to the highest peak of his aspirations. From farrier's son to Knight Templar. It had been an impossible dream, but one that had become reality. Golden light shone through the chapel window and at this moment those precious yellow rays were his. Whether it had been God or Lady Fortune that had given him this miraculous gift he knew not, so he thanked both in equal measure.

His pledges.

Yes, he pledged with all the sincerity in his heart.

This time they were vows of poverty, chastity and obedience.

There were other, smaller promises, which he made with all candour.

He would be the most devoted knight ever to have entered the Temple of Solomon and to have been accepted into that gracious and elite order of warrior-monks. He promised to obey every facet of that order. There would not be even one

362

small rule that he would break. He would keep all his vows and all the laws of the order, even those that other knights thought unnecessary or fatuous.

He would keep every single tiny one.

Except, of course, the one about hunting with falcons.

In a hallowed and private ceremony, closed to the eyes of all but fellow Templars, Andrew was finally presented with the treasured white mantle bearing its blood-red cross. He took it reverently, with a softly beating heart and bated breath. So precious, this flimsy piece of cloth. So wonderfully dear. Priceless as chapel sunlight. Certainly more valuable than gold. The first time he wore it, he was awestruck with his own grandeur. A Knight Templar! He had reached the pinnacle of his longing. The peak of most men's desire. To rise from a lowly farrier's son to become one of the most envied knights in Christendom was not only an achievement, it was a miracle. Surely there was a divine hand at work, guiding his fate? Not fairies, not witches, not demons, but an angel of the Lord had plucked Andrew from a small English village and raised him high. A warrior-monk of the greatest order in the world.

He was exalted.

On the way back to his quarters, Andrew ran into the king's tutor, Septimus Silke, who had indeed been tutoring Andrew as well.

'Septimus,' said Andrew, 'I have been made a Knight Templar! Isn't that famous news?'

Septimus Silke was a thin, reedy man with a large head and a great mass of yellow hair that hung down to his waist. On top of his head he wore a velvet cap of no particular shape or hue with a sorry looking feather drooping from it.

Septimus Silke nodded solemnly making the feather flop back and forth over his narrow nose. Septimus Silke was, of course, carrying an armful of rolled parchments, tied with coloured ribbons. There were several quills in his top pocket, the residue ink of which had stained his tunic. A large smudge of these different coloured inks had formed a nebulous blot on his pocket and had spread even beyond it.

On seeing the blot on the tutor's tunic, Andrew said, 'Oh, and by the way, I want to learn about maps.'

'Maps?'

'Yes, the shape of countries – did you not know there were such things as maps and charts?'

Septimus Silke curled back both lips, baring his teeth. 'Of course I know about charts and maps – I am a scholar. I take it you wish to learn about geography?'

'If that's what maps are all about, yes.'

'As well as learning to read and write?'

'Yes.'

'You'll be asking me to teach you algebra next – I'll have no time for the king.'

'Oh, the king knows everything anyway. What's algebra?'

'A branch of mathematics.'

'Trees?'

'No, not *trees*. Why would I be talking about trees?'

'You said *branch*,' Andrew pointed out, not without some satisfaction at having caught out his tutor.

'Never mind. Algebra is a set of formulas for . . . oh, Lord, you have so much to learn, boy, and all you want to do is rush around killing Saracens. Did you know that the Arabs invented algebra? Indeed, they are a highly intellectual race.

And here you are, trying to wipe them from the face of the Earth.'

'I don't want to do that – one of my best friends is an Arab.'

'That's what they all say.'

'I'll ask Hassan about algebra – how he invented it.'

Septimus Silke sighed deeply. 'Do that. And in the meantime, how are your private studies going? Have you finished those exercises on verbs, nouns and adjectives?'

'I've been a bit busy.'

'Killing people. Well, make sure you have them for me in two days, or we'll talk to the king.'

Andrew said, 'Aren't you going to wish me well? About the Templar thing?'

'If that is what you wish for yourself, sire, I offer you my heartfelt congratulations.'

'Of course it's what I wish. Why wouldn't I?'

He left the tutor and made his way back to his quarters where he broke the news to Tomas about his new status as a Knight of the Temple of Solomon.

'Andrew,' said Tomas, breathlessly, when he was told, 'you are the most fortunate of men.'

'I am indeed, Tomas, but don't forget you must call me *sire* now that I'm a knight.'

'Oh, yes, of course. Sorry,' replied Tomas, a little downcast. 'I shall remember in future.'

Andrew then walked about Jerusalem wearing his mantle, to let the people see what he had achieved. Those who knew him congratulated him. Those who did not stepped aside to let him pass. Andrew carefully avoided running into Hassan, who was the one person he did not want to meet. Hassan would not be pleased and Andrew understood why. The Saracens had good cause to hate the Templars.

Andrew had grown to know all the noises of the city of Jerusalem, with its mixture of races and creeds. He woke to the sound of muezzins calling the faithful to prayer, just as he had once woken to the sound of church bells in his village of Cressing. There were cockerels and dogs and geese, too, as there had been at home in England, and donkeys that brayed, but also camels hooting, kites shrieking. Here the women ululated on certain occasions, which sometimes terrified him with its eerie sound. Some sounds he loved, others he found strange and frightening.

In the backstreets he had come to know several of the professions. He knew an alchemist, and a blacksmith, and a swordsmith, and a soothsayer, having met all these people when he was with Hassan. They greeted him as if he were one of their own and he enjoyed being so accepted.

In the palace of the king, he was favoured by secular knights like Catherine, the only woman knight in Jerusalem, and Sir John and others of his kind. They liked his company, for he could be witty at times, and, being a youth, they felt maternal and paternal towards him. King Baldwin liked him because they were of the same age and laughed at the same things, and made fun of the same people, and generally shared what youth shares in any time or place. They formed a little club of two, exchanging saucy stories which were all fiction, and privately using gutter talk of which their elders would disapprove. They were barely grown boys.

Odo de St Amand treated Andrew with restrained severity and began devising missions for him to accomplish.

At first Andrew went out with other older knights to attack Saracen strongholds, or to raid enemy caravans, or to find some leader or other of a hostile tribe and destroy his camp. But Andrew proved so fearless in battle, so determined to stamp his mark on the world of the Templar Knights, that they began calling him the new 'Alexander', that once great warrior from the time of the Greeks who was also a youth when he began his career of conquering other races, other lands.

Thus the older Templars began to look to Andrew for leadership. This youth, they soon realised, could find his way through the most dense forest and across the most dreadful of wildernesses. He crossed the fastnesses of mountain ranges without any concern of being lost. When things became difficult for the band of knights, Andrew would leave them to consult with 'an angel' and return to guide his followers out of danger. He even led some men into Egypt and might have tugged the beard of Saladin himself if that great warrior had not been away on an expedition of his own.

Odo was left to wonder as this boy was praised in the Temple of Solomon and in the palace of the king. He watched through narrowed eyes as Andrew returned from his latest triumph with blood staining the white of his mantle and with dents in his precious armour. He was told that Andrew had saved the life of many another knight, on several occasions, without thought for his own life. Odo might have been impressed if he had not been suspicious as to the source of the boy's power. From where did this young man derive such courage and ferocity? If asked, Andrew would answer, the Lord, but then all Templars prayed and few matched the boy in question for cleverness and sagacity on the battlefield.

In time Andrew's exploits were sung about by minstrels who had never even met him. Songs about his deeds travelled throughout Outremer, across lands and kingdoms, and back even to the shores of his home country. When they heard about 'Andrew of Cressing' in the village of his birth, they shook their heads and told each other there must be another village of the same name somewhere else, for this Knight Templar also called Andrew was probably the son of a satrap or prince of another region. Surely, they laughed, this could not be the Andrew who had been reviled and teased by the other village youths just a few years previously?

Andrew's fame spread and spread, until one knight in particular was sick to death of hearing his name. Gondemar de Blois had been lying ill for many months, unable to move without unbearable pains shooting down his spine. But he had improved of late and was beginning to rise and take gentle rides at dawn. On those rides he could not get rid of the sour taste in his mouth, for everywhere he went he heard the same name on the lips of admirers, the name of the youth who had beaten him at single combat. Had he a right arm, that youth would be lying in his grave, but the same boy had robbed him of the limb that would have put him in the earth.

'I shall have him yet,' spat Gondemar to his squire, Gareth. 'I shall make the boy wish he were already dead.'

'Do you have a plan, sire?' asked his squire.

'I have a plan. I have many plans. There is one that is sure to bring him down. And when he is once down, I will make sure he never rises again.'

Gareth did not know whether that meant Gondemar was

going to kill Andrew once he had been stripped of his new-found glory, or whether he intended to turn Andrew into a kitchen boy washing greasy pans.

Once Gondemar was fit enough for travel, the vengeful knight set out from Antioch for Jerusalem.

24. SLAVES AND FREEMEN

Angelique visited Toby whenever she could, to smear balm on his back where he had been whipped. It did not matter that the youth was one of the strongest of the slaves working on the walls. All were given the lash as a matter of course, in the mistaken belief that it would make them work harder.

'Poor Toby,' she whispered. 'Your back is raw.'

'They won't break me,' said Toby. 'They can try and try, but I'm as strong as a horse. I have bones that would grow to oaks if they was sticks. Don't you be down about me, mistress, for I'm not about to go under, you know.'

'Oh, I know, Toby. But we're all worried about you.'

'What's it like back there, in the palace?'

'Better, but still frightening. There are executions every day. If someone displeases the sultan, they lose their head, or a limb, to his sword. Every morning he has a different slave to help him up on to his horse and most times he draws his sword as he mounts, and then strikes down the man whose cupped hands are assisting him into the saddle.'

'He is a cruel man, then?'

'The sultan does not see himself as cruel, for others are just as bad as he. And to be truthful, Toby, there are men in our own land whose cruelty shadows their souls.'

'Ah, don't we know it, mistress, us serfs and churls and those even lower in the order.'

The players at the palace were indeed having a better time of it, for Toby was sleeping in a pit full of men who formed a knot when resting. There was no room to move and those on the bottom suffered the weight of those on top, sometimes suffocating in their sleep. Arms and legs became entangled, bodies pressed against each other, and the strong fought to stay above the weak, for the need to survive turns gentle, honourable men into beasts. At least those in the palace had straw on which to sleep and a rolled coat for a pillow.

Toby ate a mess of muck which was nameless in the world of food, while Arthur, Patrick and Angelique fed on scraps of chicken and bread from the kitchen. They smuggled bits of food to Toby when they could, but it was getting more difficult as their status at the palace decreased. They were finding it harder and harder to amuse the sultan, and they could sense the day coming when they would all be working on the wall with Toby, and no hope of ever leaving the place.

One morning a miracle occurred.

Angelique was summoned to the presence of the sultan on her own and found a Christian knight was being entertained as his guest.

'Here is the boy,' cried the sultan through his interpreter, as she entered a courtyard of fountains and peacocks, 'he sings so sweetly you would swear he has the throat of a song-bird.'

Angelique started trembling. Here was a knight from her own country. Surely he had come for her?

'Approach, stripling,' said the knight in English. 'Let's hear you warble like a thrush. Make haste now, I want to be on my way. I do not want to be in this nest of vipers any longer than necessary, but I said I would hear you. You are from Britain, are you not? Let the words come out in my own tongue, then, for I do not like the gabble of the Moors.'

'I am indeed from the shores of Britain, sire, and would like to return to them as soon as possible.'

The knight, a burly man with a black beard and harsh features, leaned forward.

'Make no mistake, boy, I have come for one man only, a man of gentle birth – I can take no other with me.'

'But I, too, am of gentle birth. My father is Robert de Sonnac. If you have come to ransom a friend or relation, please take me and my friends with you? My father will reward you well, sire. Indeed he will.'

The sultan was watching this exchange with displeasure evident in his features. He could not understand what was being said, but he did not like his guests talking with slaves as if they were real people. The boy had been brought out to sing and sing he would. If not, he would be beaten, or worse.

'What are they saying?' asked the sultan of Messaoud. 'Why doesn't the boy sing? Make him sing.'

Messaoud replied, 'Lord, they talk of freedom for the boy, but the English knight does not have the money for more slaves.'

'Then let him sing!'

Messaoud said to Angelique, 'Master says you must sing – do so quickly, or he will surely kill you.'

Angelique, who had witnessed many sudden deaths at the hands of the sultan, broke instantly into song, startling the English knight. The knight watched her face as she sang the notes to an English melody. There was a frown on his forehead when she came towards the end of the song. But she did not finish where the tune ended. She added a verse.

'Sire,' she sang, 'please help myself and my three companions leave this place of Hell – indeed, my father will reward you with more than the return of the ransom.'

The knight rose from the wicker chair in which he was sitting.

'Boy,' he roared, 'I know Robert de Sonnac, and he has no son – only a daughter.'

He turned to leave the courtyard, but Angelique cried after him, 'I am she. My name is Angelique. I am my father's daughter. I had to pretend to be a boy in this place, for you know what they would do to a girl.'

'Indeed, sometimes also to boys,' said the knight, turning back. 'You are Robert de Sonnac's child? Mercy. How did you find yourself in these straits, child? I am the Earl of Ipswich. I am here for a friend's son, the captain of an English ship that was sunk by pirates.'

'I, too, was on a ship that was taken by pirates.'

Messaoud was hopping from one foot to the other, certain now that the sultan was going to behead Angelique. Swiftly, he said the sultan, 'Lord, he might purchase the boy, too – he likes him. He likes his song.'

The sultan nodded slowly, the hand that had been venturing towards his jewelled scimitar dropping away.

'How much will he pay?'

Messaoud said to the earl, 'Most Healthy Knight, the boy-girl is for sale. Have you the moneys for her with you? If you have not the moneys, the sultan will kill her.'

'What price?' asked the earl.

Then the haggling began.

At the end of it all, Angelique interrupted the bargaining: 'I cannot go without my companions – I would rather die here than leave them.'

The Earl of Ipswich looked exasperated.

'Companions? How many?'

'Three youths – two have been in the palace with me – the other is working on the wall, with the other slaves.'

'I have not the money with me to buy them all.'

'Can you send for it?'

The earl was silent for a few moments, then he said, 'You must come with me now. I'll send a man back to fetch the boys. Are they from good families? Good breeding?'

'They are strolling players from lowly families.'

'Then why bother with them?'

'The youths saved my honour, indeed my life, and I owe them theirs. I have grown to love them as brothers. Indeed, brothers could not be kinder to their sisters than these three have been to me. They have risked all to rescue me from harm and have ended up here through no fault of their own.'

The earl looked her directly in the eyes.

'But they have not touched you?'

'No, sire, they have been truly as brothers to me, nothing more, nothing less.'

'Good.' He sighed heavily. 'In that case, we will find the gold for these waifs. You, child, *must* accompany me now. Sir Robert would not forgive me if I left you here a second longer. God forbid. The boys will be ransomed. I'm sure they're not worth much to the sultan, if all they are is players.' He said the last word with some contempt. 'We shall work out

374

a good price and fetch them their freedom. I'll make sure they're put on the road somewhere well out of the way of Moorish domination. But you, you must come with me.'

'Yes, sire,' Angelique was so relieved she burst into tears. 'Oh, sir,' she sobbed, 'forgive me for being a weak female.'

'Weak?' he roared. 'I've never met a girl like you – you must be made of steel to have survived all this! Pirates. Slavery. If I ever have a daughter like you, I'll lock her in a tower. The world would be an unbearable place if all daughters had the same steel in their blood. God forbid! God forbid indeed.'

The ransomed man was a sea captain by the name of Peter Mariner. The Earl of Ipswich paid one hundred gold coins for him, and fifty silver coins for Angelique, since she was only a weak boy, albeit one with a pretty voice, and not worth a great deal to the sultan as a slave. It was true the sultan was getting tired of her singing now, for he was a man with the mind of a gadfly, whose interests darted from one thing to another on a whim.

The earl had six men-at-arms with him, more for show than for protection, since they were in the land of the Moors who numbered them in their thousands. The earl had been sent a banner to fly as he travelled, which proclaimed him to be under the protection of the sultan. No Moor would violate that truce, for the sultan was feared even among his own people. They rode to a small harbour the Iberians had called La Herradura, which means *The Horseshoe*, named for the shape of the bay. It lay on the coast below the city of Granada and the Sierra Nevada, close to the rivers known as the Seco and the Jate. There the earl signalled for a rowing boat to take them to a Genoese vessel which was bound for the port of Syracuse with a fleet of Christian ships.

Earlier the earl had told Angelique, 'It's better you remain a boy for the time being – just until we set sail.'

So, she was still posing as a youth and even the men-at-arms and Peter Mariner were not aware of her gender.

The rowing boat set off from the shore, but unfortunately on boarding the small craft a man-at-arms had dropped the sultan's banner in the water. They thus no longer had protection from the local population. Immediately, a horde of Moors began firing arrows at them from the cliffs of La Herradura.

Angelique was small enough to crouch down underneath one of the boat's seats, but the men-at-arms and the earl were exposed. Arrows rained down on the craft. An arrow hit the earl in the chest and he fell overboard. Two of the men-at-arms were then struck, killing one, wounding the other. Arrows struck the boat from stem to stern. The rowers kept pulling furiously, until the small craft finally put enough water between them and the shore to be out of range.

Those on board the Genoese ship were furious at this unspeakable breach of a truce. Even as Angelique was hauled aboard by strong hands, there was talk of retribution. Several languages were flying around the vessel: English, Italian, French, German, Scandinavian. All were crying for revenge for the earl's death. A signal went out to the other ships in the bay, twenty-eight of them in number. There was a rush to arms.

'What's happening?' asked Angelique of one of the sailors from a French kingdom.

'We will attack the heathens,' said the sailor. 'They must

pay for the death of the English knight. Get yourself a weapon, lad. You'll be coming with us. We need all the men we can get, even shavelings like you.'

Angelique found herself being bundled into a skiff and once more heading for the shore of Iberia.

The Moors on the mainland now realised what a mistake they had made. They saw the activity in the bay and decided to retreat into the hills. There were some farmers, fishermen and tradesmen, but many of them were warriors. Nearly two thousand Christians were heading towards their beaches.

The Moors were heavily outnumbered. They began to climb the foothills of the mountains – the Sierra Nevada – scrambling up the gorges towards the high valleys where they could find natural fortifications. There were millions of Moors in Iberia, but this was an enclosed region, and it would take time to get help from their neighbours.

The sailors set fire to the village that ran along the curved shoreline, then with the men-at-arms followed the Moors up dry river beds into the mountainous interior. Wildlife scattered before them as they clattered over shale and rocks, disturbing wild goats, bee-eater birds and small mammals. The inflamed Christians were yelling for blood. Angelique was swept along in this furious tide of men baying at running quarry.

The leader of the men from the ships was the Marquis of Léon, a man not normally given to rash action, and he began to advise caution. However, there was another knight there, a hot-headed Hungarian, whose name was unpronounceable to any who did not share his language. They called him the Torch because of his fiery temper. 'Do not light the Torch' had been the watchword in the fleet, 'or you'll get severely burned.' The Torch was not the leader of the invasion, but he led in the sense that he was the first man up the crags.

'Come on!' yelled the Torch, turning and waving his sword. 'Follow me! We'll take their skins.'

There were regional men among the pursuers – Catalans and Basques – who hated the fact that the Iberian peninsula had been overrun by Moors. Many had the same kind of temperament as the Torch and answered his bidding, racing up the inclines to be by his side.

Angelique hung back with the main body of men, staying close to the Marquis of Léon. She was frightened by the blood-lust which was evident in the mob of soldiers, sailors and gentlemen chasing the Moors. It seemed there was no control, no order among them. They were like a huge pack of dogs after another smaller pack of dogs, each pack wanting to rip the other to pieces.

The Moors finally reached three small villages high in the mountains, a trio called Los Guajares, where they were re-inforced by more of their own people. Still they were outnumbered by their attackers. They made a stand in the crags above the highest village, Guajar Alto. There they began rolling rocks down the slopes on those chasing them.

Ignoring the calls of the Marquis to regroup, the Torch led his keen followers in hot pursuit. Dodging the rocks that came down, the Torch and his men scrambled up the steep-sided gorge to reach the Moors above. However, breathlessness and exhaustion began to take its toll on those who came with him. Soon his numbers had dwindled to not more than two score.

Still the Torch continued to climb towards the peak where he could see Moorish heads looking over.

Suddenly there was an assault from above. With the main body of their enemy far below, the Moors poured over their natural ramparts and threw themselves down on the Torch and his men. A slaughter ensued. The sailors and soldiers were exhausted after their climb, having no energy now to fight, and they were surprised by the speed of the Moors. All turned to flee, but were stabbed and stuck with blades. Others actually fell down the steep slopes, rolling down on razor-sharp rocks and shredding their bodies. The Torch fought furiously but was set upon by four or five Moors, who lunged at him with their weapons and cut many holes in his body. His limp and lifeless corpse was thrown down the mountainside, to land near the Marquis and the rest of the army.

The Marquis kicked the body. 'This is a disgrace,' he cried. 'You deserved to die, you stupid man.'

The Marquis then settled down with his captains and worked out a plan of attack on the Moorish position.

When he was ready he calmly sent out two groups of men, one on the right, the other on the left, to take the Moors on their flanks. With shields in front of them to protect them from arrows and rocks, the main body of men began a slow crawl up the mountainside. Unlike the Torch, they were in no hurry. The idea was to get there unscathed with as many men as possible. There were to be no prisoners: all the Moors were to be cut down where they stood. Only their leader was to be taken alive.

The army ascended stealthily, not getting their ranks entangled as the Torch's lines had been. Gradually, gradually, they made the ground and the Moors became more frantic in their efforts to dislodge the climbers. Eventually the top was reached, the flanking groups timing their assault to coordinate with the main body. The Moorish position was overrun and the massacre began. Angelique held back, a short sword in her hand, unwilling to take part, yet unable to withdraw. In the blood-letting no one noticed her inactivity. When it was all over, the Marquis ordered his men back to their vessels. They had to leave before the news of the battle reached the ears of the larger number of Moors in nearby towns.

The leader of the Moors, a local official of the sultan, was taken live aboard the admiral's ship. There he was torn apart by two men with large iron pincers, who ripped off his fingers one by one, then his toes, then lips, nose, ears, and other appendages, before beginning to tear chunks of flesh from his bones. His screams reached Angelique on board one of the other vessels. They filled the bay of La Herradura with the horror of an undescribably savage death. Once the pincers reached his heart a sickening silence fell over the scene. The remains were then thrown into the water for the fish and the fleet set sail.

Angelique went to Peter Mariner, the man who had been ransomed from the sultan.

'That was a disgusting thing to do,' she said, shuddering. 'Why did they do it?'

Peter Mariner shrugged. 'As a lesson,' he replied.

Angelique said, 'I would rather not have witnessed such teachings.'

'No.'

'But, sir,' she continued, 'do you remember the earl saying

380

that we were to send a man with a ransom for my friends, who remain slaves of the sultan?'

Peter Mariner shook his head. 'No – he said nothing to me.'

'Well, he promised. I said my father, Robert de Sonnac, would repay the ransom.'

'Boy,' said Peter Mariner, looking into Angelique's face with pale blue eyes, 'no one can go back there now. After what we've done here today the sultan would rather eat live coals than accept a ransom for any slave.'

'He likes money.'

'Not that much. In fact, it's my opinion that the sultan will now execute any slave with a white skin. He will be blind to anything but revenge for this slaughter. Your friends are gone. Forget them. There is no hope they will survive. Just pray they do not fall to the same fate as that poor Moorish scribe on the admiral's ship.'

25. THE FIRST TRIAL

'You are wanted by the king,' said Tomas, breathless from having run from another part of the palace. 'Odious de St Amand is there, and also that pig Gondemar.'

'Gondemar?' replied Andrew. 'How he shadows me, that sorry man.'

'I think there is trouble for you, sire,' Tomas said, his expression full of sympathy. 'I shall pray for you.'

Something occurred to Andrew.

'Do angels pray? I ask because they are not mortals with souls, but beings from Heaven itself. Are they not of hallowed stock?'

'They praise the Lord, of course,' replied Tomas, as if he had been privy to such a thing, 'which amounts to praying.'

'Does it?' sighed Andrew. 'Well, you must know Tomas – oh, well, I'd better answer the king's call. How do I look? Am I not the prince of dressers?'

'You are everything any man would desire to be, Andrew – that is to say, my lord.'

Andrew left his companion and made his way through the passageways to the room where the king held court. He was more troubled than he liked to show to Tomas. Gondemar was extremely devious. What new attack had this troublesome knight devised to burden Andrew with? Andrew could think of nothing he had done wrong. In fact, he had done everything required of a Knight Templar, and more. His praises were sung in every quarter of the kingdoms of the East. He led men into places where others dared not go. What was more, he emerged with them at the other end. He would even have attacked the Assassins in their stronghold if King Baldwin had not had a peace treaty with these secret murderers of men.

As he followed the passageways, he suddenly remembered it was 24 March – New Year's Eve. Tomorrow was New Year's Day, the first day of 1177. He was not sure whether that was good luck, or bad. Surely a new year brought change for the better, did it not?

When he finally entered the hall he saw a deep frown on the brow of Odo and the king's face was also troubled.

Gondemar stood to the side, nursing the stump on the end of his right arm. There were other knights and nobles in the room, including Catherine of Tortosa and John of Reims. One or two were smirking, though most looked fairly serious. A few of the women were looking downcast and unhappy. Andrew was popular among the ladies of the court.

'Andrew,' said the king, 'Sir Gondemar de Blois has made a very serious charge against you – Sir Gondemar . . .?' Baldwin looked at the knight as if to say, do your own dirty work and make it stick if you value your honour.

Gondemar turned a sneer on Andrew. 'Youth,' he said, 'is it true you are not of noble birth?'

Andrew's heart sank. 'You know it to be true – you took me to squire knowing I was not of noble birth.'

A gasp went through the court. All in *that* room knew that a knight had to come from a noble father.

'Whether or not I took you on as a squire is of no material worth here. I did so as a favour to a dear friend. You have proved false, boy. Why did you not reveal to the king, and to the Master of the Temple, that you were a churl? Your father is a blacksmith – a common farrier – and your mother is a slattern . . .'

Andrew's hand went swiftly to his sword hilt, but other hands gripped it and held it tight, the hands of a sergeant-at-arms posted at his side. The strong, calloused fingers of the sergeant only relaxed when it seemed certain Andrew's flash of temper had subsided. They were withdrawn though their owner stood close by, ready to restrain Andrew again if necessary.

'. . . thus, boy, you are only fit to shoe horses, not ride them with fine armour on your back. You surely knew this day would come? Did you not guess that your secret would be revealed to the world?'

'It was no secret,' said Andrew. 'I told no lies.'

'You were not asked,' admitted King Baldwin, 'but that does not excuse you for staying silent about such a thing.'

Andrew felt wretched. He stared at Gondemar with contempt, then at the king with a pleading expression.

He and Baldwin were soul mates. They ran wild together around the town, the king disguised as a commoner. They had ridden together on hunts, the king keeping this information from the strict Odo. They played tricks on the court, they laughed at the same jokes, they wagered on the turn of the same cards. They were like brothers under the skin.

'Sire, forgive me,' he said in choked voice. 'I had no idea it was so important. I thought – well, I thought it was merely something that was desired, but not – what's the word – mandatory, sire. I did not know I was obliged to be of noble birth. I believed it could be obtained by showing courage and skill in warfare. I thought . . . well, it matters not what I thought. What am I to do now, my liege?'

'You must surrender your knighthood, Andrew of Cressing,' replied Odo de St Amand.

'And become a blacksmith's boy,' added Gondemar, with another of his sneers.

'That's enough, Sir Gondemar,' snapped Baldwin, 'this *blacksmith's* boy has beaten you in single combat and do not forget it. You come out of this with an extremely poor reputation.'

Gondemar's face filled with hot blood. His eyes started from his head in fury, a retort on his lips. He looked as if he were about to brook the boy king himself. In the end he managed to hold his temper, his valour fortunately failing him in this endeavour. Many knights were looking at him with expressions of contempt. He was not a popular courtier, while Andrew had been. Andrew had his enemies too, of course, but never so many as Gondemar de Blois.

King Baldwin now turned to Andrew again.

Miserably, Andrew went down on one knee and said, 'I must do as my king bids me – once again, forgive my transgressions, my liege.' His head rose and turned to the court, 'All of you, I hope you will all find it in your hearts to forgive me for this unwitting pretence. However,' he paused for a moment or two, staring round at the faces, 'there are several here who I have led to glory. One or two I have saved from death. Yet none of you have stepped forward to support me against this accursed knight, a man I spared in mortal combat, a man who would be dead of black rot if not for my intervention. For shame, sirs. For shame. And you, de Blois, you deserve to burn in Hell for your ingratitude and malice.'

Many there he had led to glory. Many there he had saved from death. Many there loved him as a knight.

Baldwin called as he left the court.

'I'm sorry, Andrew. I can do nothing. There are rules. Even a king must follow rules. Leave us, now. Come and say goodbye before you go. My advice is to take a ship back to England and return to your village, where you'll be safe from all those you've roused to anger here. I'm not just speaking of vile knights, but also of Saracens with a long reach. Without the protection of other knights, you will not survive.'

Andrew went back to his quarters in utter misery to break the news to Tomas.

'Oh, Tomas, my dear friend, I have been cast down!'

Tomas was almost as distressed as Andrew.

'Sire – Andrew – I am so sorry for your unhappiness.'

Hot tears of anger rolled down Andrew's cheeks. He tasted his own body salt as he sat on the edge of his bed. He was so distraught that it was some time before he realised Tomas was kissing away his tears and holding him with loose but loving arms. Tomas was humming a tune in between the kisses he rained on Andrew's face.

Andrew roughly pushed his companion away.

'What are you doing, Tomas?' he exclaimed. 'What is this?'

'Oh, Andrew, I have loved you for a long time,' said the boy with the hair of clouds and eyes the colour of a summer sky. 'I could not tell you before, because you were too busy being raised above me – far above me – but now you are thrown down to my level again I cannot hold it back any longer. My heart beats in my breast for love of you. Do you not love me, Andrew? Say you do and make my world complete.'

Andrew was in shock for a few moments. He stared at his friend, his constant assistant and helper. It took him several long minutes to absorb what Tomas had revealed to him. This, on top of losing his knighthood, was too much. Surely, surely this was the worst moment for Tomas to confess to such feelings. Any tenderness which might have tempered Andrew's reaction to this news was lost in a black whirl of horrible inner chaos.

He said grimly, almost bitterly, 'Tomas, leave me. I have no such feelings in my body or soul. Not for men.'

'You – you do not return my love?' said Tomas, in despair. 'We have done so much together – been so much to each other.'

'No, no, not in that way. Yes, you've been a good friend to me, but nothing else. Get out of my sight for now, Tomas. I can't stand all this. I can't stand the sight of *you* at the moment.'

'Will you never feel any different?'

Andrew shouted, 'Never, not ever, not in a hundred thousand years. I'm not made that way, can't you see? What's the matter with you? Don't you understand what I'm saying? There's not a shred of anything like you're suggesting in my whole being. I am a brave and lusty youth. If I have any feelings of that kind, it is for the gentler sex – girls, wenches, ladies, maidens. Not other boys. When you speak that way,

I feel as if I am made of wood. That's how much feeling such talk arouses in me. Now go from me, Tomas.'

A pale and dismayed Tomas turned and left without another word.

Andrew lay on his bed and mourned the loss of his knight-hood. He felt absolutely wretched. How could he be, in Tomas's words, raised up so high one moment, and then dashed to the lowest level the next? It was unjust. It was more than unjust. Surely God would not allow such a foul thing to happen to one of his most ardent soldiers? The mantle. He would have to take off his beloved mantle, with the blood-red cross of the Templars, and never wear it again. It was not right, it was terribly wrong. Such woe could not be borne.

When he thought of Gondemar, his grief turned to rage. Why had he let that loathsome knight live? It would have been the work of a moment to plunge his sword into Gondemar's heart and all those watching would have under-stood. Single combat. You took your chance and if you failed it was expected that you die. It had been Gondemar who had challenged *him*, so no one would have blamed Andrew if he had cut off the man's head and thrown it to the pigs.

These thoughts, and many others of a similar kind, whirled round Andrew's brain. Finally, he slept. When he woke he remembered all and almost choked on his sorrow. He got up and left the chamber straight away and went to seek his friend Hassan. Now that he was no longer a Templar Knight he did not need to concern himself over such things as the frivolity of hunting with hawks and hounds. Yes, he would get himself a hound. The king had several. They would go hunting wild boar together, he and Baldwin. The king would still treat him as a friend, would he not? Yet he had suggested that Andrew leave the land and return to England. Did that sound like the king was still an ally? Perhaps not?

Hassan was pleased to see him. Andrew's Arab friend told him that he had just returned from the baths where he had taken the ritual wash demanded by his faith. He looked smooth-skinned and glowed. Andrew decided the bathing must do something for Hassan's spirit, as well as his body.

'How are you, my friend? Shall we take the saker out? Yes? I am glad.'

With the saker falcon on his wrist, Andrew felt a little more whole again. He stroked the head of the bird with his finger. Raptors always spoke to him in some way. It was as if they were his brothers and sisters, these wonders of the wind. This bird, particularly, filled Andrew's heart with a pleasant yearning for something. The blue sky and frothy clouds perhaps? The high currents of air above the world? The peaks of high mountains? The tips of tall, swaying cedars? Something. It struck a chord deep within Andrew's spirit and his feelings always grew more gentle when he was handling such a creature, which was strange because they were killers of their own kind, savage birds of prey. But gentleness and tenderness entered Andrew's soul, nevertheless, when he was in their company.

'I can see you are happy to be with your saker, Andrew – but you seem quite sad in your heart?'

Andrew sighed. 'Yes, I am, my friend. I – I did not tell you before now, but I became a Knight Templar.'

Hassan nodded. 'I knew. I was told. There are few secrets in this kingdom.'

389

'Ah, you knew – I tried to keep it from you, because I thought it would displease you.'

'It did, but I would not let that stand in the way of friendship. We are brothers under the skin, Andrew, and even if brother is forced to fight brother, there is still love between them. Since you did not mention it, I thought it better not to say anything either. It was but a shadow between us.'

Andrew said, 'I feel humbled. You are a better person than I gave you credit for, Hassan – better than me.'

'No, not better. We are the same, you and I. I hear also that the Leper King is your friend, too, but that friendship is based on games and riotous behaviour? Is that true?'

'True enough, I suppose. Yet now the king has rejected me. I am to be punished for something not my fault. Not one man has come forward to speak in my defence. Not even Baldwin.'

Hassan put an arm around his friend's shoulder.

'I am sorry you are so unhappy. I understand. I would feel the same if Saladin had chosen me for one of his band of Immortal Guards, then cast me aside. But this is just one of those lessons in life, Andrew. You must put yourself in the hands of Allah, or your God, and let fate carry you where you are destined to go. We call it *kismet*.'

'We talk of fate, too – perhaps you're right, Hassan. I have had my taste of glory, now I should wait for what's next in store for me. Come on, let us fly this wonderful bird. Ah, you have put new jesses and bells on his legs . . .'

They left the city and went out into the wilderness. There they flew the falcon on the desert winds. Andrew was able to forget for a moment his devastation. His bird was in tune with the wind, and he was in tune with his bird, so he was able to fly above the drifting sands and forget.

There was one moment, the strangest of moments, when he was watching the saker. Something unusual – an apparition or a wraith – passed in the sky between the sun and the wheeling falcon. The spectre moved so quickly that Andrew could not be sure of what he had witnessed, but he was absolutely certain he had seen something curious.

'Did you see that?' he asked Hassan.

'Yes.'

'What was it?'

'I don't know. It was as fast as an arrow.'

There was nothing more to be said. Neither youth knew what had occurred and words were redundant. You cannot describe properly what you have not seen in detail. A shadow with wings, a quicker-than-lightning shade. So they spoke no more of it and continued with the hunt.

Andrew enjoyed the afternoon, but when he left Hassan's family, after taking tea, his spirits plunged again. He was going back to ignominy. Gondemar would be laughing up his sleeve at Andrew's humiliation. The pit of Andrew's stomach was leaden at the thought of meeting anyone at the palace. There were men who would be jovial and pooh-pooh his disgrace as something trivial. There were those who would smile sweetly, while their hearts rejoiced at his unsavoury downfall. There were those who would pass him by with faces of stone, cutting him dead, pleased not to have to speak.

He managed to avoid seeing anyone he knew and went straight to his quarters. However, the door would not open when he turned the iron ring. Andrew wondered if he had been locked out of his quarters, but then a hard push made it give way a little. Something was blocking the way on the other side. He forced his body through the narrow gap and entered the room, only to gasp in fright at what he saw.

There was a body hanging from a rope tied to a beam just inside the doorway.

Andrew looked up into the lifeless face of Tomas.

The cloud-white hair fell over his friend's shoulders and the sky-blue eyes were wide and unseeing.

'Oh, my poor Tomas,' whispered Andrew. 'What have I done to you?'

There was a note pinned to the hem of Tomas's jerkin. Andrew reached up and tore it from its pin. Since he had been attending his lessons he was able to read what it said:

Andrew, do not be sad – I have gone home.

Outside, in the church belfries of the city, the bells began chiming – midnight had arrived.

'Happy New Year, Tomas,' whispered Andrew, his face pale and his heart cramped with grief. 'God have mercy on you.'

26. CONSTANTINOPLE

Toby was almost at breaking point. He was a big youth, a strong boy, but hauling huge stones for the walls of the sultan's palace drained him of his very life. He would rise at dawn – they would have had the slaves up earlier if it had not been dark – and would be given a bowl of gritty mush to eat. He never did find out what the mush consisted of. There was little taste to it and even less nourishment. Then he would be given a wooden cup and told to drink from the stream nearby, which flowed with filthy water. His bowels were constantly troubled, which further weakened his poor condition.

Once 'breakfast' was over Toby and the other slaves, the hundreds of blacks and a handful of whites, would be whipped into line and marched to the quarry. There, those who were skilled masons cut the granite blocks. Those like Toby, who had no building skills, hauled them on ropes up on to roller logs. The blocks were then pushed and pulled on their rollers to the place where the Master Builder, an Egyptian, would supervise the handling of them into place on the wall. This last exercise was the most dangerous, for the blocks were immensely heavy and had been known to topple on to slaves, sometimes more than one, and crush them to death.

Only the previous day Toby had witnessed a piece of support timber falling on to an African's legs, breaking both of them. The guards put the poor man out of his misery, the way one might do with a wounded beast. They clubbed him to death. The sultan had no hospital for sick slaves. If they were ill and unlikely to get better he always expected their execution. Otherwise they might eat him out of house and home without any possibility of returning to work. A building site was no place for an idle man, injured or not.

In the winter hauling stones had been bad enough. In the heat of coming summer it was worse than being in Hell. Toby had suffered without complaint until now, but recently he found himself waking from his sleep – in that hole in the ground where the slaves rested like a knot of wintering snakes – crying for his mother to take him away.

Toby was at the end of his tether.

He trudged back to the quarry after he and a score of others had delivered the first stone block to the Master Builder. He was lashed along by the guards, who shouted obscenities at him and his fellow slaves. Indeed, the slaves were not humans, but animals that walked on two legs. They had become animals the moment they entered slavery. A pet dog at the palace was considered far more worthy of sympathy, or interest of any kind, than one of the slaves at the quarry.

'Hello, Toby, how are you?'

Toby turned wearily, his back aching, to see his two friends Patrick and Arthur. A faint spark of hope flared in his soul.

'I'm sick. Have you come to take me away from here?' he asked.

'No, old fellow, we've come to join you,' Patrick replied. 'The sultan has at last grown tired of us. He threw us out this morning. As a gesture he set us free, but of course we asked to take you with us, or we weren't going.'

'You shouldn't have done that,' croaked Toby, his throat already parched with the effort of his tasks. 'Patrick, you should have run. You and Arthur. You must go back to the sultan and say you've changed your mind.'

'Oh, but I haven't. Nor has Arthur. And, anyway, the sultan wouldn't listen to us now. Letting us go was the whim of a moment. He really couldn't care less whether we live or die. No, old churl, we're stuck with you on the stone line.'

Toby groaned pitifully. 'You – you won't last a week out here, Patrick. Neither of you. This work is hell. I'm broken now – a broken man. You must walk away this instant, or you'll be worked to death, you really will. Please go, both of you. I – I can keep on for a little longer if I know you're safe.'

Patrick felt the lash of the whip on his back, but he did not turn and acknowledge it, nor did he move.

'Very noble of you, I'm sure. But here we are and here we'll stay. For a little while, at least.'

Crack! The whip came down again, this time on Arthur as well as Patrick. A guard began screaming at them. Arthur moved into the line of walking men. Patrick acted as if he had been hit with a flyswat. He brushed his shoulder with his right hand and finished with, 'Only a little while.'

They did the day's work together without any accidents or incidents. As they were walking in the dusk towards the pit where they were to sleep, Patrick said to Toby, 'Tonight we're going to escape, Toby.'

'What?' A light stirred in the big youth's eyes at last. 'Tonight?'

'Escape – or die. One of the two. Better a quick death than this slow erosion of life. Messaoud wants to come with us.

395

He's bringing weapons under cover of darkness. He says the guards are fewer and less cautious at night, when the slaves have been bundled into the sleeping pit.'

'He's right.'

When they had been thrown into the hole and the limbs and torsos had untangled themselves, Toby whispered to those slaves who were nearest to him. The message was passed from mouth to ear throughout the pit. Everyone was told that there was to be an escape that night. It seemed as if most were ready to risk their lives for freedom. What had begun as a plan for an escape for a few became a plan for a mass breakout.

'I wish I had a black skin,' said Arthur, indicating the excited Africans whose cheeks were pressed against his own. 'Those lucky fellows – they'll be harder to find than us in the dark.'

'New Year's Day, today,' murmured Patrick. 'I hope this new year will bring us better luck than the old.'

Messaoud managed to smuggle weapons into the pit under cover of darkness. Then he went on to find a boat in the harbour. The slaves waited until dawn before they struck at the guards. After a long night the guards were at their least vigilant in the early morning. The slaves rose up, climbing the slopes of the sleeping pit, and overwhelmed them. They killed and wounded some, but others escaped and sounded the alarm. Then it was a general flight for the port, some two miles away.

'Run like the wind,' cried Patrick as he flew along. 'Come on Toby, keep up.'

He and Arthur were used to Toby being the fittest of the

three, but poor Toby was worn out with work. He stumbled along, heavy footed and plainly weary before the run had even started. The guards mounted on their horses would soon be on them. Two of the newer black slaves grabbed Toby under the arms and ran with him. They were young, strong fellows, quick on their feet, from a high-altitude country. This meant the air was richer for them at this level and they were faster and stronger than a lower-level man would be.

'Thank you, Umbeka. Thank you, Asolo,' Toby gasped. 'You are good men.'

The two Africans did not bother answering. They saved their breath for the run.

Soon the horsemen came and began cutting down the stragglers. Some of the runners fought with the savagery of slaves who had spent their last few years nurturing a poisonous hatred towards their masters. It became a battle, with losses on both sides. Guards were dragged from their mounts and had their heads dashed in with stones. Slaves were decapitated as they ran, or had their heads split open by a sword stroke, or were speared in the back. It was a bloody slaughter, though the guards did try to round up many of the runaways, rather than kill them, for they were valuable people. Without his slaves the sultan would never finish building his palace.

Out near the front, Arthur, Patrick and Toby, and Umbeka and Asolo, were the last to be reached by the riders. With swords in hand the English youths fought wildly but with determination. They knew only death awaited them back at the palace, so they had nothing to lose. In the event they managed to capture three horses. Arthur and Umbeka took one, Patrick and Toby another, and the third was taken by

Asolo. They rode hard and furiously for the port, followed by several guards.

On nearing the port they saw Messaoud standing on the dock with a xebec moored nearby. On his back was a quiver of arrows. In his hands was a Parthian bow, one of the best and strongest in the world. He strung an arrow and fired over the heads of the youths. One by one he began to pick off the guards as they rode behind Patrick and his players and the two Africans.

When the runaways arrived Messaoud continued to hold the guards at bay as the slaves scrambled aboard the xebec. None of the three English youths knew how to sail a boat, but Umbeka had been a fisherman in his own country and quickly issued instructions. Umbeka himself raised the mainsail and turned the craft towards open sea.

'Messaoud!' cried Patrick. 'Come quickly!'

The Barbary pirate abandoned his post on the quay, ran and jumped – and missed the boat. He let go of the bow and clung to the gunwales by his fingertips. The boys grabbed his arms and hauled him into the boat. The guards on the dockside had no bows, but they picked up rocks and began throwing them at the craft. A pebble, hurled from a sling, struck Arthur in the right eye and he went down with a little sigh, into the bilge water at the bottom of the craft. Toby turned Arthur over quickly before the youth could drown in three inches of dirty seawater.

Umbeka and Messaoud trimmed the sail and they set off over the blue Mediterranean, looking back at the shore as they retreated from it. Some of the other slaves had managed to steal boats and were out on the water, too. Others had no been so lucky. The shore was littered with pepper-black bodies, a few salt-white ones among them. It was difficult to grieve for the dead at such a time, for they too had escaped in a way. The sun had killed a lot more. The whip had taken a few. And the sultan's sword had many names invisibly etched upon its blade. Some of the slaves had been recaptured and probably the lucky ones, of those who had not escaped, were lying dead upon the sands of the Sultanate of Granada.

Out on the sea, a salty taste in his mouth, Patrick asked Messaoud a question.

'Why did you come with us? You were not a slave.'

Messaoud laughed. 'Was I not? Yes, sultan-man he fed me and gave me little moneys. Gave me bed to sleep and roof over Messaoud's head. But sultan-man have bad temper. One day he will kill Messaoud because I make his mother cross with me, or I forget to bow low. Yes, yes, he kill me in the end, you wait all right. Did he not kill his own brothers? So what protection for Messaoud? That he be a free mans? Ha! This mean nothing to sultan. All men when they become king, or sultan, or captain of pirate ship, their heart go to stone. They no longer have pity. They kill mans if breakfast not hot enough, or bed is cold, or pet cat scratch them.'

Toby stared at the ocean, wide and blue. The sun was loving and warm on his face, not hated and hot on his back. Flying fish leapt over the bows of the skimming xebec like silver darts, but not aimed at him. There was a gentle swish of the prow cutting through the waves, instead of the swish of the whip in his head. The moan of the wind was in his ears instead of the groans of labouring men in pain. Otherwise, all was stillness.

Overhead white clouds floated on another sea of blue. Toby had not looked at the clouds for a long, long time now, his head being bent over while hauling stone, his whole body being curved downwards towards the earth.

Spray flew in the faces of the others and they wore smiles as broad as the sea itself. They were free again. And for Umbeka and Asolo, taken from their villages only two months previously, it was a miracle. They thought they would never have the chance to return to their wives and children again. They danced up and down the boat like meercats on hot stones. They sang, they laughed, they yelled at the tops of their voices. Freedom! The wind tasted sweet in their mouths.

They set their mark towards Africa, to let Umbeka and Asolo ashore first. Obviously they could not let the two black men down on their own native shores, for they were further down the great continent, but Messaoud said Egypt would be a good place for them to start. Egypt was ruled by Saladin, who was known to be a man of compassion. Also the two former slaves could find a boat which would take them down the River Nile, the longest in the world, and place them somewhere where they could reach their homelands. They came from different regions, these two – one from the east, one from the west, but they were willing to take their chances.

Once Umbeka and Asolo had been dropped off, Messaoud asked the white youths where they wanted to go.

'Constantinople,' said Patrick. 'Is that near?'

'Nearer than your own land, to be sure,' said Messaoud 'and a place where East is meeting West. On the one hand you have my brothers, on the two hand your brothers. It is a city split by two, yet not so, for it mingles. Yes, a good choice

400

There we buy spices and make food taste well – yellow saffron and cinnamon bark, and good wine, and such is this city it is full of merchants and traders. It is *alive*, my friends, like a hive full of bees. And what knows, perhaps we see your friend the boy-girl there, what do you think?'

'Well,' said Patrick grimly, 'I'm not sure I *want* to meet her again, after she abandoned us. No, she left with a promise that was never fulfilled. I think I'd rather not see her again.'

Their one concern was Arthur, who had not wakened again since the stone had struck his face. He lay on the bottom of the boat with a pale face and one eye closed. He still breathed, it was true, but there was no life in his features.

27. A NOBLE GESTURE

Andrew woke to see an ugly grey imp with scruffy, feather-less wings squatting on the end of his bed. He let out a stran-gled scream and drew himself away. The creature leaned forward, its claws holding it fast to the bed frame.

'What?' said the imp in a gravelly voice, 'aren't you pleased to see me, Andrew?'

Andrew faltered. Who was this who greeted him by name? Was he from the Lord or the Devil?

'Tomas?' he tried.

'Tomas? My name isn't Tomas. Try Grindel.'

'Godfather?' cried Andrew, sitting up. Of course, this made sense. This was magic and his godfather was a magician. 'I'm so glad you aren't a fiend from Hell.'

'Well, now. I fly out here in the night, hoping to find you in the prime, only to discover you're in disgrace. The shadows here are dripping with whispers and the whispers speak of your downfall, Andrew.'

Andrew hung his head. 'Yes, I am in disgrace.'

'Who has done this thing to you?'

'Gondemar de Blois. Ever since I cut off his hand he has been haunting my very life, Godfather. It seems he will not rest until I am disgraced or dead.'

'Ah, that man, is it? Well, I too have a score to settle with Sir Gondemar.' The imp lifted a bird-like leg to scratch itself

402

under its many layered chin. 'But I can't do anything in this shape and I can't change my shape here in this foreign place – only in my hut in the forest – which is not the same hut you once knew, Andrew, for I had to flee from Cressing.'

'How so, Godfather?'

'Why, haven't I just told you? That knight, Gondemar, burned my wife at the stake.'

The breath left Andrew's body in a rush.

'Burned? What, my godmother? When was this?'

'Not long after he sent you here, to prepare for his coming to the Holy Land. He sent villagers with brands, to drag us from the forest. We were taken to the village square. The monks tried to save us, but to no avail. They were brushed aside by Gondemar's men-at-arms. It was Harold the butcher's son who set light to the pyres, one at a time. It was Harold who asked Sir Gondemar if they could fetch the two of us from the forest and Gondemar was pleased to sanction it. I watched Blodwyn die.

'She burned as if she were made of straw. She *was* made of straw, I saw to that. It was the last, the only, thing I could do for my wife, to speed her death. Then it was my turn, but I managed to twist myself into a knot while they were watching Blodwyn flaring and lighting up the darkness. I put my head up through my legs and bit through my bonds. I've always been quite supple in my bones. The villagers scattered when they saw I was free. You know I always terrified them. Then I remembered an old spell and turned myself into darkness, losing myself in the swirling of the night.'

'Were – were my parents there?'

'They could do nothing to help us. No one could. The

frenzy had overcome the other villagers. It was a witch-hunt. There's nothing that raises fear and hatred like a witch-hunt. The villagers were full of madness – the lunar sickness was on them – and nothing could stop them in that mood.'

'Oh, I am so sorry for my godmother.'

'Well, some might call her your devilmother, but no matter, she loved you like a godmother.'

'Did you not want to take revenge on Gondemar for the death of your wife?'

'I did take my revenge – long-distance, as warlocks are wont to do – I hear he is not the same man without his hand.'

'His hand was crushed in battle!'

'Ah, but who caused the injury, eh? Or indeed, what caused it? But, enough of Gondemar, I am after news of you, for your parents. Tell me all that's happened. Be quick, for I must return when the dawn comes creeping over the landscape looking for wayward men disguised as imps.'

'You still see my parents? How are they?'

'The same as ever, boy, for nothing happens in an English village, now does it? They live, they survive. Your sisters also. As do your friends and your enemies. Friar Nottidge asks after you – not of me, but from your mother and father – and the other monks. Your fame has spread throughout England to Cressing. Those who are your enemies fear your return. Those who are your friends rejoice in your ascendancy. But quick, tell me of all your joys and your woes.'

Andrew did as he was told, recounting all his adventures since he had been in the Holy Land. He told him about his friendship with King Baldwin, and with Hassan, and about his failure to keep Tomas alive. He spoke about his knighthood and his admittance to the Temple of Solomon. Then he told his godfather about his single combat with Gondemar and about that knight's vendetta against him. Once all the important things had been recounted, Andrew went over the smaller details of his life. When he got to the part about the gift of the saker falcon, the imp nodded thoughtfully.

'Ah, yes – you have an affinity with such birds.'

'Yes, yes, I do, Godfather. How did you know?'

'Why, because of the wolf, the hawk and the hare, all present at your birth.'

Andrew blinked. 'What – what about them? I don't understand. A wolf, a hawk and a hare?'

'Ah, you've never been told, have you, about those three?'

'Is this the secret the two dead men would not speak of?'

'No, this is another secret, a much smaller one, but, then again, not so much a secret – it's just never been told to you.'

'These creatures were at my birth?'

The imp nodded its huge head, the grey cowl flopping back and forth above its eyes.

'They were indeed. The story is this. It was a bleak, freezing winter, that year. Many creatures died of starvation and cold, some of them men and women. A goshawk had managed to kill a hare on the run, a remarkable feat in itself. But the carcass was too heavy for the bird to fly off with, so it had to eat it where it fell. Nearby was a starving wolf which smelled the blood of the hare and went to find it. Of course, the goshawk would not have stood a chance against a starving wolf, but her kill was close to the ditch where your mother was giving birth, and the wolf saw the humans and was loath to approach, even though its stomach was empty.

'Thus your birth allowed the goshawk to eat her fill, before she took to the air again, without the wolf stealing her quarry. Since then, she has told many of her kind and you are looked on favourably by birds of prey everywhere. The wolf ate the remains of the hare afterwards, but this particular wolf was a bit testy and ill humoured and in consequence wolves do not like you very much, so stay away from them.'

'I will, Godfather, but that poor hare – I expect he was starving, too.'

'No doubt, but he shouldn't have been born as prey, should he? If he'd been born a predator he'd have lived. In any case, it was an unusually inclement winter. Snow and ice covered any vegetation. The hare would probably have died anyway. Whoa, there're the first rays poking above the edge of the world. Got to go. I'll give your greetings to your parents and others. Keep well, Andrew of Cressing. Lost your knight-hood, eh? Can it ever be retrieved? I don't know about these things.'

'I can't see how, Godfather.'

'Well, that's life,' said Grindel, as if it did not matter at all that Andrew had been brought down low. 'The other one's not doing well either, but then that's life too . . .'

'Other one? What other one?' asked Andrew.

But Grindel had hopped to the sill of the arrowloop and had somehow squeezed his fat, impish body through the slit. He was gone into the coming morning. Only the stink of his unearthly body was left in the room.

Other one? thought Andrew. No doubt another person here in Outremer with connections to Grindel. Maybe he and his wife had had a son? If so, Andrew had never heard of one.

If Grindel came again he would ask the warlock what he meant and who it was he knew in this place. After all, such a person could prove a good ally to the warlock's godson.

A wave of sadness now washed over Andrew. He had looked around for Tomas, only to remember that the angel-boy had gone. It was at times like this that he missed his unearthly companion. Tomas was always there to sympathise when things were not good. Andrew could always rely on Tomas for advice when it came to the nature of things like feelings and whether he ought to do something about a silly remark he might have made to Sir So-and-So, or Lady Whatsit. Tomas seemed to know instinctively whether a thing like that was important or inconsequential. Huge problems shrunk to insignificance on speaking with Tomas about them. Now there was no more Tomas. He was walking the clouds above Andrew's head, probably smiling.

Andrew considered what he might do next. The king had told him to go, to take a ship back to England. But Andrew would rather die than go home in disgrace. It was not his fault that he had not been born of a noble father. Nor, indeed, was it his father's fault for not being noble. This was an accident of birth. One man was born to rule, another to be ruled. That was the nature of things. But Andrew had boasted that he would return to England a knight. A Templar knight. Now that he had been stripped of his knighthood, he had to try to do something to earn it back. Would they take notice of a truly great exploit? What could he do to retrieve his position?

'I could kill a lion,' he said to himself. 'Bring back the lion's hide for the king to use as a rug?'

Somehow he knew that would not do it.

'I could explore the East, keep on going until I reach the edge of the world!'

That would probably do it, especially if he brought back the riches of the Orient with him: silk, jade, precious stones, gold, fine pottery, ivory, tiger skins.

'But when I came back – if I ever came back, for death would be my constant companion – I would be too old to enjoy the fruits of my knighthood. My parents would be dead, my sisters become crones, my friends lost to others.'

No, that was no good. A good idea in principle, but in practice unworkable.

There was a shout outside the walls of the palace. A band of knights were approaching, probably from Gaza. Suddenly Andrew hit upon the perfect exploit.

'I shall capture de Mesnil's rogue knights,' he cried to the empty room. 'I shall defeat them and bring in those I do not kill to await the king's pleasure.'

De Mesnil's band of *Chevaliers Noirs*, called such not because they wore black armour, but because their souls were the colour of darkness, were out in the wilderness, a constant threat to Christian and Saracen alike. They raided villages killing both strong and weak. They destroyed caravans and waggoners. They killed herders and stole their flocks. They ravaged towns, raped and pillaged, and cared not a fig for the immorality of their actions. They burned, they crushed, they rode over children: they were despicable.

'I shall take them in ones and twos,' murmured Andrew, strapping on his armour, 'until I have them all.'

Out in the courtyard he passed a youth whose face looked familiar to him.

'Walter, isn't it?' asked Andrew. 'Another sword for another knight?'

'Yes, sire, it is I, Walter, son of Pugh, the swordsmith.'

'That's it, I remember now. Walter, Pugh's son.'

'Yes, my lord, they begin to call me Walter Pughson.'

Andrew said, as he led Warlock out of his stable, 'No need to call me "my lord" or even "sire". The king has taken away my knighthood. I'm just an ordinary youth, like you.'

'In that case,' muttered Walter, his face changing, 'why am I wasting my time in idle chatter while a *real* knight waits for his weapon?'

The swordsmith's son strode off, the long parcel in his hands.

Andrew stared after the youth, feeling rather put down by the sudden change in attitude.

'Well, I like that! Be polite to someone and, just because you've had some hard luck, they snub you. I might just give that boy a bloody nose, next time I see him. He's getting above himself, that one.'

Still feeling aggrieved, Andrew led his warhorse out of the courtyard, through the gates, and mounted him before riding through the town. Once out in the countryside he took out the magic astrolabe given him by Hassan. He knew that if he concentrated hard enough the brass compass would show him the way to the hideout of the *Chevaliers Noirs*. That was the first job, to find them. Then, once he had them in his sight, he could devise a plan for capturing them. His tutor had taught him to read stories from *The Arabian Nights* and he remembered the one about Ali Baba and the Forty Thieves. If a Saracen could capture forty thieves, then surely Andrew could come up with a clever scheme, too, to capture forty knights.

Andrew was pleased with himself for finding a use for his education in bookish things. His tutor would be pleased with him, too. Septimus Silke had talked of such a time that would come, when Andrew would actually use something from his reading which would assist him in his knightly duties. Septimus Silke might be a soft egg with no spine, but he had read books that stood taller than men, in libraries that were bigger than the palaces of sultans, and no one could doubt his learning. Andrew was beginning to realise that knowledge was power.

True to its wisdom and light, the astrolabe led Andrew through wild beast country, where savage wolves and hungry wildcats roamed, to a ruined city on the edge of the desert. This ruin had once been a magnificent city, built by a Median emperor for one of his favourite cousins. It had once owned beautiful parks and gardens, that were filled with fruit trees and maple shrubs, with grassy lawns and fizzing fountains. It once had buildings that blazed with gold and jewels in the sun. It once had cedar gates that reached high up into the air, studded with copper nails, the heads of which were the size of a man's fist. The walls of this crumbled city once claimed to be impregnable, being thicker than their height and taller than twenty men. Dates dripped from the trees of the palace within, which was fashioned of white marble brought from the banks of the Indus. Oranges and lemons hung like globes from the branches of the trees which filled its inner court yards. A veil of wisteria fell from every sill of every window and gave it the name of the Azure Palace.

Yet now it was a ruin, testament only to the fact that nothing lasts on this Earth, unless it remains loved. Clearly this city *was* once loved, but that love was not enduring. Another more austere emperor, a later son of a son, despised its opulence and brought the walls to their knees and the buildings to the ground, and slaughtered those who tried to save it. Love died with those who fell defending this now dusty maze of ghosts, the haunt of a rough band of outlawed knights.

Andrew stayed out of sight, in the hills, watching the rogue knights as they came and went. On some days they simply sat around eating and drinking wine, arguing, and sometimes fighting among themselves. On others they rode out intent on murder and mayhem, returning always with camels laden with trophies, or the carcasses of sheep and goats, or captive men and women strung in a line with hemp. No live thing ever came out of that ruined city, once it entered, if it were not one of the dark knights who carried it in there.

One night Andrew shed his armour and crept in close, so that he could observe his enemies. He found them sitting around a campfire. Brutish men with foul manners. They were unshaven and coarse-looking, most of them heavy-set with bull necks and broad bodies. Their hair hung down their backs, either plaited and tied with a rag or dangling loose in greasy ropes. Their hands were thick-fingered, with palms like trenchers. The legs of these men might have been made of walnut trunks and their shoulders of oak. Indeed, they were powerful beasts created by some malevolent god, who cared not that they were filthy hogs who never washed and whose teeth were stained yellow by the bile thrown up into their throats by their own gut, but only that this god's altar

411

should continue to run with the blood of innocents.

Andrew stayed long enough to see one of these beast-men stab another for stealing his bread. Then Andrew crept back to his own cave. There, with trembling hands, he donned his armour, mounted his steed and rode from that place of horror. If anyone was to destroy those knights, it would not be him, for they would crush him in his own armour with their strength and toss him away like a piece of scrap.

When he reached Jerusalem he went straight to his old quarters and lay on his bed, drenched with the sweat of anxiety and fear. It seemed that all had now been tried. His one great idea had turned out to be the worst of ideas. There was a limit to his spirit's stamina. A youth could take only so much, then he must crumple. Andrew was only flesh and blood. He did not have unlimited resources of hope and energy.

There came a knock on the door of his room.

'Who is it?'

'Gerrald, the king's page.'

Andrew rose and opened the door.

'Yes, what is it?'

'The king wishes to see you,' replied Gerrald, a smug look on his face. 'Immediately, he said.'

Andrew's heart sank even further. Had the king heard about his cowardice already?

'Do you know what it's about?'

'Yes, I do,' trilled the page, 'but I'm not empowered to tell you – if I were you, I'd be quick. Very quick.'

'Well, you're not me,' snapped Andrew, and closed the door on the boy's face.

Now what? More humiliation? Andrew did not think he could take any further punishment.

What to do?

'I will have to go and see what it is,' he told himself miserably, 'or run to the port of Jaffa, hire me a passage on a ship, and take me to England. What is it to be? Face the displeasure of the king – or run?'

PART THREE

28. THE RUBY

Ezra's mother was horrified when she learned what her son had done. She was as evil and ambitious as Ezra himself, but never so rash. What he had accomplished in a night and a day, by his hot-headedness, she knew would bring ruin on them both.

'We must think what to do,' she said, biting her fingernails to the bleeding quick as she always did when she was concentrating on something difficult. 'When your uncle returns and finds his daughter gone, his steward dead, and all by your hand, he will kill you where you stand.'

'Not if I kill him first,' said Ezra, squaring his shoulders.

His mother snapped, 'Don't be a fool, Ezra. Robert de Sonnac has never been beaten in single combat. He is a born warrior, while you are a born idiot . . .'

'Don't call me an idiot, Mother – or a fool – I am neither.'

'You are both, and you have ruined any chance of ever inheriting this house and its lands. Now we must concentrate on keeping you alive. If you stay in England he will surely find you. You must leave for the continent.'

Ezra was only now beginning to see the consequences of his hasty actions.

'Where will I go?' he asked, despairingly. 'What will I do?'

'France, perhaps? You might go to Aquitaine? No, no, he will find you there, for sure. Russia would be too near and

Chinese Tartary too far. Wait,' she snapped her skinny, wrinkled fingers, 'I have it. You must hide in an institution as well as a place. You will go to Constantinople.'

'But Mother,' wailed Ezra, 'what will I do there?'

'You will take up holy orders.'

'Become a priest?' Ezra cried. 'What do I want to become a priest for? I hate the Church. All that caterwauling and incense. It would bore me to death. I won't do it. I *won't*. I'd rather face my uncle's wrath. I think I could beat him in any case. He's an old man. He must be at least forty. Or,' Ezra's eyes narrowed, 'I could have him murdered for a few coins. There are rogues in the backstreets of London who for a handful of coppers would cut the throats of their mothers – I mean, well, you know what I mean, Mother. I don't want to go to Constantinople. I'd rather stay here.'

'You'll go,' she commanded, 'and as a priest. It might be a good idea to get you ordained before you leave. Once in priest's robes you'll be hard to recognise. Your uncle hasn't seen you since you were an infant. Change your name. Become someone else. Attach yourself to some thriving church and, who knows, you'll probably be a wealthy man before long. There are pilgrims passing through who need absolution of their sins and need to confess. It's not difficult if you flatter such men, tell them what they want to hear, creep round the hem of their garment. Not difficult to become rich if you fawn well enough. Yes, that's the plan.'

'No . . .'

'Yes, and my word is final.'

And so it was. Ezra was taken by his mother to an archbishop who owed her a favour and he was ordained. Then he set out for France and travelled down to Italy where he took a ship to the city that was once called Byzantium but now took on the name of its first emperor, Constantine. Constantinople. City of two continents, Europe and Asia. In Constantinople you could easily become lost. In Constantinople, you could just as easily be found. It depended upon your wish. It was a place where you could be both lost and found.

You could vanish into a suq the size of a large English town, or in one of the labyrinthine alleys, or on that fabled waterway, the Golden Horn. There were swarms of people coming into the city every day, there were swarms leaving, by land, by sea, this way, that way, into Europe, out of Europe, into Asia, out of Asia. It was not just a crossroads, it was a hub of many, many roads, which went out like the spokes of a wheel in all directions, and returned. There were nationalities from every corner of the known world, and some having drifted in from the unknown world. Black skins, white skins, brown, olive, red and pink, and so on. There were those who knew where they were and those who were truly lost. In such a maze of streets and such a haze of creeds and cultures, it was not a difficult task to disappear into nowhere.

You could be found by leaving a note in a shop that sold milk sweets, a place called the Pudding Shop, which was at the heart of this great city. There was a huge board in the Pudding Shop, covered in such messages. From an intrepid traveller in antique lands: *Antonius, I was here. Follow me to Cathay, Frederick.* Or from a former ambassador to the French court: *Rosalind, adorable one, if you have managed to escape your father's turret, you will find me in Egypt, your heavenly lover, Mustapha.* Or more poignantly, *Son, I forgive you. If you read this, come home. Your mother pines. Your father, Adolphus.* And even such mysterious ones as: *Sweet man, knowing your love of rivers I have looked everywhere for you – along the Indus, far down the Nile, on the Euphrates – but alas, to no avail. SH.*

But though Ezra was travelling to this wonderful city in order to be lost, not found, he did not change his name. He balked at losing the identity with which he was familiar. Why, to take on another name was to become someone else. And he was Ezra of Warwick. It would destroy him as a person to change into another man. There would be no Ezra left, and therefore it would be like that horrible death he had always imagined. In his deeper moments, when he thought of dying and going to the Hereafter, he often wondered what would be the nature of his spirit, or soul. In essence, would it retain a memory of the life spent on Earth? He had concluded that, if it did not, then the Afterlife was useless. What was the point of becoming some ethereal being which had no identity? There was no point, for it would not be *him*, Ezra, it would be this wandering mindless creature with no name.

'I am *me*,' he stated to himself. 'I will not be someone I do not know, for that would be such a death.'

Thus, in the robes of a priest, he ventured forth, blessing those who bowed before him, administering the sacraments to wayfarers, turning innocent maidens into women. These he began to see as his duties, especially the latter, for young girls were there to be made ready for marriage: he taught them what to expect from their inexperienced swains. The blessings and the communions brought in the money which he needed for the journey. Many will, of course, pay to have a clean soul.

Andrew went to the king not long after Gerrald left the room, despite his pique at being summoned. He was in no mood to be chastised again and he could not imagine any other reason why the king would send for him.

The court was full of knights and courtiers, priests and prelates, ambassadors and even one Assassin who had come to Baldwin to reassure him of the continued pact which remained in force between the Kingdom of Jerusalem and those who lived in the Alamut Valley, the Assassin sect. Andrew dragged himself into that great room and heads turned to see him enter. He cursed them as their conversations ceased. In silence he crossed to where the king sat eating sweet dates.

Young Baldwin said, 'Ah, Andrew of Cressing – you deigned to come and see the Leper at last.'

'Please, my liege, do not call yourself that,' Andrew said, forgetting his own plight and remembering how ill was the King of Jerusalem.

Baldwin smiled and shrugged. 'It's how I'm known and I have no great objection to it. I do, after all, have that terrible disease, which I'm told I caught from a miasma at birth – the drains of Jerusalem throw up such foul smells at times. My bishop tells me it has nothing to do with my soul, which is as pure as the damask silk from Damascus. But, enough of me and my trivial concerns – what of you, young Andrew?'

'What of me, sire? I wish to serve you as always.'

'Of course you do, no one has ever doubted your loyalty, even though you have a friend among the Saracens.'

Andrew blushed hotly. 'Do you speak of Hassan, of the house of . . .' and he gave the name of Hassan's father. 'They are from a land they call Al Yemen, where the Queen of Sheba held sway when Solomon was king.'

'Ah, that's who it is. Well, my spies have seen you with the Arab youth, but this is the first time we've learned the Saracen's name. So, am I to understand there is no treachery in this friendship, Andrew?'

'My liege,' cried Andrew, aghast, 'I could never betray *you*. You who made a friend of me? You who are my king and my protector? You who are – are Baldwin, who ran in the streets with me, and made me laugh, and deigned to treat me as your companion? Never, sire, in this life, nor in the next.'

'Glad to hear it,' said Baldwin, chuckling, 'for I'm happy to inform you that you are restored to knighthood. So we can continue to have great fun together. And you must not mind, Andrew, that my spies follow you and report to me, for they follow everyone, even Odo here . . .'

Odo actually looked alarmed at this.

'. . . who is much more likely to betray me than you, for he owes me nothing and is such an ambitious fellow.'

'My liege!' protested Odo.

'No, no, it's true, Odo. You would betray your own mother if it meant progression. But I digress; we're here to talk of Andrew's restoration.'

Andrew said, 'My king, if this is a jest, it is very funny, but . . .'

'No jest, Andrew. You now have a noble father.'

'I don't understand, sire.'

'A knight recently passed through Jerusalem, while you

were out looking for something or someone in the wilderness.'

'I was seeking the *Chevaliers Noirs*, my liege. I intended to destroy them and so regain your good favour.'

'You have never lost it – but did you find them?'

'I did, but I'm ashamed to say I ran from them, for they looked too strong for just one man, being more than two score of ruffians and cut-throats.'

'Ah, who would not run? I would. They are the dregs of the earth, those rogue knights.'

'But, my lord, you say I have a noble father. How can this be, unless my own father has been knighted?'

Baldwin said, 'That I doubt. But Sir Robert de Sonnac has adopted you as his son. When he heard what Sir Gondemar de Blois had done to you, he made the necessary arrangements. You are not of noble birth, Andrew, but we are prepared to accept that you now have a noble father, and are therefore of a noble family. Welcome back to the court.'

'I – I don't know what to say. Is Sir Robert still here?'

'No, he has left for Tripoli, where he has business.'

'Will he return?'

'I think not. But we're satisfied as to his intentions, and you may continue your good work here. But – Andrew – the *Chevaliers Noirs*? They would have eaten you alive for breakfast and thrown your bones to the dogs.'

The court burst out laughing. Even Odo smiled.

'Well, I could think of nothing else.'

'Then you are not a thinking man, Andrew, and I should give up that practice if I were you. Stick to poking swords into the enemies of your king. Now, what do you say we ride out and do some hunting? I hear there are gazelle just a few miles north of the city.'

Andrew looked at Odo de St Amand, the Master of the Temple of Solomon, knowing that Templars were forbidden the frivolities of hunting.

'Oh, never mind that old man,' cried Baldwin, leaping up. 'I am your king and I *order* you to accompany me. I'd order Odo, too, if he didn't wear such a long face all the time, but he'd spoil it with his whining and moaning. Come on, knights, let's get out of here and into the fresh air. I feel my disability dropping from me today. I feel very alive. Kings get first jabs at the prey, by the by, so all of you let me go first – or find yourselves in the one of the dungeons for the weekend. Andrew, help me on to my horse, will you? You won't catch anything. It's dry leprosy, you know, not the wet kind.'

'As if that mattered, my liege,' said Andrew, glowing in great contentment. 'As if I cared.'

As they rode out, in the broad sunshine of the outdoors, Andrew thought about the kindness of Robert de Sonnac. It was no mean thing to adopt a young man of small consequence and low birth. It was a huge undertaking. He would be rebuked for it, by others, perhaps even by Henry, King of England, for diluting the knighthood of the land. Yes, there would be some who would criticise Robert de Sonnac for such an action. And Andrew would be equally despised, for being the recipient of de Sonnac's generosity. A blacksmith's boy a knight? What a mutation of the ordained order of things! Surely, every man to his station or barons must fear for their wealth and position? Indeed, a serf might usurp a king and bring all to chaos.

Yet, Robert had dared to cock a snook at the right order. Andrew did not really understand why, though, for he was willing to wager that Sir Robert de Sonnac had gone against his own beliefs. Had it been another knight, another Andrew, Robert himself might have pursed his lips and called it wrong, for Robert was just as defensive of the right order as the next knight. Sir Robert was a proud man, a man who believed in status, and yet he had bent his own rules to save Andrew's knighthood?

It did not make a great deal of sense, unless the knight still believed himself to be beholden to the youth who had saved his daughter's life. In which case, Robert de Sonnac had an extraordinary love for his child. Other knights went away to war and forgot their daughters completely. Angelique must have been the most precious thing in Robert de Sonnac's life for him still to feel an obligation.

Indeed, Andrew admitted to himself that Angelique was a unique jewel among many sparkling maidens. But that was from the point of view of a passionate youth whose needs and interests were the raw emotions of a virile young man. A father's love was purer and more considered, with no ultimate carnal goals embedded in that love, and therefore the more worthy if he were to sacrifice his good name to it.

Andrew thoroughly enjoyed the hunt. He was not greatly successful at killing anything, but he loved the chase on his charger, his hair flying in the wind. When they got back to the palace there was a great feast laid out for the hunters. Lady Catherine had lanced a gazelle and she wanted it to be served up to the table immediately, but the king told her it was best hung for a night, which put her in a sulk. John of Reims was in great form, telling stories of deeds of derring-do, when he escorted some pilgrims who had got lost along the Silk Road and found themselves in a city called Samarkand.

There were three new Knights Hospitaller at the king's table that evening. John of Reims was a Templar, and so was Andrew, so they sat together and glared at the Hospitallers, who glared back. There was great jealousy and enmity between the two Orders of monk-knights. The evening could not pass before someone started an argument. It just happened to be the visiting Hospitallers.

'So,' called the flare-bearded Hospitaller whose name was Gustaf Munich, 'you are two *poor* Templars, are you? I have heard that your Order is so rich that kings are beholden to you for your loans. Are you still claiming poverty?'

King Baldwin groaned. 'Oh, don't start this again, please? We were having such a good time.'

John of Reims, however, could not stomach these sarcastic jibes.

'Yes, we are poor as individuals. I own nothing which is not essential to my status as a knight. Do you see any wealth on us? Any gold rings? Any pendants? See, my pocket is empty of silver coins. You may have whatever you admire upon my person – take anything you might lack – except my courage. I'm afraid you'll have to find that in yourself, if you can.'

'Since we arrived,' said the second Hospitaller, 'I have seen that young one in armour so splendid it would purchase a dukedom.'

Andrew felt himself going hot. He could see Catherine staring at him, waiting for his riposte.

'You know a suit of armour is quite a different thing from

426

having a full purse,' Andrew said. 'All knights, be they secular or of a holy order, need their armour.'

'But none so grand as yours,' retorted the same Hospitaller. 'I would hazard a guess that it was made by Helmschmid of Austria? Yes, I see by your face it was so. Helmschmid is the armourer of kings. Are you a king, sir?'

'I am king of myself. I have my horse, my armour and my weapons. Would you have me give them up and ride into battle naked on a goat? I am not a Hospitaller, sir, I am a Templar, and Templars need to be well armoured to protect the pilgrims and the weak. Stick to your bandages and your balms, sir; do not assume to know the private matters of other knights. The suit of armour was given to me by Robert de Sonnac, for an act of valour. It would be a churlish act indeed if I spurned his gift and wore some inferior garb.'

'Bravo!' cried Baldwin, clapping his hands. 'What do you say to that, Sir Dieter?'

Sir Dieter's lip curled. 'So, putting the armour aside, there are stories of gems that are in your possession. Speaking of goats, I was told by an Arab goatherd that it was a young Templar by the name of Andrew of Cressing who discovered a casket of jewels in a cave at the foot of Mount Ghatt.'

Andrew went red again. 'A goatherd?'

'He saw you and a boy with white hair and blue eyes enter a robber's cave in which there was stashed a trunk full of precious stones. He was certain you did not emerge empty-handed, for who would leave such wealth behind, even a Templar? If you did not want it for yourself, you could have given it to your king.'

Andrew looked around the room wildly, and saw that all

knew this story was true by the look on his own face. He glanced at John of Reims, but that knight was not going to intervene on his behalf. He would have to get himself out of this predicament.

'If – if this goatherd of whom you speak knew there was a fortune in the cave, why did he not make himself rich?'

'Because,' replied the Hospitaller, 'he was afraid. The robbers who left the casket in the cave would at some time return for it. They would certainly track down and kill anyone who stole their spoils. Also, the goatherd was terrified of the curse that was put on any thieves who entered the cave, by the wizard who ran with the robbers.'

'Curse?' said Andrew, swallowing hard. 'What curse?'

'That whoever took but a single jewel from that casket would surely hang himself before the year was out.'

'Hang himself?'

'And he would go to Hell for the rest of eternity – unless the jewel were restored to the casket.'

'Wait,' cried Lady Catherine, 'I see a loophole here.' All eyes went to this formidable lady knight and Andrew was grateful to her for this intervention. He was wallowing in a confusion of thoughts at this moment, none of them particularly pleasant. 'If the casket had a curse on it, then he who stole a gem from it would be bound to commit suicide. Therefore that suicide cannot be a sin. The thief can't help it if magic forces him to hang himself.'

'Therein lies the remedy,' said Sir Dieter. 'Restore the jewel and nullify the curse.'

King Baldwin said, 'Did you indeed find such a cave containing a casket, Andrew?'

The eyes were back on him again.

'Yes,' he said, his throat dry. 'Yes. Tomas and I discovered a casket of precious stones.'

'And did you take any?'

'No – no, my liege, I did not.'

'But Tomas did.'

All in the room, except perhaps the Hospitallers, knew that Tomas had hanged himself.

'Yes – he took one. A ruby.'

'Ah!' Baldwin nodded, thoughtfully. 'And what did he do with it?'

'I have no idea, my liege,' said Andrew, lying for the first time that evening. 'Perhaps he threw it into the sea? You knew Tomas. He was not interested in earthly things.'

Baldwin stroked his chin. 'Indeed, it does sound like your Tomas, to be unconcerned with precious stones. And you were not aware of this curse?'

'No – no, I was not.'

'And yet,' interrupted one of the Hospitallers, 'you did not think to tell your king where the casket lay, so that he could go there and get it for himself?'

Andrew did not know what to say to this.

'I did not think to – no.'

'And why was that?' cried the Hospitaller. 'I would say such secrecy is close to treachery, my lord.'

John of Reims smashed the table with his fist, making trenchers and knives jump and rattle.

'This knight is not on trial here,' he shouted, angrily. 'Who are you to come here and accuse men of treachery? This knight has proved himself loyal to his king, time and time again in battle. Where were you when we were at Montgisard? I did not see your face on the field. Where were you when the Saracens were cutting down our men with their scimitars? Not with King Baldwin, that much is certain.' He fumed for a moment, before becoming calmer. 'I'll tell you why he did not tell his king where these jewels were. Because to him they are not precious stones. They are pieces of coal, chips of granite, lumps of marble. Such trinkets have no more worth to a Templar than a pebble from the beach. We spurn such baubles. We see not jewels, but stones from the ground. We are Templars, sir, and we scorn all riches – gold is no more precious than iron – ivory is common bone – silver is ordinary steel – a diamond is but a piece of glass.'

'Very commendable, I'm sure,' said the Hospitaller, smugly, 'but what does your king think?'

'Me?' said Baldwin, after the eyes had been on him for an extremely long time. 'I, sir, am a leper – what need have I of precious stones? Give me an elixir, not a ruby or an emerald. There was no magical elixir in that casket, was there, Andrew? Some potion that would help me live forever?'

'To my knowledge, sire, there was not.'

'Then it is all one to me. Come, let's have the musicians in, and the tumblers. I need to be entertained . . .'

Later, after the evening was over, Andrew requested an audience with the king. He was admitted to the king's sleeping quarters, where Baldwin was preparing for bed. The king had been praying by his bedside, just like an infant, and he rose to his feet wearing his nightshirt and cap as Andrew entered.

'Yes, Andrew? Quickly, because I feel ridiculous standing before one of my subjects in my night attire.'

The king looked fatigued. Andrew knew that the leprosy was increasing in its ferociousness. Young King Baldwin was a youth with great spirit, having not only the courage it took to fight a battle, but also the bravery needed to fight against a disease that was gradually eating him away. Not only did he fight, he tried to carry out all his normal duties and have fun besides, which made him a remarkable person. He never complained and frequently made a joke of his disability.

'Sire – I – I have come to apologise.'

'For what?'

'That I did not tell you about the jewels.'

Baldwin made a face. 'Well, I'm not saying they wouldn't have been useful to me. A king needs money to run a kingdom, especially here, where we need a standing army. But, I believe what John said. You gave it no second thought. It was not an act of betrayal, but an act of thoughtlessness. I'll probably forgive you, soon enough.'

'I am truly sorry.'

'And I'm truly exhausted, Andrew.'

'Yes, my liege. Goodnight.'

'Goodnight, dear friend. Oh, do not have troubled sleep over me. These things happen. The sun will rise again tomorrow. The world will waken to greet it. Let's forget about it.'

'Thank you, sire.'

Andrew left.

The next morning Andrew went to see the Master of the Temple, Odo de St Amand.

'Sire, you have a ruby which was given to you by my erstwhile companion, Tomas.'

431

Odo looked at him imperiously.

'Have I?'

'Yes – Tomas said he gave it to you. Sire, his soul is in great peril unless I take that ruby back to the place where we found it.'

'And that is of consequence to me?'

'It should be, Master – you are a man of holy orders.'

Odo's eyes narrowed.

'Why was the jewel given to me?'

'Why? Well, Tomas – that is, yes, Tomas thought it would help to have me appointed as a Templar.'

'So it was a bribe?'

Andrew said nothing.

'You realise,' said Odo, 'that simony is one of the three crimes for which your mantle can be taken from you?'

'Simony?'

'Simony, sodomy and desertion. Simony is the giving of gifts in order to obtain advancement.'

'Sire, the jewel . . .'

'Is in safe-keeping. I am holding it for King Baldwin, for a time when he might need to purchase troops. That has always been my intention. But, Sir Andrew of Cressing, your admittance to such a crime cannot go unpunished. You will be tried by your fellow Templars tomorrow.'

'I – I never intended – that is, I haven't admitted anything.'

Odo smiled. 'Please, young man, give me credit for some sense, if nothing else. It was you who told me that Tomas had given me the gem in exchange for your advancement.'

Andrew had nothing to say. It was true. Tomas had given the ruby to Odo in order that Andrew be given admittance to the Temple of Solomon. And Andrew had learned of the act later, but let it stand. He had not confessed to Odo before admittance. It had been a bribe. There was no argument. He would have to face the consequences of his actions.

A man with ambition was always caught in a double bind. Those who gave men advancement expected gifts in return for their generosity. Any one of those gifts could, at a later date, be considered to be a bribe. The Templar knights who would sit and discuss Andrew's case in the morning would all have given Odo gifts, either before or after being admitted to the Temple. Yet at any time they could be called forward to account for the action, which was illegal under Templar laws.

'Could I have the ruby, sire – to save my friend's soul?'

'No.'

'He will be damned for all eternity.'

Odo smiled. 'You think God will take any notice of a heathen curse, moreover a curse made by criminals who rob and murder? I think not, Andrew. Tomas was a good lad – his soul is safe. Which is more than I can say for your mantle. Come to me at noon tomorrow and I'll inform you of the decision made by the Templars who sit in judgement over you.'

29. NEW WEAPONS, OLD FRIENDS

Harold, the Cressing butcher's son, was practising. He had received a weapon from Wales. It was something he had asked his uncle, a peddler, to bring back with him from the land of the western Celts. It was an instrument of war and was extremely difficult to use. But once you built up your right-arm strength, and got used to using it, the weapon was lethal.

A longbow.

Harold was going to kill Andrew the farrier's son with it, if that youth ever returned to the village.

This new weapon which had its origins in Sweden, or Norway, one of those countries across the sea, was said to be so powerful that its arrow could pierce armour. Henry, King of England, was becoming extremely interested in the longbow. It was predicted that soon English archers would be using the longbow in place of their shorter weapons.

Harold spent hours on his upper-body strength. Once he felt able, he picked up the longbow and tried to draw it. It was far from easy. Even when he had it at full stretch along the shaft of the arrow, the effort made him shake so much he could not hit anything. The village fletcher had made him some shorter arrows which he used at first. Even then the effort needed to draw the longbow was immense.

Harold was determined to master the weapon. He was physically sick of hearing of Andrew's exploits. Friar Nottidge had taken to standing on the speaker's stone in the village square every day at noon to shout the great deeds which had reached his ears and eyes concerning his old pupil.

Andrew was a great friend of King Baldwin IV. Andrew had slain a giant. Andrew had fought in the Battle of Montgisard with great bravery and honour. Andrew had beaten back a huge pack of wolves, wild dogs, savage bears. Andrew had saved the life of Robert de Sonnac's daughter. Andrew had single-handedly defeated a man-eating lion which was attacking pilgrims. Andrew had fought Saracens, bandits, Assassins, Seljuk Turks, Mamluks. In fact, there seemed very little that Andrew had not done and very few enemies of England that he had not been victorious over.

Andrew. Andrew. Andrew.

'Give it a rest, for pity's sake!' shouted Harold one day, as Friar Nottidge was bragging about the new exploits of his former pupil. 'We're sick of hearing about sodding Andrew of Cressing.'

'Shame on you, Harold Butcher,' cried the good friar. 'Andrew's parents over there are delighted to hear of the heroic son of our own village.'

'Well, tell them in private, can't you? I've had bloody Andrew of Cressing up to my crop.' He chopped his own throat with the edge of his hand. 'Who cares what he's done in Jerusalem, or wherever? People here work hard, in the fields, with the cattle. They're heroes, too, you know. Hard winters we've had while that bastard has been riding in the sun. Floods, fires, and landlord barons grabbing all they can. Let him come and fight some of *our* enemies.'

'Careful, boy,' growled one of the elders of the village. 'Don't you go badmouthing the lords of the county.'

'Bollocks to the lords of the county,' grunted Harold, under his breath. And more loudly, 'I'm just fed up with all this trumpeting of someone who was driven out of the village. Have you forgotten what he did to us?'

'To you, you mean,' said another youth. 'You turned us against him, if you remember.'

'You were easily led, Joseph Baker. You and your field-worker friends.'

'Well, we've seen the error of our ways. Andrew is a great warrior. You should be proud he comes from our village, as the friar says. Minstrels are singing about him in Chelmsford and London. It doesn't do any good to harbour old grudges, Harold. You should cast off such evil moods.'

But Harold could not drive out the black thoughts which Andrew engendered in his mind. He was going to kill his old foe even if he was hanged for murder afterwards. Day after day he practised with the longbow. It became an obsession with him. Finally, he was able to draw a full-length longbow arrow. Not a week after that he managed to shoot a hare with the weapon. The arrow picked up the hare with great force and pinned it to the base of an oak tree.

'Just come home, Andrew of bloody Cressing,' muttered Harold, retrieving his arrow from the carcass of the hare, 'and see what I've got for you. Your knighthood won't protect you from this. Neither will your armour. I'll pin you to one of the doors of the great barns and leave you to dangle . . .'

* * *

Robert de Sonnac had been some time in Venice, discussing business with the merchants there, when he received a message from a friend in Constantinople to say that his daughter was in that city. He was both shocked and astonished. How had she come to be thousands of miles from where he had left her, safely in the hands of his sister? There were many questions to be answered and Robert was anxious and determined to find all the answers. He set sail from Venice the next day.

When he arrived in Constantinople he went directly to his friend's home situated near the port, a rather grand house in the Islamic style. There he greeted his friend, a Turkish merchant who dealt in dyes, and begged his forgiveness for wanting to see his daughter immediately rather than take tea with his host. The Turk said he understood completely and would wait until after the reunion before the pair of them exchanged the courtesies proper to the manner and custom of both creeds and cultures.

Robert was led to a room on the far side of a courtyard decorated with breeze-blown fountains, myrtle bushes and tiled pools. There he found his daughter, her hair cut extraordinarily short, her face showing signs of early maturity, her carriage still rather too straight and uncompromising for a female, beautiful in a white gown. He could see she was still the forthright young woman he had left behind, but there was a deal of new experience in her eyes. He took her in his arms immediately and whispered with immense relief into her ear, 'Thank God you are safe.'

This was to his great credit as a parent, for most fathers would have first demanded to know whether their daughters had been violated.

Then Robert held his precious offspring at arm's length and studied her again.

'You've changed, my child. Are you unharmed? Are you well?'

Angelique suddenly burst into tears and hugged her father again, before wiping her face with her forearm and saying, 'It is so good to see you, Father.' She smiled now, her eyes shining. 'My Father. How safe you make me feel. You're such a big, strong man. I doubt you've ever known fear, have you?'

He smiled in return. 'Many times, my child – but, you have no idea how good it feels to see you, too, Angelique. When I received that note . . .' His face then became stern. 'Angelique, what are you *doing* here? Have you come overland? By ship? Where is your aunt? Where are my retainers? My servants? Do not tell me you're alone and unattended? And what *have* you done to your beautiful hair?'

'We must sit down, Father, for my story is a long one.'

Once they were comfortable, though Robert was still quite agitated inside, Angelique began her story. 'Firstly, Father, I am by the grace of Our Lady unharmed in any way, though I have had many adventures and have come close to death a number of times . . .', Robert sucked in his breath at these words, but otherwise remained silent, allowing his daughter to unfold her experiences over the last many months '. . . much of this good fortune is due to the fact that I have been disguised as a boy . . .'

As the tale was recounted calmly and clearly by Angelique Robert felt himself growing more and more astonished at the amazing adventures of his daughter, and, increasingly, blisteringly angry. By the time she had finished he was internall on fire with fury, although, as was his wont, he rarely revealed his passion in his bearing. If he could have his nephew there at that moment, the youth would have lost his head with one sweep of the knight's sword. Indeed, the boy would have to die and Robert begged the Lord it could be by his hand. Robert was also furious with his sister and wondered whether he would be able to restrain himself from killing her, too. His daughter, his precious Angelique, had suffered immense mental harm and it was only by the grace of God that she was physically unhurt. There would be a reckoning. Robert was determined on that. Such a flagrant attack on his family and household could not go unpunished. There would be bloody times ahead, if left to his will.

'Well, my daughter,' he said, 'we must both go home. I will pay my respects to my friend, who owns this house . . . by the way, how came you to be here?'

'Why, you forget,' Angelique said, smiling, 'that I always help you with your books. I remembered the name of Al Jebel, the man from the mountains, when we did the accounts, how fondly you spoke of him. When we arrived here in Constantinople I was still a boy and allowed to go my own way. I made enquiries and revealed myself to him. He took me in and immediately set about finding your whereabouts, Father.'

'A good friend,' grunted Robert. 'A very good friend. I must reward him well.'

'If what I know of him is correct, he will take no reward.'

'Then he shall have my heartfelt thanks and gratitude. I will owe him until the end of my days. But, child, what of your friends, the players? We must send a rescue party immediately to negotiate their release. Perhaps this poor Toby is no longer alive? You must 'prepare yourself for such an event.'

'Our host has already sent his son to the sultan, but the son was rebuffed and almost lost his own life. The sultan was in a frenzy of distress. It seems the boys organised an escape and though many slaves were killed in the attempt, a great many more managed to get away. The blacks will have set sail for Africa. Goodness knows where the boys are, but I know they have an endurably strong ability for survival. I'm hopeful they'll be somewhere safe by now.'

Patrick, Toby and Arthur finally reached Constantinople, the city that stood astride two continents. Arthur had only one eye by that time, the pebble from the sling having taken out the other one. However, the youths were relieved to find themselves in a friendly city, ruled by a Christian emperor. They had no idea why Angelique had not sent someone back to rescue them from slavery, but Patrick and Toby were both fervent in their defence of her, though Arthur was unsure.

'Something must have happened to prevent Angelique from organising another visit to save us,' said Patrick. 'She would never abandon us.'

Toby said, 'She might even be dead, Arthur, have you thought of that?'

Arthur was not inclined to feel remorse or guilt for something that might never have occurred.

'I doubt it,' he said, 'that girl's got more lives than a cat. I swear she *is* a cat. She had her captors eating out of her hand.

'I'll hear no word against her, Arthur,' said the magnanimous Toby. 'Not a word, mind! I'm sorry for your wound, bu if you speak bad words against Angelique I'll blacken your good eye.'

After that warning Arthur wisely kept his mouth closed on the subject.

Messaoud was still with them and keen to begin a new career as a player. He had been many things in his life: camel driver, pirate, overseer of slaves, translator and now actor.

'I will play the womans with great joy and passion,' he told Patrick. 'You will make my face beautifuls for me.'

'We'll do our best,' said a dubious Toby, 'but you're a bit old – and your skin's been dried by the sun.'

'Little oil here, little ointment there, and Messaoud shall be Nefertiti of the Nile. Her loveliness shall be spoken of from the Pillars of Hercules to far shores of Black Sea. Men will die for just a glancing at Messaoud. Womans will tear out their hair because they cannot be matching Messaoud's beauty.'

'Really?' said Arthur, looking quite dashing with a black patch over his right eye socket. 'You think?'

Patrick said, 'Well, it looks a lively place to earn our bread, this once-Byzantium. There are rich merchants everywhere. There are sea captains and generals. There are soldans and satraps, princes and bishops. Money everywhere. Here is the market of the world. I can smell a thousand spices, see a myriad fruits, hear the babble of a multitude of languages. We'll soon have the money to return to Eng—'

As he was speaking a priest passed by on the far side of the market. He was a tall man with a large flaring beard. Patrick stared at this figure for some while until the priest was out of sight among the thronging crowds.

441

'Patrick,' said Toby, looking concerned, 'whatever is the matter?'

'Oh, I just thought I saw someone we knew.'

'It was a clergyman,' Arthur said. 'Do we know any clerics?'

'Not as such.'

'Then why should we know this one?' insisted Toby.

Patrick shook his head. 'No, you're right. But a shiver went through me. I don't know why.'

Messaoud replied, 'Because you no like the Church, eh? They take the moneys off people like you and make himself rich.'

Patrick laughed. 'Well, there is that – many priests these days are corrupt.'

'There it is then,' said Arthur. 'That's why you shivered.'

Patrick nodded. 'Priests,' he said, then, 'well, what are we standing around for? Best place to start is right here in the suq. Messaoud. You put on your rouge and powder. Arthur? You're our hero for today . . .'

'Oh, but you usually play the lead, Patrick,' argued this now one-eyed actor.

'But you have the eye patch and today's play is *The Barbary Pirates*. You have centre stage. Toby, I'm afraid you're going to be a sailor, while I'm a victim of the . . .'

And so it went on, with Patrick in charge, and the others confident under his direction.

30. ASSASSINS

Andrew was filthy, bedraggled and darkly hollow-eyed. He might have been concerned about his outer state if it had not been for the fact that he was ravenous. At this moment in time he was crawling about under a table. The only thing of any importance to him was to get the next piece of food that accidentally dropped from that table. Seated around it, the Templar knights were eating. Close by Andrew were the dogs, fighting with him for scraps of food. He had been tried and found guilty of simony. His mantle had been taken from him, and his padded jacket, which he wore under his armour, and the armour itself. All his outer clothes had been locked away. He was left in thin undergarments on cold nights to fend for himself. He was not allowed to walk upright. As a criminal within the Knights Templar, he had to stay down on all fours. The knuckles of his hands were his second pair of feet.

'Get away from me, cur,' cried a knight, kicking him under the table. 'Fight for your supper!'

The Templar knights spoke to him only to abuse him. No one had a kind word. No one was allowed to give him succour, or treat him civilly, or offer him help. Even John of Reims would have nothing to do with him. This was the law. Odo would discipline any knight who showed compassion. The last knight who had suffered such indignities and oppression from his fellows died of dog bites that poisoned his blood. He received no honours at his funeral.

'Six months,' Odo had told him, 'you will be spurned, rejected and abused. If you do not like it, you may leave at any time, but you will forfeit your place in the Temple of Solomon thereafter. You will be permitted to wear the Templars' mantle no more. You will be forever banned from our ranks.'

Such punishment as he was receiving was worth it if he would once again be allowed his white mantle with the blood-red cross emblazoned on its front.

He sobbed at night, from the daily pain of kicks and punches. He slept in dirty corners until he was moved on by those who saw him hunched there. He was dragged by laughing kitchen boys by his feet and thrown down stone steps, or hauled by scullery wenches for them to spit on. He suffered such treatment so long as he was given a scrap of food after the sport was over. He was indeed an abject figure, filthy to look at, covered in sores and welts, crawling with lice.

An outcast.

What was more, when he was eventually restored to knighthood he was forbidden to take revenge on the lower orders of the Temple for abusing him. It was their right while he was a dog to treat him as one. He could not, on restoration, enter the kitchens and start beating everyone in sight. This was part of the punishment, to be treated with contempt by the sweepers, cooks, pot-grease peelers, and the like. Indeed, if they did not ill treat him, use him as a dog, they themselves would be rebuked by the Master and his knights. It was their duty to make his life a living hell while he went on all fours.

One morning he was scuttling back and forth under a dining table like a crab, escaping a tide of boots. A large ham bone with meat on it fell to the floor. One of the hounds raced for it, but Andrew took its head in an arm lock and then flung the beast the length of the tables. He then snarled at the other dogs like a wild beast and they cringed from him.

Just as he turned to grab the ham bone a hand came down and went to pick it up.

He bit the hand.

A bench scraped backwards as a knight leapt to his feet, sucking his hand.

'Jesus Lord!' cried a voice above. 'The dog's brought blood – it's almost bitten through my thumb.'

Someone else bent down and looked.

'It wasn't a dog, it was the outcast!' cried the looker. 'He's here, gnawing that bone you dropped.'

There was the ring of a dagger being unsheathed.

'I'll kill the . . .'

Andrew scuttled out of the way, across the dining room floor, and into the passageway, with the bone still in his mouth.

A knight raced from the table, the dagger glinting in a hand that poured with blood.

Andrew was cornered by a window. He turned and faced his attacker. Bracing himself, his back went up like the hackles of a trapped dog. He bared his teeth and snarled at the incoming knight, who suddenly stopped in his tracks.

'Come near me,' hissed Andrew, now lean with hunger but with a new savagery in his breast, 'and I'll rip out your throat.'

He was like a coiled snake, ready to strike at the knight's face if that man dared to come forward. His eyes were hot with fury. There was that taut feeling of needing to survive at any cost in his chest.

'I mean it. I'll tear your throat open and bite through your windpipe, you swine.'

'You – you can't speak to me like that,' thundered the knight. 'You're under punishment.'

'I'll take everything they throw at me,' replied Andrew, 'but I won't sit meekly while you stab me with that weapon. I have a right to defend myself. If I am a dog, I will be a dog. Even a hound would not let itself be cut without a fight. Do not mistake my servility for submissiveness. I will take my punishment, but nothing more than I deserve.'

'You bit me, you animal.'

'And I'll bite you again, if you steal what's mine. That which falls on the floor is the food of the dogs. I am a dog. I'll take off your fingers the next time.'

The knight seemed uncertain what to do next. He could not go back into the hall without some sort of retaliation. All the other knights, including the Master, were watching for him, waiting to see what would happen. This was good breakfast entertainment. Finally, he turned as if to go back in, then swiftly swung round again to kick Andrew in the ribs.

'Take that, you snivelling mongrel,' he said, savagely. 'Next time I'll break your head.'

Andrew took the kick like a dog would take it, yelping then slinking off with his prize. The kick had hurt but he ha established a precedent. No one would again try to retriev food that had fallen from the table. The ham on that bon tasted so good. Nothing had been as good before. It had bee hard won, but it was his. He threw the stripped bone to th other hounds when he had done. They gave him a chorus of barks and howls. Their thanks for his offering.

That night was a particularly cold one. He crawled in among the other dogs for warmth. They accepted him as one of their own. A hound for a pillow and a hound for a comforting bolster. By now he even smelled like a dog. Servants turned up their noses when he scampered past them on all fours. They threw shoes at him to keep him at bay.

'I'll remember you,' he called out like a musical jingle. 'I know you. I'll remember your faces.'

This stopped them for they knew that in a few months he would be a knight again and they would suffer. It was true they knew he could not whip them in retaliation for such as this, but the mocking threat unnerved them and made them wonder whether he might get back at them by some other method, some sly, underhand way. They had limited imaginations and had been abused and downtrodden for so long the suspicion of injustice in the hands of the knights lay close to the surface of their minds.

'Perhaps he will die, like the other one who went into disgrace,' said one servant to another within his hearing.

'Not a chance,' called Andrew to the man. 'I am made of sterner stuff, my friend. Don't count on such luck.'

The servant slunk away, into the shadows.

One day John of Reims came to Andrew and placed a parcel on the floor before him. He left without a word. Andrew scuttled forward, ripped away the wrapping with his fingers and found a huge date cake inside. There was also a letter in the neat copperplate handwriting of a scribe who wrote letters for money in the markets.

'Knight Andrew', read the note, 'I have heard from those who travel between lands that you are in need. I baked this cake with my own hands. You will find it sweet. I hope you enjoy it. I have a husband now and he knows nothing of this, so please do not send me any letters or gifts in return. Ulmurra, or She-of-the-Leopard-Eyes.'

Ulmurra? Surely that was the black slave he had saved from being eaten by the goat-ogre? Andrew had expected her to be far away by now, in some deep, dark country in the middle of Africa. Yet, as she had said, those who travel carry news of all kinds. Somehow, someone had managed to tell her of his plight and she had sent him this wonderful cake.

Like a fool he ate far too much of it and suffered stomach cramps for the rest of the day.

The rest he hid in a crevice in a wall, to visit every so often when he was really hungry.

He reread the note several times and pangs of yearning went through him.

'She has a husband,' he sighed, 'and thinks nothing of me in that way.'

Still, a cake was better than love at this point in his life. Love would not have kept him from starving. Love would not fill his belly. Love was pretty useless stuff when you were a dog with a hundred masters and no one to tend to your needs. No, a cake was much better, when all was said and done.

Yet the cake only lasted so long. Soon he was back to fighting with the dogs under the tables. A strange thing happened while the hunger pangs were on him. The phantom of a she-wolf suddenly appeared among the domestic canines. Andrew was afraid of this insubstantial creature, whose ferociousness kept him back when choice bits fell from above, so that one of the dogs got them. If Andrew tried to go forward to get any sliver of meat, the wolf would growl at him and shake its head.

'Not you,' snarled the big grey beast with the yellow glaring eyes. 'These succulent pieces are not for you.'

It did not matter that the wolf was a ghost-wolf; it owned a powerful spiritual force which made its presence appear physical.

'Why are you against me?' asked the youth. 'I have done nothing to you?'

'Oh, have you not?' cried the wolf. 'Well, think again.'

Andrew tried to recall any incident out in the wilderness when he had attacked a wolf. True, wolf packs had been near his camp sometimes. But he had not chased them out of spite or kept prey from them.

Andrew said, 'I don't understand why you hate me.'

'Were you not present at your own birth?'

Now Andrew had it. The wolf, the hawk and the hare!

'You are the wolf who starved because you could not steal the hawk's prey, there being humans nearby.'

'Humans, yes. You. You were the human. And the other three. I had young,' snarled the she-wolf. 'My babies died because they had no food.'

Andrew sympathised. 'I did not know this. But still, if I did, I would not have been able to do anything about it. I was a baby myself, just born. What could I have done to help you?'

The wolf said, 'It matters not that you were helpless. Humans always have some excuse. They have hunted and killed my kind since the dawn of time.'

'You steal their cattle and sheep.'

'Only to eat. Only to live.'

The quarrel went on for several hours. Gradually, as Andrew's logic began to defeat the wolf's emotional argument, the wolf began to disappear. It faded like mist in sunlight. Finally, it vanished altogether. Andrew was once again left able to fight for scraps with the domestic dogs. It was while he was chewing on a piece of chicken skin, thrown down by a fastidious knight who liked his drumsticks clean, that he remembered something the wolf had said.

'*And the other three.*'

Surely, at his birth in the snow on the edge of the forest, there had only been him, the warlock's wife and his mother present? Who was the fourth?

Perhaps the wolf was lying, trying to bait him? Or maybe the creature could not count. 'That must be it,' murmured Andrew, trying to get to sleep in a corner of a passageway one night. 'The animal was unnumbered.'

Yet. Yet, why mention a number at all? If the beast was confused by arithmetic, why mention a specific figure? Why not say, 'There was a crowd of you' or 'Several humans'. The wolf had said the figure with surety. No, it did seem as if there was another person present at his birth that no one had ever told him about. Could it have been his own father?

But he had been told by his mother that his father had been away shoeing horses at a distant village called Tattingstone, in Suffolk, where the local farrier had fallen sick. She had said it with some asperity, as if she were quite bitter about the fact that her husband had not been on hand when she delivered her baby. What about the warlock himself, then?

Surely it could not have been another woman from the village, or why would his mother have allowed the warlock's wife to deliver?

Such a mystery. Andrew now wished he had asked the wolf what she had meant by it. But the pair of them had been so intent on winning their argument that Andrew had thought of nothing other than putting the wolf in her place.

The chicken skin tasted good. Andrew crawled around under the table looking for John of Reims' leg, so that he could tug the knight's hose. At times John risked the wrath of the Master by slipping some tidbits to the unfortunate outcast.

It was a miserable time for the youth. A most dismal period. Those who did not like him took to kicking him at every opportunity. Those who liked him spurned him because of his crime. Fortunately, the minstrels who had sung of his glorious deeds did not sing of his misfortune. There was no advantage in it for the songsters. People in the street did not want to hear of failures, they wanted to hear only of successes. So, instead of singing about Andrew, they sung about some other knight, who had defeated this or that Saracen horde.

His punishment period seemed to last forever, yet it had only been two months when something happened which was to cause a monumental change in Andrew's life.

Walter Pughson was working at the forge when his father asked him to go to an apothecary.

'What is it, Father?' asked the swordsmith's youth. 'You have been looking quite pale of late.'

'I have a pain in my chest, my son – a little to the left side.

451

I'm sure a powder will make it go away. It's probably something I've eaten that's stuck there.'

'What shall I say to the apothecary?'

Pugh sat down on the anvil, breathing a little heavily.

'Just repeat to him what I have said to you. He'll know what to send. Go to Abraham of Nineveh. He's the one right at the end of the Street of Apothecaries. Tell him I'll pay him when I see him next.'

Walter left his father looking grey. He was only a little concerned. Pugh had never enjoyed good health, yet here he was, still alive and making swords. Still, Walter was anxious to get medicine for him as soon as possible. He did not like to see his adopted father in distress. So he hurried along the alleys, heading for the Street of Apothecaries, which lay in Jerusalem's Jewish quarter. There was none so good as a Jewish apothecary. They had studied the art of medicine for longer than most.

Suddenly, as he turned a corner, a swarthy man in a Berber's thick woollen hooded cloak confronted him. Eyes glinted from within the cloak's hood. The dark face with the hawk-beak nose smiled at him.

The man said, 'It's time.'

'Time?' repeated Walter, attempting to walk round this tall, lean creature.

'Time to perform your duty.'

'Who are you?' cried Walter, looking around for assistance. 'I have no money. You would be wasting your time trying to rob me.'

'Money?' The man spat the word. 'It's you I want. You surely remember your time in a fortress a long way from here?

452

You surely recall that you have an act to perform. You know what will happen if you do *not* do as I say?'

Walter's heart sank to his boots.

'You – you are from the Assassins.'

The man smiled again, the crescent mouth curving up the sides of his face, almost touching his ears.

'Ah – *now* you remember.'

'I – I cannot do this thing. Have mercy, sir. Please do not make me. I am not a killer. It is not in my character . . .'

'We have trained you, *Infidel*. We have given you the skill to carry out the act. You *will* do it. You should be proud to do it, for it will make you one of us. If you do not, or, indeed, if you fail to make the kill, you will be put to death yourself within the month. Also your father will die. He will be the first to go and then, when you have suffered the knowledge that you were responsible for his death, you will be next.'

Walter's hands went to his face, where he buried it in his slim fingers.

'This is so cruel.'

'Cruel? What is cruelty? The word means nothing to me.'

Walter's hands fell to his sides again.

'I still do not properly understand why you do not kill this man yourself, whoever he is.'

'Because he is a Christian. We are allies of King Baldwin. If we kill this person, the pact will be deemed to be broken. It is necessary that the deed is done by another Christian. You are that Christian.'

'God help me,' murmured Walter. 'And the name of the man I am to kill?'

The Assassin told him.

Walter gasped. 'But he . . . how will I carry it out? I have no access . . .'

'You will find a way. It must be done before the week is out.'

After this encounter, the Assassin disappeared into the streets beyond the alley. Walter continued on his way, stunned by a tremendous burden he carried in his heart. To kill a man in cold blood! And such an important personage. Of course Walter knew he would be caught. There was no way he could carry out this foul act and escape with his life. But at least his father would survive. At least Pugh would live.

Abraham the apothecary listened to this pale, babbling youth and was surprised to learn that the medicine was for someone other than the messenger, for the boy looked as if he were about to succumb to some nervous disorder himself.

31. REVELATIONS

Andrew had had another desperate day of scrapping with the hounds for his share of the detritus. A kitchen maid had burned his ear with a hot fire iron. He had found some stale crusts that had dropped between the floorboards, but they had been so hard there was a danger of breaking his teeth on them. His lice were active. He was as filthy with grease and dirt as any man could be. Stinking rags hung from his thin frame like those of a beggar. Andrew could not have sunk any lower if he actually put his mind to doing so.

That night he slept away from the other dogs, in a dark corner below a window niche. Yet those whom he sought to escape still found him out. The rats wanted the grease on his rags and came to gnaw on them in the middle hours. He fought them off with desperate kicks and punches, until finally they left him alone to sleep on the cold stone floor.

At about two o'clock in the morning Andrew woke with a start. A stalking figure had broken the moonbeam shining through the window above his head. This black shape slunk silently along the passageway towards the chamber where Odo de St Amand slept. Andrew's fuzzy mind was immediately alert. Who was this? It suddenly occurred to the outcast that perhaps the Master of the Temple was not so white and pure as he pretended to be. Was it possible that Odo had a tryst with a lover? What a revelation that would be! What a weapon in the possession of a young unfrocked Templar knight!

Andrew rose on all fours to follow the creeping figure, who was now opening the door to Odo's room.

Suddenly the figure turned and peered into the deep gloom of the passageway. The figure stood for a long while, staring in Andrew's direction. The intruder's face was stark white in the semi-darkness of the passageway. By his attire it seemed to be a man. His breathing was rapid and shallow. There was fear there, but whether of being attacked or something else was impossible to tell. Andrew slipped back into the shadows again. He settled down on his haunches, simply watching.

'That's it. Stay, boy. Stay there. Good dog.'

The words were hissed in a low voice.

So, this creeping person thought Andrew was indeed a canine beast. Well enough. He smelled like a dog. He moved like a dog. He lay down like a dog. In the half-light he could easily be mistaken for one. Well enough, then.

Let him, or indeed her, inside Odo's room – thought Andrew – then I shall burst in.

But in the next second a shout of alarm came from within the Master's chamber.

'Help, ho! Murder!' came the yell. 'Assist me, someone! I am attacked . . .'

Andrew rose unsteadily to his feet, then dropped again on to all fours when a dizziness overtook him. He was so unused to an erect position. So then, like a dog, he crashed through the doorway into the Master's room, to see two figures struggling on the bed. A knife glinted in the moonlight

456

spearing the small window on the far side of the room. The knife was in the hand of an assailant who was raising it to stab Odo.

Andrew leapt like a wolf, through the air, to sink his teeth into the wrist of Odo's attacker.

'My hand!' screamed the man.

Andrew bit down hard, into bone. The knife fell on to the blankets of the Master's bed. Andrew gripped the assailant now in his strong arms, holding him fast. The man struggled, sobbing now. In the next minute men-at-arms entered the chamber and pulled the two fighters apart. Both were held and dragged to the far side of the chamber. There were lights of torches then, which filled the room with flickering flames.

'Not him!' cried Odo, pointing. 'Not Sir Andrew. It was he who saved me from that fiend.'

Andrew was released. He stayed on his feet, swaying unsteadily.

The assailant was studied in the torchlight.

'It's not an Assassin,' said a sergeant-at-arms. 'It's the sword-smith's son.'

Walter Pughson hung there between two servants of Odo, a pathetic figure, sobbing his heart out.

Odo de St Amand sat on the edge of his bed, blood seeping from a wound in his shoulder. His white nightshirt was stained ed in various places. The Temple physician was sent for and he arrived, sleep in the corners of his eyes, to treat the wounds of the Master. He proclaimed them not to be life-threatening. Odo gathered his faculties now and stared across the room at his attacker.

'Why have you done this thing?' he asked, as he was being

bandaged. 'What have I done to you? An unpaid bill? Surely nothing else? A brother or father wronged by me? I do not think so, boy. Tell me.'

But Walter would say nothing. He looked drained of all energy. He glanced only once at Andrew and then without any malice, before being led away to the dungeon.

'Well,' Odo said, a little later, 'we'll soon find out what it is – a white-hot poker will get it out of him.'

The following morning Andrew found himself reinstated into the Templars. His mantle was returned to him. His golden spurs. His wonderful Ulfberht sword. And his Helmschmid armour. All was forgiven. Odo was grateful for his life and privately confessed that it had been Gondemar de Blois who had put gold into the Temple of Solomon's coffers in order that Andrew should be disgraced.

'I am sorry now for the wrong I have inflicted on you,' said Odo, 'and ask you to overlook the actions forced upon me by that false knight, Gondemar de Blois.'

Andrew did not think the Master had been *forced* into anything, but was so relieved to be back in the service of the Templars that he let the matter drop. He had suffered greatly through Odo's spurious judgement and injustice, but it would do no good to confront the Master. Odo was still the head of the Temple and could not be seriously challenged.

He went back to his room walking upright, using the walls on either side of the passageway to keep himself steady. I was not so much that his legs felt strange: it was more tha he felt unnatural on two legs. His inclination was to dro down on all fours again, where it was comfortable. H resisted this urge with all his mental strength. It would d no good to give in to canine habits. They had to be broken quickly.

'What are you doing, you worthless cur?' cried a voice behind him. 'For pity's sake get you down on the knuckles of your hands where you belong.'

A swift kick sent a sharp pain up Andrew's spine.

He spun round, hurt and angry, to find a greasy youth from the kitchens smirking at him.

'Joseph,' warned Andrew, 'I should not continue to do that.'

'Yes, and why, you mongrel knight?'

'Because I shall take you to task if you do. I'll allow that last kick, to remind me of what I was. But another will have you running with a bloody nose to the kitchens.'

A sweeper, whose job it was to clean the passageways and common areas of the Temple, came up behind the pair. He glanced at Andrew and then at Joseph, and quickly gauged what was passing between them. Clearly this fellow had been informed of the latest development because his eyes went as round as full moons as Joseph delivered another swift kick at Andrew's thigh and cried, 'Ha! Down on all fours, you dirty dog, you.'

'Joseph . . .' the sweeper was about to warn his colleague, but it was too late. Joseph was flat on his back, his nose gushing, while Andrew was rubbing his knuckles.

'Sorry, Joseph – I know I'm not permitted to take revenge for your behaviour towards me while I was a dog – but I'm a man again, and you kicked me after I'd been restored to that state. Now go and put a cold-water clout on that nose.'

Joseph was escorted to the kitchen by the sweeper, who said he sympathised with the grizzling kitchen boy but was later heard telling the story to others amid howls of laughter.

After a long hot bath, a good meal and a haircut, Andrew went out to the stables to find Warlock. The war horse seemed delighted to see his master, not knowing why he had been in disgrace, for why else would his master stay away from him for so long? Andrew took him out for a ride, went to take tea with Hassan and his family, telling them of his misfortunes, then returned to the palace to find that Pugh, the swordsmith, had dropped dead on being told of his son's crime.

'Turned as grey as stale bread,' said John of Reims, 'then fainted away to strike his head on his anvil as he fell.'

'Poor man,' murmured Andrew. 'To find his son was an assassin.'

'The boy was adopted, of course,' said John. 'Obviously bad blood. You never know where these waifs have come from, eh? They should be grateful, to be taken in by a good tradesman and taught skills, but bad blood will out in the end. A bastard of some thief or other, I've no doubt. Well, he'll join his poor father soon enough, at the end of a rope.'

Yet, still, no one had any idea why Walter Pughson had wanted to murder Odo. Was it for money? Was it for some sort of revenge? No one knew. The youth would not speak, even under torture. No one had told him of his father's death. They were saving that until the very last. There were still a few tricks from the store of tortures known to the dungeon master to be carried out.

In Outremer there were tortures previously unknown to homely folk. Dungeon masters learned these secrets with great relish, having ample opportunity for trying them out. The screams of the victims were like the music of a lute to their ears. They played with hot irons, scalding water, pincers sharp knives, salt, corrosive liquids, heavy stones, spiked boxes and many, many other toys. There was one particular torture Odo's dungeon master loved, which involved the victim swallowing a thick cord until it went all the way through his body and out the other end. Then the poor creature was strung up like a hammock over burning faggots.

One had to hope that those who caused such pain on Earth would be welcomed into Hell, where they would suffer for eternity what they had so casually inflicted on others.

Andrew actually felt sorry for Walter Pughson. Yes, you could not go about trying to murder lords, but being given to the dungeon master as a plaything was an ugly fate. Andrew went to Odo and asked permission to visit the criminal.

'Perhaps I can get out of him why he committed this deed?' said Andrew. 'Then we can hang him and have done with it.'

Odo shrugged. 'As you wish – for mine own part I would like to see him suffer a little more, but I confess to being intrigued by his reasons.'

So Andrew was admitted to the cell where the criminal was being held. He found an abject figure crouched in filthy straw, head bowed, cramped by manacles and chains. The youth looked up at Andrew when he entered, his eyes blinking in the sudden light of his lamp, for there were no windows in the cell. Andrew sat down in front of the youth and stared at him.

'How's your wrist?' asked Andrew, genuinely concerned. 'The one I bit.'

'That was you? You look different. I thought you were a beast. You looked like a mad dog – one of those which pass on the disease of madness to men. Are you mad?'

'Only a little, and not in the way of a dog.'

461

'Pity,' muttered Walter, 'for such a disease would assist me to my grave, where I wish to be.'

'The madness of dogs is an ugly way to die – there are much easier ways.'

'Give me one, for I am bound and tethered, and unable to choke myself to death, which I sorely wish to do.'

'I might be able to help you if you tell me why you tried to kill the Master of Solomon's Temple.'

'What?' muttered Walter, thickly. 'You want to know why I did it?'

'It might save you more pain.'

'If – if I told you, harm might come to an innocent old man,' replied Walter. 'I would rather suffer those hot irons than anything happen to him.'

'You mean Pugh, the swordsmith.'

'Yes.'

Andrew decided to take something on himself.

'I'm afraid he's dead, Walter. He died on hearing of your crime. I think his heart broke in his chest.'

Walter began to cry. 'Oh God, bless my father – take him into Your arms, Lord. Oh dear Jesus, why did he have to die? He hurt no one . . .'

Andrew let the grief flood from the youth before him waiting patiently until the tears subsided.

'Well, then,' said Walter, fiercely, once he had stopped weeping, 'I shall tell you. It was those damned Assassins who put me up to this. They said they would kill me and my father if I didn't murder Odo de St Amand. They wanted revenge for sending Walter de Mesnil to kill their ambassadors. Walter de Mesnil! I am even named for a killer.'

'But Walter de Mesnil did that murder of his own accord – so far as I know he was not sent by anyone.'

'The Assassins do not believe that. They think the killings were ordered by the Master of the Temple.'

It was while Walter was spitting out this sentence with all the venom of a youth who felt wronged that Andrew glanced down at the prisoner's feet. They were manacled at the ankles, with chains holding him fast to iron rings in the floor. But the lamplight revealed something else, something amazing to the visitor. He stared disbelievingly at some marks.

'Where did you get those?' shouted Andrew, leaping up.

'What?' answered a bewildered Walter, looking down at the manacles. 'These were locked to my ankles.'

'No! Not the irons. Those dark stains on your feet!'

'These birthmarks? Why, I was told they were the hand-prints of a witch.'

'Who told you that?' asked Andrew, sharply.

'A tall, dark stranger came to me one night, when I was a small boy in England. The stranger said my mother had given birth to me in the winter snows and the only one there to help was his wife. This woman pulled me from my mother's womb with hands that burned these marks into my feet.'

'You lie!' cried Andrew, terrified and confused by Walter's words. 'How could that be, for *I* am the child pulled from my mother's womb by the warlock's wife.'

Walter shook his head, equally confused. 'I don't understand,' he said. 'I am simply repeating the words of the tall stranger.'

'What did he look like, this stranger?'

And Walter proceeded to describe the warlock who had lived in the forest beyond Cressing village.

Andrew's mind whirled with thoughts. He could not understand what was going on here. Was this some trickery, some evil workings of Eastern magic? Where did this Walter learn of Andrew's birth? Perhaps Harold the butcher's son had somehow got word to the swordsmith's apprentice?

'I ought to kill you,' said Andrew, still in a state of confusion. 'I could do that now, with my sword.'

'Please do,' Walter replied, calmly. 'It would end my misery.'

'Do – do you have webbed toes?'

'Yes,' replied Walter.'

'And what of hawks and their kind?'

'They are my friends.'

'Oh Lord,' cried Andrew, 'I think I'm going mad.'

At that moment a weird thing happened. Through the walls of the dungeon came marching a troop of spectres. Ghosts from another world. They were ashen in aspect, gaunt in feature, morbid in expression. Dreadful creatures who tramped through one outside wall, across the floor of the cell, and out through the opposite wall. Mournful beings, silent as the grave, simply intent on some destination beyond the imagination of the two mortals in the room.

One of these marchers suddenly broke ranks and stood before the two terrified youths. Andrew recognised this ghoul immediately. It was one of the two dead men who had met him in the wood before he left home. The one who had prophesied his future knighthood. It was the axe murderer, the other, of course, being his victim, who was not present.

'Ah,' said the murderer, in the hollow tones of the dead, 'you have discovered the secret.'

'Have we?' cried Andrew, not quite in his right mind. 'I have not.'

'If you have not now guessed, then, bless you, you are about as bright as an inbred pig.'

Walter said, 'I think I have – we are twins.'

Andrew, stunned, stared at Walter and then at the ghostly figure of the murderer.

'Twins?' he said.

'Of course,' groaned the murderer in that horrible voice from the other side of the grave, 'what else? The warlock's wife took one of you, knowing that if your mother carried both home you would be killed by superstitious villagers. You know that twins are both considered unlucky and evil? The villagers would have impaled the pair of you.

'Thus the second child was given to a passing peddler, who sold the boy on, who was traded yet again, until finally he ended up the adopted son of Pugh the swordsmith.'

Andrew stared at his brother.

'But we don't look alike.'

The ghoul laughed. 'Not all twins are identical, boy – many are not. There are certain features which are similar. The nose. The eyes. But you are taller and stockier than him, and he is much more intelligent than you. The hair would be the same if yours was longer and his was shorter.'

'My brother,' said Andrew, now in hushed tones. 'Walter, we are brothers.'

'Twin brothers,' agreed Walter, then adding sardonically, 'one of whom is about to hang for attempted murder.'

'I must go,' moaned the ghost. 'My Company calls me.'

Andrew said, 'Your what?'

'The Company of the Damned. My victim is now in a better place than I shall ever be. I must tramp with these wraiths without bodies, without hope, without minds, forever and forever and forever. On and on they stamp, without any end in sight, travelling the wastelands of the Otherworld, always marching, marching, marching.'

He groaned audibly, filling the cell with his deep distress.

Andrew pointed out to the spectre that he was in a temple built of stone, not out on a wasteland.

The ghoul looked around him, his eye sockets dark pits in his phantom skull.

'We are in different places. I see peat hags and misty moors. Farewell, I must be with the unhappy doomed.'

Once the ghost had left to join his regiment of lost souls, Walter turned to his brother.

'What do we do now?' he asked.

Andrew said a little waspishly. 'Why don't you tell me? You're supposed to be the bright one.'

'Odo is not going to release me, is he?'

'The fact that you're my brother will make no difference to whether you hang or not,' agreed Andrew. 'You tried to kill the Master of Solomon's Temple. I could speak to the king, but I doubt if he would hold any sway with Odo on this matter. So there is only one course left to us.'

He drew his sword and Walter closed his eyes.

'Yes, better to die by the sword than dangle from a rope with my eyes starting from my head and my throat gasping for breath, while my body jumps and twitches . . .'

'What are you talking about? I'm going to loosen these chains,' said Andrew, using the sword as a lever beneath the iron rings embedded in the floor. 'Then we shall ride away from Jerusalem and head for a port.'

Walter's eyes opened again.

'You would do this for *me*?'

'Good lord, Walter, I'm your *brother*.'

The Ulfberht blade was incredibly strong, being fashioned from crucible steel from Persia. It was the strongest steel in the world. Any other blade would have snapped, but the Ulfberht sword, forged in the Rhineland, forced the rings out of the stone into which they had been hammered. Once they were out, Andrew told Walter to hide behind the door. Then he shouted for the turnkey in a shrill, panicky tone.

The door was opened and the jailer poked his head cautiously inside the cell.

'What is it?'

Andrew said, 'He's gone! The prisoner's gone!'

'Gone?' cried the turnkey, coming into the cell now. 'Gone where?'

'He went over there, somewhere at the back of the cell.'

The jailer peered into the dimly lit corner of the room. Andrew snuffed out his lamp and stepped smartly towards the doorway. Walter was already halfway out of the cell. The pair of them slammed the door on the turnkey, just as he was exclaiming 'Hey!' to an empty dungeon.

Andrew found a lump of wood in the fireplace of the turnkey's room and jammed it under the door. The turnkey started hammering on the other side, but his shouts were muffled by the thick, nail-studded wood. Stone walls without windows were not the best carriers of sound either. It would be a long time before he was discovered.

'We must get something to cover those irons,' said Andrew. 'Stay here while I fetch a cloak.'

He ran along the passageway and down the stairs, the dungeons being, as most dungeons are, on the top floor of the building. There were some brown woollen monks' habits hanging in the hallway which the Templar knights sometimes wore on bitterly cold days. Andrew grabbed one of these and went back to the jailer's room.

'Here, put this on,' he said to Walter; 'throw up the hood and follow me out to the stables.'

Walter did as he was told.

They passed two knights on their way across the courtyard, who nodded to Andrew.

'So I said to Sir Alphonse,' Andrew said in a loud voice, 'that he could not tilt at a pig riding a goat, let alone a man on a horse. Of course he challenged me to single combat . . .'

Walter made muttering noises from deep within the hood of his habit. When they were just past the two knights one of Walter's chains clinked on the cobblestones. Both knights turned to look down.

Andrew immediately dropped to one knee, as if looking for something.

'My coin!' he said. 'I was going to give that to the stableboy.' He rose again on two legs. 'Oh well, no doubt he'll find the thing himself if he has any gumption.'

The two knights turned again and moved on.

Andrew and Walter continued to the stables, where Andrew called to the boys to saddle Warlock.

While this was going on, Andrew told Walter he was going to fetch his armour.

It was a nervous time for both youths.

'Can't you leave it?' asked Walter.

'Not on your life. It's worth a fortune. Besides, it was given me by my adopter father.'

'Ah, in that case you must collect it.'

Andrew left Walter talking and went to get his armour. He came back with it in a sack. By that time Warlock was ready to ride. Andrew handed the bag of armour to Walter to hold and then climbed up on his steed. He then took the sack, tied it to the saddle and handed up his brother. They then rode casually away from the Temple of Solomon. A pang of sorrow went through Andrew as they did so. All his young life he had wanted to be a resident of this temple. Now he was having to turn his back on it forever. He could not return. Odo would have him executed for assisting in Walter's escape.

'You are sad, Andrew,' said Walter.

'Oh, we have far more things to worry about than me being sad,' replied Andrew. 'We have to get to Tyre or Sidon without being tracked down. It's no good trying Jaffa or Acre. Those are the first ports they'll look for us. Food. We need food for a journey. I have a friend in the city. We must go there . . .'

And so they went to the house of Hassan's father, who gave them supplies and another horse. Walter's chains were removed from his wrists and ankles. From there they rode for the gates of the city. It was clear that a hue and cry was already in progress once they reached the main gates so they turned back and managed to leave Jerusalem by a secret gate in the garden of one of Hassan's cousins. There they struck out east, heading for the desert, rather than following the coastline to a port, knowing that there was danger down by the shores of the sea, where Odo's men would be searching.

'I wish I'd said goodbye to the king,' Andrew said, sighing. 'I shall miss him.'

'Won't King Baldwin be angry with you?'

'He has no love for Odo de St Amand,' replied Andrew. 'He'll laugh when he hears what we have done.'

Then Andrew fell into silence. They rode until deep into the evening, stopping only when the sun had gone down behind distant hills. There they remained until the following dawn without a fire, concerned in case Odo had guessed what they were doing and had sent out parties in their direction.

That evening, under the starlight, Walter asked to see his brother's sword.

'It must be made of strong steel, to tear those iron rings from the dungeon floor,' said Walter, as the blade was handed reverently to him. 'Who fashioned it?'

'It's an Ulfberht,' said Andrew.

There was an intake of breath from Walter, who held up the sword in the poor light.

'I have never seen an Ulfberht, let alone touched one. My father . . .' his voice had a catch in it. 'My adopted father would have loved to handle this blade. There are many fakes, of course. Iron swords made harder by plunging them into cold water when they are red hot. But such treatment leaves a sword brittle and they break easily. An Ulfberht is the king of swords. You must have done something quite wonderful to be given such a weapon, Andrew.'

'I – I helped someone in trouble.'

'What sort of trouble?'

Andrew was reluctant to speak of his exploit.

'Oh, nothing much.'

'You must have saved a life at the very least?'

'Oh, all right – yes. I dived into the River Thames for a girl who was drowning.'

'And her name?'

'Angelique de Sonnac.'

'Ah. A knight's lady?'

'His daughter.'

'A beautiful maiden, no doubt?'

Andrew shrugged. 'Quite pretty. But very young.'

'A lot younger than we are?'

'Two years perhaps. Not so young, I suppose. Anyway, she will have forgotten all about me, that's certain.'

'But an Ulfberht!'

'Yes,' Andrew said, smiling, as his brother again held up the blade so that the light from the stars glanced off it in flashes of silver. 'Now *there's* a beautiful maiden.'

When the sun rose again, they restarted their journey, striking north now, heading for the County of Edessa, which neighboured the Principality of Antioch. Once they were past these gateways to the south, they could strike north-west and try to cross the Rum of the Seljuks to reach Constantinople.

It would be a long and dangerous journey, through enemy territory. There would be bandits, wild beasts and other hazards to contend with. And they had to stay ahead of any pursuers. Their chances were slim, to say the least. But they were two brothers who had found each other. Twin brothers. That knowledge instilled a great deal of courage in both youths.

And they had magic on their side.

They rode through a forest of cedars, and then out on to a shimmering plain. There were mountains in the far distance, like a line of black clouds crushed against the ground. When they had almost crossed the plain, a fast-flowing river blocked their path. Then, from behind, they heard the note of a horn hanging on the wind. Looking back, Andrew could see knights, their banners flowing from their lances. It was not the *Chevaliers Noirs* but most probably Odo's Templars.

'They've caught up with us,' said Andrew. 'We'll have to fight.'

Walter said, 'I can't fight with our own knights, Andrew. I was in the wrong, after all.'

Andrew understood his brother's dilemma. If they fought and killed Odo's men they would end up being hunted for the rest of their lives. King Baldwin might forgive an attempted murder, so long as the excuses were acceptable, but not an actual killing. Andrew looked at the river in front of them.

'We'll have to swim.'

'What about your armour?'

'Warlock will carry that. Can you swim, Walter?'

'Me? I've never tried, though I've feet like a duck.'

'Ah, of course you have!'

The horns of the pursuing knights sounded again, nearer now, and had an urgency about them. They announced that the 'quarry' had been seen. The riders were moving in for the kill.

Andrew put all his armour, his sword, in fact everything he had, into the one sack. He tied this on to Warlock's saddle. Then he led the charger into the rushing flood. Warlock was anything but keen, kicking and jerking his head away from the leaping spray. But once he saw his master entering the water without concern he calmed down and started to swim.

Walter came last. Walter's horse followed Warlock, who was clearly the leader. The swordsmith's apprentice was shaking, both with the cold water and with terror. Yet he found, once he was out of his depth, that he was not sinking. So long as he kicked his feet as he had seen Andrew do, he remained afloat. Still, the river water rushed up his nostrils and down his mouth, causing him to panic once or twice. The force of the current seemed intent on wrenching his hand from the horse's tail, but somehow he managed to cling on without losing his grip. He coughed and spluttered, gasping for air and swallowing water, but gradually, gradually, he realised they were making the crossing.

Though they made progress over the watery divide, the current swept them at a sharp angle westwards, so that one yard forward was six yards sideways. The knights chasing them had ridden hard and furiously to the banks, where they were only just in time to see the two youths and the horse sweeping around a bend. Andrew's prowess as a swimmer was put severely to the test. He saw his brother struggling with cramp and had to let go of Warlock's reins to slide back and assist Walter.

'Keep your head up,' he yelled against the noise of the rushing water. 'Grab breaths when you can – don't try to breath as you do on dry land. Just snatch at the air and swallow it quickly. Kick, kick, that's it. Use your free hand like a paddle. We're nearly there. . .'

In fact, it took another ten long minutes or more to make

the far bank. When Walter crawled out he was utterly spent. He fell on his back and sucked down air, staring up at the boating clouds above and swearing to himself that he would never ever again enter deep water.

Andrew lay beside his brother and suddenly burst out laughing. 'So funny,' he said, 'their faces! They were willing us to go under, you know. They hate being thwarted, Templar knights, and they knew they were beaten. But still they hoped the river would take us. Well, it didn't. Here we are, safe and sound, and ready for any other adventure.'

Walter gasped out, 'I'm glad you told me about our webbed toes – that it was impossible to sink.'

'Oh, I just said that to cheer you up.'

Walter sat up, abruptly. 'You mean – you mean it wasn't true?'

'Of course not, you gull. Anyone can drown in a fast-flowing river. Oh, I suppose our webbed toes help us somewhat, but only in the calm water of a mill pond. In a raging flood like that, webbed toes don't make a jot of difference. We should have drowned, if truth be known.'

Walter was horrified, more by the fact that his brother was so casual with the truth than by the nature of his mendacity.

'How – how can you tell lies like that?'

'Oh, easily,' said Andrew, airily. 'All I do is open my mouth and out they come.'

Walter was beginning to wonder what sort of disreputable creature he had gained as a brother.

32. A BAND OF ROGUES

The two youths had much to think about as they rode north-
wards.

Walter was still grieving over the death of the only father
he had ever known. Andrew had told him about his *real*
family – a farrier father, a mother and two sisters beside. But
there were no images in Walter's head of these people. The
man he remembered – the kind, thoughtful man who had
taken him in as an orphan, as a slave boy – he was now dead.
It was this figure who gripped Walter's thoughts. Pugh, the
swordsmith, whose soft words were still in Walter's head;
whose features were still in Walter's mind's eye. It would be
some time before Walter would come to terms with his adopter-
father's passing. He had loved him as any son loves his own.

Andrew was grieving, too, but over the loss of his status
and reputation. Oh, he told himself, he did not regret giving
these things up for a brother. A brother was worth a king's
ransom. But still he missed them. Was he still entitled to call
himself a knight? He believed so. Many other knights had
done worse things and were still called 'Sir'. But there would
be no more riding with kings, or jesting with Templar knights
around the feasting table, or receiving respectful bows from
merchants and clerics in the street. Most of what Andrew had
worked for had now been thrown away in a single gesture:
that of saving his brother's life.

'Tell me about your time with the Assassins,' said Andrew, as they rode together. 'What are their fortresses like?'

Walter told him, and also told Andrew about his previous life as a swordsmith's apprentice. It was interesting, but Walter had not had as many adventures as Andrew. Andrew then proceeded to tell Walter about life at Cressing, about Friar Nottidge, about Gondemar and the evils he had visited on Andrew, about Patrick and the players, and all the other adventures he had experienced since leaving home.

While the two youths were discussing their histories, messengers were still going out from Jerusalem on racing camels, to all the far corners of the region. Even now a messenger had reached Antioch well ahead of the twins and spread the word that if Andrew of Cressing was seen he was to be apprehended and brought to the justice of Odo de St Amand. One man was particularly pleased to hear of the young knight's downfall: that was, of course, Sir Gondemar de Blois.

Gondemar tried to raise a group of knights to go out with him to find the renegades, but there was a religious festival in full flow in Antioch and others were reluctant to leave. So instead the knight took a purse of gold and sent word out that he wanted to recruit the rogue knights of Walter de Mesnil. The *Chevaliers Noirs* were happy to oblige him. They met him near a bridge over a small river and asked him the name of his enemy.

'A youth named Andrew of Cressing.'

'Ah,' said one, 'we have heard of this knight.'

Gondemar said to them, 'Knight? He does not deserve to be called such – he is the grubby son of a blacksmith.'

'Then he should be easy to despatch,' cried a huge bull of a man. 'We shall kill him before breaking our fast.'

'And I shall be there to assist,' said Gondemar.

'If you ride with us, you will be one of us for all time,' came the reply. 'They will not take you back into Antioch.'

'Then so be it,' said Gondemar.

Since they were knights of the wilderness, of the mountain and plain, robbers, thieves and brigands, they knew all the paths and passes. They paid goatboys and shepherds to watch for two riders coming from the south. Odo's men might be lost out here in the marches, but Gondemar's new friends were quite familiar with the land. It was not long before they received word of the twins from men in a watchtower which guarded a narrow pass into a wilder region than their own. The youths were coming at an ordinary pace.

A travelling man walking with a dancing bear told the twins that the *Chevaliers Noirs,* 'those bloody cut-throats', were waiting for them a short way ahead, 'led by a knight with one hand missing'.

'Gondemar,' said Andrew. 'He must want my head very badly to join with that evil crew.'

The twins rode out together not long after dawn. The sun was bright, almost white on the sands. Bleached seashells, left by an age when the ocean had covered the land, shone like ivory here and there. Dust devils rose, whirled and died. Balls of tumbleweed rolled with the breeze, running along the sands as if they were live creatures. There were dry animals' skulls and other bones lying among the rocks. It was warm, but not as hot as it would become near to noon.

Now the lizards and snakes came out of their rocky holes

to gather warmth to their cold-blooded bodies. Later, when the world was even more parched and arid, they would seek the shade again. Mountains were already hazy with curtains of heat rising before them. The sea, far behind to the west, dazzled the sky with its silvery sheen.

Walter was unused to being on a horse. He looked uncomfortable in the saddle. He rode like a scarecrow stuck on a donkey. However, Andrew had chosen him a gentle mare, which would not have great fire in a battle, but would not bite or bolt or do anything silly because there was a novice on her back. Walter looked determined and he was a swordsmith's son: he knew a blade and how to wield it, probably even more expertly than his twin brother. He had been testing such swords since the day he had been adopted.

But he had never before used a sword in a serious fight against another man.

'How far do we have to go, brother?' he asked Andrew. 'Is it miles or hundreds of miles?'

'I honestly don't know,' came the reply. 'The astrolabe doesn't give us the distance.'

'We have to do this thing?'

'I do. Gondemar will never let me rest. There must be a reckoning between us. You do not have to, Walter. This is my fight.'

Walter said, 'You are my brother – and you saved my life. I must die by your side or forever live in shame.'

The idea of having a brother was still fresh enough for Walter to use the word with great pride. He had a brother! He, Walter Pughson, had a flesh-and-blood brother. Nothing could be more wonderful. The fact was that he also had two

478

sisters, a real mother and a real father. But a brother was enough for the moment. If he thought about family in England, he still put them below his adopter father. Pugh had taken him in, treated him like a son and was therefore entitled to be treated like a father. If Walter thought too much about yet another father he felt he was betraying Pugh. It was too confusing at present.

They rode through valley and across plain, until finally they came to a river. On the near bank of this river was a group of knights, some forty of them. They were indeed the *Chevaliers Noirs*, those despicable rogues who had murdered ambassadors from the Assassins. Murdered them in a cowardly attack while their prey was defenceless. Now they were prepared to murder Andrew and Walter. At their head was Andrew's hated enemy, Gondemar de Blois. Gondemar's white armour stood out clearly against the river bank. His banner fluttered from his white-wood lance.

'My goodness,' said Walter, mildly, 'they look a rough lot.' Understatement.

Thirty horses, forty men. Burly knights. Their steeds were churning dust. Brutes of men. Huge figures in dirty armour and tattered mantles. Close to savage beasts. They took what they wanted, when they wanted, and killed those who tried to stop them. Might was right. Their habit was to crush. Stand in the way and they would stamp you into the ground. They milled now, in the haze, waiting. They were waiting to kill. They were certain in their belief that they would triumph. When did they not? Those who held other beliefs were dead. Left to rot, burned or buried. These were killers. No honour in their bones. Only selfish wills. They waited, staring, unconcerned by the foe. Two young men, one without armour. It would be easy. Very easy.

'They are formidable,' murmured Andrew, his stomach fluttering with fear. 'You need not stay, Walter. I will handle this alone.'

'That does not even warrant a reply,' said his brother.

At that moment, out of the south, came another band of men. Andrew groaned. Had the rogue knights called for reinforcements? Perhaps they had formed a pact with Odo de St Amand for just a day, to get rid of a troublesome pest? There were but a dozen of these newcomers, who actually looked too gaudy and flamboyant to be Templars.

'Saracens,' muttered Walter. 'Look, you can see their banners with the Arabic writing!'

One of the Saracens rode out in front, galloping to where Andrew and Walter waited on their steeds.

'*Salaam ali kum*,' cried the youth on the white horse. 'My very good friend, Andrew. I come to assist.'

Hassan! It was his great comrade and ally, Hassan. Andrew was overjoyed.

'*Ali kum salaam*,' shouted Andrew. 'What are you doing here, you fool? Does your older brother know you have come?'

'My brother rides with us,' said Hassan, pointing back at the men behind him. 'We have come to wipe these parasites from the face of the Earth. Too long they have been allowed to rape and plunder. Today will be the reckoning.'

So they gathered there, facing a vicious and formidable foe, two youths from the British Isles and twelve Arab horsemen.

'They have lances,' said Andrew, looking at the rogue knights.

Hassan, resplendent in his decorated Saracen armour, called forth one of his riders.

'We too have lances,' he told Andrew. 'This man carries them – choose one for yourself. And you, Walter.'

'They all look the same,' said Walter.

'They are all the same, but one of them is yours – do you not feel any attraction?'

'This one,' Walter said, extracting a long spear-like lance from the sheath carried by the Saracen warrior. 'It seems to want to be used.'

'You are all riding white horses,' Andrew remarked. 'Is there a reason?'

Hassan's brother said, 'In the heat of the battle you will look for someone to strike. Do not cut down a man on a white horse, for he will be your friend. See, even the rogue knight yonder who rides a big grey will not be mistaken for one of us – his steed is so filthy it is almost brown with river dust.'

'Ah, good thinking. And you will know us? Walter and me?'

'We are cooler in our battle-mind than Christian knights – we shall not make any mistakes.'

'The time has come,' Andrew said. 'Form a line!'

The Saracens were not used to fighting in formation but they drew up in a ragged line as ordered.

'Ready?'

'Aye,' cried Walter, excited by his first battle on horseback, ready, my brother.'

Andrew was about to cry, 'For God, King Baldwin and erusalem!' but he remembered in time who he was riding vith, so he simply cried, 'Death to the Black Knights!' and icked an already impatient Warlock into his stride.

481

The chestnut steed surged forward. Warlock was in his element. This was what he had been trained for and this was what he loved. Full gallop into a hot fight. The clash of swords. The rip of the lance. The clatter of shields. He felt the energy surge through his frame. All his muscles rippled with anticipation. His hooves struck hard earth and back came the sound of thunder. His ears were like spear points, his mane whipped the wind, his tail flew straight out behind him as the banner of a great war horse.

Andrew's men were outnumbered three to one, but, as they rode at the enemy, Andrew noticed two extra riders.

The jinn. A green jinnee and a blue jinnee, both riding hellhounds, both protected by flaming shields of red fire. Walter had seen them, too. The brothers knew they were the only ones who could see these warriors from the Otherworld; no one else even glanced at the jinn. The naked jinn carried a scimitar in each hand and daggers in their teeth. The pair looked up at the two brothers and grinned with such evil delight that Andrew and Walter laughed.

The rogue knights now came forth. They presented a solid block of weapons and metal. Gondemar was out front. This was the final battle, the final reckoning. One of them would die today: Gondemar de Blois or Andrew of Cressing. There would be no quarter. The dark figure of Death was waiting to do the body count, patient as ever, knowing that all would come to him in the end, no matter what.

The first clash unseated several men. Lances skewed of shields, or found their mark. Men fell with cries on their lips. Blood spilled and droplets flew through the air. Horse screamed and tumbled. Blades appeared and clashed, ringing in the hollow morning of that desolate place. The wilderness was suddenly echoing with grunts, groans and the curses of those who fought. Dust billowed, fogging men's eyes. Sweat made for slippery palms. Helmets muffled many a death rattle as a rider toppled from his mount to the earth.

Andrew felt a blade hack at his shoulder. He turned Warlock, and, yes, there was Gondemar. No face could be seen, for a helmet hid his foe's features. But Andrew noted the missing hand, the hand he had removed in all good faith. Gondemar hammered down on Andrew's helmet with his great sword, the sound intolerable within. *Crang! Crang! Crang! Crang!* The strokes fell mercilessly on the metal helmet. Andrew wheeled and wheeled about, trying to get out of range of the blows. Trying to get in some strokes of his own.

The armour held. The armour blessed by Tomas, who was even now looking down from his country of cloud.

Finally, Andrew was able to back away without hitting another horse. Andrew then launched Warlock forward, rampant, hooves flailing, to strike Gondemar in the chest. The other knight fell, his heavy body thumping the dust. But Gondemar clambered to his feet, even before Andrew could turn his mount again. The one-handed knight unclipped a mace from his waistband. With this spiked-ball weapon he struck Andrew in the knee. Andrew yelled in pain and dropped from the saddle, down on the far side of Warlock.

In the meantime the fighting around the pair had reached its peak. The jinn had been creating mayhem, striking knights from their saddles and leaving them for Walter to despatch into the Hereafter. At the height of the fighting a lone saker falcon stooped from the sky and caused great confusion among the rogue knights. It touched no one, but flew close to the faces of Gondemar's knights, blurring their vision. Once those knights were thoroughly disconcerted, it flew off again with a loud 'kark', as if triumphant in it dealings with wickedness.

Hassan and his Saracens fought bravely. One or two of them had been killed, some injured. Walter had been wounded in the thigh. But they had put many of the enemy to the sword. The end was clear. The rogue knights were going to lose. Those who thought to save their skins threw off any loose armour and plunged their horses into the river. They hoped to swim to the other side. The current was strong, however. These men were swept off their saddles, taken with the fast torrent, and further along the river several were drowned. Others went down fighting, even on foot, slashing about them with hopeless abandon, until they too were struck down by jinnee, Saracen or Walter Pughson.

Gondemar must have seen that all was lost.

This troublesome knight stood over Andrew wielding the deadly mace like a hammer. Once, twice, he hit Andrew's head with his weapon. Inside the helmet Andrew's ears rang and his skull felt like an anvil. The third stroke would surely break his neck. He stared up through the slit in his helmet at the white knight, who was gathering all his strength for a final double-handed blow. Andrew's sword came up quickly, found the gap in Gondemar's armour where the separate pieces met at the waist, and drove the blade deep into flesh. The Ulfberht sword was forced upwards to where it pierced the heart.

Gondemar's eyes widened and he screamed.

'Mercy, for pity's sake!'

Andrew replied, grimly, 'No mercy for the man who burned my godmother.'

Gondemar let the mace fall to the ground, clutching at his stomach where blood gushed forth.

First he went down on his knees.

Then on to his face.

A few struggles in the dust with an unseen enemy – and then he was dead.

Andrew was helped awkwardly to his feet.

'It is over, my friend,' said Hassan. 'You are free of this despicable knight forever.'

'Thank God,' Andrew said, drained of all energy and spirit for a short while. 'Thank God it is over.'

33. THE SELJUK TURKS

The wound in Walter's thigh proved not to be serious. It was treated with a healing ointment and then bandaged. The dead rogue knights were buried in a mass grave. The two Saracens who had been killed in the battle were bound with winding sheets and strapped to horses. Hassan and his older brother would take them back to their families for the last rites.

The time had come to say goodbye properly and forever, for Andrew knew he would never again visit this region.

He and Hassan embraced.

Andrew said in a choking voice, 'We are from different sides, but I shall always think of you as my dearest friend.'

Hassan hugged him hard. 'You and I, we will meet in some other place where such differences are no longer important.'

It was an emotional farewell. The two youths had difficulty in restraining their feelings. When they rode off, in separate directions, neither looked back. Andrew kept his face to the north and Hassan his to the south. Neither would ever forget the other, no matter how far into old age their bodies travelled, nor how faint their minds became.

Walter and Andrew threaded their way between the cities of Antioch and Edessa. They crossed the narrow stretch of Armenia and into Rum. Here they were in enemy territory. Only the previous year Emperor Manuel Comnenus of Constantinople had taken his Byzantine troops, and merce

486

naries, into this vast region. He had been soundly beaten by
the Sultan of Rum, Kilij Arslan, whose capital was at Konya.
The emperor had survived the battle, but thousands of his
soldiers had been slaughtered. It was in this battle that
Gondemar had received his crushed hand.

Hostilities were still at a high. Manuel had sent a fleet of
one hundred and fifty ships to attack both Turk and Saracen.
One of his generals, John Vatatzes, was wreaking havoc in
Rum at this very moment, cutting down Seljuk Turks where
and when he found them in retaliation for the massacre of
Byzantines by Kilij Arslan. It was the worst possible time to
be crossing Rum, especially if you were a Christian knight.

Walter and Andrew were almost entirely ignorant of the
great danger as they left the territory of the Cilician Arme-
nians which bordered Anatolia and the eastern Mediterranean.
They had heard of the battles, of course, and knew they were
in a land that was hostile to them, but were oblivious to the
frenzied hatreds that hung in the wind. There were bands of
Turks roaming the whole of the Sultanate of Rum, feverish
for the sight of foreign knights so that they could cut them
down.

The brothers reached the Goksu river and followed it north-
west, heading towards Philadelphia. They travelled through
the Valley of Fairy Chimneys, keeping formidable mountain
ranges on either side of them. The fastnesses around the edge
of Rum created impassable walls of towering rock. The high
crags seemed part of the sky: twisted and gnarled, they hooked
the passing clouds. Bleak and totally forbidding, this mountainous region cast a grim warning to strangers that it would
take lives if its heights were attempted. The two youths skirted

these natural fortifications knowing they could never climb them, especially on horseback.

They had half a thousand miles to travel to relative safety. Many thousands of knights had died in this region – hundreds of thousands – some through disease, some through hunger or thirst, and some had simply become lost – but many had fallen at the hands of an enemy, be it tribesman or warrior. Two lone youths stood little chance of success. Yet they battled on, day after day, suffering hot winds, flying dust, wild tribesmen and, once, a desperate fight with three lone Seljuks.

It could not last.

They met a whole regiment of Seljuks just beyond the site of an earlier battle at a place called Heraclea. They were stripped almost naked and forced to ride camels to the capital of the sultanate, Konya, called Iconium by some. There they were led through the streets while citizens threw raw eggs at them, spat on them and beat them with sticks. They were thrown into a dark earthen dungeon and told to eat worms if they wished to continue living.

'But think about this,' said the Seljuk Turk who was the commander of the band, 'because death might be preferable to what the future holds for such as you.'

They crouched in their dungeon, which was half the height of a man, and sank into misery.

'I'm so sorry to have led you to this,' said Walter. 'It would have been better perhaps if I had been left to the mercy of Odo de St Amand.'

'You would have got no mercy there, brother. And what we do, we do together from now on. We are bound by our birth and, if need be, we will die together.'

'You have lost everything – your magnificent armour, your beautiful sword, your magic astrolabe – even the golden spurs given you by King Baldwin – everything. Oh, and woe on woe, your horse. They took Warlock.'

'Things,' said Andrew, shrugging in the dark. 'I shall miss Warlock, of course, but the rest . . .'

'There must be so much hatred in your heart at this moment. Do you still think of that bully you told me of? What is his name, Harold?'

'Harold Butcher? Not any more. Once upon a time all I wanted to do was ride through my village, a Templar knight, and cut him down where he stood. Now? He means nothing to me. Perhaps those humiliations as a boy were necessary to me? Perhaps not? I don't know and I no longer care. I am humbled now. As we rode over those plains and mountains, I had time to think about what it means to be a knight.

'Certainly war is not what I imagined it would be. No one can feel elation after a battle, win or lose, when men lie dead by the thousand all around. Men with families – children and wives, mothers and fathers, who would suffer great distress when their son or husband could no longer walk through the doorway. One can only feel sorrow and, yes, anger, at being part of the slaughter trade. I have lost friends on the battlefield, and seen personal enemies go down, and at the end I have wondered what was the gain? A city for a king here, a piece of land for a sultan there? And ideals? We can't force other people to think as we do, nor can they make us into copies of them. War is a useless, destructive thing with nothing at the end but a change of rulers' names. You or I do not become any better for winning a war and in any case there will be another war coming along which we might lose.'

'Futility,' said Walter.

Andrew continued. 'I became a knight because I thought it would be a glorious feeling to ride above the heads of lesser men. I was told that Templars were warriors with holy orders: strong men who protected helpless pilgrims from attack by hostile people and beasts. That was just a small part. The larger part is following fat barons into battle so that they might become fatter. A knight is used as a tool by those they follow. Just as my father uses a hammer to fashion a horseshoe, so an earl, lord or baron uses the words 'honour and glory' to fashion a killer out of a man with high but mistaken ideals.'

'You have become a philosopher, my brother.'

'In this place,' Andrew said, looking around him in the dark, 'with rats and lice for company, philosophy comes as naturally as day follows night. All we are left with is our thoughts. In the ordinary course of life we are too busy to think. It's only when we're forced to do so, because there is nothing else to do, that we search ourselves. You – you are better than me, Walter. You do not fight for a living.'

'I make swords for those who do, and I enjoy the money which such a trade brings. Perhaps I'm worse? People are killed by those I arm, with no personal danger to me. I am a second-hand killer, Andrew.'

Andrew sighed. 'Well, now that we've bared our souls, and have made our confessions, perhaps we will be able to argue our way into a better place when the time comes?'

'I wouldn't wager on that,' replied his brother, 'it might come while we're feeling smug about it.'

Andrew laughed out loud. Walter laughed, too.

The guard above them hammered on the grille with the butt of his spear, telling them to be quiet.

They laughed even louder and invited him to join them in their merriment.

The next day they were again led through the streets. Stones and eggs came at them. Sticks were used on their legs and shoulders. The hisses and jeers came in their hundreds. They thought they were being led to torture, or to their execution, but when they reached the walls of a palace they had buckets of cold water thrown over them to clean them down. Their cuts and bruises were treated by men with ointments and balms. Then they were dressed in plain white shifts and taken into the palace.

Confused, the pair were shunted down passageways and across courtyards, until they found themselves in a great hall where men in splendid robes were gathered. Elephants' tusks decorated the doorways. Precious tapestries hung on the walls. Curtains of strung pearls hung over latticed windows. Sitting on a seat in the centre of the hall was a man whose garb showed him to be someone of great importance and stature. Standing by him was a giant of a man, naked from the waist up, leaning on a huge scimitar which must have stood in the stead of an executioner's axe. Beautiful women were feeding the important man, who must have been at least a vizier, if not a sultan. Andrew decided on the second, for no one would meet the man's eyes.

An interpreter translated this man's words.

'I am the sultan. Bow low before me.'

The two young men did as they were told, watched by that

burly, unsmiling guard wielding the huge scimitar. Andrew and Walter touched the marble floor with their foreheads, their palms flat on the ground.

'Now sit and face me.'

They sat cross-legged, their backs straight.

'You are knights of Emperor Manuel.'

'No,' said Andrew through the interpreter, 'I am a knight of King Baldwin of Jerusalem. This is my brother, who is a swordmaker's assistant.'

'You have come to my kingdom to assassinate me.'

'No, we are trying to get to our homeland, which is England.'

'I can cut off your heads in an instant.'

'Yes,' said Walter, 'you can.'

'We shall see.'

The sultan then clicked his fingers and the nobles in the room parted to allow two lines of men to form into a narrow alley. These men all carried what appeared to be a small, loose sacks the size of flour bags. These sacks contained something which turned them into plum-shaped clubs.

'Now you will run,' said the sultan, 'while you are beaten.'

'The gauntlet,' muttered Andrew. 'We're being made to run the gauntlet. I'll wager those sacks are full of stones. Make sure you stay on your feet, Walter. If you fall, they'll beat you where you lie and won't let you get up again. I'll go first . . .'

And Andrew ran down between the lines. The men swung their bags, which were in fact full of sand, and struck him on the head and shoulders, some on the stomach, some aimed for the kidneys. The blows hurt but they were not meant to be fatal. Walter followed him soon afterwards. They both reached the other end without falling. They were breathless and hurting badly from the blows which had thudded into their bodies: bodies that were already weak from lack of food.

'And again,' ordered the sultan.

Once more they did as they were told, resulting in several bruises the size of a man's fist.

'And yet again!'

This time Walter fell. The wound he had received in his thigh while fighting the rogue knights had opened. It caused him great pain and hampered his running. Those wielding the sacks of sand stood over him and beat him with great enthusiasm. They yelled as they did so, having a victim at their feet at last. Andrew heard his brother's cries of pain and turned, braving the flailing clubs of sand, to where Walter lay trying to protect his head with his hands.

Andrew reached out and pulled Walter to his feet, both youths still getting a pounding from their antagonists. The pair clung to each other, struggling back to the end of the two rows once more. They were absolutely exhausted, the pair of them, and fought for breath. Walter's legs were buckling under him.

'And yet . . .' began the sultan, but then he smiled and paused before adding, '. . . no more. You did well. Brother helping brother. Now, can you give me the name of one family – just one – who is of my faith? A family who would speak well of you?'

Without hesitation, Andrew gave the sultan Hassan's family name, the first names of his father and brother, Hassan himself, and the names of his mother and sisters.

'And where are they from?' asked the sultan.

'From a country called the Yemen. A land where they grow at grass and where no rivers ever reach the sea.'

493

'Ah, the Maalouf family from Al Yemen – very good,' the sultan said, nodding.

Andrew was surprised.

'You know this family?'

The sultan smiled. 'No, but you put great feeling into names which must be difficult for you to pronounce. I do not know this family, but I believe you when you say you do.'

The sultan suddenly looked stern, but actually the words, when they were spoken, were sweet to Andrew's ears.

'I am now going to let you go free on the understanding that you tell the Emperor Manuel that I am a gracious and merciful ruler, far more worthy to rule than he is. You must repeat my words without changing them,' said the sultan. 'I trust you on your honour to take this rebuke to him.'

'We promise,' said Andrew.

Andrew was thinking, quite rightly, that this was a whim of the moment. The sultan might just as easily have ordered their execution. Absolute rulers were unpredictable. One minute they granted a life, the next they took it away. Today luck was with the brothers. Tomorrow, or even in an hour's time, and the judgement might be completely different.

Walter now said, 'What about our clothes?'

'We will give you new clothes.'

'And my brother's horse, sword and armour?'

'Never mind,' hissed Andrew, under his breath, 'let's get out of here . . .'

But the sultan replied. 'We have searched for the armour but it has been broken up and passed among my troops. It irretrievable. You must leave without it. Your horse is in my stable. A handsome steed. You may take him with you. Th

494

sword – ah, yes, the remarkable sword. That, too, has been found, for it was too valuable to be given to common warriors. One of my officers took it for his own. It shall be returned to you as you ride from my city.'

'And the golden spurs?' insisted Walter.

'Alas, gone forever,' mourned the sultan, shaking his head from side to side. Andrew guessed the sultan had taken the golden spurs for himself.

'There will be no more eggs and stones then?' said Walter, not without some indignation in his tone. 'We take offence at being pelted with eggs and stones.'

The sultan raised his eyebrows and turned round to look at his vizier. This man gave Walter a look which a mother might give a son about to be spanked by his father. The sultan studied this look and nodded thoughtfully.

'Oh, yes,' said the sultan, turning back again. 'There will be eggs, and several stones of a smallish size. My citizens look upon this sport as their given right. But what are a few eggs and stones compared to freedom?'

'Nothing, my lord,' said Andrew, hastily, treading on Walter's instep on purpose. 'Nothing at all.'

The youths bowed their way backwards out of the hall.

An hour later, their bruises like black and yellow badges on their bodies, with Walter's thigh wound weeping again, the youths passed through the city gates. A Seljuk officer stepped forward and reluctantly handed Andrew his sword, complete with scabbard and belt. Andrew was also given a banner to carry. This was the sultan's flag which would ensure their safety in his kingdom.

There were no egg or stone throwers. The brothers did not

know whether the sultan had been joking, or whether he had decided temporarily to remove the rights of his citizens. There were insults thrown, with some venom in their tone, but no solid objects. There was no doubt as to the hostility of the crowd which had gathered on both sides of the gates. Some of these people had lost friends and relations in the recent wars.

Dressed in Turkish clothes, with billowing pantaloons and a flowing white shift, the two youths left Konya.

In true warrior-monk style – like Templars who had taken a vow of poverty – they shared a single horse.

34. HALFWAY HOUSE

Andrew and Walter entered Constantinople on a hot summer's day without a breath of wind in it. The heat was stifling, especially in the streets, which were crammed with people. The overpowering scent of spices and herbs filled every corner of the city. The noise was astonishing. No one took the least bit of notice of these two youths dressed like Seljuks riding one mount. The heat and dust demanded too much attention. People were far more interested in finding shade to carry out their daily pleasure or business.

'No sense in seeking any Templars,' Andrew said to Walter as they dismounted to cross a bridge in the throng. 'Bad news travels fast and may have got here ahead of us.'

'Let's find a swordsmith, then? My father's name is well known in the profession. We may get some help there.'

'Good idea.'

Indeed, only the second swordsmith they visited announced that Pugh was known to him.

'We worked in different English towns,' said the man. 'He in Middle Wallop and I in Winchester – but we knew of each other and respected each other's work.'

'I am his adopted son,' Walter said. 'My brother and I are on our way back to England from the Holy Land. My brother is a famous knight – you may have heard of him? Andrew of Cressing?'

'Andrew of . . . why, yes, yes, the minstrels sing of the boy knight's deeds,' replied the swordsmith, excitedly. 'Is this really him, in the flesh? Sir Andrew of Cressing, eh? He looks a little shorter than I expected him to be, but . . . would he mark one or two of my swords? They would fetch more money with his initials etched personally on the blades . . . but first, some proof of identity? Ah, the Ulfberht! Yes, that will do it, most certainly. Given him by Sir Robert de Sonnac, his adopter father, according to the verses. May I see it? Oh, what a blade! What a marvellous blade. Yes, yes. Each of these Ulfberhts has an individual mark – here it is. Here is the mark, just below the hilt. Most surely, this indeed is the sword once owned by Sir Robert.

'So, Andrew of Cressing, well, well – astonishing – I can't believe it, I really can't. Here, shake my hand. Wait until I see my own dear brother at the market next Tuesday . . .'

Borrowing money, it turned out, was easier than either of the brothers thought it was going to be.

They found lodgings and a stable for Warlock.

The next few days Andrew spent making arrangements to return to England. One hot noon he went to a shop which sold milk puddings. There the walls were covered in notes from people who wanted to find people, and from people who had left people and wanted them to know where they had gone. Reading these idly with his newly found skill he came across one which said, *Angelique. We are here in the city, making money. Please look for us in the suq on Wednesdays and Saturdays. Patrick and the Players.*

'PATRICK!' cried Andrew, making an elderly gentleman drop his milk pudding with a splat on the flagstones. 'Patrick is here – in Constantinople!'

'Indeed,' said the old gentleman, staring at the mess at his feet, 'and I am without pudding.'

Andrew purchased him another then went to find Walter. The following morning they raced to the suq and searched through it. It was Saturday, but they had no success. Andrew then remembered that the players usually worked at midday and in the evening. He and Walter took tea then at twelve o'clock they set off once more to find the players.

They found Patrick deep in the role of hero. There was a huge crowd around the players and Andrew and Walter had to elbow their way to the front. True, some of the people with language other than English were looking rather bemused, but were presumably entertained by the tone of the voices and the gestures. Andrew was quite impressed with the numbers of the audience. In England they would be lucky to get a crowd half that size. It was perhaps the novelty of these players that drew the customers.

'Oh, that I could see the light of another day . . .' began Patrick, and then suddenly saw Andrew and let out a high-pitched squeal. Some of those watching believed it to be something to do with his death throes and clapped enthusiastically. However, they were not prepared for the next action, which involved both Patrick and Toby jumping forward and slapping one of the members of the audience repeatedly on the back, several times. 'Andrew, Andrew,' cried Patrick. 'You're still alive?'

'Just about,' Andrew replied, laughing.

Arthur and a female lead joined Patrick at his side.

The audience now began grumbling, aware that the play had ended abruptly, and began to disperse without putting coins in the hat.

'How are you all? Indeed, how are you?' cried Andrew. 'Look!' He did a twirl. 'See that? That is a knight, my friends, a full-blooded knight of the realm. A Templar, no less.'

'We heard,' said Arthur, sourly. 'Braggart.'

'Well, he's got something to brag about,' defended Toby. 'I think it's a wonderful achievement.'

'Not so great,' said Andrew, wryly, 'but here – I found a brother in the East. A real live brother. Meet my twin, Walter.'

The three players and an odd-looking wench, with a dark face covered in rouge, stared at Walter as if he were a creature from some strange, exotic place beyond the Earth's pale.

'Really?' said Patrick. 'He is your twin?'

'Given away at birth, because of the mistaken belief that twins bring evil and bad luck . . .'

'Ah, the bad luck and evilness is real,' muttered the dark-faced man, taller than the rest, 'not a mistake.'

'And just who is this grotesque being?' asked Andrew, pointing at the rouged figure.

'Oh, meet our leading lady, Messaoud,' replied Toby. 'He was a Barbary pirate, whose captain sold us as slaves to a sultan. Messaoud came with us when we escaped . . . but that's a long story and not for today.'

'So, he's a brigand!' growled Andrew, a hand going to the hilt of his sword. 'And I a knight who slays such creatures.'

'Poohf,' sneered Messaoud, the many folds of his voluminous green gown rustling, 'I shall blow you over with one quick fart.'

'Now, now, we're all friends here,' said Patrick, laughing. 'Messaoud, Andrew is jesting, so stop pouting. Lads, we need a drink. Who's for a flagon of ale? Walter's buying.'

'What?' cried Walter.

500

'Now Patrick's jesting,' said Andrew, laughing along with the leader of the players. 'Yes, come on – and take off that silly eye-patch, Arthur – you've left the stage for the day.'

All went quiet among the players.

'I'm a bit sensitive about this,' muttered Arthur, lifting the patch, 'so you just get one look, damn you.'

He lifted the patch and showed Andrew the empty socket underneath.

Andrew was suitably shocked.

'Oh, I'm truly sorry, Arthur.'

'That's all right. You didn't know.'

'Walter here has a wounded thigh – we fought a great battle with false knights.'

'I thought he was limping,' said Arthur. 'Look, Walter, I can recommend a healing balm that I purchased from an Armenian . . .' They talked as they walked.

They found a hostel that would provide them with beer. It was cool inside, though rather noisy. Men with ale in their fists are not quiet creatures. They grumble mostly, about local affairs, world affairs and their ailments.

With pots of ale in front of them, and trenchers of bread and meat, Andrew asked about Angelique.

'I saw that you left a note to her, in the pudding shop,' he said.

Patrick recounted the adventures of the players and Angelique both in England and abroad.

'She is now in England, I think. I forgot to take that note down from the pudding shop board. Sir Robert's men are seeking her cousin, Ezra, who has much to answer for. Ezra was last seen taking a ship to Normandy, but he could be anywhere by now. Even here.'

'Poor Angelique,' said Andrew. 'But dressed as a boy! Why, that must have been she who watched me at her father's house, while Old Foggarty trained me. Of course! Velvet cap to hide the curls. It *was* she. But you think she may be with her father now?'

'I'm certain of it,' said Patrick. 'She was here in Constantinople, but once her father arrived we saw her no more.'

'Did he not reward you for helping her?'

Patrick took Andrew aside for a moment and whispered to him.

'Yes, he did. He offered us passage home to England and he gave me a purse of money. It was a lot. I've got it all about my person, stitched into two belts, but don't tell the others. Oh, I'm not trying to cheat them, Andrew, you know better than that; they're my best friends. But if I reveal the amount they'll all want to go home and sit on their backsides and do nothing. It'll be the ruin of us as a group of players. This is my life, Andrew – the play's the thing. I love it to death. It would destroy me if I could not act in front of an audience. And without Toby and Arthur?'

'So you'll keep the money?'

'I'll eke it out, when we have bad times. At the moment here in this city we seem to be doing well, but who knows what the future will bring? I promise you they'll receive their share, one way or another.'

They went back to the group and the next hour was spent in stories, some of which were completely true, but many of which were embellished. Those who have had adventures know that the facts can always be improved and enhanced by a few changes to an actual account.

The boys gasped at Walter's nightmare abduction and his

time in the fortress of the Assassins. They gasped even louder when he informed them that there was a death sentence on his head, and that at any time an Assassin might leap out of an alley or dark corner and end his life. They listened in awe to Andrew's tale of the goat-ogre and nodded solemnly as he described the beauty of Ulmurra. They cheered when he recounted the last fight with Gondemar de Blois.

As to the Battle of Montgisard, Andrew skated over his part in that encounter. He himself was not sure why he did so. Like many who had been on killing fields, the recall was emotionally disturbing and reawakened deep mental wounds. Likewise Toby had great difficulty in talking about his time as a slave. The other two did not, but then they had been house slaves and were not almost worked to death.

As the stories flowed, back and forth, Walter began to feel out of it. He was a newcomer to this group. Most of his adventures had been experienced before he had known Andrew, let alone Patrick, Toby and Arthur. After a while he excused himself, saying he had something important to do. The others hardly noticed him leave the room.

Walter went from their company and began to search the streets for a place of worship. He wandered the area around the suq rejecting this church and that church. This cathedral was too big, that church was too busy. Finally, he came to a small, quiet chapel at a crossroads. It was perfect for a private time with a priest who was not too arrogant or too harassed really to pay attention to a troubled mind.

After his flight from England, Ezra of Warwick had made his way down through the kingdoms of Lotharingia, Saxony and

Franconia down to Venice, until finally he stopped running when he stepped off a ship at Constantinople. Here was a place where one could get lost for a few years. He was, of course, dressed as a priest and had decided that was the way to make his living. His mother had given him a certain amount of money and he used some of this to purchase a small chapel at a crossroads.

'There's a small fortune to be made here,' he told himself, 'from pilgrims passing through.'

He charged for confessions, of course, but there were papal bulls to sell and even votive candles. It was money for nothing. The papal bulls – fake letters of absolution supposedly signed and sealed by the Pope – were written by young clerks and could be purchased by the score if you were in the trade. Votive candles came in batches of a hundred. It was a nice little living which no one questioned.

A small chapel was also a good hideout. He kept the place dimly lit, with only a little daylight entering. Ezra had grown a huge beard which covered most of his face, leaving just his nose and eyes visible. He had also grown a good deal fatter since he had left the shores of Britain, which he padded even further with thick layers of clothing. A corpulent priest was often more successful than a thin one. Visitors to the chapel saw him as a man at peace with himself and the Lord, and a willing listener, a patient man of God who took time to sympathise with their troubles. It was a good little business, if you knew how to deal with your customers.

Yet Ezra was still quite fearful.

Robert de Sonnac's agents were everywhere. The enraged knight seemed determined to track down the killer of his

504

steward, the man who had driven his daughter out of her own house by threatening her with rape. The man responsible for sending his daughter into the hands of Barbary pirates and eventually into Moorish slavery. Ezra knew that some day his Uncle Robert would tire of looking for him, but that time was not now, and Ezra needed further disguise.

He now wanted what he once swore he would never wish for: a false name and a fictitious history.

He wanted a new, believable identity. His imagination and indeed his intellect were not powerful enough to be able to *invent* one for himself out of nothing. That took a mind more lively than Ezra of Warwick owned. So he was now on the look-out for this new person he wanted to become. People entered the chapel every day. He questioned them gently, as if out of concern for their welfare, but he had not as yet found a suitable other self in which he could immerse himself and – if questioned – be convincing enough to fool agents of his uncle.

As he was lighting one of the altar candles a youth entered the chapel and came down to a front pew. The young man went down on his knees and began to pray. Ezra watched him carefully. After about an hour he went to the youth and said quietly, 'Perhaps you would like a candle for your father?'

'How did you . . .? Oh, I was praying out loud.'

'Well, a whisper, but in here, where silence reigns . . .'

'Yes, I would like to light a candle for my father.'

'And then a confession, perhaps?'

'Oh,' replied the youth, 'I have had little opportunity to sin lately – perhaps next time?'

'Hmmm.'

Ezra watched as the youth lit the candle and placed it in the box of sand, his lips moving and a tear in his eye.

Just as the boy was about to leave, Ezra asked, 'Might I know your name, young man?'

'Walter – Walter Pughson.'

'Ah, a good name. You have a trade, no doubt?'

'I was apprenticed to my father, a swordsmith in Jerusalem, but tomorrow I leave for England. My father – my father died. His heart broke. There was little reason for me to stay after that. I should like to see the land of my birth.'

'Naturally. An apprentice swordsmith? Now what does that entail? Sit. Sit down. Talk to me for a while. I get so lonely in this small chapel. I should like to listen to you for a while. Tell me the secrets of the work. They are safe with me. I have my own profession, as you see.'

'Well – all right. But they are not so much secrets as just small skills, easily learned over time . . .'

Over the next half an hour Ezra learned the intimacies of swordmaking. He took it all in. As the youth had suggested, there was nothing difficult to understand. This Walter Pughson seemed an ideal subject. He must have been an orphan, for no mother was mentioned. He had no history except for his years in Jerusalem with his father. And now he was on his way back to Britain, where presumably he would remain.

'And where did you stay? It must have been most interesting to live in such a city?'

Ezra learned the name of the street which housed Walter and his father, where Walter bought his bread, which butcher he preferred for his daily meat. In fact, it seemed that this Walter had never before had anyone interested in his day-to-day life and he was eager to talk about it. In a short while Ezra knew just about every detail of an ordinary day in Walter's life, which hardly seemed to vary from one week to the next. He even learned the name of Walter's cat, his neighbours on both sides and what colour his bedclothes were.

It would be easy to become this very ordinary youth, with his believable past, a past which would surely fool any enquiring agent of Robert de Sonnac. Yes, Ezra was now an ex-apprentice swordmaker from Jerusalem, who had left his trade and taken up the priesthood when he received a call from the Lord. *I walked by the shore at Jaffa one night and the Virgin rose from the waves and beckoned me.* The real Walter Pughson was such a simple soul he was easy to duplicate.

'Well, well,' he murmured, as another customer entered the chapel, 'thank you for talking with me, Walter. I feel comforted by your interest. God speed tomorrow and may the blessings of the Lord be on you for your journey.'

'Thank you, Father.'

The youth left the chapel.

Then the person who had just entered the chapel, a woman with her head covered by a white cloth, knelt in the same pew as Walter had vacated, it being the closest to the altar.

'You have come to speak with Our Lady?' murmured Ezra, in velvet tones. 'If I can help?'

'Yes, please, Father . . .?'

'Father Walter.'

'Oh, Father Walter, I have sinned . . .'

35. HOME

The players did not want to return to England. At least, not until they had spent more time in Constantinople. The pickings were just too good there. The citizens of this bridge between East and West seemed to appreciate players more than did London or Chelmsford. Patrick thought that perhaps it was because English cities and towns had more bands of wandering players and the audiences were jaded.

'Anyway, we intend to stay a little longer,' he told Andrew and Walter.

A ship was found to take the twins to England. Andrew and Patrick firmly shook hands on the quay. Toby warranted a hug because he was Andrew's favourite. Arthur was lucky to get a brief touch of the fingers. Then Messaoud started weeping and dived in and kissed the brothers on both cheeks, several times. The pirate had only known them for a few days, but he acted as if he was an old friend of both. It was his way of disrupting a carefully planned farewell. Messaoud just had to be the centre of attention.

'Goodbye, dear brothers,' cried Messaoud, 'may you be finding your loved ones upright and healthful.'

The twins ignored him.

Once on board the vessel, Andrew had misgivings about the money they had borrowed. He was unsure of ever being able to pay it back. The swordsmith had advanced most o this. Andrew had promised on his mother's life that he would somehow repay the debt. The swordsmith said he believed him because he was Sir Andrew of Cressing.

'It's rather daunting,' Andrew told Walter, as they sailed from the port, 'to be so trusted just because a few minstrels have made so much out of so little.'

'Well, brother, we will both work to get the money – it will be sent back somehow.'

The voyage was uneventful. They were both sick at first but found their sea legs within a day or so. The wind hummed through the rigging. The sails cracked and banged when the wind changed. The sailors sang their songs at night. It was all quite smooth and pleasant after so many turbulent months. It seemed a short journey from Constantinople to Venice, and thence to the shores of England.

The ship was small enough to go up the Thames to London. Andrew and Walter disembarked and found lodgings for one night, before they set out for the estate of Sir Robert de Sonnac. Andrew had no idea what sort of reception he would get from his adopter father. It was possible that word had been sent to England regarding events in Jerusalem. There might even be a warrant out for the arrest of the twins.

The first person Andrew saw when he rode through the gate to the estate was the one-armed Old Foggarty. The elder's shock of hair had turned even whiter, if that were possible. His face was more like a relief map than ever, with wrinkles etching dry river beds into his brow and cheeks. Two more teeth were missing from his gums and his three limbs looked thinner.

But his blue eyes were just as bright and intelligent looking as Andrew remembered.

'Ho!' cried the old man. 'The wayward scallywag returns, like a prodigal or such. What have you been up to, you young rascal? Causin' all sorts of bother, eh?'

'Any bother caused was not of our making, Old Foggarty,' he said, leaning down to take the old man's hand. 'Here, meet my brother, Walter.'

Old Foggarty nodded at the other youth.

'Well, you'd better go and see the master. He's here, you know.'

'I will.'

Andrew's stomach was churning now. Sir Robert had been kind to him in the past, but what would he think of his escapades regarding Odo de St Amand? Would he understand that a brother could not be left to die? Andrew had, after all, saved the Master of the Temple's life. Surely it should be left to him to decide the fate of the would-be killer? Somehow, though, he did not think Sir Robert would be of the same mind. Andrew expected a fierce reception, even though he was determined to face it out with dignity.

Walter held back, clearly awestruck by the opulence and grandeur of this great estate.

Sir Robert met Andrew in the entrance to the house.

Sternly the great knight said, 'Ah, my adopted son. And where is your armour, sir?'

Andrew had not expected such a question.

'Why, sire, it is in the hands of the Seljuk Turks.'

'Are you aware, young man, that your armour cost me a fortune? Fortunately I am a very rich man, though I balk at throwing away expensive suits of armour. I see you still have your Ulfberht sword at least. Did the Seljuk Turks not want such a blade? Were they ignorant of its value and status?'

510

'The – er – the sultan gave it back to me.'

'Oh, you were on intimate terms with the Sultan of Rum, were you?'

'No, sire – I'm sure you jest. We were captives and made to run a gauntlet of sand-filled clubs. He – that is, the sultan, seemed impressed by our performance . . .'

'Andrew came back for me when I went down, sire, even though he was sorely beaten for it.'

Sir Robert glared at Walter for his interruption.

'And this is?'

'My brother, Walter.'

'He who tried to kill Odo de St Amand?'

'Ah,' said Andrew, 'you have heard. Well, sire, it was not as it seemed. Walter was forced by the Assassins to attempt the deed, or the cut-throats would have killed his father, Pugh the swordsmith. Walter is the mildest creature alive, sire, but he owed his adopter father everything . . .'

'As indeed do you,' murmured Sir Robert.

'Yes indeed, sire. I have yet to thank you, most profusely, for adopting me as your son. Without your support I might have been stripped of my knighthood. I am ever in your debt and will do anything to repay you for your kindness.'

Sir Robert stared at the two youths for a long time, before sighing and bidding them enter his house.

'Fortunately for you, young man, King Henry has no love for the Templars in general or Odo de St Amand in particular. He dislikes the fellow intensely and when told of the attempt on his life cursed not Walter, but you, Andrew, for preventing the action. Come, come and eat and drink with me and tell me all your tales of derring-do. Then we'll discuss what will come next. I have some news for you, my boy. Good news, I think. We'll see . . . oh, what a surprise,' he interrupted himself with irony in his tone, 'here is my daughter, Angelique, sitting at the table waiting for us. My dear, I never expected you to join us.'

'Stop it, Father.' She looked at Andrew and he was astonished by how beautiful she had become in the few years they had been apart. He remembered her only as a slim, pretty girl and here she was almost a woman. 'Sir Andrew,' she said, 'how nice it is to meet you again.'

'And you,' he stammered. 'You look – very fine.'

'Is this your brother, Walter? I heard you talking to Foggarty.'

'Indeed it is,' said Andrew, glad the attention was off him for a moment during which he could gather his faculties. 'Walter, the Lady Angelique de Sonnac.'

Walter almost curtsied in his confusion, but he managed to stop himself and turn it into a bow.

'My lady,' he said. 'Andrew has spoken of you often.'

'Liar,' she retorted. 'He forgot me completely.'

Andrew flushed. 'That I did not – not completely, that is. I recalled, quite often, the image of you dressed as a boy in a velvet cap.'

'Now, now,' said Sir Robert, sitting down heavily at the head of the table. 'Angelique – grace, if you please.'

Angelique delivered a grace in Latin very prettily.

Over the meal Andrew recounted his adventures in the Holy Land. Angelique then told Andrew what had happened to her regarding her cousin, Ezra. Though the youths had heard it all before from Patrick and the others, they listened politely as if this were the first telling. Then Sir Robert spoke of his travels and his meeting up with his daughter in Constantinople at the end of them.

'When I get hold of that murdering whelp of a nephew,' he said, waving his dinner knife, 'you can be sure he will wish he had drowned on the crossing to the continent.'

When they had finished eating, Andrew said, 'Sire, you spoke of some good news for me?'

'Ah, yes,' Sir Robert put his elbows on the table and linked the fingers of his hands. 'I wanted to see how full grown you were before I told you this, but I'm satisfied by your manners and the modest way you recounted your adventures that you have matured a great deal since leaving England.

'Andrew,' he continued, solemnly, 'you are to be the new lord of Cressing.'

'What?' Andrew dropped his knife on his trencher with a thud. 'I'm sorry, sire – did you say . . . lord?'

'I'm not speaking of the Templar grounds, you understand – the barns, priory, walled garden and the fields they own. Just the village itself. The Templars are, of course, a law unto themselves and you are not in their good books at the moment in any case. I would stay away from them for a while. No, just the village with its few shops and hovels. There is village land that has nothing to do with the Templars themselves, ancient land with rights which go to you. The living this land will produce is not great, but it is – well, ample. You will have certain duties which the king will expect you to carry out with diligence and wisdom. There'll be judgements to make, when arguments occur. You will oversee . . . well, that will come later. I shall instruct you on your duties.'

Andrew was quite shocked by the enormity of this position he was being offered.

'Sire, who gives me this lordship?'

'Why, the only man who *can* give such things – the king – King Henry.'

'You spoke to him?'

'Well, you wouldn't have got it if I hadn't, now would you? He's heard of you, of course. The songs and poems praising your exploits at the crusade were all over London at one time, though they've died down now, which is a good thing – you don't want to become one of those knights who are more famous than the king himself. He doesn't like that.'

'No, no, I don't expect he does. I – I am greatly honoured, sire, to be given this . . . Walter, did you hear? Of course you did, you're sitting there beside me. What do you think?'

'I think it is richly deserved, Andrew.'

'Well, you would – you're my brother. What about you, Lady Angelique? Am I worthy of this honour?'

Angelique made a face. 'Honour and pride are things men are concerned with. The lady of a house is a keeper of two things: the keys and the morals. She is concerned with the safe-keeping of all that belongs to her lord and master, and with the integrity of her lord's actions. When she believes her husband to be acting wrongly, she should be able to tell him quite plainly and openly without any fear of rebuke. In fact, women do not care whether a man is a prince or a peasant, so long as he gives her rightful due – and loves her exclusively.'

There was silence around the table, broken by Sir Robert, who asked, 'Who said anything above love?'

'I did,' replied Angelique, and took a segment of preserved peach and popped it in her mouth.

The men preferred not to explore this new avenue opened up by the one lady in the room, and began talking of more important matters.

'We shall have to get you some new armour, Andrew,' said Sir Robert.

Andrew replied, 'Not as grand as the last, sire. It would not feel right. A plain suit of armour, for which I will repay you once I begin to earn, Sir Robert. I will be the lord of a small Essex village. I do not want to look like some earl from Canterbury or York. I am what I am, a farrier's son risen to knighthood. The villagers must feel they can approach me.'

'Very good. Very commendable,' murmured Sir Robert. Then he turned to Walter. 'And what about you, young man?'

'I have a trade, sir, taught me by the father who adopted me. I shall continue making swords.'

'Good. Good.'

'And I wish to go with Andrew,' said Angelique, 'when he returns to Cressing.'

'Why?' asked her father.

'I want the villagers to get used to seeing us together.'

Again the men went silent. Two of them were aware of the direction in which they were being herded. Sir Robert had long since given up trying to manage his daughter, so he made no further comment. Angelique had a mind of her own which was quite out of the ordinary. It probably came of there being no mother to guide her in the niceties of feminine ways. Andrew found, a little to his surprise, that he did not mind being nudged along this track with its misty end. Walter was quite oblivious of any undercurrents and reached for a chicken leg, then, after a bite, announced it to be delicious.

'Isn't there a lord of Cressing already?' Andrew questioned. 'When I left he was in full health, out on wild hunts most days – boar, deer, even marsh birds.'

'He has been moved on to a higher position, still in Essex, a place with a large priory at the south end of Prittlewell, near the sea.'

'Oh.'

Three weeks later Andrew, Walter, Old Foggarty and Angelique set out for the village of Cressing. After a night's stop in Chelmsford, they continued the next morning and entered the village after skirting the Templar enclave. Andrew had already renounced his membership of the Order of the Templars, the news of which had gone ahead of him.

'There are the great barns,' said Andrew to Angelique, 'the symbol of the Templars' wealth in this region.'

Angelique studied the high rooftops of the two monster corn barns as they appeared to dominate the landscape.

'Indeed,' she said, 'they are magnificent.'

'I laid the Horkey Branch in the second one,' he said, proudly. 'You have to climb up into the rafters of the roof, which, as you can see, is quite high.'

Indeed, Andrew was almost prouder of that moment than all his achievements since, in the Holy Land, and now as a lord.

The quartet had been seen from a long way off by workers in the fields and some had run down to the village to warn of their coming. Andrew had been recognised. He wore his breastplate, but no other armour. His helmet hung from one side of his saddle and his greaves from the other. He was, of course, riding Warlock, who had had as many adventures as his master and was probably just as proud of them.

When the four rode into the village Andrew and Angelique were side by side, with Old Foggarty and Walter behind. Above them several hundred geese flew over, making a terrible racket with their rhonking. They had come all the way from Scandinavia to winter in the Essex marshes. They darkened the sky with their numbers.

Suddenly, from behind an oak tree, a man stepped out with a longbow, an arrow ready to fire.

Andrew halted his mount.

'Harold,' he said. 'You already stand accused of a heinous crime. Would you add another to it? Put up your weapon.'

'No,' the hand that drew the bow trembled a little. 'I must do this thing.' But he was already on the back foot. 'What crime?'

'The burning of Blodwyn.'

'She was a witch. 'Tis no crime to burn a witch. I shall send you to her, if you but wait a moment . . .'

Angelique, riding side-saddle, sat up quite straight.

'Would you slay the lord of your village?' she asked. 'A hideous punishment awaits a man who commits such a dishonourable act. Let me tell you, you would be hanged by the neck until almost dead, then your arms and legs torn from your body by four heavy horses, and finally your torso would be cut into quarters.'

Andrew still made no move towards his sword and when Old Foggarty began to advance, he held out an arm to halt the elder's progress.

517

'Who is this?' cried Harold, his voice wavering. 'Who is this lady?'

Andrew said, quietly, 'She is my companion.'

Harold could not quite get his mind around this unexpected twist in circumstances.

'You are married?'

'No.'

The bow was lowered slightly, the right arm relaxed on the drawing of the arrow.

'No? I don't understand. Will you *then* be married to this lady?'

'You ask questions that we have not voiced among ourselves yet,' said Angelique. 'Do you think we speak with strangers about such matters, when we have not held any conversation on the subject ourselves?'

Harold looked totally bewildered.

'I don't understand.'

'Put down the bow, churl,' ordered Old Foggarty. 'And stand aside. You would do well to forget old quarrels. This is your lord, your master. For mine own part, I would cut you down in an instant, but Sir Andrew seems reluctant to let me. Think on this. You have been granted a reprieve, but hold that bow one more minute and you will die.'

The old man drew his sword with a warning ring.

Harold let down the longbow and put the arrow in his belt. He then turned and walked from the village. Those who watched him go realised he would not come back. He could not. Not after threatening the village lord. Harold would go north or south, find some other town or hamlet, and set up a trade as a butcher. This was Blood-month and butchers would be needed more than usual on farms, in markets, to slaughter the beasts that had grown fat in the summer months.

Andrew and Walter now left Old Foggarty and Angelique to go on to the lord's estate on the hill above the village, while the brothers went to the farrier's house.

Andrew stepped through the doorway of the house and found his mother and father sitting at the table, watching for him coming through. They looked rather dazed. They had been dazed for a long time, in fact. Their rather ordinary son had been the subject of many songs and poems. Now he was here, lord of Cressing village. It was all a bit too much.

Still, his mother got up to kiss him, and was in the process of doing so when a nervous, smiling Walter walked through the doorway.

'Mother, Father,' said Andrew, 'this is your other son – the twin brother you had to give away – his name is Walter.'

Their mother swooned into their father's arms.

A long way away, in another land, in a thriving, bustling city, a priest was walking along a narrow street. A swarthy man came towards him and stopped him with a brief enquiry.

'They say you are Walter Pughson?'

The priest smiled through his dark beard and folded his hands over his silk-robed stomach.

'Yes, that is who I am.'

Whereupon the man, an Assassin, rammed a dagger into the priest's chest and opened his heart like a book.

AFTERWORD

The Templar barns at Cressing, which are well preserved, can be seen today by visitors to Cressing Temple, in Essex. They were not erected in the twelfth century as this story suggests. They were in fact built in the thirteenth century, but since I wished to include both the Battle of Montgisard and the raising of the barns in the few years during which this novel is set, I had to make an historical twist. I decided to move the date of the building of Cressing barns, so I ask the reader to forgive this deliberate error in chronology. It might also interest the reader to know other certain facts of history which followed this story. Saladin, that great Islamic warrior, later drove the crusaders from the Holy Land. In 1187, at the Battle of Hattin, he destroyed the armies of the Kingdom of Jerusalem and recovered Jerusalem for his people. The courageous young King Baldwin IV, 'The Leper', died in 1185 at the age of twenty-four. His passing was the death knell for the kingdom he ruled during his short life. The Knights Templar themselves eventually fell into disrepute. Although the individual knights were poor, the Order itself became immensely rich in land and gold. It made the mistake of lending money to the kings of France and England, then asking for it back. In the fourteenth century they were outlawed and many, including the Grand Master of the time, were burned at the stake. Much of their wealth was given to their rivals, the Knights Hospitaller.

In medieval times New Year's Day was 25 March, not 1 January as we have it now.

The wall of the Pudding Shop in Constantinople (now Istanbul) continues to be covered with messages left by travellers for other travellers, the great city being the gateway between Europe and Asia, having one foot in each continent.

Copies of the famous Ulfberht swords are still being made in the USA.

Richard Argent is married with children. He is happiest in the wilderness, is a keen skygazer and is a long-standing member of the Cloud Appreciation Society. His main home is near Sutton Hoo in East Anglia but he spends his winters in Andalucía.

Find out more about Richard and other Atom authors at www.atombooks.co.uk